Rosemillion

J. Helen Elza

Rosemillion
J. Helen Elza
A Four Star Press Book
Published by Four Star Press
Athens, TN

This is a work of fiction. Names, characters, places and incidents either are the product of the author's imagination or are used fictitiously. Any resemblance to actual persons, living or dead, events, or locales is entirely coincidental.

J. Helen Elza
Printed in the United States of America
First CreateSpace Printing: February 2014
ISBN 13: 978-1493793716 (CreateSpace Assigned)
ISBN 10:   1493793713
Library of Congress Control Number:

Acknowledgements

The miraculous unseen that abide with us daily.

Judy Belshe-Toernblom, Long Beach, CA. casting director, producer, award winning script writer, talent agent and author, thanks for the Castor Oil, puka shells, and for forty eight years and counting.
http://www.christianfilmdatabase.com/review/boonville-redemption-2/

Todd Anderson, Sarasota, Bradenton, Florida, for your artistic passion, creative skills, and excellence in book and cover design, website creation, and marketing pace setting.
http://parrish-design.com/

And to readers and fans worldwide, for loving this book beginning with the first version released in 2010.

For

Rose Million

Forward

Do you believe in angels? I do. It was summer, 1985, between 2:00 and 3:00 AM. Following a clash of tempers with a male friend, I walked out of a local club, leaving behind my shoes, purse, and good sense. I proceeded, drunk and barefoot, walking beside the railroad track that runs along the outskirts of downtown Ft. Worth, Texas, when a Yellow Cab approached.

The driver leaned across the front seat, rolled down his window and offered me a ride. I waved him off, claiming to be fine, when the cab's back door opened. A little silver-haired woman who looked to be in her eighties insisted "This is my cab; you get in here right now. My driver will take you home."

Her driver did take me home, fourteen miles to my front door in North Richland Hills. I asked the woman her name as I exited *her* cab. Upon learning her name I blurted "Someday I will write a novel and title it with your name." At the time, I had written a few short stories, some essays, a little poetry, but never had I entertained the notion of writing a novel. Why would I tell her such a thing? *Drunken stupor*—I told myself.

Later, when I tried to find the woman to thank her for her kindness, I could not. And I was not surprised, not really. I never believed that this cab owner was an ordinary stranger. I believed then as I do now that she was/is an angel.

As a result of our meeting, I quit drinking. And I began to write novels. That was twenty-five years ago. There have been other encounters. But I will save them for another day.

Hebrews 13:2 Be not forgetful to entertain strangers: for thereby some have entertained angels unawares.

May God bless us everyone.

J. Helen Elza

Prologue

Freezing rain and dark clouds lingered above the Cumberland Mountains in Eastern Kentucky, mountains known to the locals as the *Big Black.*

Far below, drenched in the foul waters of Big Black's foothills, a little community shivered in the downpour. For five of the community's children, life itself had stalled.

Sixteen-year-old Pick was the oldest. Tall and bony, with a mass of heavy red hair, Pick's flawless skin claimed none of the freckles that are as expected of one with red hair as jelly is to *peanut butter and....* But the fire that folks expect of a redhead was there, in Pick's temper and in her eyes.

Pick's green eyes had always sparkled with the confidence of a well-loved child, a well-loved child who, by design, had been spared close encounters of any kind with strangers.

Strangers—those who lived beyond the stench of the coal carnage, beyond the creeping chemical death that lurked in the live pits and deserted slag heaps of Colter's Coal Mines. The uninvited who stumbled blind, awkward and fearful onto the maze of fallen trees and vapory vegetation that concealed the hidden valleys in the remote ravines and withered washes of Appalachia.

Hidden valleys--like Widows Hollow, where horizontal trees lie dying beneath the mold of former leaf. Where leaves of the grapevine canopy whisper and crackle like burnt toast on wilted vines.

Where Joseph McKinley met and married Isabel Carter. Where they had welcomed and loved their five offspring. And where they both rest in peace—now.

Chapter One

"Aaahhh!"

Pick screamed and fell face first in the sticky muck. She kicked free of the unlaced boot the mud had sucked from her foot and rolled off the squalling toddler who had slipped from Pick's arms in the fall.

"Sissy, Sissy! You all right?" Pick pushed herself to her knees. She wiped mud from her hands on her overalls and scooped up her sister who lay cocooned in a stiff blanket that crackled, icy, at Pick's touch.

"Huh, huh, huh!" The child's wails indicated that clearly, Sissy was not all right.

"I'm sorry, Sissy. I couldn't help it. Don't cry, baby, we're home now, don't cry." Pick clutched her three-year-old sister Olivia closer and bent her head to protect the child from the stinging ran when she felt a touch at her elbow.

Pick glimpsed the dimpled cheeks of her six-year-old brother, Buddy, who peeked at her from under the jacket he had pulled over his head. He held her boot in one hand and with the other, tried his best to pull her from the mud.

Pick summoned a smile to her lips. The smile balked with the single tear she saw slip from Buddy's eyes.

Pick clamped a hand over her mouth too late to stop the wail that escaped.

She tore her eyes from Buddy's face and forced her chin in the air. *Don't you do it, Pick McKinley!* She silently commanded herself. *This ain't the time. Git these younguns out of this freezin rain, git em washed, fed and into bed. Then you kin....*

"Pick, you comin or not?" Jimmy Joe hollered. The tall, lantern-jawed blonde who held the door with his foot swore at the wind and yelled at his brothers.

"Willie, you and Buddy get in here fore you get blowed to the next county!" Jimmy Joe cried. He grabbed at their sleeves and collars and hauled the little boys through the door and into the cabin the McKinleys called home.

Jimmy Joe's stomach growled as he felt his way in the dark to the fireplace mantel. He fumbled with the coal oil lamp, struck a match, and held it to the cotton wick.

"It's freezin in here!" He complained as he clattered the chimney glass into place. He blew foggy breaths on his hands and rubbed them together as the meager flame spluttered to life.

He shrugged out of his jacket, raked water from his hair, and said with a nod to his younger brothers "Take off them wet jackets."

Buddy and Willie, his older brother by two years, took off their jackets. Side by side, the boys inched backward to Jimmy Joe until they felt his legs against their backs.

Jimmy Joe dropped to one knee and encircled the little boys in his arms. Together the three raised their eyes to Pick who stood in a puddle of muddy water with her bare foot resting on her booted foot.

2

Weighed down with Papa's old coat that was sizes too big for her, Pick looked like a corn crop scarecrow. She held Olivia in one arm while she peeled wet blankets from the child with the other.

Pick swung Olivia to her hip and stared at her brothers' faces. They could not have looked more forlorn.

She scraped rivulets of soot from her cheeks with the heel of her hand, tossed her knotted, mud-clotted hair off her shoulders, sucked up her tears, and issued orders:

"Jimmy Joe, fetch in some wood and lay a fire. Willie, you and Buddy hang up them jackets you throwed on the floor. I'll see to Vee, and warm up the stew Mama John brung us."

The little boys did as Pick asked. They picked up their jackets and hung them on wall hooks near the front door.

Jimmy Joe stomped louder than usual the short distance to his bed. He plopped himself on the end of the handmade bunk and peeled a wet sock from his foot. He removed the second sock, dried his feet, and then turned in anger to Pick. "What business you got tellin us what to do? Ain't nobody give you leave to be bossin us around!"

Like a deer startled in headlights, Willie swung his eyes from Jimmy Joe to Pick.

Buddy looked to Willie with fear in his eyes, took silent steps backward and reached for Willie's hand.

"Our Mama died, Jimmy Joe! Now we ain't got no Mama or Papa. Pick's our Mama now. She kin boss us if she wants to!" Olivia cried and burst into tears.

"Sshh, sshh, Vee, don't you worry none," Pick said, forcing a smile as she wiped the child's tears. "Everthing's gonna be just fine, you'll see. You'll feel all better when we git you into yer nightclothes and git some warm food in yer belly." Pick poked a finger in Olivia's belly button. "Hands up!" She ordered.

Olivia raised her arms over her head.

Pick stripped the child of her wet clothes, dressed Olivia in a flannel nightgown, and carried her to the front room, tickling her chin.

With her foot, Pick caught one of the runners of a rocking chair to drag it nearer the fire.

"Hey!"

Startled, Pick peered over Olivia and into Buddy's indignant eyes.

"You nearly ran over me!" he cried. He sat in a squat with his hands stretched to the fire.

"I'm sorry, Bubba, I didn't see ya."

"When are we gonna eat supper, Pick? I'm hungry," he exclaimed, looking as tortured as possible.

Pick placed Olivia in the rocker and pulled the rocker nearer the fire. "Buddy, you play with Sissy fer a minute, that'll keep yer mind off yer belly 'til I get yer supper."

Buddy nodded his curly head and rummaged through a willow basket of toys.

Pick glared at Jimmy Joe. Her boot made a squishing sound as she tromped across the faded linoleum to her unsuspecting fourteen-year-old brother.

Careful to control her voice she said, "You ain't gonna start no back-sassin in this house. If you don't do like I say these little uns ain't gonna pay me no mind neither, so we might as well get this settled right now!"

Faster than a striking rattler Pick blind-sided Jimmy Joe with a wallop that left her crimson handprint on his cheek.

Buddy, Olivia, and Willie gasped and pulled their hands to their mouths.

Jimmy Joe sprang to his feet with his fist drawn. "You better keep yer hands to yerself 'fore you have another scar to be hidin!" He threatened, but stopped cold in the angry flash of Pick's eyes.

Jimmy Joe was no stranger to his sister's temper. Pick McKinley could not abide injustice. She was not the kind to sit idly by when the strong threatened the weak.

She caught the fire around age seven. While neighbor boys had looked on, hootin and hollerin, young Pick had charged past them to beat a chicken hawk with a broom until she forced the hawk to drop her kitten from its talons. Armed with nothing but chunks of coal, she had chased foxes from the henhouse many times.

Only once she had fallen victim as a child. She traced the jagged scar in her forehead with a finger. *Never again.*

She grabbed up Buddy and Willie's muddy shoes, stomped to the kitchen, and dropped them beneath the workbench.

"Ain't nobody give me leave to do nothin, James Joseph McKinley, Junior! Ain't nobody left me nothin neither but four younguns to feed and see to, a rusted pickup that ain't likely to run and a cupboard what's barer 'n a skinned jackrabbit!"

She stormed back and forth, pointing to Olivia as she passed. "Right over there's a youngun what's needin medicines we ain't got.

And right here," she said, poking a finger in Jimmy Joe's chest, "is a smart aleck brother who can take my part and see to ever bit of it anytime he chooses and it can't be quick enough to suit me!"

She cut her eyes to the bark bits and wood chips that littered the hearth. Heading for the back door she called over her shoulder "I'll be more'n happy to fetch in firewood while you study on how to feed four younguns when you ain't got no job, ain't got no notion of no job, and can't read a lick nohow!"

"Our Mama died, Jimmy Joe. We ain't got no Mama or Papa, member? Pick's our mama now," Olivia wailed.

The look of boiling anger that Pick shot Jimmy Joe evaporated in Pick's rush to comfort Olivia. Pick pulled a handkerchief from her pocket and pressed it to Olivia's nose. "Blow," she said.

Tears streamed down Olivia's cheeks as she blew into the handkerchief. She pushed Pick's hands away and sobbed. "Is my Mama gone for always, Pick? Is she?"

The misery in her baby sister's face tore at Pick's heart. She glimpsed Jimmy Joe stacking split logs in the wood box. After allowing herself one brief moment of satisfaction she heaved a weary breath, dropped into the rocker, and pulled Olivia onto her lap.

Pick plucked damp strands of hair from Olivia's face. "No, Vee," she said, pointing to the ceiling. "Mama's not gone forever. She's right up there in Heaven, watching us, and so's Papa."

Jimmy Joe dropped the last log with a loud *thwump!* He wiped sap and wood bits from his hands on his jeans, jabbed a finger at Pick and yelled.

"Pick, quit lyin to Sissy! We buried Mama today in that run down weed patch of a cemetery. And there she'll stay forever. She ain't never comin back here and she didn't raise us to be a lyin!"

Sobs punctuated Olivia's words. "I –want-my- Mama!"

"Hush, hush, Sissy. Jimmy Joe's right. Mama's body is back there in that cemetery, but Mama and Papa's real parts, the parts the Good Lord keeps forever is in Heaven and here." Pick placed a hand over Olivia's heart. "Mama and Papa's spirits is here. I ain't lyin. Promise."

The rocker groaned. "Mama's sound," Olivia whispered.

Caught off guard by the words, Pick hugged the child closer, swallowed her tears, and steeled herself against the memories of her Mama rocking in this same chair.

"Yer Daddy made me this rocker. That's my name, right there," their mama had once said as she pointed to *Isabel*— the single word Papa had carved in the back of the hard rock maple chair.

"He done it when I told him we was gonna have us a baby, a second baby. Hit's a fine chair, Pick. I reckon this chair'll be a rockin long after me and James Joseph is gone."

Pick closed her eyes for a moment. She could see her mama rocking babies. She could hear the notes of her Mama's sweet singing.

7

The wormy pine floor beneath the chair was worn smooth from the rocking motion and from the gentle tapping of Isabel's feet.

What am I gonna do without you, Mama? Pick swallowed her tears and willed herself not to glance at her mother's empty bed. Her weak will failed. A quilt her mama had helped to make covered the bed. It smelled of rose water, her Mama's favorite fragrance.

A lump the size of a black walnut grew in Pick's throat. Her pulse raced. She squeezed her eyes shut, shook her head to keep her tears at bay, and gave herself orders:

Don't you do it Pick McKinley! You're all these younguns got. Don't you be letting on you're as skeered as them. You just get supper and keep yourself still til bedtime!

Olivia's sobs quieted to hiccups. Pick was grateful that the chair's familiar creaking had worked its magic.

"Jimmy Joe take Vee so I kin git supper."

Jimmy Joe did not argue. Glad to claim the comfortable chair near the fire, he took Olivia and settled himself in the rocker while Pick got to work.

In a few moments, supper was ready. "Ya'll wash up and come to the table," Pick called shortly from the wooden table in the middle of the cabin. A bowl of stew and hot cornbread steamed before each child's chair. The chair at the head of the table and the chair to its right sat empty.

"Hands," Pick said the word with a glance at her siblings who joined hands and bowed their heads.

Coughs and sniffles punctuated Pick's prayer as she asked God for His blessing on their food, their home, and their departed parents.

The children ate in silence when a fiery log crumbled into ashes with a loud, *thud!*

Buddy gasped, frightened by shadowy figures that played now –you- see- us, now –you- don't in the flickering firelight. He jumped at a sudden wind that screamed through the cracks in the walls and rippled pages of the Bible that lay open on the mantel.

With a sob Buddy dropped his head of thick, dark curls to his chest. Staring into his bowl he asked softly, "Pick, who's gonna read the Good Book to us?"

Olivia glanced from Willie to Buddy. Seeing that they both had tears in their eyes, Olivia let out a wail. With her small hands she covered her face and stumbled from her chair to Pick's arms.

Pick lifted the child. She thrust her body back and forth, whispering "*Ssshhh, Ssshhh,* Sissy, it's all right. Don't cry. It'll be all right."

Mama. Mama read the Good Book to us.

Pick closed her eyes tight but could not shut out the memory.

"Pick... Pick, she's gone." Brother Lester's announcement three days ago at her Mama's bedside seemed distant.

Pick had responded with a mute nod. Shedding no tears, she had turned to the task of notifying neighbors and friends and to making the necessary preparations that her Mama's passing had called for.

Neighbors with grim faces and comforting words had visited in a steady stream. They clutched baskets, jars, steaming dishes, and hands, hands of frightened children who shrank from the cold, colorless figure that looked to be sleeping in the pine box in the McKinley front room.

Pick's heart had ached each time the children shrank from her mother's still body.

Isabel McKinley had lived a life filled with love and laughter despite the hardships she had endured. She had refused to allow the stroke that had paralyzed one side of her body to stop her from smiling and singing, or from reading the Bible to her children every day.

Tears stung Pick's eyes. *I'm the oldest. It's me what's gotta read the Good Book to these younguns. But I can't. I can't read!*

Pick hid her panic. She looked into her brothers' eyes and vowed her silent vow. *Ain't no McKinley gonna be no heathen!* She crumbled cornbread into her stew and picked up her spoon. "Let's finish our supper like Mama'd want us to. You too, Vee. We got to be strong so's we kin keep our promise to Mama."

Olivia swept her tears into the corners of her mouth with her tongue and asked in a whisper "Pick, can I sleep in Mama's bed?"

"And me too?" Buddy wiped orange grease from his mouth on his shirtsleeve and raised expectant eyes to Pick.

Willie hesitated. He wiped his mouth with the back of his hand and then raised his eyes to Pick. "And me?"

"Well, Jimmy Joe, you wanna sleep in Mama's bed, too?" Pick asked, grinning the grin she used for needling him.

"No I don't!" He exclaimed. He swelled up like a bullfrog, crossed his arms and watched sullenly as Pick shooed Olivia off her lap and scraped her chair back from the table.

Pick quickly finished the supper chores and bathed the little ones. She pulled back the heavy quilt and dumped Olivia, squealing, in the middle of the feather bed.

Buddy and Willie wrestled. They played tug-of-war with a quilt before crawling into bed beside Olivia.

"All ready?" Pick asked with a look of mischief.

"Ready," the little ones said.

Pick stepped to the pine cupboard near the bed. She pulled quilts, one after another, from the shelves and spread them over the children.

"Pick, why do ya ask if we're ready? Ready fer what?" Buddy asked, blinking his solemn brown eyes.

"You always been full of questions, ain't ya, Bubba?" Pick sat beside him, rumpling his curls. "These old quilts is heavy, heavier than you or Vee. You gotta get the way you want to sleep fore yer covered up 'cause you can't change yer mind after the quilts is spread."

Buddy twisted his mouth and squeezed his brows like he was deciding if he believed this or not.

"They ain't *that* heavy…." Buddy squirmed like a beetle on its back that tried to roll to its side. "I can't move!" He cried with a burst of laughter.

"Told ya!" Pick pinched his cheeks, laughing. She tucked the quilts under the little ones' chins, kissed them, and then she knelt beside the bed. "Let's say our prayers."

"Jimmy Joe!" She called.

Jimmy Joe did not join her.

"Jimmy Joe!" She called again.

"I ain't comin! Ain't no God would kill our Papa with the black lung and kill our Mama with a broke heart pinin fer 'im. I ain't prayin no more to a God some fool made up to make like this life is bearable. It ain't and I ain't wastin no more time makin like it is!"

"James Joseph McKinley Junior, Mama and Papa'd die if they heered you denyin the Good Lord! You'll bring a curse on this house with your blasphemin!"

"Mama and Papa's done dead, Pick! Most of the folks what ever lived in this holler is dead. The ground's dead! The sky's dead! All them ol' chickens we was raisin is dead. Ain't no life here at all and I'll be leavin fore I'm dead, too!"

"I want my Mama, I don't wanna die!" Olivia and Buddy hollered.

Willie's lip quivered. He dropped his eyes at Pick's glance and wrapped an arm around Olivia.

The corners of Pick's mouth lifted in a smile. In her mind, she heard singing, her parents' singing *Take it to the Lord in Prayer.*

Logs shifted in the fireplace. Pick rose from her knees singing. *"Oh, what peace we often forfeit, oh, what needless pain we bear..."*

She added logs to the glowing embers and returned to her siblings. "I'm singin with Mama and Papa, I kin hear 'em. If you listen, the Good Lord'll let you hear 'em too."

The three young children listened. *"Are we weak and heavy laden, cumbered with a load of care? Precious Savior, still our refuge, take it to the Lord in prayer."*

The tight muscles in their faces relaxed into ever-so-slight smiles. In their minds, sweet memories painted images of their rugged, red-bearded Irish father, and their beautiful mother with her milky skin and long, silky red hair.

After saying her prayers alone, Pick kissed Olivia. "Good night, sleep tight."

Before Pick could get away, Olivia clutched Pick's cheeks with her small hands. "Pick, sleep with us."

"Yeah, Pick, sleep with us," Buddy echoed.

Pick made a face. "It's awful crowded in there, but I'll sleep with you fer a little while if I can get the mud outta my hair first."

Pick added hot water to the cold water that remained in the galvanized tub from the children's baths. She pulled a quilt across the kitchen doorway for privacy and sank into the warm water.

She scrubbed with homemade lye soap until her skin tingled, washed her hair, and then dried herself with a linen towel.

Isabel had embroidered the towel with the words, *Tuesday's Child*, in red, Pick's favorite color.

Pick pulled her flannel nightgown over her head. She emptied the tub, mopped up the spills, and replaced the tub on its nail on the back porch. After tidying the workbench, she wrung out the washcloth and then stood for a few minutes before the fire, tossing her hair to dry it a bit.

At last, she fell into the crowded bed, exclaiming on a weary breath, "Thank the Lord this day is over!"

"Tell us about the roses. Pick, please tell us about the roses!"

Pick groaned.

Wide-awake, Olivia and Buddy pleaded with her to tell them the story of the little girl who magically transformed bleak and black Widows Hollow into an enchanted garden, alive with beauty, laughter, and light. The story was a fairy tale, Isabel McKinley's fairy tale and she had called it Rosemillion.

"Oh, all right," Pick said, thinking it would do no harm to start the story at least. Maybe it would calm the little ones. "Once upon a time, there lived a sad woman named Isabel. She lived in a bleak, barren place where the sun refused to shine."

"Stephen! Stephen!" Vivian Stalworth called out to her son as she limped to the nearest stall door of her state-of-the-art thoroughbred stable. Grass stains spoiled her tweed riding outfit. Her typically neatly coiled hair, having lost its pins, hung in disarray over her shoulder.

She pulled a black glove from her hand, lifted a telephone receiver from its cradle on the wall, and punched a single digit to ring the main house of the Stalworth Country estate.

The housekeeper answered on the first ring. "Stalworth residence, Maggie speaking."

"Maggie, tell Stephen I need him. I'm in the front stable. Tell him to dress for riding and to be quick about it."

"Yes Mam, Madam, I'll go up and tell him right now." The housekeeper hung up and hurried up the winding stairs to deliver her employer's message to her son.

"Mommy! What happened? Are you all right? Did you take a fall? Stephen Stalworth asked in alarm. He ran to his mother's side, clearly shocked at her untidy appearance.

"Of course I didn't take a fall! Someone fired a shot into the pasture. It was so close, the sound was deafening. It frightened Sheba so badly she reared and threw me! We'll have to go find her."

"Mommy, you walked from the pasture?" A glaze of anger filled Stephen's eyes.

"Did I have a choice? Sheba ran off. I can't imagine who would fire a shot into our pasture. I'm certain it was none of our neighbors. They have more respect for us than that."

"Mommy, it takes no imagination at all to know who fired that shot. It was one of those damned heathen hillbillies from that vile hollow in the county. Those heathens have no regard for legitimate landowners. They poach anything that breathes and don't care that we're riding on our own grounds. If they spot a rabbit, squirrel, or armadillo, they shoot, regardless of whose life they endanger!"

The anger melted from Stalworth's face. His concern was genuine. He offered an arm to his beautiful, petite mother and said in a softer voice, "Are you all right? Let me help you to the house. I'll saddle Sir Gill, find Sheba, and bring her home."

As he brushed leaves and grass burrs from his mother's jacket Stephen's face took on all the characteristics of a small boy who was about to cry. "I'm so sorry this happened to you, Mommy. If I could, I would bulldoze that white trash ghetto to the ground and run every one of those low-bred heathens out of this state!"

Stephen's mother glanced at him in surprise. "But of course you wouldn't, my pet. Your superior breeding would never allow you do to stoop to such vulgar behavior."

Vivian Stalworth pocketed her glove. Continuing across the lawn arm in arm with her beloved son, she had no idea how quickly he would prove her wrong.

Olivia and Buddy listened, picturing scene after scene in their mind's eye as Pick led them deep into their Mama's tale.

"An evil spirit had cursed the land. He took the reds, and yellows, and blues, and greens. He took the whispering of the trees and the sighs of the rivers. The evil spirit was mean--he took everything. Isabel's neighbors and friends were sad in the blackness. Without flowers and trees, the birds, squirrels, and rabbits ran away. They were sad, too. They had no place to play."

"Pick, kin the evil spirit come here? Kin he take us away?" Buddy asked.

"Not with the Good Lord watchin over us, Bubba. Evil spirits don't like to mess with folks the Good Lord's got His eye on."

"Tell us some more, Pick," Olivia said through a yawn.

Pick stifled her own yawn and continued. "Then one day in the dark, silent land, a child was born. The child was a happy child and so full of love, she brought joy to Isabel and her neighbors. The evil spirit did not like that one bit. He tried to steal the child's laughter but he could not. The child laughed and sang beautiful songs as she walked through the dark land."

"The evil spirit hated the little girl's beautiful singing so bad! He made like he was gonna hurt her, but the Good Spirit stopped him. The evil one whined and begged--like you and Olivia do when yer wantin yer way and ain't gettin it," Pick said with a laugh.

The small children giggled.

"The evil one asked the Good Spirit to give him just three weeks, and he would make the child stop singing. The Good Spirit agreed, but, He told the evil one, "If you fail, I will grant the child one wish, any wish, no matter how great.""

"The evil spirit tried and tried. He made the child's family and friends sick. He wasted all their money and dried up their gardens. He made the cold come with awful winds and freezin rains. At last, he made the child sick with a fever that lasted for days and days. But the child got better and in no time, she was singin again. The evil spirit threw a tantrum."

Buddy rolled his eyes. "I know, like me and Sissy do when we're wantin our way and ain't gettin it."

"Right," Pick said with a giggle.

"Buddy, be quiet, we wanna hear the story," Willie complained.

Pick continued. "The Good Spirit smiled as the little un made her wish. Whenever the blackness made Isabel sad, the child would sing. Like magic, a garden would appear, a beautiful garden filled with roses of every color. The roses was so beautiful and smelled so sweet, the birds and squirrels come back to play. The music and laughter in the garden grew louder every day. The leaves whispered and the waters sighed, flowers and trees bloomed again in the land what had died."

Pick stole a glance at her siblings. Their eyes were heavy. Smiling, she hurried to finish the tale. "The Good Spirit smiled. He told all the people He'd call the little girl Rosemillion 'cause she brought joy and singin to all Isabel's friends and neighbors. Now, Isabel was happy 'cause Rosemillion turned Widows Hollow into an enchanted garden of beauty, laughter, and love."

Pick lifted herself on her elbows. Olivia, Buddy, and Willie slept with contented smiles on their faces.

Pick closed her eyes. "Lord, I can't read the Good Book. I'll study hard and learn quick if you send me a teacher. Fergive me fer smackin Jimmy Joe but it ain't him what's got to feed and see to these younguns. Take kindly to him, Lord. He didn't mean them hard words; he's just missin Mama and Papa. Bless this house and the younguns. Thank you, Lord. Amen."

A few minutes ticked past and Pick grew weary. But when the old bed groaned with Jimmy Joe's added weight, Pick smiled to herself and drifted off.

Chapter Two

Bright light woke Pick.

"Sunshine!" she cried. Throwing off the covers, she raced to the fire. She piled logs on kindling and fanned the flames until the fire caught.

Running on tiptoes to the pine cupboard, she snatched a pair of woolen socks.

Olivia coughed a long hacking cough.

Pick wrinkled her brow, waiting. Olivia's frailness worried her. Pick feared pneumonia might settle in the child's lungs after being out in the freezing rain yesterday.

When Olivia quieted Pick hurried again to the fire. She sat in the rocker and pulled on her socks and ragged boots. She wiggled out of her nightgown into the only dress she owned. Her overalls needed washing before she could wear them again.

She backed as close to the fire as she dared. With her hands laced behind her, she looked over the small cabin.

Sunlight spilled through cracks between the logs where plaster had crumbled away. Faded linoleum worn through in spots curled from the walls. There was Mama and Papa's room with its simple pine cupboard and handmade feather bed.

In the kitchen, a Stanley wood burning cook stove shared a corner with a rickety wooden workbench. The workbench supported a rusted pump beside a chipped enamel basin that served as a sink. There remained the main room with its river stone fireplace and oak mantel, wooden table and chairs, Mama's rocker, and the children's bunks.

Pick and Olivia shared the top bed. The boys shared the bottom one. "Don't reckon I'll have to make the bunks today," Pick said. The beds remained untouched with their frayed quilts smoothed neatly over the pillows.

Pick darted to the kitchen. She pumped the heavy black handle of the well pump and let out a sigh when cold water rushed from the spout. The temperature had dropped to below freezing last night. As a child, she had never worried about the water freezing before. Now that she was the parent, things were different.

She stooped to pull aside the thin fabric Mama had strung over the shelves beneath the workbench. "Flour, sugar, salt, leavening, meal, lard, coffee, soup beans, and oatmeal," she said aloud. Worry lines creased her face. "We ain't got no milk, no eggs, and no meat. The vegetables we put up last summer is done gone. If this family's gonna eat, I got to get me work and I got to get it fast," she said. "Jimmy Joe kin finish off them soup beans by his self."

Olivia coughed again. Buddy tossed in his sleep. He was coughing, too.

Pick pulled her fingers through her hair. "I got to git medicines fer you younguns."

She walked softly to the front of the cabin. As quietly as possible, she pulled a hand crocheted shawl from a wall hook. Wrapping the shawl about her shoulders, she stepped out the front door into the cold mountain air.

Rotting boards on the bare porch creaked beneath her feet as she stretched her arms for balance, skipping like a high wire artist across the big stones that jutted from the mud.

She reached the wash that ran dead center of Widows Hollow as an icy gust tore at her shawl. She pulled the shawl tighter and turned her back on the mountain.

Black, bleak and desolate, Widows Hollow lay before her. Rickety shanties, exhausted with the effort to stand upright, struggled to support sagging roofs.

Chains, once shiny, silver, and strong, chains that had borne young families on green timber through air scented with honeysuckle and hope, hung like forgotten skeletons above rotting porches.

The steel chains and wooden swings had surrendered, along with the human spirit, to the slow burn of chemical oxides and the raging fires of poverty. Rusted, abandoned cars, stripped of anything that could bring a dollar, sank in the mud.

Papa's old Chevy pickup was one of these. It might run. It might need gas. Pick could not be sure.

Good news, the sun was shining. If it would shine for a couple of days, if the wind would blow, just steady, the mud would dry up. The treacherous ruts that served as Widows Hollow's sole passageway would be passable, and Pick could go find work.

A door across the way creaked open. "Pick McKinley! Chile, you better get on back inside! This cold'll be the death of you!" The voice softened. "How are ya doin this mornin, baby? I know you're a missin yer Mama somethin fierce."

Pick smiled at the old woman who had come to the hollow years ago as Early Mae Johnson. Folks had called her "Mama John" for as far back as Pick could remember.

Pick worried about her. Mama John was not getting any younger. Her high blood pressure vexed the old woman with spells. Probably had something to do with her cantankerous old husband, Mule, and her six children.

"Mornin, Mama," Pick called out. "I'm doin all right, glad to see the sun a'shinin, maybe it'll dry up this rut so I kin find me work."

Pick waved the old woman back inside and said to herself, "Good folks, these is all good folks. I got to find a way to help 'em."

Smiling in the sun's warmth, she hummed a tune. "This mud'll dry in a couple of days," she mused. "I'd best be tendin to the younguns and get ready to find work."

Pick raised her eyes. "Lord, I'll be needin you close by. I'm willin to work hard as I have to but I ain't sure that old truck of Papa's can get me where I need to go.

Breathe on it, Lord, and on them that lives fancy. I got to call on 'em fer work. You know I'm skeered but I thank you now for tendin to it. Amen." Humming a familiar tune, Pick skipped back across the stones and into the cabin.

Olivia sat up in bed coughing, her blonde hair tangled against her face.

Pick felt so bad for her. She smoothed Olivia's hair and rubbed her back gently.

"My throat hurts, Pick," Olivia said. Her eyes watered. She clutched her neck with both hands.

Pick kissed the top of her head. "So, how about I make you a nice cup of tea with lots of honey, reckon that'll help?"

Olivia nodded with a meager smile.

After boiling water and making the tea, Pick stirred in raw honey. She held the cup while Olivia took small sips.

Buddy stumbled from the bed with sleep creases in his face. "Pick I'm hungry," he mumbled.

"I better git yer breakfast, then. With them brown eyes and dark curls, and with a little meat on her bones, you might grow up and be right handsome."

"Yeah, and you might not," Jimmy Joe taunted. He sailed a pair of wadded socks at Buddy.

"He will too, he looks like Papa!" Willie cried.

"Buddy, you get out of them night clothes and see to Olivia for a bit while I git yer breakfast."

"Jimmy Joe, you and Willie see if Papa's old truck kin be run. I got to find work and that truck's got to git me to it."

"That old truck ain't been run in months. It ain't gonna run and ain't no gas in it no how!" Jimmy Joe grumbled, heading for the rocker. He dropped into it, folded his arms, and spat into the fire.

"You kin git that truck runnin or you kin starve. Better decide which you'd ruther!" Pick shouted with a threatening glance.

She filled a kettle with water and placed it on the stove. The rusted oven door screeched as she removed the remaining loaf of the bread she had baked last week. She stirred oatmeal into the boiling water when she heard a familiar sound from Mama John's house across the way.

Whomp! Whomp!

That's Jimbo at his wood chopping chores. Pick thought. Jimbo was eighteen already and full grown—a six-footer and then some. Mule was getting on in his years so Jimbo carried a lot of the load for his big family. *Mule and Mama John are blessed to have Jimbo to handle the heavy chores. Speaking of chores...*

"There's wood to chop, too!" Pick yelled over her shoulder to Jimmy Joe and Willie.

"Jimbo!"

Pick glanced out the window at Mama John's yell. What followed was a blur.

Chapter Three

"Oh Jeeeesus! Lord help me! Mama! Mama!"

Pick shoved the oatmeal off the burner. "Buddy, you and Sissy stay put til we get back!" she yelled, and sprinted out the door with Jimmy Joe and Willie.

Pick's heart beat in her throat as she raced past children and adults that spilled from Mama John's shack.

Jimbo screamed and writhed on the icy ground. He had nailed his foot to the chopping block. Blood spewed like a fountain from the ax head he had accidentally buried—dead center—in his foot.

"Jimbo! My boy! Oh! Sweet Jesus-- my boy!" Mama John screamed, waving her hands. "Oh, my ba...." Her words stopped, half out. Clutching her heart, Mama John crashed to the ground like a felled tree.

Tears spurted from Pick's eyes. She gritted her teeth and wrenched the ax from Jimbo's foot. "Jimmy Joe, Willie! Help Jimbo!" She yelled.

"Mule! Mule! Get Mama John!"

"Lucy, Lottie, fetch your Mama's bucket of coal oil!" She yelled to Mama John's ten-year-old twins.

And to Mama John's eight year old, "Petey! Fetch some rags!"

Mule struggled to lift his wife. He could not. "Mama, Mama. Wake up. Ol' Mule needs ya, honey, wake up." He wagged his head, beseeching Heaven. "Lord doan take 'er, please doan take 'er!" he sobbed.

"Be careful of that foot!" Pick shouted to Jimmy Joe and Willie who half-dragged Jimbo between them.

"Mule, she's gonna be all right, I know it." Pick groaned as she strained to help lift Mama John. She clutched Mama John beneath her arms, clamped her teeth and grunted, "Younguns!"

A swarm of children squeezed together, shoulder-to-shoulder, on each side of Mama John. Together with Pick and Mule, they lifted Mama John and carried her into the house.

"Get a quilt for Mama. Put Jimbo on that rug 'fore the fire." Pick shouted, breathless. With a loud groan, she heaved with all that was in her to lift Mama John onto her bed.

"Mule, get some salts!"

"Lucy! Lottie! Where's that coal oil?"

"Petey, I need them rags."

"Mule, raise Mama John's head, put them salts to her nose. She'll wake directly."

Lucy and Lottie stumbled from the kitchen carrying a five gallon galvanized bucket of coal oil between them. Petey shoved past them with rags.

Pick threw a rag over her shoulder and knelt beside Jimbo.

"Thank you younguns," she said with a passing glance at Jimbo's face.

Unable to bear the pain etched in Jimbo's eyes, Pick turned her head. She squeezed her eyes shut, straight-lined her lips, and shoved Jimbo's mutilated foot into the greasy coal oil.

"Aaahhh!" Jimbo screamed--and fainted.

Pick exhaled in relief. "Least you ain't hollerin no more," she said.

She lifted Jimbo's foot from the oil, wrapped it in rags, and said to no one in particular, "It'll mend. It'll take some time, but it'll mend proper. Clean missed the bones—whacked right between 'em."

"Lucy, Lottie, let's clean up this blood. Yer Mama and Jimbo don't need to see it no more."

"Pick!" Mule called in excitement. "Pick, Mama's openin 'er eyes!"

Pick pushed herself from the floor to join Mule at Mama John's bedside. She squeezed his arm as the old man shuffled closer to his wife moving his stooped body slow and mechanical like a piece of rusted machinery.

Terror slid from his face in a wet stream as Mule took Mama John's hand. He pressed it to his cheek, kissed it, and then dropped his gray head into it, crying, "Oh, thank you Lord, thank you Jesus! Mama! I thought you done lef' us!"

"Why you silly old man, I can't be leavin..." Mama John blustered then glanced anxiously about. "Jimbo? Where's my Jimbo!" She cried, her voice high-pitched and frantic.

Pick patted Mama John's hand. "Look Mama, he's sleepin right there on that rug by the fire. He'll mend just fine. Clean missed the bones."

"Oh, bless you, child," Mama John gushed. "Bless you, you sweet angel baby!"

Pick smoothed the blanket over Mama John. "I got some of Mama's medicines. I'll fetch 'em for Jimbo. He's gonna be hurtin awful."

She turned to Mule with a serious look on her face. "Mule, you gotta see that Mama John stays put. I'll take Jasmine home with me so's Mama kin get some rest." Pick reached to take Jasmine, Mama John's two-year-old baby, from Lottie.

Pick propped Jasmine on her hip and then turned to go.

"Pick, thank you, child. May the Sweet Lord bless ya real good!" Mule said, pumping Pick's hand.

"Let's go, younguns," Pick shouted and headed for the door.

Halfway across the rut, she stopped in the sucking mud to hug her brothers. "I'm so proud of you boys! Thank you fer helpin when our neighbors needed help."

"Stop that, I ain't no sissy!" Jimmy Joe cried and pulled away.

Pick ignored her lanky brother's discomfort. "Lookin at you's almost the same as lookin at Papa. You're big like him, with his same square jaw and proud walk."

Willie hugged back.

"Sissy!" Jimmy Joe teased.

"Ain't no sissy! Huggin feels good and I like it!" Willie said and poked out his tongue.

"I thank you boys for helpin with Mama John and Jimbo. Mama and Papa'll be up there pesterin them angels with "Them's our younguns!" and a grinnin."

Pick followed her brothers inside the cabin.

Buddy and Olivia lay sprawled on their bellies on a quilt before the fire. They played with rag dolls their Mama had sewn by hand.

"I finished the oatmeal, Pick," Buddy said, beaming. He pointed to the kettle on the stove and to the two empty bowls on the table. "Sissy was hungry so I finished it."

"And yer just six years old!" Pick exclaimed. She gave Buddy a squeeze and placed Jasmine on the blanket. "Here, Jasmine wants to play with you and Vee. You keep her out of that fire, you hear? I'll just be a minute; I got to find medicine for Jimbo."

Pick rummaged through the collection of odd bottles, mason jars and tins on the shelves beneath the workbench until she found a small green bottle. "This will ease Jimbo's pain," she said.

She rummaged further and found a leather cord with a single key hanging from it. "The key to Papa's truck," she said. She held the key before her and raised her eyes. "Bless it Lord and make it work."

"Jimmy Joe, Willie, here's Papa's key. Now you kin see if that truck's gonna run."

Jimmy Joe scowled. "It ain't! It ain't never!"

"How do you know if you ain't even tried it yet?" Willie demanded with a scornful glance at Jimmy Joe.

"That truck ain't gonna run I'm telling ya," Jimmy Joe cried. He dropped his bowl and spoon into the soapy water in the basin and angrily yanked the key from Pick's hand.

"I'm taking this medicine to Jimbo. You and Willie be getting that truck runnin. Buddy, you tend Sissy til I get back," Pick said, and reached for Jasmine.

Pick rolled her eyes. "I shoulda knowed you'd be up," she said to Mama John who sat at the kitchen table peeling potatoes.

"There's my baby. Come here, baby girl." Mama John wiped her hands on her apron. Cooing and clucking like a mother hen, she took Jasmine from Pick and hugged and kissed the baby with noisy kisses.

Pick shook her head. "There ain't no keeping you down is there Mama?"

Mama John nodded to Jimbo. "He's hurtin awful, Pick."

Pick followed Mama John to Jimbo and knelt beside the boy.

"I know yer hurtin, Jimbo," she said.

She took a single pill from the green bottle, placed it in Jimbo's open palm, and lifted his head.

Jimbo slapped the pill in his mouth and washed it down with the cup of water Mama John gave him.

"It'll be a few minutes, but ease is comin," Pick said, grateful to see the rigid muscles in Jimbo's ebony face relax. She inspected his bandaged foot. "Looks like it quit bleedin," she said.

"You'll be good as new and ornery as ever in no time." She patted his shoulder and tucked the covers tighter. "You rest now and don't worry none fer yer Ma and Pa. We'll see to 'em and to these younguns til yer fit again."

Pick's eyes sparkled with mischief. "I 'spect I'd best keep a close eye on Jimmy Joe when he's swingin that ax. He might just take a swing at me!"

Clattering and banging from the back of the cabin drew Pick's attention from Jimbo.

"What is that racket?" Mama John demanded. She slapped her hands on her hips and wobbled her head like a metronome. "Mule! Mule! Whatever is you up to, you noisy old man?"

"You just tend to yore business, I'll tend to mine," Mule replied. He stepped into the room toting a leather pouch and shotgun.

Mama John stared wide-eyed at her husband. "Have you done lost yore senses? You ain't leavin this house you old fool! You gonna hurt yourself or another'n. What crazy notion has done got you now?"

Mule directed a casual glance at his blustering wife. He squared his scrawny shoulders and said with a tilt of his chin "We's all tired of soup beans. I'm aimin to fetch us some meat!"

"Pa, I'll be healed soon, we kin go huntin then," Jimbo called. "Ain't no need in your traipsing through them woods by yerself!"

"I'm goin. It's settled!" Mule pulled a battered hat from a peg, smacked it on his head, and marched out the door.

"Don't fret, Mama, I'll send Jimmy Joe and Willie, they kin watch out fer 'im," Pick said.

Delighted at the prospect of hunting with Mule, Jimmy Joe wasted no time fetching his Papa's gun and leather pouch.

Willie eyed Jimmy Joe with the gun on his shoulder. "I don't care nothing fer killin," he said and continued his play with Buddy and Olivia.

Pick yanked Willie to his feet. "Yer goin just the same. Time may be when you don't care nothin for starvin and killin will be all that's fillin yer belly!"

"Yeah, hug this!" Jimmy Joe shoved his Papa's shotgun at Willie.

Willie slapped at the gun and snatched his jacket from Pick who watched from the doorway and shook her head at the heated words that accompanied her brothers into the night.

Chapter Four

Mama John twisted her kerchief in knots. She peered through the front window of her cabin into darkness black as coal dust. Worried, she glanced at her children and Pick's. They played quietly so as not to disturb Jimbo or the stifling tension that cramped the cabin like an unwelcome visitor.

"That ol fool should of listened. His eyes ain't what they used to be. He's prob'ly lost out in them deep woods with nary a blanket nor a match!"

"Mama, Jimmy Joe and Willie know their way 'round these woods. They know the cabins where to call if need be. Don't work yerself into a spell, they'll be in directly," Pick said.

She tried to carry on like everything was all right when the sudden sound of footsteps on the porch startled her and Mama John.

Mama John raccd to the door with her bosoms bouncing and her kerchief flying. "I'm gonna light into Mule *Jackass* Johnson fer scarin the life outta us like this!" She cried and yanked open the door.

She narrowed her eyes in mock anger. "You get on in here," Mama John gasped.

She passed Pick a fleeting glance then stammered, "Why Mose, Mose Tate, come on in this house."

The meek little man entered. He stood with his head partially bowed, his hands twisted around one another. He wore a threadbare denim jacket over denim overalls and a plaid flannel shirt. He snatched a worn hat from his head and raised shy eyes to Mama John and Pick.

"I'm sorry fer callin on you good folks at this late hour, but hit's nearing Amy Beth's time and I, I can't... can't take no more of her hollerin." The little man's lip quivered. He looked like he might burst into tears at any moment.

Mama John and Pick took a minute to absorb this news.

Mose Tate was only twenty-five, his tiny wife, Amy Beth, twenty-two. They had mourned the passing of childless years with "Maybe we ain't meant to have no babies."

Pick smiled with the memory. She had been present the day Mose had come home from the mines, black-faced and exhausted. Amy Beth had greeted him at the door with a bright ribbon wrapped around her shining black hair and with an equally bright smile. "We's gonna have us a baby!"

The desperate look on Moses' face snapped Pick from her musings.

"Mama John, if you'll mind Buddy and Sissy, I'll tend to Amy Beth and the birthin. Lucy and Lottie kin come with me if you don't care." Pick pulled on her jacket with a hurried warning to Buddy and Olivia to mind their manners.

Mama John shooed her twins before her. "Get your coats girls, hurry now. You go on along with Pick and mind her words. Pick, if you run into a bad turn, send one of these girls to fetch me."

Mama John pulled Lucy and Lottie's collars tight about their throats. She pecked their cheeks with a kiss and then waved them off with Mose and Pick.

Amy Beth's moans filled the Tate's small cabin. Pick ordered Mose outside the quilt-curtained corner that served as his and Amy Beth's bedroom.

Lucy and Lottie boiled water and gathered towels.

Mose chain-smoked. His rolled his own cigarettes with hands that shook so badly he could hardly grip the flimsy white papers or his Bugler tobacco pouch.

Hours passed. Amy Beth's pains that had started earlier in the day came with a steady frequency and then stopped.

Lucy and Lottie slept curled together, wrapped in quilts that Mose had placed before the fire.

Pick slept in a rocker beside the bed, waking with a start each time Amy Beth moaned.

Pick squinted in the bright sunlight and rose stiffly from the chair. "You're gonna hafta call this one Mule, Amy Beth. He shore ain't in no hurry to get here," she said with a laugh.

Pick tended Amy Beth with a nagging fear that something might not be right. Amy Beth's belly was swollen like she was carrying two watermelons. *And fer her size....*

Pick did not let on that she was troubled. She walked outside into the sunshine and a gentle breeze. She glanced up the road to Mama John's, anxious for word from Mule and her brothers.

Mama John's door slammed open. Peach, age seven, burst through it. The child raced to Pick with her coat flapping about her in the wind.

"Pick, Mama sent me to tell ya Pa and Jimmy Joe and Willie is home. They come in early while we was sleepin. And Mama wants to know if you need her," Peach cried, breathless.

"No, Peach, tell Mama we're fine. This youngun's decided to stay put fer a while yet, he may not show up 'til spring."

Pick was wrong as morning passed into early afternoon. Amy Beth screamed, red-faced and frightened. The pains were less than a minute apart.

"Breathe, Amy Beth, breathe! Now push, push!" Pick instructed.

"Oh, Sweet Jesus in Heaven!" A look of horror washed over Pick's face. "It ain't comin' right! That's a shoulder or a backside maybe, but it ain't no younguns' head!"

Pick's breath came in short, frantic spurts. She tucked the covers around Amy Beth and prayed a silent prayer. "Lord, we gotta get 'er to the county. I can't do no knife birthin. Please show me what to do, I ain't got no notion what to do." Pick hid her face from Amy Beth and swiped at the tears that blurred her vision.

Plup! Plup! Plup! Plup! Plup! Plup!

Pick threw her hands over her head with a joyful shout. "I know that sound like my own heartbeat. It's Papa's truck!"

"Pick, hit's Mule in yer Papa's truck, he's right here," Mose gushed.

"And please dry the mud," Pick said with a quick glance at the ceiling.

Pick grabbed her jacket and Moses' shouting "Mose, get Amy Beth in the truck, we got to get 'er to the county!"

Amy Beth screamed and Mose whimpered as he cradled his wife in his arms. "My wife, my baby…."

Pick pushed Mose out the door. "God didn't send this chariot to be takin'. He sent it to be a bringin'!"

With Amy Beth in his lap, Mose squeezed into the pickup beside Mule.

"We'll get 'er there, Mose, you just hold on tight," Mule said. He carefully guided the old truck through the bumps and ruts, watching in the mirror to see that Pick, Lucy and Lottie did not bounce out of the truck bed.

The old truck ticked and stalled. Inching forward with a groan, it spun mud with every rotation of the tires.

Crawling past Mama John's, the rickety pickup with its burden of passengers lurched forward. The tires spun with an angry whine as the rut became a swamp. Mule pushed on the gas. The truck spit, sputtered, and churned mud but would not move forward.

Fighting panic, Pick jumped to her feet. "Help us, we gotta get to the county, help!" She screamed and scrambled over the side of the truck.

She flattened her hands against the rusted tailgate and shoved to no avail. Lucy and Lottie splashed into the mud hole with her and pushed. Whining louder, the tires continued to spin mud.

Jimmy Joe, Willie, and Mama John raced from Mama John's porch. Brother Lester, Sonny Simpson, Luke and Kenny O'Connor sprinted from their homes, stuffing shirttails into their pants. Levi Thompson came hopping on one leg, fumbling his boot on the other.

Together, the neighbors of Widows Hollow pressed hands and shoulders against the tailgate. Grunting and gritting their teeth, they shoved.

"Try it again, Mule, turn the wheel! Straighten it out! Again! One more time! Heave!" The truck shuddered, spinning mud and muddy water over every soul that slogged through the rut. The truck ticked, gathering speed, moving…moving….moving!

Pick dived for the truck bed and landed in a belly flop. "Owww!"

Shouts of "Good luck, be careful, we'll be prayin fer ye," mixed in the air with the black exhaust that followed the truck from the hollow.

Edward Moses Tate Jr. arrived by cesarean section shortly after Pick and company arrived at the County Hospital. Edward's identical twin, Joseph Aaron Tate, arrived a few minutes later.

"Twins! We got us twins!" Mose cried and hugged Pick with joy.

Mud-splattered and exhausted, Pick threw her arms around her neighbor. "Ain't it wonderful, Mose?"

Pick lingered at the nursery window. She watched the pediatric nurses gently enclose the tiny premature newborns in heated incubators. Tears sparkled in Pick's eyes as she turned to Mose and said, "Ain't God good?"

Chapter Five

"Pick, why ain't ya sleepin?" Olivia whispered.

"What're you doin awake, Sissy?"

"You been awake all night, so I been, too. Yer skeered, ain't ya?" Olivia asked, holding Pick's face in her small hands.

"You don't want to go to town by yerself cause yer skeered of them strangers. But you got to go to git work." She added after a moment "And they don't like younguns nohow."

Olivia's words mystified Pick. "Sissy, why do you say them fancy city folk don't like younguns? Where'd you get such a notion?"

"Mama John told me."

"Mama John?" Pick repeated. She could not imagine Mama John telling Olivia such a thing. Pick tickled Olivia. "Tell me what Mama John told you," she said playfully.

"She said the fancy folk send their younguns off. They put 'em in striped clothes and send 'em off."

"What? Striped clothes—like what them on the chain gangs wear what's working on the roads?" Pick burst into laughter. "Olivia, them city folks don't send their younguns off fer good and they don't dress 'em in striped clothes. They dress em in school uniforms and send em off to private schools fer a little while."

"Pick..." Olivia grew serious. "You ain't never gonna send us away are ya, not even fer a little while?"

"Oh, Sissy! No, I ain't ever, never gonna send you off!" Pick vowed. She added playfully, "I'm gonna keep you right here so when you git bigger, you kin do all the cookin and cleanin and I'll be one of them ladies of leisure."

Olivia giggled in Pick's arms.

"That you'll do," Jimmy Joe blurted.

"Yeah," Willie added.

"She won't neither, Pick's our Mama now and she ain't never gonna be no leisure lady," Buddy cried in Pick's defense.

"Did anybody in this house sleep last night?" Pick asked.

"No," the children shouted as they laughed and talked back and forth in the early dawn.

"Well, I'd best be gettin to it. Today's the day," Pick said. She gave Olivia a squeeze and slid from beneath the covers.

Pick finished her chores feeling more burdened than ever. She had not realized that her siblings knew her best kept secrets, but why wouldn't they? Widows Hollow and each other was all they had.

Pick felt a stab of guilt. *I gotta be careful with my thinkin. These younguns can't read nothing else, but they kin read my thoughts just fine.*

After tidying up the dishes from an oatmeal breakfast, she put on a kettle of soup beans. "Jimmy Joe, you keep an eye on these beans. Add water when they need it. I'll finish up supper when I git back."

"Sissy, you and Buddy stay inside today," Pick said and scattered toys on the quilt where they played.

"But I wanna play with Petey," Buddy protested.

Pick lifted Buddy's chin with a finger. "Petey ain't coughin like you and Sissy."

"Aawww," Buddy grumbled.

Pick peered into the oval mirror above the pine cupboard. Her eyes looked sick with fear as she ran a finger over the scar in her forehead. As always, touching the scar transported her back to age five.

One morning back then, she gathered ginseng near Stump's place when she heard drunken laughter followed by loud shouts.

"Well, looky here, we got us a real live hillbilly!"

She had looked up to see four city boys sitting on the tailgate of a shiny red pickup, passing a jug. A boy with a mouthful of braces dressed in jeans with rolled up cuffs and with his hair slicked back in a ducktail leered at her.

He slurred the words he made up to a 1950s cheer; "If I was Lil' Abner and you was Daisy Mae, we'd make whoopee the Dog Patch way." The boy laughed an evil laugh, slid from the tailgate, and lurched toward her with a shout. "Hey Daisy, where's your slingshot?"

Pick hated being called a hillbilly. She was not a hillbilly, she was a survivor. Her daddy had told her so. She snatched up a rock and hurled it at the boy who ducked just in time. The rock whistled past, inches from his head.

"She don't need a slingshot!" His friends laughed. "She just parted your hair with a rock!"

"Oh yeah?" The boy jerked the jug to his mouth and took loud gulps.

He wiped his mouth, picked up a rock, and said with a snarl "So this little white trash hillbilly thinks she can throw a rock…." With a glance at his buddies to be sure they watched, he took aim at Pick's head and hurled the rock.

Pick grabbed her forehead and screamed a scream that echoed off the mountain. Blinded by the blood that gushed between her fingers, she crumpled to her knees from the force of the blow.

Hysterical, she screamed and bit at the weathered arms that snatched her from the ground.

"Sshh, sshh, hush child, yer all right. Stump's got ye now," the familiar voice reassured her. She had clung to the old man's neck as he dropped to one knee, leveled his shotgun in silence, and fired. *Kaboom! Kaboom! Kaboom! Kaboom!*

The boys bailed out of that Chevy. Hollerin for their lives, they tore out of Widows Hollow. They ran as fast as their legs could carry them without a single backward glance.

Stump stood and lifted Pick to his shoulder. She caught a glimpse of the shiny red pickup and smiled. All four tires were flat. And smoking.

Time passed but no one ever returned for the pickup. After a while, like other things that had no business in Widows Hollow, it vanished.

Pick's fear gnawed at her. And I ain't never been alone close to no strangers since. A lump formed in her throat with the thought, *but I got to go among 'em today, alone.*

She cut her eyes to Buddy and Olivia. They played with plastic soldiers and paid her no mind.

Pick tried without success to pull a comb through her fresh washed hair. Frustrated, she gave up. She scrubbed her face as tears leaked from her eyes.

"Pick!"

Pick wiped away her tears. Mama John's voice had never sounded more welcome.

"I figured you'd be up early baby, and that you'd be a frettin to be on yer way. Hit's snowin, Pick Honey." Mama John brushed flakes from her head and from her dress. She continued with a worried glance. "So you better hurry on."

"What would I do without ya, Mama?" Pick cried.

Mama John shook her head. "Chile, yer hair looks like them sparras been nestin in it. Come here, baby, let me fix it." In no time, Mama John had Pick's copper hair shining to her waist smooth as silk.

Mama John had not slept well either. The dark circles under her eyes confirmed it. She grieved the loss of her friend, Isabel, and now circumstances forced Isabel's child to leave the fiercely protective community of Widows Hollow to find work among the strangers in town.

43

"What's waiting fer you out there beyond the mountain, Chile?" Mama John asked herself, feeling sick with worry for Pick.

She stared at Pick's smooth skin, high cheekbones, and lanky frame. Pick's hipbones poked at the thin fabric of her dress. With an aching heart, Mama John blessed the girl that she loved like one of her own.

Isabel and Joseph, I'm asking the Good Lord to be with your chile today. She's goin off by herself among strangers. I can't be settled with it. There's something won't let me be.... Mama John hoped that her prayer would banish the nagging fear that shadowed her like a black cloud.

Mama John smiled a smile that she did not feel as she reached into the pocket of her house dress. She withdrew a kerchief and unfolded it. "Tie this roun yo hair, baby, so you won't be a fussin with it."

Pick's smile at the gift of a blue satin ribbon faded quickly. She fumbled with it, spewed a breath, and then dangled the ribbon over her shoulder.

Mama John took the ribbon. "Ain't no need to start carryin on! Yer gonna be just fine. Where's yer pretty smile?" Mama John tied the ribbon in a neat bow around Pick's hair. "There, that's better, Baby," she said and nodded her approval.

"It ain't too early to call on 'em, is it, Mama?" Pick's eyes were anxious.

"No, Chile, it's just right. You go on Baby, and doan you worry. I'll see to these younguns and to yer supper. Now, bundle up tight."

Pick pulled on her Papa's coat and gloves, determined to calm her fears when Olivia ran to her, threw her arms about Pick's legs, and pleaded, "Don't cry, Pick, it'll be all right."

Pick hugged the child with a fierce hug. She raised wet eyes to Mama John who gently pulled Olivia away despite Olivia's tearful protests.

"It'll be fine, I'm gonna git me work this morning," Pick said with a voice full of tears. She tore her eyes from her siblings and Mama John and raced out the door.

Navigating the maze of gravel ridges and pitted washes, Pick tried to remember the last time she had come with Papa to fetch Mama from her work.

She babied the truck along and stared at the unfamiliar sights. Buildings stood where she remembered trees and fields. Beside the buildings, felled trees lay stripped and naked, discarded in haphazard heaps.

Pick imagined herself shrinking. Her heart thundered. She wiped her eyes and took comfort in the gummy gray layers of coal dust and sweat Joseph McKinley had molded to the steering wheel with his callused hands.

She straightened herself in the seat. *Papa made his turn at the big fence made with red bricks. It was this way, I'm sure it was this way....*

Miles up the road Pick cried in relief. "That's the fence!"

The red brick wall ran alongside the four-lane in perfect symmetry, curving into tall, columnar pedestals that rose to an arch above the two-lane entrance to the neighborhood where Isabel McKinley had worked, cleaning and mending, before her stroke.

Slowing the truck to a crawl, Pick turned beneath the arch. "These homes ain't fancy, they're grand, grander than I remember," she breathed. "I ain't never seen so much color. There's color in the big yards, color in the windows, and color in the fancy brick drives."

She cranked down the window and filled her lungs with the tempting smells that seeped from the chimneys. "The smoke from these chimneys is thick and black. It smells different. Good."

Pick stared, breathless. The garden here was not imaginary nor was the beauty. Trees and shrubs sculpted to look like animals and children added an air of enchantment to the lawns of the grand estates.

Tears filled Pick's eyes. She stared at a little girl in a bonnet with a basket on her arm bending to pick flowers from banks of them at her feet. The little girl, the basket and the bonnet were sculpted from an evergreen.

"Once upon a time there was a sad woman named Isabel." In her mind, Pick heard the words in her mother's voice.

Now she understood. The fairy tale—Rosemillion-- her mama had made it up so that she could bring this beauty home to Pick and her siblings.

Pick scraped open the door and told herself, "I'm gonna walk right up to that fancy home, speak to them God-fearing folks, and get me work."

The drive, inlaid with smooth paving stones, seemed to stretch on forever. *It must be near a mile up it,* she mused.

Pick kept her mind off her fears by catching snowflakes on her tongue. She kept her hands in her pocket in case the temptation to reach and touch the little evergreen girl became too great to resist.

Pick drew in a sudden sharp breath.

Magnificent quarter horses raced to the fence that ran alongside the drive. The beautiful animals with their glistening coats came so close she could see their foggy breaths as they whinnied and snorted at her. As quickly as they had appeared, they raced off again with their manes and tails flying.

Pick approached the porch and hurried up the steps. Without thinking, she whistled through her teeth at her reflection in the porches' shiny surface. She felt so small. She tilted her head to see the great white stone columns that soared to the second story.

Tall windows on each side of the massive oak doors shimmered with multi-colored lights. "Like a puzzle made out of pieces of the rainbow," she whispered.

The scent of the pine wreaths that hung from the doors was powerful and fragrant. Festive red ribbon tied in splendid bows decorated the wreaths. Evergreen trees wrapped in spirals of lights sparkled from great clay pots beside the doors. Red ribbon tied with fancy bows decorated the pots and the great columns, too.

"Just like in a fairy tale," Pick mused. She straightened her shoulders and knocked on the door.

No one answered.

There were people inside, she could hear them talking. A square brass box beside the doors caught her eye. Pick pushed a button on the box then jumped in fright. Chimes rang out, chimes like the church bells at the Church of the

Little Flock, the church that she and her neighbors attended.

"Now I've done it!" Pick's throat went dry as one of the great doors swung open.

"Yes, may I help you?" The stout woman who answered the door dressed in a black dress with a white apron and a white ruffled cap raised curious eyes to Pick.

"I, I beg yer pardon, Miss. My name's Pick McKinley, from Widows Hollow. I'm lookin to do cleanin and mendin chores fer wages."

"Please…. Come in…. Child…," The woman spoke in halted words as though she searched for a vocabulary that might be suitable for communicating with this, this—*vagrant?*

With narrowed eyes, the woman scrutinized Pick from the toes of her worn out boots with their broken and knotted laces, to her flimsy blue gingham with its flour sack patches.

No smile threatened to soften the hard lines of the woman's face as she stared at Pick's dirty coat. Ragged threads poked through the busted seams in the collar. The coat hung from Pick the same way that plaid flannels hung from scarecrows.

The woman folded four fingers and bent them toward herself.

Pick took this to mean "Follow me."

"Madam Stalworth will be down shortly for breakfast, I will announce you... What are you doing!" The woman shrank from Pick with a dark scowl.

Pick straightened herself. "I was smellin yer perfume. It smells awful good," she said with an innocent smile.

The woman pruned her lips and clasped her hands. "May I take your wrap?"

"My wrap?" Pick repeated with eyes that said *I have no idea what you are asking.*

"Your coat Miss." The woman glanced at Pick with a fleeting glance. Her eyes darted off as if to follow something small and invisible above her head.

"No, thank you Mam, I'll keep it if it's all the same to you," Pick stammered.

The woman spun on her thick, sensible heels and departed down the hallway with heavy steps.

Pick remained where she stood, rooted to the polished marble floor.

The woman had retreated halfway down the hall before she realized that Pick was not beside her. Scowling, she turned and beckoned with a raised hand. "Please follow me, Miss, Miss…Pick."

Pick followed but stopped often to stare wide-eyed at the collections of museum quality art, rugs, furnishings and life-sized portraits that graced the oversized rooms of the lavish estate.

"You may wait in the library, Miss. Madam Stalworth will be down shor...."

"These books is stacked so high, folks gotta use a ladder to reach 'em!" Pick exclaimed. She whistled at row after row of glossy volumes and leather-bound classics that lined twelve vertical feet of the polished oak shelves that comprised three walls of the impressive library.

Entranced as she was in these rich folks' surroundings, Pick did not notice that she was alone until she heard voices.

"Imagine Colter's audacity! He thinks that he can buy that forest, level the trees, ship them down river and turn what's left into another of his slag heaps."

"Daddy stopped him dead in his tracks, didn't he, Stephen?"

"Yes, yes he did," Stephen Stalworth replied. He flashed a smile at his sister, Victoria Talbot Stalworth and added "Doesn't it make you wonder?"

"Wonder what?" Victoria swept her blue eyes past Stephen to watch the high-spirited thoroughbreds in the pasture beyond the window.

"What can Daddy hope to gain by threatening an old business associate like Colter over that dump in the county? There's nothing there but rickety shanties in a God-forsaken breeding ground for illiterates and poachers. Daddy despises that white trash. Wonder why the sudden interest…." Stalworth sipped his coffee and awaited Victoria's answer.

Pick listened from the library in alarm. She lived in the county. She knew the words white trash, illiterates and poachers. She had heard them all before. These people could not be talking about Widows Hollow. *Could they?* Pick bit her lip and listened as the two continued talking.

"Maybe that's it," Victoria said. She swung her long blonde hair off her shoulders and reached into a linen-lined basket for a blueberry muffin. With her knife, she chased melting butter across the warm muffin.

"What's it?" Stephen raised his eyes to Victoria's.

"Maybe Daddy doesn't want coal miners and lumberjacks for neighbors any more than he wants those low bred heathens in the county."

Stephen said with a laugh "As though that were possible."

"Brother Dear, you're spending too much time at the County Hospital among those low class heathens that you loathe. You have no idea what's going on right here in our beloved city."

"So enlighten me." Stephen reached for a muffin and waved his empty coffee cup at the housekeeper who busied herself wiping down kitchen counters. "Maggie, get me some coffee."

"They call it consolidation." Victoria grew solemn. "There are weak souls among us who believe that we should gather up our scattered little counties, consolidate them into fewer and larger counties, eliminate a number of those pesky county offices and their salaried officers, and use the savings to benefit the less fortunate."

"Like?" Stalworth accepted his coffee from the housekeeper with the same warmth as a traveler accepting coffee from a vending machine.

"Like educating those illiterates, for example," Victoria said with a wave of her hand. "Some of our own neighbors think that we should invest the savings building schools and hiring teachers for those heathens. They believe then that we should create jobs for them!"

"Imagine it. They want to create a resource management board and call it *The Southern Mountain Authority*. This board would designate portions of the state as park and recreational areas and others as areas for industry. The board members would decide where we could mine coal and what trees we could cut down in which forests."

"Supporters of this foolishness want to take the acreage that Colter destroys with his strip-mining, and restore it, turn it into tourist attractions that will generate state revenues."

"You don't like hearing this, do you Stephen?" Victoria noted that her revelations seemed to agitate her brother.

"Understand, Dear Brother, that consolidation to us means that those poachers and their pilfering progeny become neighbors in *our own* county. *Our money* will be wasted *on them*."

"Not necessarily."

"Whatever are you talking about?" Victoria demanded. "That smug grin of yours is maddening!"

"So, Daddy has no plans for that land, but he stopped Colter from acquiring it.… Tory, I have a wonderful idea. Maybe consolidation wouldn't be so bad if it is handled properly."

The young woman that breezed into the room startled Pick. The woman smiled and brushed snowflakes from her hair. She pulled a lipstick from her coat pocket, peered into a mirror, and applied it.

"This here's what's called a library, ain't it?" Pick asked the pretty woman. "I ain't never seen so many books in all my life. Has these folks read 'em all, do ya reckon?"

The pretty woman turned from the mirror. She pointed the lipstick to the bookshelves. "These? Have they read all of these books? Hardly," she said with a laugh.

"Some people might call this a library, but mausoleum would be more accurate in this case. Nobody reads these books. I doubt that any of them have ever been opened. Like the baby grand and the Persian rugs, they're strictly for show. No decorator in Ashford would dare present a home without them."

"You mean these fancy folks got all these books and they don't read 'em?"

The look on Pick's face startled the woman. The girl looked devastated.

"Uh, yes, they…." The woman fell silent. She turned with Pick to the sound of voices from the breakfast room.

"Daddy's worked very hard to keep our kind separate from their kind. Now, bleeding heart busy bodies want nothing more than to move these misfits into our beautiful city among *us*. Somebody must stop them. If there is any justice at all, somebody will!" Victoria exclaimed.

"Oh, I think there may be justice after all little sister." Stephen glanced at his watch and rose from the table. "Suzanne's late. We're supposed to drive in together so she can drop off her car for a tune up. You'd think she could be on time just once!"

"Oh, and don't worry too much about that consolidation, Tory. It might prove to be the best thing that ever happened to us." His words drifted behind him as Stephen strode from the room and into the foyer.

Peering into an oversized gilt mirror, Stephen straightened his collar and silk tie. He tugged at the crisp cuffs of his tailor-made shirt. He ran manicured fingers through his black hair, noting with satisfaction that it was streaked with premature gray at the temples when a sudden movement behind him jarred him out of his self-admiration.

He bristled like a cornered cat. "How in the hell! It can't be, not in my own home!" He screamed.

Victoria raced to him as Stephen spun in fury on the object of his wrath.

"How in the devil's own hell did you get in this house? How dare you drag your ill-bred, vermin-infested body inside this door, infecting our home with God only knows what manner of pox?" He stomped to the front door and slung it open with a force that rattled the gilt mirror on the wall.

"Get out white-trash! You are not welcome here!" He jabbed a finger at the frigid outdoors. "Get out and crawl back to the sewer where you were spawned!"

Pick's screams froze in her throat. She clapped her hands over her mouth and ran in terror. Stumbling on the lace of a ragged boot, she tumbled down the steps, ripping her dress beyond repair.

Her face and knees bled bright red drops of blood as she picked herself up, raced to her Papa's pickup, and dived inside.

"Please! Please!" She screamed. Her hands trembled so violently she could not fit the key in the ignition.

"Pleeeease!" She screamed again. She stomped the accelerator. She fumbled the key in the ignition and pumped the pedal wildly. The engine rattled, ticked, and died.

Sobbing in hysterics she tried again. The engine rattled, ticked, and died.

Fearing that her heart would explode, Pick swung her eyes to the house.

She pumped the gas and pounded the wheel. Realizing that the truck was not going to start, Pick let out a howl. She grabbed the key, rammed the door with her shoulder, bolted from the truck and ran into the pelting snow.

"Stephen! If I hadn't seen it with my own eyes, I would never have believed it! How could you? How could you!"

Suzanne Claiborne wrenched the diamond solitaire from her finger and threw it at her fiancé, Stephen Stalworth.

"That was the cruelest, foulest, lowest display of inhumanity I have ever witnessed!"

"Dr. Stalworth!" She spat the words. "You are not fit to wipe the mud from that poor child's boots! The only pox in this house is you! God help you, that child's poverty will never match your own! Don't bother to throw me out and don't bother to call me again, ever!"

Suzanne was too upset to apologize to the wide-eyed domestics that witnessed her outburst. She ran past them from the house and jumped into her two-toned salmon Chevy Bel Air. The Chevy fishtailed in reverse from the drive.

Suzanne drove up beside Pick's truck and peered inside but the young woman was gone.

Chapter Six

Back in the hollow Mama John suddenly called to her daughter. "Lottie, look after these beans, I'll be back directly."

"Yes, Mama, I'll…." Lottie stared after her Mama who grabbed her coat and raced out the door clutching a dripping spoon in her hand.

"I feel it in my bones, something's wrong, something terrible bad has happened!" The dread feeling that seized Mama John hurried her across Pick's porch with surprising speed. She shoved open the door to four pairs of eyes that blinked at her in surprise.

"Everthing all right here, babies?" She asked, near tears.

"What's wrong, Mama John? You look like you seen a ghost!" Pointing, Jimmy Joe added with a grin. "You gonna chase him off with that spoon?"

Mama John patted her heart. "Don't pay me no mind, babies. Pick'll be back directly and I mean to see you children is behavin. Jimmy Joe, you call me if you need me."

Panting every step of the way home, Mama John burst through the door. "Mule, Mule! Old man, somethin is wrong. Somethin is bad wrong! It ain't with the children so hit's got to be with Pick! You tell me, old man, you did return the gas in her Papa's truck, didn't you?"

Guilt washed over Mule's face. He hung his head and whispered. "No Mama, I s'pose I didn't."

"Oh, Sweet Jesus! That poor baby is out in this freezin storm and hasn't a way home. Old man, we done let that baby down!" Tears streamed from her eyes as Mama John buried her face in Mule's slumped shoulder.

Snow fell in torrents. It obliterated any landmark that Pick might have recognized. She looked for the thick stand of trees that marked the highest rise this side of the Big Black Mountain. Gum trees. Stump's gum trees. She saw nothing but a blizzard of snow.

Pick's hands grew numb from the cold. She blew on them until the warmth in her breath turned as cold as the frigid wind that stung her face and legs. She bent her head into the blinding snow, tucked her hands beneath her arms, and sobbed.

Mama John paced from the window to the door peering frequently out at the snow that blanketed Widows Hollow.

The fire Jimmy Joe had blazing in her front room could not chase the chill from the cabin. Mama John's children played quietly with Pick's siblings. There was no horseplay and no laughter to lighten the burden of fear.

Coal oil lamps that never burned this late in Widows Hollow flickered brightly in Mama John's window. Similar lights shone from windows up and down the hollow, lights that were meant to guide Pick home.

Jimmy Joe, Jimbo, Mule, and Mama John talked in hushed tones.

"Mama, me and these boys kin go find 'er. Ain't no use in Pick bein out there all alone."

"Hush up, old man! There ain't no use in yer being lost out there in this blizzard, too. The Good Lord's got His eye on my little sparra. He'll bring 'er in shortly, we just got to keep prayin."

"EeeeeAwwwwww."

Mama John snapped her head to the sound at the front door. Straining to hear, she raised her hand for silence.

"EeeeeAwwwwww."

"He done sent her home!" she exclaimed. Mama John waved her kerchief joyfully and tripped over Mule's feet in her hurry to open the door.

"I know that raggity hat and neck scarf!" Mama John dropped one hand to her hip and pointed with the other. "Stump Simpson, what on earth is you doin' out in this freezin storm this late of an evenin?"

Bundled up in his long johns, overalls, and barn coat, Stump Simpson looked like a plump snowman. He wore his hat wrapped onto his head with a muffler and stomped snow from his boots on Mama John's porch.

He spit a dark stain of tobacco juice in the snow, wiped his mouth, and said, "Old Buster's been agitated all evenin. Wouldn't give me a minute's peace. I was gonna take a hick'ry to 'im when I saw the cause of his misbehavin. What's happenin Early Mae, causin all the lamps to be lit?"

"Hit's my doin, Stump," Mule cried as he pushed past Mama John. "I done gone and let that old truck of Joseph's run clean out of gas. Pick's in it other side of the holler. She went callin on the rich folks fer work this mornin. She shuda been back by supper but we ain't seen nothin of her. Mama's bout wore out this floor with her pacin and carryin on."

"Nuf said," Stump replied. "Early Mae, you and Mule git on back in the house and git yerselfs some sleep. Me and Buster'll go find Pick. We'll bring 'er home."

Stump's retreating steps thudded across the porch. He untied his mule and swung his stout, compact body onto the animal's back. He gently toed the mule in his side and said with a cluck of his tongue, "Buster, find Pick."

The new construction on the other side of the hollow was familiar to Stump. He and his aging mule knew every inch of this territory.

Stump, who had lived too long to be surprised, practiced what his Pa had taught him when Stump was no bigger than an acorn. "A wise man has more than he shows and tells less than he knows."

Though Stump was first to admit that he could talk a blue streak, he had never admitted how much more he knew than he told.

Mule and rider plodded along mile after mile. They turned beneath the brick arch unaware of the car that followed.

The car stopped. The sound of a door scraping open was followed by the sound of rapid footsteps that crunched through the snow.

Stump flailed at the blinding glare. He swiped dangerously close to the nose of the familiar young policeman who shined the flashlight in his eyes.

"Stump Simpson! What in the hell are you and your crippled old mule doing in town in this blizzard this late at night?"

"We're lookin' fer a friend, Billy Ray. Joe McKinley's girl, Pick. She come early lookin fer work. That'd be her Papa's pickup yonder," Stump said, nodding at the old Chevy. "Let's pay a visit to young Master Stalworth."

"Stump! You can't disturb the Stalworths at this hour!" Billy Ray's eyes stretched wide as pancakes.

"This hour or any other! I ain't beholdin to them nary a mite and I've a fair mind there's the reason Pick ain't to home. I'll be goin with ye or without ye!" Stump cried.

He emphasized his words with a nod and with a stream of tobacco juice he sent flying within an inch of Billy Ray's boots.

At Stump's insistent pounding, the Stalworths' housekeeper answered the door. She raised her brows, dropped her jaw-- and never got a word in. The curious little man at the door with Billy Ray by his side made no polite inquiry. He sought no assistance. He issued orders.

"Fetch yer Master Stephen!"

Billy Ray shot the woman a "do as he says" look.

With a wide-eyed glare at Stump, the woman snapped her jaw shut and marched off mumbling something about "unwashed, beggarly heathens."

Stephen Stalworth stomped into the foyer. "Has the whole world gone mad, Billy Ra…?"

"Save yer breath! I'm lookin fer a friend that come callin this mornin. She ain't to home yet and I'm here aimin to fetch 'er. Might you be knowin where I kin find 'er?" Stump demanded, glowering at Stalworth.

Unaccustomed as he was to being forced to answer questions he was not prepared to answer, Stalworth stammered. "She left early this morning, and, and her truck wouldn't start...."

"And I reckon you bout broke yore neck offerin to help 'er with it!" Stump stormed.

"Ah, well no, actually, I was late for work and...."

Stump turned his back on Stalworth. With the toe of his boot he scraped snow from the porch steps.

He bent close to the cleared steps and ran a finger across a dark, rust-colored stain.

Stump stood. He fixed Stalworth with a glare, pointed to the sky, and cried. "There is a God up there in Heaven. He's the very one you better be prayin to," he jabbed a finger at Stalworth, "that this" he pointed to the blood stains on the steps, "ain't her'n!"

"He's threatening me! This demented old hermit is threatening me!" Stalworth screamed at Billy Ray.

The young officer cowered beside Stump.

"What in thunder is going on here?" The voice that boomed behind Stephen boomed from a broad shouldered, white-haired man who swept into the foyer like a fullback dressed in a velour bathrobe. He clamped a hand on Stephen's shoulder and shoved him aside.

"Stephen, what's going on here? Who are these peo...?"

"I'm what's going on here! I'm looking for Joe McKinley's girl and I've a fair mind this book-rich, brain-poor young buck of yer'n is the reason she's lost in this sufferin snow! I ain't threatened 'im yet, but he kin count on hit's comin if'n I don't find 'er quick!" Stump shouted and angrily waved a finger at the junior Stalworth.

The bluster drained from Clay Stalworth's face. Better known as Henry Claymore Stalworth, by far the town's most powerful and respected man, he wasted no time greeting his visitor with his hand outstretched.

"Why, Samuel Simpson! Come in, friend, come in! I am certain we can take care of any problem that my boy may have caused!" He cut his eyes to his son who stared back in disbelief. "Stephen! Get Mr. Simpson anything he likes and be quick about it!"

"What I like, Clay Stalworth is Pick McKinley, safe at home where she belongs. But if I'm hearin' correctly, she came callin here this mornin and was shown the door with some powerful showin."

"Yer steps say she fell down em and got hurt in the doin. That old truck of her Pa's is out of fuel at yer curb and she was so full a'fright she run into this storm and's been lost since."

"Stephen, what do you know about this?" Clay demanded. "Was the girl here or wasn't she?"

"Well, Father, I...."

"I ain't got time to waste with yer family matters. The child is like froze a'ready!" Stump insisted.

"Stephen, get the car. We'll drive Mr. Simpson."

"Billy Ray'll drive me," Stump said with a nod to the young officer. He pointed to Buster. "My mule's tuckered out, though. He'd appreciate a lift, Stephen."

Stephen glowered at Stump and at Buster.

"Load that mule and be careful with him!" Clay barked as he climbed in the back seat of the patrol car behind Stump and Billy Ray.

Furious, but unwilling to further anger his father, Stephen shouted at the ranch hands who, in his opinion, moved too slowly loading Buster in a horse trailer.

The snow fell faster than the wipers could clear it from the patrol car windows. Stump strained to see beyond miles and miles of fences, split rail, barbed wire, and iron, wrought iron that rose skyward, post by post, and was graced with spires that rivaled anything that had or might ornament the hood of a Rolls Silver-Cloud.

The road stretched and wound past palatial estates, the private residences of some of Kentucky's best-known horse breeders.

Bronzed images of many of the Derby's immortal champions stood like silent sentinels, guarding the vast accumulations of wealth their breed and speed afforded their owners.

Stump pulled a Red Horse pouch from his pocket and bit off a chew of tobacco. He pocketed the pouch as the road ended abruptly at the tree-lined entrance to the ranch of Klaus and Olga Vandeventer.

Bronze images of the couple's top moneymakers reared on pedestals supporting an iron arch that announced,

"Vandeventer Farms." Heavy iron gates, chained and padlocked, swung across the road beneath the arch.

"This is the end of the line, Stump," Billy Ray said and switched off the spotlight.

"The end of the line is at the back of this property Billy Ray." Stump pushed open the door, spat another dark stain of tobacco juice in the snow and hurried to the locked gate.

"We can't open that gate! We'll have to wait until morning," Billy Ray cried.

"You get on yer fancy little talkin radio and have yer captain wake em' to let us in, or I'll be a goin in, no matter."

With sweat beads popping on his brow Billy Ray cried, "Captain Bradley ain't going to disturb the Vandeventers in the middle of the night Stump, it ain't decent."

"I ain't never been accused of bein decent no how," Stump said. He pulled his Smith & Wesson K-38 Masterpiece from his coat and fired. The lock shattered. Heavy chains rattled to the ground with a thud.

"Oh good God, the man's insane!" Stephen swore from his '51 Chevy pickup that idled a few feet behind the patrol car.

"Let's go!" Stump ordered and swung the gate open. He motioned Billy Ray forward, shoved his gun beneath his coat, and returned to the front seat.

"Klaus could use a little excitement in his life," Clay said with a nervous laugh.

As the party approached the main house, lights flickered on inside. Lights flooded the grounds in an instant, illuminating tennis courts, a swimming pool, and the grand house itself with its marble columns and second story verandas.

Riders on horseback circled the cars. "Halt, you're on private property!" A cowboy with reins in his fist and a shotgun across his arm issued the order to the men who exited the patrol car and the pickup.

The oak doors of the stately mansion swung open.

Klaus and Olga Vandeventer, dressed in jeans, sheepskin coats and boots, hurried to identify their uninvited guests.

Chapter Seven

Olga Vandeventer clutched the arm of her husband, Klaus, a short, stout man with blue eyes and a halo of silver hair that matched his beard and moustache.

"Tanner," Olga called, swinging her waist-long silver hair as she turned to address the ranch foreman. "Who are dese people?"

Stump, Billy Ray and the Stalworths approached the house. Clay advanced ahead and offered his hand. "Klaus, Olga, it's…."

Smiling, Klaus nodded at Clay and stepped past him to Stump. He wrapped his short arms around the man and embraced him with enthusiasm.

"Stump!" He cried in his thick Dutch accent. "Vot brings you shootin up my gates in da middle of da night?"

Stump returned the man's embrace and touched his hat brim to Olga. "Mam," he said with a nod of respect.

Henry Stalworth shook Klauses' hand with a look of surprise. "Klaus, you know Mr. Simpson?"

"Know Mr. Simpson?" Klaus replied with a laugh. "You mean Stump? Dis man teach me to fish and he teach me about da horses. Me and Mama, ve vould 'ave no business vidout Stump."

Stephen took Klauses' hand and asked with a note of skepticism, "He, Simpson, taught you about horses?"

Klaus nodded. "Stump teach jour father, too." He turned from Stephen who appeared thunderstruck, to Stump.

Stump made a face and swung his head to a banging noise in the horse trailer that was attached to Stephen's pickup.

"Buster, you settle down in there," Stump shouted. "I'll get to ye in a minute."

"Blame mule's spoiled, wantin attention," Stump said with a grin. He pulled his hat from his head and slapped it against his leg, spilling snow to the ground.

He replaced the hat and said to Klaus "Pick McKinley's lost in this storm." He pointed to the pasture behind the house. "And I'm thinkin she's out there, back of yer place."

"Zho-sef's leetle red haired dotter?"

"The same, Klaus, only she ain't so little no more. I'm afeared fer 'er. She ain't fittin dressed fer this blizzard and she's been out in it fer hours. What's back of the house?"

"Vy, de woods and de lake."

"How fer they go Klaus?"

"Few mi'els, not so bery many."

"I'll be needin Buster," Stump said. He tied the muffler around his hat and cast a glance at Stephen.

Stephen responded with an angry glare.

"Now!" The senior Stalworth barked. He snapped his fingers and met Stephen's eyes with a threat in his own.

Ranch hands, armed and mounted, awaited the Vandeventers' instructions.

In an accent thicker than her husband's, Olga addressed her ranch foreman. "Saddle Starbuck and Rogue quickly please, ve appreciate if you help us find de lost child."

Klaus led the way on Rogue, his black stallion. Olga followed on her pet buckskin, Starbuck. Stump lagged behind on Buster.

The Stalworths and Billy Ray rode double behind ranch hands that reined their horses for the sprawling acres behind the Vandeventer home.

"Peek! Peek!" The name, shouted with an accent, mixed with the muted rumble of thundering hooves across the snowy fields.

"Buster, find Pick," Stump commanded. He reined the mule toward the gently rolling hills that sloped to a small lake.

Klaus and Olga led the others in the opposite direction.

Fighting gusting winds that piled snow in deep drifts, Buster picked up his pace. He followed the lake's curving shoreline to its farthest end where he stopped abruptly. He pitched his head up and down, brayed loudly, and pawed the ground.

"What is it, Buster?" Stump squinted into the darkness but saw nothing but endless fields of snow.

Buster brayed again and pawed the ground.

Stump patted his mule's neck and slid from his back. Carefully, he kicked at snowdrifts until his boot touched something solid. He dropped to his knees to feel with his hands. His excitement grew as he identified the object as a boat, a small skiff of some kind, turned upside down.

Stump's pulse raced as he lifted the boat and shoved it over. "She's here, I kin feel 'er!" He said to Buster. Stump took a minute to adjust his eyes, then he fell to his knees—and screamed.

"Klaus, Klaus!" Stump pulled his gun from beneath his coat and fired it in the air. Before the smoke cleared, the ground beneath him rumbled with the approach of galloping horses.

A car engine whined behind him, blinding Stump in its headlights. Horses snorted and whinnied, leather saddles popped and crackled as horses, riders, and young Klaus Janssen Vandeventer converged on Stump.

Stump's speckled hands trembled as he pulled away the ragged coat that covered Pick's face and shoulders. He let out a groan, pulled a knotted fist to his eyes, and cried. "Joseph! I'm so sorry, Joseph!"

Pick's bloody hands lay frozen to her swollen face. Blue and lifeless, she lay curled in a tight knot with her thin arms crossed over her chest.

Her legs were bloody and bruised, with one bluish-black foot bare and exposed, missing a boot.

Placing a gentle hand on Stump's shoulder, Jan reached past him. He lifted Pick's wrist and met his mother's eyes with a look of dread. Suddenly, Jan sought Stump's eyes. "She's alive!" He exclaimed. "Mama, bring blankets!"

Olga slid from Starbuck's saddle and hurried to her son's Jeep for blankets.

Stump wrapped his arms around his mule's neck and sobbed.

Klaus, Olga, and two of their ranch hands stretched a blanket open between them. Jan carefully shoveled his arms beneath Pick's body and lifted her as she lay onto the blanket.

Jan helped Stump into the cargo area of his Jeep and helped him pull the blanket with Pick's body curled on top, to him. Jan climbed in after Stump.

"Tanner, see to our mounts. Feed Mr. Simpson's mule and take 'im 'ome, please. You boys ged some sleep now. Thank you for your help."

Klaus took his leave of the Stalworths with a handshake. "Clay, Stephen, it vas good to see you, do nod be strangers. I do nod vant to be rude, but you understand ve must hurry."

"Of course, Klaus. Please keep us posted on the girl's condition and let us know if there's anything we can do to help."

Klaus released Rogue and Starbuck to Tanner and then slid into the driver's seat beside Olga.

"Mr. Stalworth, Sir, ride Rogue if you like, your son can take Starbuck back to the house," the ranch foreman offered.

"That sounds good to me," Clay said, then added, "Stephen, you lead Buster and don't hurry him. That mule is older than you are."

Klaus drove as fast as he dared to the hospital, cautiously ignoring red lights and yield signs.

Olga sat in silence, praying they had not found the girl too late.

With his eyes on Pick's face, Jan ripped through her tattered dress with his pocketknife and gently encircled her icy, fetal-positioned body with his own.

Falling forward on his knees, Stump wrapped Pick and Jan in his arms, then covered them both with his tears—and his prayers.

Chapter Eight

Mama John dragged the tail of her nightgown over sleeping children that lay like logs before the fire in her front room. Breathless, she tugged open the door. Peering into the snowy dawn, she could just make out the shape of a patrol car.

She gathered her gown in hand and flew across the porch to the yard before Billy Ray opened the car door.

Mama John had wrestled with guilt and worry all night. This morning, Pick's continued absence had pushed Mama John's blood pressure to new heights.

She about yanked the door off its hinges, startling the weary young officer who apologized through his yawn. "I'm sorry for waking you, Mam, but Stump, he sent me to tell you Miss McKinley's all right."

With one hand on the door handle, Mama John dropped her wagging head and froze.

Alarmed, Billy Ray scrambled from the car.

"Hallelujah! Oh, hallelujah, Jesus!" Mama John shouted, bursting in exaltations and waving her arms to Heaven. Jumping in Pentecostal profundity, she locked her arms around Billy Ray and swung him like a puppet on a pogo stick.

Squashed between her plump arms and her bountiful bosoms, Billy Ray gasped.

He staggered when Mama John released him, folded himself hands on knees, and drew in great gulps of air.

"They found 'er, early this morning back of the Vandeventers' by the lake. She was near froze."

Mama John's wide eyes, shaking head and threatening arms prompted him to add quickly "But she's all right. Stable. Up county. They're gonna keep her for a while to make sure."

With her face tilted skyward, Mama John waved to the angels that she felt certain rejoiced with her.

Billy Ray hiked a thumb at the horse trailer that was hitched to the patrol car. "Stump's mule's in there. Stump said you'd see to him until Stump gets back."

"Don't you worry none bout ol' Buster, we'll take good care of 'im," Mama John said. "You better come on in and warm up with some nice coffee, hot biscuits and gravy."

Without waiting for his reply, Mama John pulled the boy along, shouting, "Mule! Mule! Our baby's all right! They done found Pick. She's all right!"

Mama John waved her kerchief at the yawning youngsters that poked their heads out the door. "You boys fetch Buster out of that horse carrier. Give him some water and somethin to eat."

Giddy with joy, Mama John hugged Billy Ray and Mule, who hurried to join them in his nightclothes.

73

The clerk peered over her reading glasses at the strange pair that slept on the sofa in Pick's hospital room.

"Miss, Miss," she spoke in low tones to Pick. "Miss... Pick," the woman repeated. Pick did not open her eyes.

The old man who slept on the sofa did. "What'er you a doin?" Stump demanded.

"I'm from accounting," the clerk replied. "I need billing information on this patient." She stared at the unkempt spectacle and muttered quietly to herself, "As if that's any of your business."

"You don't be wakin 'er fer no billin purposes," Stump said. He pushed himself from the sofa, fumbled his hat on his head and added, "Samuel Simpson's all the information you'll be needin. Now go on, git out of here, let the child sleep."

Clearly irritated at the gall of this arrogant *hillbilly*, the clerk narrowed her eyes to slits. "I am authorized to question this patient to determine who is responsible for her medical expenses," she insisted.

If Stump had been a cursing man, he would have cursed the clerk. Instead, he approached her with rapid steps, repeating, "I just told ye, now I'm a tellin ye agin, git!"

The woman's jaw dropped. "See here, you can't just...."

"Is there a problem, Sandy?" A young brunette addressed the clerk upon entering the room.

Pointing at Stump, the clerk said, "This old, er, this man, ordered me to leave. I need billing information on this patient. We have only her name and Widows Hollow for an address. He claims that Samuel Simpson is all the billing information we need," the clerk said and rolled her eyes.

"Leave the clipboard, Sandy, I'll take care of it for you," the brunette said in a pleasant voice.

The clerk turned over the clipboard and glared at Stump on her way out.

"You don't be wakin 'er, neither!" Stump barked at the brunette who replied "I don't plan to wake her, Mr. Simpson. Are you related?"

"I don't hardly see as how that's any of yer business," Stump replied, twisting his beard.

The woman smiled and rested a hand on Stump's forearm. "Sir, let me buy you a cup of coffee so that we can discuss this young lady, please."

The kindness in the woman's eyes, the sincerity in her voice touched the old man.

"Fine!" He huffed, then added in a softer voice "But I'll be buyin the coffee."

The woman glanced from Pick to the young man who slept in an uncomfortable looking slump on the sofa.

She raised a finger and mouthed to Stump. "One moment," as she stepped to the closet at the foot of Pick's bed, removed a pillow and blanket, and returned to the sofa. She dropped the pillow near the sofa arm and gently pushed the young man toward it.

He fell onto the pillow and stretched his long legs over the opposite end of the sofa.

The woman covered him with the blanket and followed Stump from the room.

Walking through the hospital corridors, the woman introduced herself. "I'm Suzanne Claiborne, Dr. Suzanne Claiborne. And you are Samuel Simpson?"

"Samuel Llewellyn Simpson proper, but folks these parts been callin me Stump fer years. I'm obliged if'n you'd do the same."

"Stump it is," Suzanne said.

Stump's gnarly appearance and barnyard odor invoked waves of gasps and snickers that followed the pair like a wake. Suzanne flashed disapproving scowls at gawking kids and adults. Stump seemed not to notice.

Prompted by some maternal instinct, Suzanne moved closer to Stump who took Suzanne's arm in his own. Without a flicker of an eyelash he said, "Pay 'em no mind, Miss. They's hollower'n a cane pole and not nearly so useful."

Suzanne blinked in surprise. She had regarded Stump as a simple, naïve old man who had wandered too far from home, one who needed the savvy and sophistication of a city-wise female doctor. In a sentence, he cleared that up.

Stump purchased the coffee and seated himself with Suzanne in the noisy cafeteria.

While she detailed the events following Pick's admission to the County Hospital, Suzanne assessed Stump with an innocent eye. "So you see, Mr. Simpson, the prognosis is really very good."

"He throwed her out, didn't he?" Stump blurted, keeping his eyes on the coffee that he swirled in his saucer. He lifted the saucer to his lips, blew across the steaming liquid, and sipped. With the saucer in his hands, he propped his elbows on the table and raised unreadable eyes to Suzanne.

Rattled by Stump's sudden question, Suzanne avoided his gaze and stirred her coffee with vigor. "Why would you ask me that, Mr. Simpson? How would I...?"

"You and him work at the same hospital. A man like him lets git around what others would keep to their selves. You'd know if he throwed 'er out."

Suzanne felt like she and Stump were in a foot race that she was losing. She needed to be a lot faster to keep up with him. "Unfortunately, I was there when he threw her out. It was not a very pleasant experience for your friend or for me."

Stump rattled his saucer to the table and then stood to his feet.

Suzanne clutched his arm. "Wait, Mr. Simpson, please wait. He's not worth...."

Stump flashed Suzanne a genuine, country-bred smile. "Ain't often I kin enjoy a cup a'coffee with a purty young lady," he quipped with a wink.

Suzanne blinked, bewildered.

Stump returned with two cups of coffee. Wrapped in his ragged coat and muffler, he looked like a portly gnome. His beard cascaded down his chest in shades of yellow and white. His wreath of long snowy hair strayed from beneath the old hat that he wore like an appendage.

Suzanne had heard stories about Widows Hollow. The place could have been a leper's colony as far as the townspeople were concerned. The highway that ran between the county and the City of Ashford divided a lot more than prime real estate from rural acreage. Suzanne felt a tug at her heart.

This volatile little creature was one of *them*. She glanced at him thinking, I'm sure he's penniless. How can he possibly pay Pick's medical bills?

Stump poured coffee from his cup in his saucer and raised the saucer to his lips. He slurped the coffee, wiped his mouth with the back of his hand and said, "You a friend of his?"

Suzanne blinked--*his*?

"Stalworth's..."

"I, uh..., no." Suzanne frowned. "We were engaged. If it hadn't been for your Pick, I would have made a terrible mistake and married him. Stephen was difficult. He was impatient and demanding." Her eyes clouded, her voice faded. "But I had no idea that he could be so heartless."

Stump raised an unsteady hand to stroke his beard. The look that crossed his face made Suzanne feel uneasy but she continued.

"Stephen is very class conscious. He's a snob and I can't imagine why he wants to practice medicine. He doesn't need the money. And his heart is not in helping people. I pity him."

The look in Stump's eyes startled Suzanne. He looks troubled. Guilty? She argued herself out of the notion.

"I'll never forget what he said to that poor child. It made me sick! Are you related to her, Mr. Simpson?"

"Stump," he said. "No, she ain't no relation, but might's well be. My own are passed. I ain't got nobody ceptin' my mule, Buster. Pick's pap, Joe McKinley was my friend, my best friend."

"Coal come and took 'em all. Took Joseph. The hard times and the sorrow crippled Isabel, Pick's mama. She put by what she could, cleanin and mendin fer the city folk. Now the hard times is passed on to Pick."

"With four younguns to see to, she went callin on Stalworth lookin fer work. I ain't likely to fergit his treatin of 'er. I ain't never had no quarrel with Clay, but that young buck...." Stump fell silent. His face clouded with a clash of emotions that his beard and stained hat brim could not hide.

"How old is Pick, Mr. Simpson?"

A coughing fit seized the old man. He coughed a violent cough and dropped his head. His hat hid his face. It did not hide the hand he darted under his coat to rub his chest.

Stump dismissed Suzanne's look of alarm with a wave of his hand and continued. "As near as I kin recollect she's sixteen year old and ain't had no schoolin. None of 'em had any schoolin."

"Mr. Simpson, are you telling me that none of the children in that hollow can read or write?"

"Stump," he said, and directed a pointed glance at Suzanne. "Nary a one of 'em. The folks in town are spoilt. They got more'n they know what to do with, they're ruined with it. They can't be bothered with the likes a'neighbors, can't see past their own winders, if ye know what I mean."

Suzanne watched and listened.

Stump had her full attention. He spoke easily now. The fire had returned to his eyes.

Suzanne would admit that she did not know much about the strange, clannish people from the interior of the Appalachian Mountains. The one thing that she did know was that a sixteen-year-old girl named Pick McKinley was powerful kindling to Samuel Llewellyn Simpson.

Chapter Nine

Bright lights. Warm. So warm. Pick floated through the fog of medicated sleep as she slowly roused to consciousness.

A tall man dressed in white scrubs bent over her. He had black hair streaked gray at the temple, and green eyes. She saw no wings. *Shouldn't there be wings?*

The face came into focus as the cloud vapors vanished.

"Aaaaaahhhhhhh!" Pick screamed like a condemned sinner who had wakened in hell to the leering face of Satan himself.

Jolted from sleep by Pick's screams, Jan sprang to her side.

"Why is she so upset? This girl is terrified of you," he cried with a glance at Pick's face. "Call another doctor!"

Dr. Stephen Stalworth snatched the clipboard from the foot rail of Pick's bed and snapped at Jan. "I will not call another doctor. Wait outside or I will call security and have you removed."

"I don't thing your fadder vould like dat," Olga said upon entering the room. She reminded Stalworth of the long-standing friendship that she and Klaus shared with his parents.

"Zhan, help me vis dese packages, please."

Pick kept fearful eyes fixed on Stalworth. She pulled at the IV that she found taped to her hand.

"Please don't." Jan gently touched Pick's hand with two fingers. "You don't need to be afraid. You're safe now," he said, smiling.

He turned and lifted shopping bags from Olga's arms. He piled them on the bed beside Pick and continued. "We're here with a friend of yours, Stump, I believe you call him. He's gone for coffee but he'll be back any minute."

Stump. Tears of relief leaked from Pick's eyes. She took the tissue Olga offered her, wiped her tears, blew her nose, and followed Jan's every move with her eyes.

He was so handsome Pick could not help herself. He had a rugged, smooth face that dimpled when he smiled. His eyes were bluer than a clear mountain sky. The sandy blonde hair that fell across his forehead made him look gentle and boyish, but the broad shoulders, muscled arms, and square jaw defined a man. He might be a little older than Pick, but not much, she felt certain.

"I'm Klaus Janssen Vandeventer, Jr.," he said and raked a wayward shock of hair from his forehead.

"I reckon that's a mouthful." Pick made a face and crossed her eyes.

Jan laughed. "I reckon it is," he said, surprised at himself for his quick retort. The dimples in his face sank deeper. "And this is my mother, Olga."

Pick smiled at the little woman.

Olga's face shone with a kindness that Pick rarely saw. She was dressed in a light blue sweater with satin appliqués and tailored pants of gray wool. Her shining silver hair hung to her waist behind a blue velvet headband.

"We've had quite a night," Jan said through his lopsided grin. "Stump came calling a bit late and woke us with a gunshot."

"A gunshot?" Pick cried.

"Stump wasn't about to let our locked fences keep him from finding you before you froze to death."

Jan's eyes softened. "And you almost did, you know. Stump and his mule found you under a boat at the back of our property."

Pick's cheeks flamed crimson. "I'm sorry fer causin so much trouble. I just wanted to git home. Home!" She cried, darting her eyes to the window. "The younguns must be worried clean out of their skin. They ain't got no idea where I'm off to. I got to git home right now!" Pick threw off the covers and pulled again at the tape that held the IV in place.

"Whoa! You can't go anywhere," Jan cried and grabbed Pick's wrist in a reflex.

Pick yanked her hand from his grasp. She pulled it to her chest and recoiled like a threatened animal.

Jan instantly regretted putting his hands on her. The pain on her face tore at him. Fearing that he had frightened her and compromised his credibility beyond redemption, he felt tongue-tied and unsure of himself.

"I'm sorry. I didn't mean to frighten you. Really," Jan said. He looked into her eyes and found himself mesmerized. *Those green eyes….*

"Yer bout the handsomest boy I ever seen," Pick said with her eyes locked on Jan's eyes.

Jan let out a burst of laughter. "Mama, did she really say what I think she said?"

Olga nodded. "I agree vis Peek," she said with a wink.

"Mama!" Jan cried, blushing.

Realizing that Pick had caught him in her gaze, Jan felt as if he relived the dream in which he was naked in public with no place to hide. The lump in his throat felt like a football. *Great! Melt-down!* He chided himself and tugged at the neck of his sweater.

Jan grew increasingly irritated with himself. His mind went blank. His vocabulary vanished. He grasped for a thought, a sentence, a word….

"Stump sent the policeman that drove him to our home to tell, uh, Mama John, is it? And your family that we found you, that you are all right and that you will be home tomorrow. So quit pulling on that needle." He grimaced, then added, "Ain't nobody worryin out of their skins."

Pick's face crinkled with an impish grin. "Glad you got that out, ain't cha?"

Jan stared, unable to answer. *What's happening to me? My tongue won't move. My palms are wet. Her eyes are like magnets, her speech-unbelievable. And she's making ME sweat!* He wiped his palms on his jeans.

"Peek… May I call you Peek?" Olga asked, patting Pick's hand.

Peek?" Pick pointed to Olga. "Is that my name she's sayin?"

Jan laughed. "Yes, my parents are natives of Amsterdam. They came to America after they married and their Dutch accents came with them.

Pick's eyes lingered on Jan's face. *Such beautiful dimples....*

Jan stood smiling with his arms crossed. He nodded to Pick and without uncrossing his arms, wiggled a finger at Olga.

"Oh, yes Mam, you may call me Peek," Pick gushed.

They all let out a bit of nervous laughter.

Dr. Stephen Stalworth, however, did not laugh. He cleared his throat. "Ahem, I have duties to attend. Since you are not related, please wait outside while I examine my patient."

Pick shook her head violently. She grabbed Jan's hand and with her eyes she pleaded. "Don't leave me alone with him!"

Olga exchanged startled glances with Jan as Suzanne Claiborne entered the room at a brisk pace.

"Dr. Stalworth, I'll be responsible for this patient now," Suzanne said and took Pick's file from Stalworth.

"Mrs. Vandeventer, Mr. Vandeventer, if you will please give us a moment."

"Ah, Suzanne, who authorized this reassignment?" Stalworth asked, frowning.

"That's *Doctor* Claiborne, Dr. Stalworth," Suzanne snapped. She moved to Pick's bedside, careful to keep her back to Stalworth.

"Check with Dr. Hollingsworth. Perhaps as the hospital Chief of Staff *he* will meet with your approval! He reassigned this patient."

"Ve vill be back, Peek," Olga said.

Jan let go Pick's hand but he held her eyes. He hesitated before leaving the room with his mother and Stalworth.

"You need to get some rest young lady," Suzanne said to Pick who watched with interest as Suzanne wrapped a cuff around Pick's forearm.

"You was there, wasn't ya, Miss?" Pick blurted.

Suzanne had hoped to avoid this conversation. Careful not to meet Pick's eyes, she replied, "Yes, I was there."

"You heerd him, didn't ya?"

Suzanne fought an overwhelming urge to burst into tears. *It must have taken enormous courage for this frail young woman to leave her safe, familiar environment to drive to the city and ask powerful strangers for work. Then, to be thrown out so cruelly, and called such heartless names....*

"Miss? Miss, why are you cying?" Tears glazed Pick's eyes. Her lip quivered. She pulled Kleenex from a box and wadded them in Suzanne's hand.

"Oh, I'm so sorry! I didn't realize I was... I didn't mean to...," Suzanne fell silent and patted her eyes with the Kleenex.

Pick burst into tears. Looking shattered and forlorn, she cried to Suzanne. "What is it I done, Miss?"

Suzanne looked horrified. "What? Oh, no, child, you have done nothing!"

"Then what are you cryin fer?"

Suzanne took Pick's hand. "I apologize Pick, I didn't mean to upset you, it's just that, that," Suzanne broke into sobs.

"I can't understand such cruelty! I felt so bad for you when he threw you out, I wanted to stop him, to find you and take you home, but you were gone!"

"I am so sorry! Oh, please Pick, please don't believe that all strangers are like Stalworth. It's not true. He's a bad apple in a world full of good people. You'll see. I promise."

Suzanne dried her eyes and composed herself. She noted Pick's unique beauty as she checked her blood pressure.

"Why did he call me white-trash? He took on like I done him wrong and I never." Pick's eyes filled with tears.

"There is no easy answer to your question, Pick. Some people have never experienced hardship. They live life as if they are in a bubble.

All is well as long as all is well *with them*. But the minute tragedy strikes and they find themselves as vulnerable as the rest of us, they begin to see things differently very quickly."

"They realize that despite all their money, power, and success, they really aren't so different from those who have none."

"People like Mr. Stalworth choose to believe that they are insulated from hardship and tragedy forever. When Mr. Stalworth saw you in his home, he had to face reality. He didn't like that. But I'm sure if he got to know you and your friends, he would see things differently."

"Has times been easy fer you, Mam?"

Suzanne caught her bottom lip with her teeth. "I guess they have been. I can't say that I've had to struggle, but I don't try to isolate myself from people that do. I met one of your friends this morning." Suzanne's cheeks dimpled. "I like him a lot."

"That'd be Stump," Pick said with a grin. "Do you like Mose and Amy Beth and their new twins?"

"Mose?" Suzanne knit her brows.

"Mose Tate and his wife, Amy Beth. They come here to have their younguns. I come with 'em."

"Mr..., Mose Tate is your friend?" Suzanne looked surprised.

"Yes'm. They live up holler from us. They's bout bustin their buttons, they's so proud of them boys."

"The Tates took one of the babies home yesterday. The smaller twin, Joseph, I believe, isn't strong enough yet. He'll be staying with us for a few more days."

"Kin I see 'im?"

"I see no reason why you can't," Suzanne said and stuck a thermometer in Pick's mouth. She wondered at this young girl who showed such concern for others when she herself had nearly frozen to death the night before.

Suzanne Claiborne lived by a code that cautioned against becoming emotionally involved with patients. Suzanne never had. But as she contemplated this incredible, determined orphan, she suspected that all of that was going to change. Today.

The furrows in Pick's brow disappeared. Her sudden smile caused Suzanne to wonder if Pick had read her thoughts.

Suzanne removed the thermometer, noted Pick's temperature, shook the mercury down, and asked on impulse. "Pick, if a good fairy could grant you one wish, any wish at all, what would you wish for?"

"Oh, I already got me a good fairy, Miss."

"You do?" Suzanne tucked Pick's chart under her arm, then gave Pick her undivided attention.

"Oh, yes'm. Her name is Rosemillion."

"Rosemillion," Suzanne repeated. "I've never heard that name. It's beautiful."

"You want I should tell you about her?"

"Please."

"Once upon a time there was a...."

A small group that had gathered outside her door listened as Pick told the tale.

"Dat's a beautiful story," Olga said.

Stump scratched his chin with a speckled hand and with a faraway look in his eyes.

And Jan asked himself what held him here at the County Hospital in the company of this eccentric old man.

Jan felt certain that he knew and felt equally certain that he could not explain it even to himself. It was this illiterate, impoverished, unpredictable straight-talking, orphan from Widows Hollow.

Chapter Ten

Suzanne finished examining Pick. "Looks like you're gonna be fit as a fiddle by tomorrow young lady and that means that you may see the Tate's youngun!"

"May ve come in now?" Olga asked from the doorway.

"Yes, please do," Suzanne said with a wave. "Pick's going to be fine. She's ready to go visiting."

Olga scowled at Pick's gaunt, mud and blood-streaked frame and at her knotted hair. Pick was not ready to go anywhere but the shower.

Olga shook her head. "Peek, Sweetie, I do nod thing you are ready to go visiting, but Olga fix dat. Open dese packages, I show you," she invited.

Pick pulled a fancy shopping bag close and removed pastel shirts, jeans, socks, shoes, satiny underclothes, a pink nightgown, and a soft pink bathrobe. A second bag contained fragrant lotions, hair care products, a hairbrush and mirror, a pink satin hair ribbon and a book.

Pick opened the book then closed it quickly. Shame-faced she stammered. "I thank you kindly Miss Olga, but there ain't no pictures in this book and I can't read."

Seeing Pick's spirits nosedive beneath this new humiliation, Suzanne's heart went out to the girl. Suzanne could not dismiss the mental image of Stalworth screaming at Pick and calling Pick names.

Suzanne questioned herself. "What do I have to offer her that might guarantee that Pick will never suffer such humiliation again?"

Suzanne folded Pick's new items of clothing. "Pick, would you mind if a lonely human with too much time on her hands perhaps made one of your wishes come true?"

"I don't reckon I would, Miss," Pick said, her eyes downcast, her voice hollow.

"Consider it done!" Suzanne cried and felt the sudden warmth and satisfaction that comes with doing for others.

She leaned close to Pick. "I have a library in my home too and I've read most of the books in it. I love to read. I think it's a shame to let good books sit on the shelves collecting dust. So, if you will allow me, I would like very much to teach you and your friends to read."

Speechless, Pick stared at Suzanne. After a moment Pick let out a squeal of delight and hugged the petite doctor.

Suzanne responded with "This is my chance Pick, to prove to you that not all strangers are bad. And thank you for giving me this opportunity. I look forward to it."

"And one more thing, Miss Pick." Suzanne's eyes were playful.

"Yes, Miss?"

"I would be most *obliged* if you would call me Suzanne."

"Yes, Mam—Suzanne."

"Oh, Peek, how vunderfal!" Olga cried as Suzanne excused herself to attend other patients. Olga waved limp palms at Stump and Jan. "You boys shoo now, Peek and I have verk to do."

Suddenly, like a woman possessed, Pick ripped the IV from her hand and threw off the covers. With the pink ribbon clutched in her hand, she shoved past Olga and Jan and raced from the room.

"Peek! Peek, you mustn't!" Olga cried.

Breathless, and despite her swollen foot, Pick ran as fast as she could down the corridor where she found Mose Tate sobbing. Dr. Stephen Stalworth had the man by the arm.

"What's wrong, Mose? What's wrong?"

"Pick, Pick! He's sayin my Joseph ain't gonna live!"

"Amy Beth's to home with Edward Moses, I come to stay with Joseph and this doctor's tellin me my boy ain't gonna live. He's tellin me to fetch Amy Beth so's she kin say good-bye."

"Pick, my baby! I can't be losin my baby! Lord, help me, I can't tell Amy Beth we's losin Joseph!"

Suzanne stepped off an elevator to see Mose in tears with Pick at his side. Alarmed, Suzanne hurried to them.

Olga, Jan and Stump were not far behind.

"Mose, you go git Amy Beth and Edward. Hurry now!" Pick ordered.

"Mr. Tate, Sir, I'll drive you," Jan offered.

With wet eyes Mose stared blankly at Jan.

Stump clamped a hand on Moses' shoulder. "Jan's a friend, Mose. I'll come with ye if ye don't mind."

"Let me see 'im, Suzanne. Please kin I see 'im?" Pick begged after the men had departed.

Suzanne shook her head. "You need to be in bed young lady."

Olga wrapped the pink bathrobe she bought for Pick around Pick's shoulders and dropped the pink slippers at Pick's feet. "You vear dese. Olga come vis you."

"Thank you, Olga," Suzanne said. "Maybe the two of us can take care of her since she refuses to take care of herself."

Hand in hand, Pick and Olga followed Suzanne into an elevator. The elevator rumbled to the second floor where the women exited and continued on to a set of swinging doors marked Maternity Ward.

A swarm of new parents, friends, and relatives made fools of themselves before the glass. They made faces and strange noises at the newborns that slept undisturbed in their transparent plastic cradles or that flailed the air with tiny fists, wailing for attention.

Suzanne led the way through a second set of doors. These were marked No Visitors Past This Point. The women stopped before a glass nursery.

Inside the nursery a doctor dressed in green scrubs and wearing a sterile face mask performed procedures on a tiny infant through portals in an incubator. Nurses huddled near the doctor.

After a few moments the doctor peered at data on a glowing screen. He shook his head, withdrew his hands from inside the portals and peeled off his latex gloves.

Pick caught the sparkle of tears in the nurses' eyes as they turned in haste from the window.

She heard a whisper in her mind. It was a voice, a beautiful sweet voice, singing. Pick searched her memory. *I know that tune...and I remember some of the words!* Pick repeated the words to herself in silence. *"Sing, Rosamond, sing, let your beautiful music take wing."*

Pick dropped her head against the glass. She felt Suzanne's touch on her shoulder and looked up. "What's wrong with the baby? Why ain't he strong as the other'n?"

"Pick, his lungs aren't fully developed. He can't breathe very well and if he can't breathe, he can't live. He's getting weaker by the minute. I'm afraid his mother may not make it."

Suzanne squeezed Pick's shoulders and then joined her peers inside the nursery just moments ahead of Dr. Stalworth who pushed through the door in a rush.

Pick lingered at the window with Olga. Together they watched the medical team monitor the still, tiny baby when Pick turned away at the sound of rapid footsteps.

Mose, Stump and Jan had returned with Amy Beth. Amy Beth's face was red, her eyes swollen with tears. With Edward Moses clutched to her chest, she burst into sobs at the sight of his still, pale twin. Her pitiful sobs echoed through the hospital corridors. "Please don't take him Lord, please don't take him!" Pick had never felt so helpless. Her heart broke for the grieving young mother. She was desperate to help Mose and Amy Beth, but what could she say? What could she do? Amy Beth's sobs became more than Pick could bear. She buried her face in her hands and ran in search of a washroom.

Grateful to be alone in the washroom, Pick grabbed the edge of a stainless sink and fell to her knees on the floor. "Lord, this is Pick. I'm needin you sorely now. Mose and Amy Beth's youngun is dyin. Them doctors say he's gonna die a'fore the hour passes. Show me what to do, Lord. Please show me what to do."

"He's got to git stronger so's he kin breathe. I ain't doubtin them doctors, Lord, it's just they ain't asked You to show 'em what to do. Please help Mose and Amy Beth, Lord. I'm askin in Jesus' name, Amen."

Still and silent, Pick remained on the cold tile floor. Suddenly she picked herself up. She raced out the door and back down the hallway to her friends. In her hurry, she collided with Mose. "Sorry Mose," she cried as she brushed past him.

Pick grabbed Amy Beth's hand. "Amy Beth, bring Edward Moses!" Pick insisted, breathless.

With Amy Beth in tow Pick ran to the nursery window. "Come here!" She demanded. She beat on the window with her fist.

Stalworth turned to the racket. He stormed from the nursery in a fury. "What is the meaning of this?" He demanded.

"I ain't meanin to tell you yer business, but you gotta git that sick little baby and put 'im in a crib with his twin. Put their feet together and tie 'em with this ribbon. Edward Moses kin make Joseph Aaron strong!"

Anger boiled behind Stalworth's eyes. "Surely you don't expect… Are you mad?" Stalworth glared at the spectacle before him.

Pick was battered and bruised. She had streaks of mud on her face, arms and legs. She was half-covered in a faded hospital gown and her wild red hair was twisted in muddy ropes.

And yet she stood before him, an educated and respected member of the medical community, and presumed to tell him how to save a critically ill newborn that would unquestionably expire in seconds.

"Is there no end to the insolence of you intolerable heathens?" Stalworth swore.

Hearing the loud confrontation, Suzanne rushed from the nursery. "What's going on here? What's all the shouting about?"

Stalworth pointed to Pick. "This, this—*person*," he spluttered, "is telling me to take that dying baby from the incubator and put him in a crib with his twin and tie their feet together. That baby will expire the minute we take him off life support!" Stalworth yelled.

Suzanne swung her eyes to Pick.

Pick angrily wagged a finger at Stalworth and cried in tones that grew increasingly louder. "You said he would die a'fore the hour passes. I asked the Good Lord how to make Joseph Aaron strong and it's Himself what told me!"

Pick looked to Suzanne with pleading eyes.

"Pick, I…."

Pick spun to Stalworth. "You may call me white trash. You may hate me and my kind, BUT YOU AIN'T GONNA

CAUSE THAT LITTLE BABY TO BE A DYIN!" Pick snatched Edward Moses Tate, Jr., from Amy Beth. She kissed the baby's forehead and then shoved him in Stalworth's arms.

"Now you tie 'em together at the feet! I ain't the One doin the telling, I'm just deliverin His words!"

"I will never! I refuse to be responsible for this madness!" Stalworth spluttered.

"So I'll be responsible."

"Dr. Hollingsworth!" Suzanne cried.

She was relieved to see the hospital's Chief of Staff, Dr. Dan Hollingsworth, the highly esteemed M.D., Ph.D., Pediatrics and M.D., Ph.D., Orthopedic surgery.

Hollingsworth gave Stalworth a brief nod before entering the nursery with Suzanne.

Nurses responded in quiet voices to Hollingsworth's request for an update on the baby's condition. Hollingsworth read some charts and scanned the data on a computer screen. After a moment he announced in a flat monotone, "The baby's blood pressure is falling. He's losing color. His lungs will collapse any minute. Death is imminent."

Hollingsworth opened the incubator. He removed the tube from the baby's nose that fed the baby oxygen. He disconnected wires and sensors and then lifted the baby up to his eye level.

"Lord, he's in Your hands," he said as he gently placed the tiny Joseph Aaron into a crib.

News of Pick's angry exchange with Stalworth traveled quickly through the hospital. Surgeons, interns, and medical practitioners made their way to the nursery as Hollingsworth motioned through the window for Stalworth to bring baby Edward inside.

Stalworth stomped past Pick in disgust. He carried Edward Moses the same way that he carried vials of toxic bacteria that could prove fatal to humans upon contact.

Hollingsworth took the baby from Stalworth and placed him in the crib with his twin. He took Pick's ribbon from Suzanne and gently tied the babies' feet together.

A hush fell over the nursery and the adjacent corridor.

Pick looked up, stirred by a sudden breeze. She turned to identify its source and found only the empty corridor and music, music that swelled into her consciousness like the voices of an invisible choir singing *How Great Thou Art*.

Goosebumps prickled Pick's arms, for in that same instant, Edward Moses Tate Jr. let out a scream, a loud, lusty, robust scream.

Doubting scowls vanished from the grim-faced MDs who abandoned their bedside manners and elbowed one another in their clamor to get nearer the crib.

Hairs stood on their arms and exclamations spilled from their throats as they witnessed the transformation.

The pink color traveled as visibly as mercury in a thermometer beneath the surface of the baby's skin, from the tips of his tiny toes, across his curled feet, through his legs, waist, chest, and into his face where the pastel tint radiated into a richer hue.

The baby's blue lips quivered and parted. The tiny fists clenched. Joseph Aaron Tate, whose lungs were not fully developed and who, seconds earlier, could not expel a breath, let out a matching scream, just as loud, just as lusty and just as robust as that of his healthier twin.

One after another, doctors bent over the squalling infant with stethoscopes and looks of disbelief. And one after another, they reached the same conclusion. Joseph Aaron Tate's survival and instantaneous recovery were medically *impossible*.

"Mose, do you hear 'im? Do you hear our youngun? That's Joseph a yellin! Mose, Oh, Mose!" Amy Beth cried. Tears spilled from her dark eyes as she joyfully hugged her husband.

Dr. Claiborne and Dr. Hollingsworth laughed. Clutching one another, they rocked in a joyful embrace. Suzanne pointed to Hollingsworth's name tag. "Guess you're still a doctor," she said.

Hollingsworth raked his fingers through his hair. "I've never witnessed anything like it. I hate to question my own competence, but I *saw* it and I'm still not certain that I believe what I saw! That baby didn't have the lung capacity to draw a breath or to make a sound, and to let out a yell like that?"

Hollingsworth shook his head and turned back to the crib. "Listen to him! He's wailing as loud as his brother!"

Mose squeezed Pick in a bear hug. "Pick, it was you what done it! Them doctors said our boy was a dyin, but you wouldn't hear 'em. You knowed how to save our Joseph and you told them doctors! We ain't never gonna fergit it, Pick, we ain't never!"

Pick flashed Mose a happy smile, a happy smile that quickly turned to a look of horror.

Doctors, patients and strangers bombarded Pick with questions. In no time, reporters from the local stations surrounded her with microphones and cameras.

Pick shunned the attention. "I ain't got no answers fer 'em Suzanne! I just want to git home, kin I go home now?"

The reporters ignored Pick's protests. "Are you from Widows Hollow?"

"What is your name?"

"This isn't the first life you've saved, is it?"

"Can you tell us how you do it?"

"Are you the girl they call the Healer from the Hollow? You worked another miracle here today, didn't you?" Reporters shouted their questions in rapid-fire succession.

Suzanne darted her eyes to Pick. *It can't be…* Suzanne recalled reading a newspaper story about a mysterious young girl from Appalachia. The headlines read "The Healer from the Hollows." The story claimed that the girl worked healing miracles but always vanished before she could be photographed or interviewed.

Pick shrank from the camera flashes. She let out a cry and crossed her arms over her face.

"Git 'er outta there!" Stump commanded and shoved Jan forward.

Jan charged through the crowd ahead of Stump who slapped at microphones, cameras, cameramen, and reporters.

A local news cameraman who fired off one blinding shot after another cut Jan off as Jan reached for Pick's hand.

Stump fared no better.

Jan broke through the crowd and caught a glimpse of Pick's face. "Look at her, Stump, she's terrified!"

Jan dropped his head and plowed forward. He bulldozed cameras, cameramen, and indignant reporters out of his way.

A local news anchorman with a microphone in his hand grabbed for Jan's sleeve.

Jan slapped a palm against the young man's chest and shoved him backward, hard. With his free hand, Jan yanked Pick from the crowd, scooped her in his arms, reversed his direction, and charged anyone who stepped into his path.

"Aren't you Jan Vandeventer of Vandeventer Farms?"

Jan set his jaw and kept silent.

"Where is she from? Is she from Widows Hollow?"

"Are you related to this girl?"

"What is your relationship to the healer, Jan?

Jan hastened his step. He refused the reporters so much as a "No comment," and flashed Suzanne a grateful smile for the elevator that she held for him.

"Take her back to her room. We'll get rid of this crowd," Suzanne instructed.

With Pick in his arms Jan ducked in the elevator with Stump. "Where's my mother?" Jan shouted and wedged a boot between the closing doors.

"Zhan!" Olga waved from behind a lanky reporter.

"Move!" Stump yelled to the startled young man who scrambled out of Olga's way.

Stump muttered something about vultures and bones as he grabbed Olga's hand and hauled her into the elevator.

Before the elevator doors closed Pick struggled to free herself from Jan's arms. "Put me down, I kin walk!" She demanded.

With a dazed grin, Jan considered the girl in his arms. How could Pick be so fragile and at the same time be so equally defiant and independent? In all his life Jan had never met anyone like Pick.

"Put me down!" Pick repeated. She slugged Jan in the chest with her fist.

"All right, Miss McKinley, I'll put you down," he said and stared at her with a maddening smile. "But first tell me, are you a miracle worker?"

"No more'n you!" she snapped. Her bare feet hit the floor with a thud. The elevator doors slid open and in an instant, she was gone.

Jan had been chased like a fox in a hunt since high school. Panting packs of females had followed after him, each trying to outdo the other to attract his attention, to win his affection, to inspire his awe. None had succeeded.

But this obstinate orphan, this penniless outcast with the peculiar name who had nearly died in his arms, this *Pick....* Jan shook his head and stared after her retreating figure in awe.

Chapter Eleven

Suzanne watched her neighbor, Andy Welch, shovel snow from his drive with his golden retrievers yapping about him.

Snowplows hummed in the distance, clearing roads for the bustling citizens of Ashford. Andy's garage door opened.

Carla, his wife, appeared inside, dressed in bulky layers of white. *She looks like a snowman,* Suzanne mused. That reminds me, I need to speak with Andy to get some tips on becoming a reading instructor.

The ringing telephone shook her. Suzanne scowled and grabbed the phone. "Hello. Yes, this is Ms. Claiborne," she said, emphasizing the Ms. as dutifully as the caller had. She listened for a moment. "Thank you Mrs. Mainard, I will be there at 4:00 O'clock sharp, with a dish."

"Damn!" She muttered. Why didn't I cancel?" Suzanne's status as a successful doctor qualified her for Ashford society's *B* list. When the emerald green gasps of envy had subsided following the announced *Engagement*, her status had magically levitated into an *A*.

Finding oneself betrothed to the son of Ashford's First Couple had its privileges. Vivian Vinsant Stalworth and Henry Claymore Stalworth came by the First Couple title honestly. The Stalworths were simply victorious in the game called *He who has the most money wins.*

He who has the most money can have any title he wants, along with the strings to a plethora of puppets with little power allotments of their own.

When invited, Suzanne had eagerly joined the Ashford Women's League. She wondered if news of her broken engagement to the First Couple's Firstborn had made the circuit and smiled to herself.

Since *The Announcement*, her mailbox had been bloated with invitations from people with names she recognized solely from the society pages of the Ashford Sentinel.

As soon as this, uh, let's see, what would *they* call it? Tidbit? Bombshell? No, outrage, preposterous outrage, flew from mouth to mouth between every wrinkled old prune on Ashford's party line, she would be lucky to receive anything other than billing statements.

Suzanne laughed. Yes, as soon as *they* heard the news, *they* would see to it that she made no list at all. And the best part? She did not care.

It had been exciting at first, the balls, dinners, galas, and weekends at country estates. But recently, the clink of crystal raised in toasts beneath the tinkling of exquisite multi-tiered crystal chandeliers had become monotonous.

The predictable parade of internationally acclaimed designer fashions had become tedious. The subtle innuendoes, "My dear, Charles can work absolute miracles on the *dreariest* of hair."

Suzanne inflated her cheeks and spewed air from a corner of her mouth. "I wonder which fashionable frock I'll have to drag from the closet to properly impress the ladies."

Suddenly, her mind flew back to her neighbor. *Andy. Andy.* She wrinkled her forehead. *Why did I want to see Andy?* Her subconscious waved flags: Reading. Reading. And then, she had it.

As Superintendent of the Wade County Schools, Andy could help Suzanne in her new venture as a reading instructor. She glanced at her watch which told her she'd missed her opportunity. Andy would be at work now. She would have to speak to him after the meeting.

Take charge, Suzanne, she urged herself. What do I really want to do with these few hours?

She looked at the tiny Christmas tree she had decorated last week. She had placed packages beneath it for her only living relatives, her sister, Dr. Claire Richardson, Claire's husband, Dr. Ross Richardson, and their children, Anthony and Yvette.

Her invitation to the Richardson Estate for Claire's annual Christmas dinner had arrived this week, an invitation to take part in all of the Richardson's traditions like gift opening.

"Ugh, rituals! God, how I hate rituals!" She cried and sailed a sofa pillow at the wall. The pillow hit and bounced off near the tree.

Suzanne glanced at the fragrant spruce with the packages piled beneath it and spoke as if she addressed the tree.

"Christmas this year will be no celebration. I'll attend Claire's dinner, smile and make all the proper noises, then return home to this empty house. The only animated thing in this house besides me is the clock that ticks with a mocking impertinence there on the mantel."

Tingles of excitement followed by an impulsive grin sent Suzanne racing to her bedroom.

Rummaging through her closet, she snatched her favorite, well-worn jeans and a bright red cable knit sweater.

She pulled them on, brushed her hair into a ponytail, and fastened it with a red bow. She smiled at her reflection in the mirror, thumped the Rolex Stephen had given her last Christmas, grabbed her worn Timex, and fastened it to her wrist.

She returned to her closet and slid garments on hangers past her eyes; there was her black mink, blue fox, brown leather, faded, who-cares denim. *Yes!*

Suzanne bounced a triple pirouette on her bare toes. She grabbed the aging denim jacket with its sheepskin cuffs and collar with such energy, the hanger spun, clattering in a circle, around the rod.

She pulled on the coat and a pair of not-so-gently-worn boots, drop-kicked a pillow back onto her bed, and headed for the garage.

Skipping down the steps from the laundry room to the garage, Suzanne glowed. Energized by the thought of her new freedom and independence, she threw back her head, opened her mouth to the sky and falling snow, and threw her arms in the air. "Wahooo!"

She jumped behind the wheel of her Chevy Bel Air, backed from the drive, and headed to Ashford. She would attend the meeting later this afternoon and her past would be behind her. She hoped.

Driving past estate after elaborately decorated estate, Suzanne's mind wandered. She saw smiling faces and heard innocent voices.

"Pay 'em no mind, miss."

"It ain't my words I'm a givin ya."

And whispers. "It's a miracle."

Suzanne peered into her rearview mirror. She had a few hours before the meeting and she could think of no one that she'd rather spend the morning with than Pick McKinley.

Suzanne spun the Chevy in an abrupt, rubber-laying U-turn. Ashford disappeared behind her as she sped toward the county and Widows Hollow.

She replayed the childhood tales that she had heard about the place, tales her parents and others had invented to keep city kids separated from the county kids with their alleged contagious miseries.

Like most of her friends in their teen-age years, Suzanne had visited the wrong side of the tracks on a dare.

Some parents had told tales of the tainted hollows with such conviction and threats of punishment that their offspring had never ventured into any hollow.

Henry Claymore Stalworth must be First Storyteller, too, Suzanne mused. His son had a terror of Widows Hollow. Stephen Stalworth would go to any length to avoid contact with the place or its people.

"Why would Clay Stalworth instill such a horror of Widows Hollow in his own son? It doesn't make sense," Suzanne told herself and glanced at the road ahead. "But most of what I know about the Stalworths doesn't make sense. Not to me, anyway," she said aloud.

She crossed the highway into the county. Entering the maze of trees, ruts, and ravines, Suzanne chided herself. What was I thinking? I don't even have Pick's address. I have nothing but a mental picture of her pickup.

Suzanne grimaced and tightened her grip on the wheel. Her tires spun on solid ice as the Chevy balked at the steep incline. She was losing her confidence. "Maybe this wasn't such a good idea," she told herself.

Suzanne steered the car up the steep grade, onto a one-horse briar ridge that twisted and curved into a dead end.

She backed up and turned onto a pot-holed rut filled with jagged rocks and storm debris.

The rut roller-coastered up and down, following a washboard breech that spilled into a moldy leaf gutter of a drop-dead decline. Suzanne spewed air from her lungs. She was grateful that the violently bouncing car had settled at last on a gravel road that leveled abruptly into an unexpected clearing.

Suzanne leaned over the wheel to stare at the primitive panorama. The valley below was surprisingly populated. She knew that many who lived in Appalachia and all across the Cumberland Plateau lived a primitive existence well below the poverty line, but this... Suzanne wrinkled her brow.

"These people can't read. And those are real log cabins down there!" Suzanne cried, feeling as though she had arrived at this place by way of a time machine that had spit her out half a century into the past.

A sudden *splat!* Jolted Suzanne from her thoughts.

Someone had thrown a snowball from an icy slope to her left. The icy slope was a playground to a number of children who were dressed in ill-fitting jackets and lumpy layers of sweatshirts.

Despite their inadequate clothing, the laughing children swooshed down the slope on cardboard sleds and metal trashcan lids, exhaling frost clouds from their cracked lips.

Some of them raised hands gloved in mismatched socks to their mouths when they coughed, others to wipe filmy mucus from their red noses.

Suzanne guessed the children ranged in age from four and five to their very late teens. A tall, large-framed black boy sat on a rock at the foot of the slope. A younger white boy sat beside him. Two pairs of crutches separated the boys.

The older boy yelled. "Lucy, Lottie, I done tole you to let them babies have a turn." He said to the boy at his side, "Eli, go on and try it. If need be, I kin catch ya."

"I rather sit here with you, Jimbo, and watch the little uns."

What is that heavenly smell? Suzanne rolled down her window and sniffed the air. *Somebody's baking bread.*

"Hey Jimbo, who's that?"

Suzanne glanced up the hill with a start. The children no longer laughed or played. They stood together quietly with their eyes on her.

The big boy stood to his feet and supported himself on crutches. Leveling wary eyes at Suzanne, he dropped a halting hand on the shoulder of the boy at his side.

Suzanne felt a stab of guilt. *I've interrupted their play, and made them feel uncomfortable.* No turning back now, though.

Suzanne climbed from the car and addressed the older boy. "Excuse me, I'm looking for a young woman named Pick."

The boy looked to the top of the slope and yelled. "Jimmy Joe! She's lookin fer Pick."

Three boys came bumping down the hill on makeshift sleds. The oldest scrambled to his feet and brushed snow from his jeans.

He herded the smaller boys behind him and faced Suzanne with eyes that he narrowed in a wary slant. He swatted the head of a curious youngster who peeped around him to see the stranger.

Suzanne felt as if she could read the boy's mind. "What're you doin here? We ain't bothering nobody. Strangers don't come to Widows Holler just wantin to be neighborly."

The boy paused for a moment before he found his voice. "You knowin Pick?" He asked, careful to keep his expression blank and to reveal nothing by word or gesture to this *stranger*.

"Yes sir," Suzanne stammered. "I'm Dr. Suzanne Claiborne, from the hospital. I met Pick with her friend . . . ah, Mr. Stump?"

The hard lines in the boy's face vanished. He dropped his defenses and yelled. "It's the nice lady Pick told us about from the hospital!"

The children scattered like baby chicks and clamored to get a better look at the pretty stranger.

"If you'll follow us, Miss?"

Relieved, Suzanne relaxed her shoulders. "Suzanne, please call me Suzanne."

"If you'll follow us Miss Suzanne, we'll show you the way," the boy said. Slinging his arm in a forward arc, he raced off with the younger children following in a noisy pack.

The strong ones ran sure-footed and quick through the twisted landscape. It rose and fell in hills and valleys past crumbling shanties, rusted, abandoned machinery and yawning holes that gaped like open wounds in the snow.

Ragged curtains moved in dingy windows in the car's wake. Cabins that appeared deserted but for the thin spirals of smoke that seeped from their chimneys, manifested curious crowds who pointed and whispered to one another when the car passed.

Suzanne spied the old pickup beneath a tree at the same time the boys veered off the road. They ran across the porch of a chinked log cabin shouting, "Pick! Pick! Miss Suzanne's here to see ya."

All three boys crowded against the door, holding it for Suzanne.

"Good grief, I don't think I've ever felt this nervous," Suzanne muttered under her breath.

She stepped inside the cabin where Pick sat rocking Olivia before a crackling fire. "Suzanne!" Pick exclaimed, beaming. She stood with Olivia in her arms, shifted her to her shoulder, and hugged Suzanne.

Jimmy Joe quietly took Olivia and seated himself on the hearth with the little girl in his lap.

"Please, make yerself to home," Pick said and raised her voice to be heard over Olivia's cough. Pick pulled a chair from the table for Suzanne and then seated herself.

Pick followed Suzanne's eyes to Olivia. "I asked the Good Lord to make Sissy better. Her cough'll be passin soon," Pick said, as if Olivia's cough was improving already.

Suzanne frowned. The little girl coughed a deep, rattling cough.

"'Fore I fergit my manners," Pick nodded to the little girl, "This here's my baby sister, Olivia. We mostly call her Sissy, though.

She pointed to each of her brothers and introduced them in turn. "This is Jimmy Joe, that's Willie, and this uns Buddy," Pick said.

She pulled Buddy against her knees and pinned him in the crook of her arm. She gave him a squeeze, and then rubbed her knotted fist playfully on top of his head.

"Younguns," she said, over Buddy's giggles. "This is Miss Suzanne, the nice lady from the hospital."

"I ain't a learnin to read and I ain't a gonna be made to do it, no matter!" Jimmy Joe blurted. He stared with angry eyes at Suzanne.

"Jimmy Joe! You hold yer tongue and mind yer manners 'fore guests in this house!" Pick's warning came with an angry flash of her green eyes.

"I'm sorry, Miss Suzanne, but Jimmy Joe reckons that since Papa could read and got work in the mines, that readin is the cause of Papa's dyin."

Suzanne glanced at the angry boy and noted the pain in his eyes. Jimmy Joe's anger and misguided beliefs doubled her determination to help these children.

Olivia coughed again, a cough that Suzanne felt certain was cause for alarm.

"That's a bad cough," she said. Although she longed to cuddle the pretty child and make her cough go away, Suzanne made no move to do so. The last thing that she wanted to do was to offend.

Pick lifted her chin and sniffed the air. "Excuse me, Suzanne, I gotta tend my bakin or my bread's gonna burn black as coal dust." Pick pushed her chair from the table and headed for the kitchen with Suzanne following close behind.

"That bread smells heavenly," Suzanne said. She inhaled the fragrant steam clouds that rose from a simmering kettle of beans. "And so does this."

Pick removed two pans of bread from the oven and emptied them on a plate to cool. "Well, just help yerself," she invited.

She removed a red and white checkered cheese cloth from a heavy ceramic bowl. She reached into the bowl and scooped out two handfuls of plump, elastic dough. She dropped the dough onto a board that she dusted with flour and then sank her hands in the middle of it.

Suzanne glanced about the small house.

Buddy and Willie sat at the table, arranging plastic soldiers for a skirmish. Jimmy Joe entertained Olivia with a sock puppet.

The house was void of any luxury money could buy and, Suzanne guessed, it was probably just as void of many of life's necessities. But they didn't notice. These five children who lived on bread and beans and not much more were content. They were happy.

Suzanne startled herself and hummed a tune. She felt a peace in this house that she'd forgotten existed.

Pick had nowhere to be, nothing to do but work-- baking bread. She did not have to concern herself with a mortgage, with bill collectors, with endless maintenance, or with the costly and requisite machinery that endless maintenance required.

She had no job pressure. No peer pressure, no traffic jams, no auto payments and no automotive upkeep.

Suzanne felt a sudden shame. She could not be envious of Pick! What kind of a horror of a person would that make Suzanne?

Pick looked up at Suzanne and smiled. She looked like she was having fun.

On impulse Suzanne asked. "May I help?"

Pick scratched her nose with a floury hand that left her nose smudged with flour.

Pick laughed as Suzanne brushed away the flour. "Did yer Mama teach you to bake bread, too?"

"No," Suzanne replied. "But you can teach me. How about I'll teach you to read and you teach me to bake bread?"

"Ain't nothin to bakin bread, anybody kin bake bread," Pick said. She picked up the ball of dough, patted it between her hands, returned it to the board, and squashed it with the heels of her hands.

"I wish that were true, Pick," Suzanne said and studied the girl for a moment. This young girl before her was now woman of the house and here she was, baking bread and entertaining guests. Incredible.

"Pick, people who take the time to make homemade bread are really living. Most of the people I know, myself included, are *not* living. We exist."

"We march through life like robots, controlled by the clock, by the need to gather, to accumulate, and to compete with others who gather and accumulate. Our days and our labors are dictated by the calendar and by society's ever changing whims.

"See the USA in your Chevrolet," Dinah Shore insists that we need a new car. Blah, blah, blah, insists that we need a new....... It's sad that we as a society can be so easily manipulated."

With a laugh, Pick stepped away from the dough board. She stood with her floury hands in the air and said to

Suzanne, "So why don't you take time to make homemade bread? Ain't nobody stopping ya."

With an amused grin Pick watched Suzanne look for a place to wash her hands. Pick pointed with her elbow to the black iron pump beside the basin. "Just grab that old wooden handle there and pump."

Suzanne hesitated. She made a face like a school kid who is stumped by a math problem and then she grabbed the handle and pumped.

She giggled as the cold water streamed out. Suzanne washed her hands in the rush of water and dried them on a linen towel that Isabel had embroidered with pink and blue lambs.

Feeling all happy and proud of herself, Suzanne turned at last to Pick. "I'm all yours," she said with a wide smile.

Pick nodded to the ball of dough. "Just work it a little bit," she said as Suzanne sank her hands into the soft, pliant mound. She patted and kneaded the dough, raising a cloud of fine white powder that settled on her face and in her dark hair.

"Bet them ailin folk ain't never reckoned on yer bakin bread, all painted with flour," Pick teased.

"I'm sure you're..." Suzanne began and followed Pick's eyes to the front door as footsteps sounded on the porch.

"That'd be Mama John," Pick said. Without seeing the caller, Pick shouted, "Door's open!" Pick wiped her hands on her apron and greeted Mama John.

"Pick, Baby, forgive my interruptin when you've got comp'ny," Mama John said and darted her eyes to Suzanne. "But Mule is havin a hissy fer you to try this jerky. Old fool's done been messin with his recipe and he's bustin fer you to try it."

Mama John smiled a wary smile at Suzanne and poked a loose curl beneath the kerchief that she wore tied around her head.

"Mule's jerky can't get no better," Pick insisted. "Folks come from all over wantin it." She bit into a stick of the spicy venison and waved a hand at Suzanne. "Mama John, this here's Miss Suzanne."

Suzanne caught Pick's eye and made throat-clearing noises.

"This is *Su-Zanne*," Pick corrected herself with a laugh and then crossed her eyes. "She's the nice lady from the hospital that I told you about."

"Suzanne, this here's my best friend in the world," Pick said, beaming at Mama John. "She don't count nobody as growed. We're all little chicks to her. That's why we call 'er mama John."

Suzanne dusted flour from her hands to shake hands with Mama John.

"Come here, Chile! You sweet baby! Thank you, honey. We thank you kindly fer watchin over our Pick up County. God bless ya, Baby," Mama John said and hugged Suzanne with such enthusiasm that it startled the petite woman.

Mama John held Suzanne at arm's length and said to Pick with a smile, "I never figured on 'er bein such a slight thing."

Mama John released Suzanne and reached a hand to her forehead. She said with a troubled look, "Pick, Honey, I better sit a minute. The devil's done got hold of my head and he's shakin it real good."

As Mama John dropped her plump body into a chair beside Buddy and Willie, Suzanne glimpsed the worried look on Pick's face. Mama John's hand trembled as she offered a stick of jerky to Suzanne.

"Here, Baby, try it," she said and passed the bag to Buddy and Willie.

"This jerky's wonderful; I've never tasted anything like it!" Suzanne exclaimed as she savored the tangy meat that she slowly ground between her teeth.

"Honey, God's been real good to us. There's plenty more where that come from, so you just go on and help yerself," Mama John replied, then turned to Pick who stood behind her with a hand on Mama John's shoulder.

"Pick, Honey, Mule's goin into town this afternoon. He's gonna fetch some tea and honey for that baby's cough," she said with a nod at Olivia who coughed continually.

Suzanne glanced from Olivia who sat with Jimmy Joe, coughing until her eyes watered, to Mama John who scraped her chair back from the table and stood to her feet with a measured caution.

"Mama John, if you don't mind my asking, can you read?" Suzanne asked.

"Oh, Baby! Time was when I could read. Yes'm, I could read and cipher good as you please, but these old eyes is blind as cave bats. Ol' Mist' Age, Honey, he done got my eyes and the devil hisself got my head. Fergive me, Baby, fer bein such a mess today, just meetin you 'n all."

Mama John hugged Willie and Buddy and said with a sparkle of mischief in her eyes, "The younguns is building a mighty fine snowman yonder, ain't you gonna help?"

With eyes that said he was eager to take Mama John up on her invitation, Jimmy Joe glanced from the door to the little girl that he held in his arms.

"May I?" Suzanne asked with arched brows as she reached for Olivia.

Jimmy Joe looked to Pick who said with a nod, "Drag that rocker over here Jimmy Joe so me and Suzanne kin talk without burnin supper."

Jimmy Joe released Olivia to Suzanne's outstretched arms then he picked up the rocker and placed it at the end of the table nearest the kitchen.

With a loud *whoop!* He grabbed his jacket. "Last one out's a rotten egg!" He shouted as he raced Willie and Buddy to the door.

"Isabel...," Suzanne said the name aloud before she settled into the rocker with Olivia.

"Isabel was our Mama. That's her rocker Papa made fer her 'fore I was born," Pick said as she patted the dough into baking pans. She slid the pans into the oven and then lifted the lid from the simmering beans to check them.

Olivia coughed another deep, rattling cough.

"Pick, how old is Olivia?

"She's three."

"And the boys?"

"Jimmy Joe's fourteen, Willie's eight, and Buddy's six."

"That's quite a handful for you, isn't it?" Suzanne asked innocently.

Terrror washed over Pick's face. "I've heered them stories 'bout younguns bein snatched and put in strangers' houses and orphanages when their folks is passed." Emerald fire blazed from her eyes.

"These younguns is my family and they ain't no handful! Mule's bringin medicine fer Sissy and the Good Lord Hisself sees to us! We got plenty to eat, a fine home, wood for the fire...."

Pick's words tumbled out frightened and defensive. She felt overwhelmed and confused and did not want to think of Suzanne as a threat but tears filled her eyes.

Suzanne stumbled from the rocker. She hurried to Pick. "Pick, I'm so sorry! Please believe me, I did not mean to frighten you or to make you think that your family is threatened in any way. There is no threat. Pick, I really am sorry! I just meant that, well, that you're still a child yourself and it must be very hard for you to handle all this alone."

"I don't handle nothin alone!" Pick cried. With lips that quivered, she lifted a shoulder to wipe tears from her cheek. "When I need help, I ask the Good Lord. He's my help."

A small hand touched Suzanne's face.

"Yer drownin Sissy."

"What?" Suzanne stammered and brushed her wet cheek on her shoulder.

"Yer drownin Sissy," Pick repeated, grinning.

"Oohh, I'm sorry, Little One," Suzanne said, half-laughing and half-crying as she squeezed Olivia. "I didn't mean to get you wet with my tears."

"Yer purty," Olivia said. Looking up at Suzanne with her blue eyes, she smiled a shy smile.

Suzanne looked to Pick with pleading eyes. "Pick, please, let me help you. I have no family. I live alone and have no life outside my work at the hospital."

"You're gonna let 'er teach ya to read, ain't cha, Pick?" Olivia asked, squirming to get down. She darted across the room and raised expectant eyes to Pick. "So's you kin read the Good Book to us."

"I reckon I'm gonna do that, fer sure," Pick said with a smile and a nod.

"Pick, I'm hungry," Olivia announced. She climbed bottom-up into a chair and propped her chin in her hands.

"Suzanne, would you like to stay fer dinner?"

"I'd love that, Pick. Very much," Suzanne said.

After eating dinner with Pick and her family, Suzanne helped Pick clear the dishes.

"Pick, your beans, and heavenly homemade bread with hand churned butter, was the best meal I've had in a long time. I really enjoyed it."

Suzanne dried the last bowl and folded the dishtowel. "I can't remember when I've felt so relaxed. Maybe it's the mountain air or maybe it's the good comp...."

"Help!" Willie cried as he burst through the door. "Help! The girls are beatin us. Their snowman's bigger! We gotta make the biggest snowman or we're gonna have to eat a red worm! Come on Suzanne, you gotta help us!"

Suzanne shook with laughter. Willie looked so serious tugging on her arm. She brushed snowflakes from his hair and said with a smile, "We can't have that, now can we?"

"Play nice," Pick said with a laugh and tossed Suzanne her coat. Suzanne shrugged at Pick, took Willie's hand and followed him out the door.

With kids all around her, Suzanne piled and patted snow onto the grand snowman. Laughing like a child, she fired snowball for snowball at kids who ducked, and laughed, and fired them at her.

Was it getting darker? She glanced at her Timex. "Three o'clock. It can't be!"

She hurled a final snowball with a giggle and watched it explode on Willie's shoulder. Then she dashed into the house breathless. "Pick, I'm going to be late for a meeting! I don't have time to dress for it now. I'm supposed to bring a dish too, but I don't have one prepared."

"Is it a church meetin?"

"No, I'm meeting with some ladies to plan a party."

"Then why you gotta dress fer it? You look fine to me."

Suzanne scrunched her brows and made a face. Mud and flour spotted her clothes. "I'm a mess!" She said.

"Yer beautiful, Suzanne," Olivia said

Suzanne looked at Pick and Olivia. *They mean it. I look just fine to them. And there is nobody in Ashford or its Women's League that I care to impress more than these innocent, loving children.*

With a bang of the door Lucy and Lottie ran into the house. Lucy dangled a brown paper bag before Suzanne. "Miss Suzanne, Pa sent this jerky fer you to take home."

"Thank you, girls and please tell your Pa thank you for me," Suzanne said as she accepted Mule's unexpected gift.

"There's your dish, and these," Pick said. She wrapped two loaves of warm bread in cheesecloth. "See, there ain't no need fer worry. The Good Lord provides."

Suzanne hesitated. She couldn't take bread from these children.

But then, it was a gift and refusing might hurt Pick's feelings. Suzanne opted to accept the gift.

"What they see is what they'll get!" She said with a laugh. She took the damp cloth that Pick offered and wiped mud from her face and hands. She dabbed the cloth at the stains on her sweater, too.

She said her good-byes with hugs for Pick and Olivia. There were more hugs as she crossed the yard to her car, dodging snowballs all the way.

"And don't forget, Pick, we start reading lessons next week," Suzanne shouted with a final wave.

Chapter Twelve

Suzanne pressed the doorbell and glimpsed her reflection in the door's oval glass. Her ponytail cantered off center to one side of her head. Splotches of mud and spikes of bread dough added a colorful and interesting texture to her red sweater.

The mud that was caked on her boots left Suzanne no choice but to remove them. With her parcel clenched between her teeth, she hopped on one foot while she removed her boot from the other.

Estelle's maid answered. Holding herself rigid as a fence post, the severe looking woman stared at Suzanne with the pinched look of one who had sucked the lime and spilled the tequila.

Suzanne waved her mud-encrusted boots. "Want me to leave them out here, Mina?"

The maid's eyes bulged. Her brows shot upward. "Oh, no, Miss!"

Suzanne took this to mean that her soiled boots might spoil the effect of the gleaming marble porch that was graced with hand carved Grecian columns.

She lifted the boots to eye level. The maid shot out a hand and caught the boot tops with her fingers and a perfectly extended pinkie.

"Great catch, Mina," Suzanne said with a laugh.

The maid stared at Suzanne with wide, incredulous eyes and then headed for the dining room.

Suzanne waved her off. "Don't bother to show me Mina, I remember the way."

Suzanne followed voices to a room filled with the sounds one might expect from a rowdy gaggle of magpies. Seeing Suzanne, the magpies hushed-- and waited to exhale.

"Estelle Dear, I'm sorry but my dishes need dishes." Suzanne rattled the paper bags at the hostess whose gaping mouth and staring eyes hinted that she might be stunned by Suzanne's sullied and sinful barefoot appearance.

Estelle reached for the bag of bread and jerky with the stiff arm and limp wrist one might employ when reaching for a slimed toad.

Suzanne felt carefree and giddy. She leaned a shoulder into Estelle, sniffed the air, and said, "Doesn't this bread smell divine?"

Straightening her ponytail with her hands behind her head, Suzanne beamed. "Forgive me, ladies, but I was baking bread and building snowmen this morning when the time got away from me."

Discreet leanings and whisperings followed a few audible gasps as Suzanne pruned her lips and loudly blew white clouds of flour from her sweater sleeves. Smiling, she looked about for an empty seat.

Olga Vandeventer stood. She motioned with her hand. "Su-Zhan, come sit vis me."

Suzanne seated herself next to Olga and was surprised that Olga had not learned of Suzanne's broken engagement. She was doubly surprised at Olga's reaction to the news. "Good for you! Spoilt one, dat!"

When the meeting adjourned for dinner, talk turned to favorite recipes and the catering that would be necessary for the event that the ladies had met to plan.

Well into the meal the mayor's wife, Melody Maschotte, complimented Estelle. "Darling, that chef of yours is a magician, this bread is divine. I must have this recipe."

Others joined Mrs. Maschotte in praising the bread. Somewhat mystified, Estelle confessed. "But my chef didn't bake any bread."

"Beef jerky—how quaint," Vivian Stalworth declared. Clay loves jerky and I am sure that this is outstanding. Estelle, your chef is a wonder."

Pressing a jeweled hand to her cheek, Estelle stammered. "But I, my...."

Suzanne crammed the last bite of a chocolate chip cookie in her mouth. She raised her hand. "Ladies... Ladies! Estelle's chef is a wonder, but the bread and jerky that you are raving about came from our talented neighbors in Widows Hollow."

Suzanne ignored the thinning air as the ladies sucked the oxygen from the room in a collective breath. She continued with enthusiasm. "My friend, Pick McKinley, baked the bread. Her friend Mule made the jerky."

She caught Vivian's eye and added with a grin, "Now you know why it's famous all over Kentucky."

Suzanne had no doubts how this news would be received. Widows Hollow and Leper's Colony were fairly synonymous in these ladies' minds. Loud gasps confirmed her suspicions. *Smelling salts, please, Mina.*

Olga smiled at Suzanne's revelations. When it became apparent to her that none of the other ladies shared her enthusiasm, Olga stood. "Su-Zhan, do you thing Peek vould bake this vunderful bread for our ball? And I vould like some for my Christmas dinner."

Olga's words set off a flurry of magpie chatter. Approving nods and ever-so-slight wags of the head lent emphasis to the debate. Olga and her unchallenged position at the top of Ashford's philanthropic pyramid gave the nods the win to Suzanne's delight.

"Pick will be happy to bake bread for you, Olga, and for the ball," Suzanne said. "As a matter of fact, nothing would please her more than to lend a hand, cleaning or cooking or helping with catering."

With a rattle of her fourteen carat cluster bracelets, Olga tapped a manicured finger on her chin. "I also need some help vis my home and I'm sure our friends could use some help this Christmas season." Olga swept her eyes over the crowd. "Ladies?"

They responded with quick nods.

With a bounce of her ponytail and a wide smile, Suzanne hugged Olga who produced a notebook and pen. Suzanne noted requests for bread and jerky and scheduled Pick's help for the busy holiday season. Suzanne smiled as she returned Olga's pen and pocketed the list. This afternoon was not a complete waste after all.

Shortly after arriving at home, Suzanne dialed Andy Welch. Andy's wife, Carla, answered. "Andy's wrecking the kitchen, brewing eggnog. Why don't you join us, we'll discuss your new enterprise."

As Suzanne walked through the falling snow to Andy's, she realized that her Christmas spirit was alive and well. Smiling, she pressed the doorbell.

"Merry Christmas, Neighbor!" Andy's greeting was loud and light-hearted. Tall and blonde with Scandinavian good looks and the confidence of an Ivy League graduate, Andy rubbed his hands together.

In a Boris Karloff voice he said, "Step into our parlor." Sounding very Andy Welch again he said, "We'll cram the calorie counters up the chimney and stuff our faces shamelessly."

"This is going to be an interesting evening," Suzanne said with a laugh. She followed Andy into the living room where a fire crackled in the fireplace. Christmas music by a solo guitarist played in the background.

Andy and Carla were dressed in red sweat suits, Santa hats, and house shoes with big ugly rubber toes. Suzanne giggled. "If I didn't know you two, I might be tempted to run."

"Oh, no, please stay. Wife and I are trying to make the list, "Who's Who of Lust and Lasciviousness," he said, and planted a playful kiss on Carla's cheek.

"My darling, red velour makes me, makes me... pant... to show off my culinary superiority," Andy exclaimed, bouncing his brows.

Carla shrieked. Laughing, she raced Andy to the dining table. Tempting trays of cookies, fudge, and homemade candy beckoned from nests of fragrant evergreens and colorful poinsettias.

"I would kill for a piece of this cherry pecan fudge," Andy said as he popped a piece into Suzanne's mouth.

"Oh no you don't," Carla cried. She snatched chocolates from a tray. "Those impostors pale beside my rum balls." Laughing, she waited for Suzanne to finish chewing a piece of fudge before she shoved a rum ball in her mouth.

Andy and Carla raced around the table gathering cookies here, fudge and candy there.

"Wait!" Suzanne slapped a palm in the air. "Truce, you two, or I won't be able to waddle out of here!"

"So my dear Miss Claiborne, what brings you to our humble abode this snowy evening?" Andy propped himself against the oak mantel and shoved a hand in his pocket, imitating Sherlock Holmes.

The doorbell rang, encouraging Andy's antics. "Ah, more visitors! The pot thickens, my dear Watson. Do you mind?" Andy smiled at Carla who crossed her eyes at his word play and hurried to the door.

"More house calls?" Andy asked the new arrival who shook himself like a wet retriever and then entered the room brushing snowflakes from his hair.

"Dr. Gardner, Dr. Claiborne." "Dr. Claiborne, Dr. Gardner," Andy said with a nod. He crossed his arms over his chest, pointing at Suzanne and at the newly arrived Dr. Bennett Gardner.

"We've met. Please call me Bennett," Gardner said, taking Suzanne's hand in his own.

How did Bennett the Bookworm happen to show up here? Suzanne mused, stifling a groan.

As if Andy had read her mind he glanced at Suzanne. "If you're wondering how your esteemed colleague happens to know the wife and me, it's because he's Carla's gynecologist, and because I've known the lad since he was in knickers."

"I never wore knickers!" Bennett protested.

"And it's a good thing, too, Suzanne. He has knobby knees," Andy fired back.

"The good doctor plays Santa at the Ashford Children's Home. This is the third year he's conned the wife and me into providing the goodies. We've been baking all day," Andy said with a feigned pout.

Suzanne glanced at the man's short, curly, reddish-blonde hair and at the hazel eyes he hid behind a pair of thick glasses. Despite his six-six height, broad shoulders, and athletic build, Bennett Gardner took a lot of ribbing at the hospital where they both worked.

Suzanne had never paid much attention before, but now, seeing him up close, she realized the tag *bookworm* did not fit this handsome man.

Stephen Stalworth had tagged Bennett with a few unflattering names. Gardner did not hide the fact that he was a political activist and a prominent figure in Ashford's arena of worthy causes.

"Bleeding heart Bennett," Stalworth called him when Gardner volunteered at local fundraisers.

Carla and Andy burst into simultaneous laughter. They raced again for the table of treats.

"Oh, no you don't!" Carla laughed. She grabbed a handful of rum balls and threatened to toss them at Bennett.

"Humor the child, Ben," Andy quipped. "Then tantalize those taste buds with my kumquats of culinary confections."

Carla popped a rum ball in her mouth.

Andy fired pieces of fudge at Bennett's raised hand. Bennett popped a rum ball in his mouth. He spoke as he chewed. "Better go light on that rum Mrs. W., Young Andrew might get tipsy."

Carla froze, then exchanged startled glances with Andy. Together they stared at Bennett who licked chocolate from his fingers.

"Young Andrew... we're pregnant!" Andy threw his hands in the air. He shouted the words in a hail of cherry pecan fudge.

"Ben?" Carla's eyes watered.

Bennett slowly licked the chocolate from his fingers, prolonging the agony of his friends' suspense. Finally, he raised a solemn face.

"Mr. and Mrs. Andrew Welch, it is my duty to inform you that you have suffered peace and quiet long enough. Those rotten retrievers of yours are going to have to make room for baby. Your young firecracker should make his debut with a bang, he's due on the Fourth of July."

"A baby! A baby! We're going to have a baby!" Andy grabbed Carla and crushed his lips against hers in a long, passionate kiss. He shoved Bennett toward Suzanne. "Look Benny, you do it like this!" He said with a giggle and kissed his wife again.

Caught off guard when his body collided with hers, Bennett raised uncertain eyes to Suzanne who laughed helplessly. Bennett shrugged his shoulders. "I'm game!" He bent Suzanne over his arm and planted a quick peck on her lips.

"Amateur!" Andy chided.

"Show em how it's done Suzanne!" Carla said with a wink.

Suzanne slowly pulled the red bow from her hair. She shook her mane of shining black tresses over one shoulder and cocked her head playfully.

Crooking her finger at Bennett, she said in voice that sounded so sexy, she surprised herself. "Come here, lover boy!" She grabbed the surprised doctor and kissed him passionately.

Hot blood surged through Bennett's veins. Was this the same Suzanne Claiborne that passed him every day at the hospital as though he were invisible? And hadn't Stalworth laid claim to her?

Andy grinned at his glowing wife. Breaking the spell, he blurted, "I'll fetch the bubbly."

An hour later, Andy glanced at the drained champagne bottle and at the clutter of empty glasses as he sank into an overstuffed chair and patted his knees. "Come here, pregnant wife."

Carla dropped into Andy's lap. Andy pulled off her Santa hat and kissed the top of her head.

Suzanne tucked her bare feet beneath her on the green brocade sofa. Bennett sank into the plush cushions beside her.

"Now, where were we?" Andy asked, assuming his Holmes' identity. "I believe you had a request to make of me, my dear Ms. Claiborne." Andy made a disagreeable face.

"Ms., it sounds so like mis-erable. Mrs., on the other hand, sounds so very marvelous. Come here, you!" Andy said, and pulled Carla closer. Then, "Wife! We have guests!" He grinned, met Suzanne's eyes and said, "I'm all ears."

"I've promised to teach some friends to read," Suzanne began. "But I don't know where to start...."

Bennett burst into laughter.

Caught off guard by Bennett's rude and unexpected laughter, Suzanne glared at the man. "Did I say something funny, doctor?"

"I'm sorry. It's the mental picture I get of Dr. Stephen Stalworth's wife catering to the illiterate. Forgive me, Ms. Claiborne, it's that image that I find amusing."

Andy slapped his forehead. "Pardon me, Dr. Gardner, I forgot to regret to inform you that Dr. Claiborne returned the ring with a zing a while back. Her relationship with *Stainless* was anything but painless. She ditched the good doctor."

"Adequate summation, my dear?" Andy hitched his brows at Suzanne.

"*Stainless*?" Suzanne hitched her brows at Andy.

"Long story. Nicknames. Never mind," Andy said, looking serious.

"Tacky. But adequate," Suzanne said with a laugh.

"I believe...," Andy began.

"Let me help," Bennett interrupted.

"How can you help?" Suzanne asked.

"Simple. I've been teaching reading at the First Baptist fellowship hall in the county for a couple of years. Nothing to it."

He raised a hand. "God forbid I should wax maudlin, but I grew up in an orphanage. Lots of good folks helped me along the way so I try to help others when I can."

"So, Doctor, once again you've rendered me useless," Andy said. He cocked a brow at Bennett. "My neighbor-in-distress comes calling, and you head me off at the pass with your usual pocketful of solutions. By the way, who taught you to dance? Smooth moves, Buddy Boy."

"Fred and Ginger. The movies," Bennett said.

"By Jove! I do believe the boy's blushing. It looks good on *both* of you," Andy said with a mischievous sparkle in his eyes.

Straight-faced, Bennett asked, "Dr. Claiborne, could you do that hair thing again, with the finger and the lips?"

"Next time, I promise. It's getting late. My clock's on the mantel waiting for me." Suzanne unfolded herself from the sofa and stood.

Andy and Carla walked their guests to the door. Carla hugged Bennett. "Thank you for the great news, Ben, you made our Christmas." She opened the door to a flurry of snowflakes.

Bennett batted snowflakes at Suzanne. "Can I drive you home? The roads are probably solid ice."

Before Suzanne could answer, Andy hiked a thumb at her house across the street. He whispered loudly to Bennett. "Why don't you just *walk* her home?"

Chapter Thirteen

"That wasn't luck. Your luck's not that good, Commissioner! Watch him boys, he's hot!" Stephen Stalworth shouted over the noise and laughter.

He took a sip of his drink and scanned a wall rack of cue sticks. He selected a stick, hoisted it in the air like a drum major, dipped his chin, and trumpeted a mock toast.

"My rod and my staff... and my Southern Comforts me!" He paused, waiting for the laughs that he expected his pun to inspire.

He shoved his drink into the hand of a passing butler and twisted chalk on the tip of his stick. With a nod to the player at the opposite end of the billiard table he barked, "Rack 'em, Jimmy Boy!"

An international gathering of horse breeders, politicians, and country gentlemen filled the billiard parlor of the Stalworth country estate.

Old family friends strolled the grounds, resplendent in their Stetsons and hand-tooled ostrich boots, nappy tweeds or velvet and leather riding habits.

Stalworth hospitality was legend and generous. These select few had amused themselves in genteel leisure and exquisite southern comforts for days. Others were just arriving.

Brunch, served this morning, was a prelude to a leisurely afternoon of mixing and mingling. The politicians would promote their politics from armchair podiums while the matriarchs waved the cross-stitched banners of their favorite philanthropic persuasion.

Mr. and Mrs. Henry Stalworth hosted the occasion. Ashford's society columns headlined it as The Annual Ashford Childrens' Hospital Charity Ball.

The Ashford Women's League were the organizers, and *money* was the tie that bound them all.

Calvin Colter bowed beneath his Stetson to sign over his five digit contribution. The governor's wife thanked Colter with a smile that sparkled as brightly as her three-carat solitaire.

Colter had agreed to reroute his coal trucks when the new highway opened. The coal dust that had blanketed the counties south of Ashford with a chemical shroud of dust and slag would simply become someone else's problem.

Colter had campaigned, along with most of those assembled, for the bond money that would build the new highway.

Eminent domain had reared its ugly head. It cut a swathe deep as a mortal wound through the vast bluegrass real estate holdings of Ashford businessmen.

Young Jefferson Jacoby had fallen victim, but had enjoyed a speedy recovery. He discovered that he *could* live without all those offices in that pesky business park. After all, they were nothing but brick and mortar. A good businessman with lots of *cash* could always find prime real estate.

Jacoby had eagerly packed his new Chevy Corvette for the drive to the Stalworth estate. The addition of the cherry red Corvette to Jacoby's four-car garage had helped ease the pain of eminent domain and had lent a nice patriotic touch in the doing.

This Harvard-educated, New-York-born-architect with a Jewish heritage knew that Southerners were close-knit, tight-fisted, and *patriotic*.

"Gentlemen." Stalworth raised his scotch glass to Jacoby. "I have an announcement to make. Our young friend and neighbor, Mr. Jefferson Jacoby, has agreed to design our golf course and country club.

That bluegrass blight we know as 'Widers Holler' will soon become Ashford Acres. That is of course, as soon as Jeff has completed construction of my new medical complex."

Crystal clinked against crystal, hands slapped against manicured hands as the good old boys welcomed Jacoby into their fold.

Reid Garrison pinned Stalworth in the cross hairs of his stare. "Aren't you putting the cart a wee bit before the horse?" He asked. The locked jaw beneath his steely blue eyes, thick dark lashes and rogue mustache suggested that Garrison was all business.

Six feet and eight vertical inches of him stretched across squared, muscular shoulders, a stomach that rippled like a log cabin washboard, and thighs that required custom tailoring to accommodate their circumference.

Close cropped in front, his thick, silver-shot black hair hung shoulder length over his collar in natural curls.

The genteel citizens of Ashford pardoned Garrison's casual west coast appearance in their courtrooms because he served them well with his formidable southern-grit tenacity.

As the Stalworth family attorney, Garrison handled every legal matter that arose in the multiple entities that comprised the Stalworth Empire. Horseracing and breeding, insurance, mining, excavation equipment, banks, and tobacco were just a few of the vast family enterprises.

"That's where you come in, my friend." Stalworth straightened himself from his shooting stance. He placed his stick on the table, retrieved his scotch, and said with a finger pointing beyond his drink, "Now that our good friend Mr. Colter has taken care of the black cloud, we'd like for you to do a title search on every acre of land south of the highway between Simpson Pike and Old Niles Ferry."

He paused to sip his drink and then continued over the sound of rattling ice. "And of course we will exterminate those vermin in due time," he added and loudly crunched ice between his teeth.

A snake with fangs, Garrison noted. He rolled a brandy snifter between his hands. After a moment, he arched a brow at Stalworth. "We?"

Ah, yes, this is on the Q.T., Reid," Stalworth said. He covered his scotch glass with his hand as if to conceal his secret inside the etched crystal. He stared into the glass and continued. "It's to be a surprise for Mom and Dad from Victoria and myself."

Garrison leaned a shoulder against the paneled oak wall and crossed his long legs at the ankle. "Rather an ambitious surprise, isn't it, Stephen?" He asked, his face clouding. "Golf course, country club, and if I know you like I think I know you, that's just the beginning."

Stalworth jabbed his cue, *smack!* Two balls rolled into side pockets. "You know me too well, counselor," he replied.

Without a glance at Garrison, Stalworth chalked his stick. "The citizens of Ashford deserve only the finest, so they shall have it. And you're right, Reid, why stop there?"

"We'll add a five star restaurant, pro shop, that's Tory's pet, and for golfers who want to make a weekend of it, we'll provide accommodations."

"Of course," Garrison mouthed. His lack of enthusiasm for this conversation showed in his face as he employed a baiting tactic. "Hotel?"

"With all the ambiance of Europe's finest," Stalworth retorted.

Garrison charged. "You're talking millions of dollars, Stephen!" He cornered the witness. "How do you plan to finance this *surprise*?"

Stalworth slammed his cue on the table. He turned on Garrison with his jaw clenched in anger. "You will keep in mind, Mr. Garrison, that you are a family employee. You are not paid to cross-examine us! The only pertinent questions here are the ones that I ask. Just find out who owns that land and leave the rest to me!"

Garrison drummed his fingers on his glass. Seething.

"Wagers?" Stalworth invited, holding his pool cue like a scepter.

The men clamored to place their bets.

"Gentlemen," Garrison said with a nod. He elbowed his way through the forest of waving greenbacks and descended the stairs.

Stalworth leaned over the billiard table. He squeezed one eye closed, retracted his cue, threaded it through his looped finger and smacked the cue ball. *Whack!* Balls scattered, tumbling into pockets.

Stalworth righted himself, retrieved his scotch, and said with a wink to the others, "I know I can trust my good friends to keep our little secret."

The men nodded their assurances.

One young man stood, dart in hand, with his back to the billiard table. He failed to acknowledge Stalworth's request by word or posture as he let the dart fly. It hit the dartboard, dead center. Bulls-eye.

The scorekeeper added points for Jan Vandeventer who ignored his cheering teammates to glare past them at Stalworth.

Jacques Champeaux, Jan's best friend and teammate in the dart tournament, let out a low whistle. He shook his head and said to Jan with a nudge, "If looks could ignite, Stalworth would be in flames."

Chapter Fourteen

Vivian Stalworth scanned every corner of her rambling estate with a critical eye. The staff in their crisp uniforms hurried to place fragrant linens and specially molded bars of soap throughout the many guest baths of the three-story mansion.

"Everything is in order," Vivian said to herself before she took one last glance. Satisfied, she gathered her skirts and ascended the stairs to await the arrival of the cocktail hour that preceded dinner and the Ashford Children's Hospital Charity Ball.

"Your parents have arrived, Sir," The porter announced in a discreet whisper to Jan.

"Jacques, my parents are here. I'll see you at the shindig," Jan said. He chucked his chin at the other dart players and folded green bills in the porter's hand. "Follow me, please."

With the white-gloved porter on his heels, Jan hurried from the billiard parlor to the courtyard of the Stalworth country estate.

Cars lined the sweeping, circular cobblestone drive, one behind another. Patient chauffeurs deposited guests who were decked out in tuxedoes and ball gowns into the capable hands of waiting porters and maids.

The Vandeventer family chauffeur exited the shining limo. He opened the back door and reached a gloved hand to Olga.

Olga stepped from the car, opened her full-length black mink, and stretched her white gloved arms, turning slowly for Jan's benefit.

Her black satin gown hugged Olga's curves from the lace-trimmed scoop neck and short sleeves to her pretty ankles. Earrings of diamonds and black onyx, presented hours earlier by her doting husband, Klaus, matched the bracelet that sparkled from her wrist.

"You like?" Olga beamed at Jan.

"Mama, you are gorgeous!" Jan exclaimed. "Papa, you must keep Mama close tonight, somebody might steal her from you."

Klaus laughed. "Here is jour tux, son." He nodded to the leather wardrobe bag the porter removed from the limousine. "And vill ju be keeping a partner close tonight?"

"You just worry about Mama. I can take care of myself!"

Olga led the way to the back of the limousine. Boxes of packets wrapped in green cellophane, tied with red satin bows filled the trunk.

The porter carried the boxes to a table in the foyer. An imposing centerpiece of fresh cut flowers in a sterling urn dominated the table. Olga arranged the packets in a semi-circle beneath the urn.

In elegant calligraphy, folded tags that were attached to the packets read, "Your $5.00 donation will help us help the children." The larger packets required a ten-dollar donation.

Olga placed a folded cardboard sign that read, *"Homemade for you with happy hands,"* to the right of the urn, and a matching one to the left, *"Taste...the fame of Kentucky"*

Jan arched his brows in surprise.

"Jour mama's been a bery busy lady," Klaus said. "While you and Jacques been off snow skiing in Colorado, she and Miss McKinley have taken ober the house, cooking and baking.

Jour mama looked so cute in her apron vis flour everywhere. She so beezy, she forged her hair appointment," he added with a giggle.

Jan's dimples sank deep in his cheeks with the smile he gave his mother.

Olga glanced at the baroque grandfather clock. It chimed a single chime from its corner in the vast foyer. She clutched Jan's elbow. "Zhan, you must dress quickly, the lighting is at seex."

Heading upstairs with the tuxedo over his arm, Jan's thoughts wandered. What would happen if he did have a date tonight? What if his date was Pick McKinley and she was dressed in an elegant ball gown? She would descend the stairs with her green eyes sparkling and he would *gladly* take her hand. The thought struck Jan like a thunderclap. He would gladly take her hand.

He entered the guest bedroom and tossed his tuxedo on the bed. From the window he watched a parade of guests arrive in limos and expensive luxury cars. He caught a glimpse of his face in the dresser mirror. *Quit fantasizing,* he told himself. There was no way Pick would appear here tonight.

At precisely five fifty-five P.M., Vivian Vinsant-Stalworth stepped into the brilliant circle of light that flooded the second floor landing of the grand, sweeping staircase that spilt its red-carpeted stairs into the great ballroom.

Smiling a regal smile, Vivian welcomed her guests and thanked them for their generous contributions.

A ripple of excitement pulsed through the crowd with the announcement of the new Olga Vandeventer burn center, funded entirely by Klaus Vandeventer to honor his beloved wife.

Having dispensed with the solemn business of welcoming the guests and tallying the take, Vivian Stalworth, with theatrical drama, lifted her gloved hand to her husband.

Clay Stalworth kissed her hand as Vivian sank into her mistress of the manor skirts in the cherished tradition of the southern belle.

Together, they smiled to the wildly applauding crowd. Clay nodded to a porter who waited in the foyer. The porter opened a small metallic box and pulled a lever downward.

Thousands of white lights burst into brilliance throughout the mansion, across the expansive grounds, up the tree-lined drive, and across every arch and angle of the elaborate estate.

Spotlights illuminated ice carvings of children in various poses of play as the orchestra filled the room with the strains of *This One's for You.*

The Stalworths descended the stairs, leading a parade of resplendent women dressed in sparkling sequins, silks, taffetas, and a surfeit of priceless jewels.

Jan did not notice. Uncomfortable in his tuxedo, Jan tugged at his bow tie, to Jacques' amusement.

"A little warm under the collar are we?" Jacques teased.

"This isn't my idea and you know it, Jacques!" Jan hissed. "If Claude Olliphant weren't such a good friend of Papa's, I'd have refused. I can't believe he asked Papa to have me escort Margaret tonight."

Jacques folded his arms. He said with a laugh, "There are definite possibilities here, Jan. She does have a crush on you, and if you weren't so thick headed, you'd admit she is beautiful."

"Beautiful, brainless, and bold as a Brahman bull!" Jan cried. His eyes flashed in anger. "And I'm not in the market for bull of any kind!"

"You're calf-roped and hog-tied tonight!" Jacques said. He pretended to straighten Jan's tie. "And I'm not sticking around for this little drama, friend. I'm off to join the free-men upstairs."

"Jacques, don't you dare leave me alone with her!" Jan hissed under his breath. Too late, he realized and was disappointed that Jacques had vanished in the crowd.

Jan hid his disappointment behind his gallant smile. He took Margaret's eagerly extended hand. One after another, the belles and debutantes of Ashford descended the stairs, followed by the ladies of the Ashford Women's League.

Stephen Stalworth cut short his conversation as a hush fell over the room. The woman standing at the top of the stairs commanded his full attention.

Her beauty captured and mesmerized the glittering crowd. She hesitated for a moment and then smiled as though taking cues from an invisible stage director.

She's gorgeous, Stephen mused. He could not take his eyes off her.

Suzanne's hair cascaded down her back like an ebony mantle. A simple, antique cameo suspended from a velvet ribbon adorned her neck. She looked like a porcelain doll, dressed in a red velvet sheath with puffed sleeves that fell from her shoulders.

The dress molded itself to her petite frame, revealing soft curves and shapely legs that tapered to delicate ankles above her red satin pumps.

Stalworth made his way to the bottom of the staircase. Entranced as he was, he failed to hear the sound of hastily advancing footsteps that announced the late-arriving guest who shouldered his way through the crowd.

At the top of the stairs, Suzanne raised a hand to her eyes. The spotlight blinded her.

She leaned outside the circle of light, lost her balance, and pitched forward with a shriek, leaving one red slipper to teeter on the stair's edge.

Chapter Fifteen

Stephen leaped to the stairs and collided roughly with a figure that raced past him. "Get out of my way, you idiot!" He roared.

Suzanne plummeted, screaming, into Bennett Gardner's arms.

A deafening whistle vibrated through the ballroom. The whistle was followed by the loud crunch of glass, followed by the heavy *thud!* Of a falling object.

Cameras flashed. The ballroom erupted in pandemonium.

"Oh good God! I'm ruined. Ruined! I'll be the laughing stock of Ashford!" Vivian wailed.

Margaret shook with laughter. She squeezed Jan's arm and said in a loud voice, "And another of Vi's domestics bites the dust! That moron will never work in Ashford again!"

"Oh yes she vill!" Olga exclaimed as she hurried to help the alleged *moron.* "She works vis me!"

Margaret squeaked and turned crimson.

Olga advanced a few steps before she turned back. "Zhan?" She called to her son.

Jan freed his elbow from Margaret's grip. Without offering any explanation to Margaret he hurried after his mother.

"Damn irresponsible... Ignorance! Where do these idiots come from! My leg's broken because they're too stupid to serve drinks!" The writhing, red-faced figure on the floor bent over his leg, swearing.

"I'm, I'm sorry," the horrified domestic stuttered her apology to the back of his head.

The injured man turned to her in fury. "Yooooouu!" He screamed and pointed a rigid finger at Pick.

"Mister Stalworth!" Pick choked out the words.

Bennett consoled Suzanne. "You'd do anything to get out of those shoes, wouldn't you?" With Suzanne in his arms, he balanced himself on one leg, kicked her teetering slipper off the stair, and, without taking his eyes off her, snatched it from the air.

"You might have been on time and prevented me from making a spectacle of myself," Suzanne said. She swatted Bennett with her open palm. "Why were you late, if I may ask?"

"Sheer impudence, my love. That newborn I left snuggled in his mother's arms at the hospital refused to postpone his arrival until after we returned from this charity brawl."

Suzanne sank one corner of her mouth and narrowed her eyes in a scowl.

Bennett ignored her feigned anger. He pulled her close and planted a kiss on top of her head. "I better go check on the golden boy. His bruised ego might prove fatal."

"And I'll check on Pick."

Bennett performed a quick examination of Stalworth's leg and let out a whistle. "Looks like the party's over for you, Doc. We need to get you to the hospital and have that leg set."

"Damn it!" Stalworth pounded a fist on the floor. "If you hadn't knocked me down, my leg wouldn't be broken!" He glared at Bennett with his mouth twisted in a snarl.

"If *I* hadn't...," Bennett repeated. He recoiled from the hatred in Stalworth's eyes.

"Why, you arrogant excuse for a...." Bennett checked himself. *No, I refuse to let you pull my strings. Arguing with you would be as foolish as arguing with a drunk.*

Bennett stood to his feet and beckoned nearby porters. "Please see that Mr. Stalworth gets to the hospital. He's broken his leg."

As two solemn-faced porters lifted the man between them, Stalworth yelled. "Gardner, you better stay away from Suzanne. She's out of your league!"

Bennett wrinkled his brow. After a moment he settled on the most dignified reply. "Really?"

Pick wiped her eyes with the tissue Suzanne offered. "I'm *so* sorry Suzanne. I saw you was fallin. I put that tray with them drinks on the floor to whistle cause I seen that runnin man wasn't gonna let you fall. I never meant nobody no harm, especially not *him*," she added and blew her nose.

"This ain't no place fer me. I don't belong here no more'n a jackass in the Derby. Kin I go home now, please?"

"You vill nod be leaving dis house," Olga said in a crinkle of taffeta. She knelt beside Pick and put her arm around the girl. "Bro'gen glass is no crime. Accidents happen. Bones break, dey mend," she added softly.

"Mama is right."

Jan! Pick's heart hammered. She squeezed her eyes shut. "Not now Lord, don't let 'im see me like this!"

"Pick?"

Pick opened her eyes to the cuff of Jan's elegant, creased tuxedo pants and to his expensive black Italian oxfords that were polished to a gleam. She reminded herself that moments ago he had been holding hands with Margaret.

Pick dropped her eyes.

My hands is scarred and rough as corncobs. What fingernails I ain't chewed off's got dirt under 'em! She opened her hands, spilled the glass she had picked up, and then covered her face and sobbed.

Jan knelt at her side. "Please don't cry," he said and gently pulled her hands from her face. He brushed glistening glass shards from her palms and lifted her chin in his hand.

Staring into Pick's green eyes, Jan felt an explosion of emotions that he could neither identify nor deny. He encircled Pick's wrists with his fingers, stood, and pulled her to her feet.

Don't cry. Please don't cry. I can't bear it.

"Let me go," Pick said in a whisper. She felt nothing but her racing heart. She saw nothing but his eyes.

Jan felt her pulse quicken.

You're not going anywhere. Not if I can stop you. He peered over the heads of the milling guests until he spotted Olga. "Mama," he called to her. "Waltz."

With an easy grace, Olga moved through the crowd to the orchestra. She lifted her palms and said with a nod to the conductor, "Valtz!"

Jan drew Pick so close he could feel her breath on his face. Staring into her eyes, he removed the white ruffled cap from her head.

Pick jumped in fright, but frightened or no, she could not tear her eyes from his dimpled cheeks, from his perfect white teeth, his smiling eyes. She could feel his heart beating against her own.

He's so handsome, so close....

She stole a glance at the elegant women who were dressed in fancy gowns. Real jewels sparkled from their ears, wrists, and throats. Jan could have any one of them with a snap of his fingers or with a flash of his crooked grin.

Pick struggled to find her voice. "Please let me go. I wanna go home now."

Jan smiled a smile Pick felt certain angels would envy.

Her heart somersaulted. If only she could close her eyes, feel the rhythm of his breathing, feel the safety of his arms. *No! Wake up! This ain't real!*

A frown replaced Jan's smile.

Margaret charged toward him, stomping past guests who snickered as she passed.

Jan stepped between Pick and the angry young woman.

"Jan! Is this how you treat your …?"

Olga interrupted. She looped her arm through Margaret's and said sweetly "You come vis me, please."

Margaret offered no resistance. Meekly, she allowed Olga to escort her back the way she had come.

Pick followed Margaret's angry retreat with her eyes. *Now, he'll have to let me go.*

"Just relax and follow me," Jan said. He drew Pick closer, pressed her head on his shoulder and moved in slow, dreamy circles to the strains of *As Time Goes By*.

Afraid to stay and afraid to go, Pick clung to Jan. She breathed in the scent of his cologne. "You smell better'n store-bought soap," she said.

Jan searched Pick's face for a moment and then burst into laughter.

Pick felt a shiver. She wrinkled her forehead and said, "When you touch me I feel like I got 'lectricity runnin through me." With a straight face she added, "Ain't that somethin?"

The tension melted from Jan's body. He did not like to dance, but felt he could dance with Pick all night.

Sudden laughter and loud voices jolted Jan from his thoughts.

"Margaret, I thought you were kidding! But he is. Jan really is dancing with one of the kitchen maids!"

Champagne sloshed from Victoria's glass. She draped herself on Margaret's shoulder and howled with laughter.

Margaret fanned her face with her hand. Her heart palpitated in rapid, erratic rhythms and she realized to her horror, "I'm jealous of that low class white trash!"

Mortified, Margaret sipped her champagne. "Why, Victoria, you know *our* Jan, he's just being polite. Lord knows nobody else with any class would dare be seen dancing with the hired help!"

Margaret looked to Victoria for confirmation.

Victoria wobbled unsteadily and spilled more champagne.

Victoria's tipsy! Margaret realized with a start.

Laughing uncontrollably, Victoria lurched into Margaret. "Is her name really Pick? Is that Tooth Pick or Ice Pick?"

Margaret hiccuped a tiny laugh, then with Victoria, exploded with laughter.

Pick turned at the sound of her name. She realized with a sob, *They're laughin at me!* Pick wrenched free of Jan and ran.

Jan raced after Pick who vanished into the kitchen, but Suzanne stopped him at the kitchen door.

"Let her go, Jan," Suzanne said softly.

Jan Vandeventer was not a drinking man. But right now he wanted a drink. And more than that, he wanted a handful of darts.

Chapter Sixteen

"Way to go!"

"Nice catch, Lover Boy!"

"You're not bad looking when you're smirking!"

"You really shouldn't have kicked the guy down the stairs!"

"Come on, I didn't kick anybody, I have bad knees!" Bennett protested.

More whistles and catcalls of "Oh Sweetheart!" rang out from doctors and medical professionals who were having lunch in the County Hospital's cafeteria.

Bennett bared his teeth, lifted a piece of ice from Suzanne's tea glass, and thumped it over his shoulder at the hecklers.

"The vultures are still vultching. Next time, let's meet in some sleazy hotel."

"Next time let's stay home," Suzanne said with a laugh.

"As though we'll have a choice," Bennett replied. He ducked to dodge another piece of flying ice.

"Mine's at the frame shop." Bennett limped his wrist and tapped the newspaper that lay open before them.

Suzanne smacked his shoulder. "Behave!"

The picture that was splashed across the front page of the Ashford Sentinel beneath Helvetica huge headlines read: "CHARITY BALL FREE-FALL SMASHES THE BASH!"

Suzanne looked to be suspended in mid-air, poised like a crazed diver above Bennett's outstretched arms.

Sprawled like a petrified spider, Stalworth lay with his arms and legs in the air, his face contorted in pain.

And, there in the background, stood Pick, dressed in her maid's uniform, two fingers in her mouth, executing a wild, wayward whistle, cheering Bennett on as he charged to save Suzanne from her fall.

"Think we'll be exiled?" Suzanne asked, crossing her eyes.

"No, my love, *executed* is the term that comes to my mind!"

Bennett took a gulp of Suzanne's tea. Suddenly, he slid from the cafeteria booth to the floor. He knelt, grabbed Suzanne's hand, sobered his face, and pleaded. "Please, please don't make me go back out there. Let me stay here and work. I'll do anything, but please, no more shopping!"

"Get up! People already think we're crazy!" Suzanne cried, shaking with laughter.

"Deal?" Bennett met her eyes and bounced his brows.

"No deal. Suzanne works. Ben shops. How's it going?"

"I'm halfway home. I got the chalkboard, nails, chalk, flash cards, tablets, pencils, workbooks, and coal oil."

"Coal oil? Coal oil wasn't on the list."

"Neither were lamps, but I got a couple of those, too."

"You're amazing, Dr. Gardner."

"That's Professor Gardner my Dear."

Suzanne folded the newspaper. "I thought we'd have to work around our schedules, but it appears it's Pick's schedule that we'll be working around."

"They haven't stoned her yet, I take it?"

"Stephen would if could. Thank God he got a sprained ankle and not a broken leg like we thought."

Bennett shrugged his shoulders. "I'm a gyno, not an ortho." He added with a grin "It's a good thing, huh?"

Suzanne glanced at her watch. "I'm afraid he'll get over the sprain before he gets over his hatred for Pick and her neighbors. I can't understand why he hates them so."

"Perhaps it's not hatred," Bennett said. He took half a BLT sandwich from Suzanne's plate and bit into it.

Suzanne took a bite of her sandwich. "Then what?" She asked.

"I think it's fear." Bennett glanced at Suzanne and licked Mayonnaise from the corner of his mouth.

"Fear? How is that possible? How could anyone who's been raised like a prince fear them?"

"It's because he was raised like a prince that he fears them. If the golden boy found his fortunes suddenly reversed, and himself impoverished, he would have a tough time surviving. The thought has to frighten him. Pick and her neighbors remind him of the possibility. To remove them is to remove the reminder."

"Oh, Bennett! I can't believe I forgot to tell you!" Suzanne smacked her forehead.

"Forgot what?" Bennett asked, alarmed.

"Something Olga told me. Jan heard Stephen instruct his attorney to do a title search on all the property in and around Widows Hollow. Stephen plans to buy it, develop it, and evict them all."

"You're kidding. Tell me you're kidding!" Bennett cried.

"I am not."

"Do you have any idea who owns the property?"

"None," Suzanne replied.

Bennett mulled over Suzanne's revelation. He wrinkled his brow and after a moment, said on a sigh, "I don't think the boy can swing it alone. From what I've heard about Stevie's daddy, Daddy isn't likely to fall for the boy's scheme on this one."

Bennett brightened. He snatched a potato chip from Suzanne's plate. Crunching loudly, he said, "I think the Hollow's safe, for now." He glanced at his watch. "My dear, you have to get back to work. I have to finish the shopping and find something suitable to wear to your sister's bash tomorrow night. She doesn't have a winding staircase, does she?"

"I'm afraid so," Suzanne said, laughing.

Bennett poked a finger at her. "I forbid you to step a single toe on those stairs!"

Suzanne swiped at his hand. "I have some last minute shopping to do, too. I want to get something for them," she said. She wiped her face and hands with a napkin, then crumpled it in her plate.

"Them?" Bennett gave her a quizzical look.

"Pick and her family. And that sweet old woman Mama John and her family."

"Need a loan?" Bennett smacked his back pocket.

Suzanne shook her head. "Oh, and Ben, Olga wants us to stop by there tomorrow night if we have time."

"We don't."

"Yes, we do. My house at seven, then?"

"Six thirty."

Halfway to the exit, Bennett grabbed Suzanne. He lifted her off the floor and gave her a loud smooch. "Eat your hearts out, Cretins!" He yelled to his noisy peers.

Chapter Seventeen

Stephen swatted at the pillow that Victoria fluffed. "Get that damn pillow out of Mommy's face!" In a softer voice he pleaded. "Mommy, please quit crying. These things happen when heathens mix with our kind! Do you still think that I was harsh when I threw that white trash out of this house?"

Vivian sniffled. She wiped her eyes with the delicate handkerchief that she held wadded in her fist.

"Excuse me, Madam. Mrs. Brittany is calling." Maggie, the Stalworth housekeeper, announced from the doorway.

"Damn it, Maggie, take a message! Tell them Mommy's out of town! Can't you see that my mother does not wish to be disturbed?"

Vivian sank deeper into the plush sofa cushions. "I'll never outlive this humiliation! I have devoted my life to setting a proper example for you children and for the citizens of this city. Clay and I have worked hard to maintain flawless reputations."

"And no one questions your success, Mommy!" Victoria cried from the chaise opposite her mother. "Many of our associates agree that the Stalworth name is Sterling in this community. It commands respect that borders on reverence."

"That was before the most prestigious social event of the year was referred to as a vulgar *bash* on the front page of our own newspaper! I cannot bear it. I just can't bear it, I tell you!"

"Mommy, it will take more than tacky newspaper headlines to impugn the Stalworth name. Half the people in Ashford would be unemployed if it weren't for Daddy."

Maggie answered another call, prompting Vivian to squall. "I'll never live it down! All our friends are calling to offer me their sympathy, SYM-PA-THY!"

The Stalworth home had resembled an anthill earlier this morning. Maids and butlers laden with fresh fruit, frosted drinks and sleep aids had crossed and re-crossed the elegant floral carpet in the downstairs library, rearranging the room to accommodate *Young Master* Stephen in his convalescing.

The room, with its high ceilings and woodcarvings, was Stephen's favorite. The eighteenth-century mantel and over-mantel carvings displayed intricate designs of fruit and flowers. Today and for days to come, Stephen would occupy the room's red satin brocade sofa. The staff had drawn tables close and had placed telephones and necessities within Stephen's easy reach as they closely tended the fire.

Stephen liked a roaring fire. He was especially fond of the painting that dominated the room from above the fireplace. The life-sized portrait depicted his parents in riding dress. The artist had captured the likenesses of both Vivian and Clay to the smallest detail.

Stephen's proud, powerful father stood smiling beside his mother who glowed with the youthful radiance of one who had enjoyed an unencumbered life. To Stephen's mind, the painting reflected a quiet confidence. It promised *all is well and will remain so....*

Stephen had feared the painting as a boy. At times, alone in the room, the feeling of a presence other than his own had overwhelmed him.

Times like these, he had howled in fear and run to the ever-present comfort of Vivian's arms.

Her smiles, hugs, and reassuring words had never failed to soothe him. Vivian's doting had proven instrumental in molding the confident, ambitious, self-assured personality that she believed her son had become.

Clay Stalworth charged into the room in a cloud of cigar smoke. "Oh, Good God Vivian! Are you still carrying on like someone died? And you two," he thundered, pointing at Victoria and her friend, Adrian Maxwell. "You keep pampering the boy and we'll be able to turn this place into a funeral parlor for real. Somebody, get me a scotch!"

Vivian patted her eyes. She squeezed Stephen's shoulder.

Adrian perched on the edge of the chair nearest the senior Stalworth as he seated himself in his favorite wingback chair.

He sipped the scotch Victoria gave him, puffed on his cigar, and fixed his gaze on his beautiful daughter. "Tory, dear, you plan to spend the holidays close to home, don't you?"

"Why, yes, Dad. I've no special plans."

"Adrian?"

"Yes?" Adrian stole a glance at Stephen. "I'm alone for the holidays. Whatever Victoria has planned is fine with me."

Vivian pulled herself erect. Her feminine intuition homed in on Clay's questions like sonar. She dabbed at her eyes, watching him.

Clay rose from his chair. He strode to the fire, smiling to himself.

"Clay? Why do you ask?"

He answered in a casual voice. "Your brother Claude just phoned."

"My *brother*?" Vivian repeated. She placed a hand over her heart and shot her husband a look that demanded answers. "And?"

"And he wants us to come to Santa Fe for the holidays." Clay smiled to himself. *That'll intercept her missiles and send her into a tailspin.*

Vivian arched her brows then dropped them. She lifted the corners of her mouth then sank them. She appeared inconsolable. "Clay, I would love to go. But we can't possibly, not now," she said with an anxious glance at Stephen.

"Oh, Mommy, you should go!" Victoria insisted.

Adrian swept the air with a jeweled hand. "Mother Stalworth, Victoria and I will take care of Stephen ourselves. Don't give it another thought. We'll see to his every need."

163

"When the Pope's Baptist...." Maggie mouthed the words over her flying feather duster and rolled her eyes at Adrian.

Now for the big guns, Clay chuckled to himself as he sipped his scotch. He had anticipated his wife's refusal and had prepared his argument.

"Mommy!" Stephen exclaimed as his father looked on. "Tory and I are not children! I think we can manage the holidays this once without you and Dad. I'm not crippled, you know! My sprained ankle is no excuse for you to refuse Uncle Claude's invitation. A nice holiday is exactly what you need. Maggie, Tory, Adrian, and I will manage just fine. You start packing. I insist!"

Clay turned to Vivian, careful to keep his face innocently somber.

"Clay, you can't stand Claude. You have never agreed to visit him in Santa Fe. I couldn't live with myself if I thought that dragging you out there would make you miserable."

You're good, very good. Clay smiled at his wife. *But I'm better....*

"Claude Vinsant is a bore," Clay said, puffing on his cigar. He turned from the fire to blow smoke rings at the ceiling. "But I think I can find sufficient distractions in Santa Fe this time. Prince Asad will be joining us."

"The Prince?" Vivian gasped. "Prince Asad?" She repeated.

"The same," Clay answered.

Vivian rose regally from the sofa. "Maggie Dear," she called to the maid with a smile that Scarlet O'Hara might have envied. "Who called earlier? I *must* return their call."

"And start packing," Clay and Stephen said in unison.

"So, Claude still entertains royalty?" Stephen asked as Vivian left and Clay re-settled himself in his chair.

"Yes. And for that, I am grateful," Clay said, his face relaxed and animated. "With the prince on hand, we will have no lack of amusements. He loves the races and he loves to dance. And he creates such excitement everywhere we go."

"He no longer flaunts those ridiculous tags, surely?" Stephen asked.

"But of course." Clay smiled a mischievous smile. "That's the fun of it," he added.

"Fun of what?" Adrian asked, feeling lost in the conversation.

Clay gestured with his scotch. "Prince Asad travels with a fleet of limousines, a harem of wives, and a staff of servants. The servants park his limousines side by side at the front door of every establishment the prince visits. His Majesty ignores signs like Valet Parking, Parking in Rear or No Parking."

"The limousines have identical tags that read PRINCE. Since Asad is the son of an Arabian Sheik, law enforcement looks the other way. The establishment owners love it because Asad's fleet parked at their door guarantees capacity crowds."

"Sounds like fun," Adrian said.

"And the prince is gorgeous," Victoria breathed. She fanned her face with her hand.

"And so are his wives," Clay said and bounced his brows.

"Dad, will you be flying commercial?" Victoria interrupted.

"I don't know. It may be too late to book first class. Max may have to fly us."

Stephen leaned forward, shaking his head. "This weather's too unpredictable, Dad. I'd feel better if you fly commercial."

"You may be right, Son." Clay rattled his scotch to his lips, took a gulp, and caught Victoria's eye. "Tory, call Karen at the agency. Tell her that we'll be leaving in the morning."

Clay shook his head and knit his brows. "This bruised bash or buggered ball—whatever it is your mother calls it—is just plain silly! The sooner we get out of here, the better!"

Victoria stood and motioned to Adrian with her hand. "Come on, we'll call the agency and then see if Mom wants to do some shopping."

"Do you have to?" Clay cried with a pained expression.

"Oh, Daddy!" Victoria patted her father's cheek and left the room with Adrian.

Clay blew smoke rings and watched as they floated to Stephen. "How's the ankle, Son?"

"Hurts like crazy Dad, but I'll survive. It's slowing me down a bit. If having a medical practice weren't so necessary, I'd postpone it for a while."

"It's not necessary! Damn it, Son, we've been through this a thousand times! Money comes and money goes."

Stephen's courage faltered, as always, when the Senior Stalworth got that strange, far-away look in his eyes. It was the same look that always accompanied this conversation.

Clay shook his head as though he dismissed an unwelcome thought. "Your mother thinks it prudent for you and Victoria as well to generate your own income. It will always be in your best interest to have incoming money no matter how much you think you may have," Clay's voice rose.

"Tory will be great at managing the pro...." Stephen caught himself, too late. He realized with a look of dread that his pain medication had dulled his mental faculties.

"Tory managing what? Pro what?" Clay demanded.

"The pro shop," Stephen stammered.

"What pro shop?"

"The pro shop that Tory and I are going to build along with the golf course and country club." Stephen lowered his head to avoid his father's eyes.

Clay pushed himself from his chair. He walked to the bar, poured himself a scotch, and dropped ice cubes in the glass with loud *plops!*

He returned to his chair, settled himself in, and barked with a face devoid of any expression. "Tell me about it!"

"It was to be a surprise for you and Mom."

"Skip the bullshit. I want the facts!"

Chapter Eighteen

No one knew better than Stephen Stalworth that the name, Henry Claymore Stalworth, belonged to one man with two decidedly different personalities.

Stephen knew for certain that when he accidentally mentioned "the big surprise," that Clay Stalworth, his father, had exited the room.

It was Henry Stalworth, the no-nonsense, brass tacks businessman who had armed himself with an arsenal of skepticism that stared back at Stephen.

Stephen wiped perspiration from his brow. He said with uncertainty, "We, Tory and I, plan to build a golf course, country club and pro shop."

"Where?"

"In the county, on that land around Widows Hollow."

"YOU'VE BEEN THERE?" Clay thundered.

"No!" Stephen cried his voice childlike and defensive. "I've never gone there. You said…"

Clay sliced a hand through the air. "Aren't there people living on that land?"

"Not many." Stephen struggled for words. "And we'll make them a good offer."

"Them?" Clay locked his jaw. His eyes glittered with anger.

"Whoever owns it."

"And how are you going to finance your *good offer?*"

"I, I'll sell some of my horses!" Stephen exclaimed, louder.

"You don't own any horses!" Clay bellowed.

Stephen stared at his father, incredulous. "But, the horses at the Cou..."

"You don't own any horses!" Clay repeated. "And just what if these people don't want to sell their land to you for a golf course, country club and pro shop?"

"We'll make the offer more attractive, one they can't refuse."

"And if they still refuse?" Clay's neck veins bulged. Like bellows drafting a fire, anger pumped his voice from deep within.

Stephen missed the danger signals he would have caught in normal circumstances. He cried "Then we'll force them out! Those heathens humiliated my mother and that blight of a hollow threatens to encroach on every prime bluegrass acre in Ashford. That white trash has no place in this community. They're all paupers, illiterate, useless!"

"So you would like to tie them all up in a bag and drop them in the river, is that it?"

"Something like that!" Stephen shouted.

Clay emptied his scotch in a swallow, rose from his chair, and stomped across the room to a polished oak desk.

He rummaged through a drawer and removed a key. He pulled back a rug to reveal a circular piece of metal sunk in the floor. He inserted the key, lifted the heavy metal disc, and withdrew a bundle of papers that were tied with a ribbon.

He retrieved his scotch, stomped back to the chair, and fixed a glare on Stephen that frightened the boy.

"Do you like this house?"

"Yes sir."

"Do you like the horses and stables and tennis courts?"

"Dad! What's your point?"

"My incoming money bought this land, built this house and everything you see around it. Young and reckless at the time, I got satisfied, proud, and stupid. Just like what I am seeing now, in you!"

Clay shuffled through the papers and waved a document, a contract of some sort. "You see this?"

"Yes sir!"

"It's an I.O.U. –my copy of a contract made between myself and the one man in this world to whom I will be indebted for life. You've met him once. And by the way, I've called Reid off the title search you ordered."

"You did what? But I told him..."

"You listen to me you rash, arrogant idiot! I KNOW who owns every inch of that land on the other side of the highway. Every inch as far as the eye can see and more like it. And I can tell you for certain, it is NOT for sale. Not to you and not to anyone else, for any reason!"

"He doesn't want your money. And as far as you telling my attorney to keep a secret from me, that's a little like the cart pulling the horse, isn't it?" Clay ranted, red-faced and angry. "This I.O.U. says Paid in Full," he shouted, waving the contract in the air.

Papers scattered to the floor. Clay froze. He crouched, cast a fearful glance at Stephen, and frantically gathered them up.

It must be the medicine. I'm imagining this, Stephen consoled himself.

Clay stood, shouting as though there had been no interruption. "Because the money I borrowed to save your mother from real humiliation was repaid years ago. The debt itself will never be!"

A sneer dragged at the corner of Clay's mouth beneath his salt and pepper moustache. "It was never your mother's idea that you and Tory work."

He twisted his gray head to face Stephen. "That was *my* idea. I gambled everything I owned, this house, this land, and every cent I had in the bank, on a single horse in a single race!"

"I thought then that I knew everything, like you think you do now. That horse couldn't lose. Impossible." Clay rattled the papers at Stephen. "But it did!"

"I didn't have a rich daddy to bail me out so I left the track and went searching for the nearest jug of liquor I could find. I got good and drunk and sobbed my story to the man who provided the liquor. I was too afraid to come home that night. I couldn't face your mother with the news that we were broke and homeless."

"When I did come crawling home, I guarded the door like a lunatic, expecting an eviction notice every time the bell rang. The envelope I was expecting arrived by courier." Scotch flew from the glass Clay thrust in the air like a saber.

"Before my knees buckled beneath me, I ripped open the envelope; I had to see my demons dance on that page, laughing and mocking my vanity and arrogance."

Speechless, Stephen gaped at his father. He rattled his head and squeezed his eyes to dismiss the vision that his father painted.

Tears glazed Clay's eyes. He choked. "I opened the envelope believing my heart would simply stop beating. But there was no eviction notice in that envelope. There was nothing but this packet I hold in my hands...." He chased his words with scotch.

"This I.O.U., the deed to the house and the land, and every cent I had signed over from my bank account were inside the envelope. I thought at first that it was a cruel joke-- it had to be. But as I read the contract and the signature I knew it wasn't a joke. It was my life, handed back to me, irrevocably, and the signature line below my printed name remained blank."

"Uncle Claude?" Stephen guessed.

"Uncle Claude!" Clay laughed a derisive laugh. "No Son, it wasn't Uncle Claude!"

"I would have told you sooner, but I swore to my benefactor that I would never reveal his kindness to me to anyone. But now I am forced to break that sworn oath-- because of you!"

"Because of me?" The color drained from Stephen's face.

"As I said before, you met him once—when he came to my door looking for a young girl. That same young girl you threw out of my home. That same young girl your mother now blames for your sprained ankle and her bruised social standing."

"Dad!" Stephen's expression turned to one of horror. "Dad, you can't mean...."

Clay crossed the floor to the sofa where Stephen reclined. He waved the paper in his face. "Read that signature!"

Stephen read aloud. "S. L. Simpson."

"That's Samuel Llewellyn Simpson--to you! It's "Stump" to me and to others who are fortunate enough to be his friends. To hurt one of those people in that hollow in word or in deed is to hurt him. You've already hurt one of them and he never said a word."

"Now, you want to hurt them all. Do not be fooled by his silence, Stephen! If you never heed another word I say to you, heed this: Do not tangle with Stump Simpson. Leave him and his land, and those people in that hollow alone. And as long as I live and breathe, I had better never hear that you did otherwise. And you better never breathe one word of this conversation to another living soul, do you understand me, boy!" Clay's words exploded in Stephen's ears.

"Yes Sir!" Stephen barked. He would have bowed prostrate if doing so would end his father's wrath.

With a glance at the doorway, Clay hurriedly returned the papers to the safe and the key to the drawer. He closed the drawer the same moment Victoria and Adrian returned.

"Not one available flight, Dad. I'm sorry," Victoria said and bit into a chocolate covered cherry. She offered a dish filled with them to Clay who waved it away. "Looks like Max will have to fly you," she added, licking chocolate from her fingers.

Serves me right for waiting until the last minute," Clay said with a merry laugh. "Call the estate house and see if Max is around. He can check out the plane and fly us to Santa Fe. I'll call the tower for the weather. Where's your mother?"

"Oh, she's packing and making a shopping list."

"Why did I ask?" Clay groaned and followed Victoria and Adrian from the room.

Alone again, Stephen stared at the portrait above the mantel. "Don't worry Mommy, I will make them pay. I swear it!"

The next morning, Vivian hugged her children and Adrian. "I feel so guilty about leaving you at Christmas. Are you sure you'll be all right?"

"We'll be fine, Mom," the three assured her. You and Dad have a good trip and a wonderful holiday. Now, go!"

Clay took his wife's hand and headed to the waiting car that would take them to the private airstrip behind their country estate. At the last minute, Vivian abruptly turned and ran back into the house. She hurried to the library and hugged Stephen so fiercely it took his breath.

"Mommy!" He gasped.

Vivian hugged Victoria. "I just don't feel right about leaving you!"

"Mommy, are we going to have to carry you to that plane?" Stephen demanded, smiling at his mother.

"No, Darling, it's just that I've never spent a Christmas away from you. I guess I'm getting emotional. Give me one last hug, my darlings and I promise I'm gone."

Vivian dried her eyes, forced a smile, and hugged her children and Adrian one last time.

She inexplicably burst into tears as she climbed in the limo beside her husband. Clay gathered Vivian in his arms, gave her a squeeze, and said with a grin, "My pet, he's your brother. I'm the one who should be crying!"

Chapter Nineteen

Suzanne chased the powdery residue from her makeup brush down the drain and was happy to see that the face in the mirror smiled back at her.

Look at that, I'm smiling and looking forward to this evening at Claire's because I'm going with Ben. He's so spontaneous and fun, nothing like Stephen.

The doorbell rang. Feeling like a schoolgirl on a first date, Suzanne hurried to her front door and pulled it open.

Dwayne, Stephen's valet and chauffeur, stood on her porch holding a gift -wrapped box in his open palm. "For you Madam, from Master Stalworth."

"Th, Thank you," Suzanne stammered. Stunned, she watched from the window as the sleek limo pulled away into the night.

She stared at the small box in her hand. "Why is Stephen sending me gifts?"

"Don't think I'm going to be manipulated by this," she said aloud. She lifted the lid and gasped. With breathtaking brilliance, the engagement ring that she had hurled at Stephen sparkled from the box. A heart shaped pendant of fiery diamonds lay beside the ring. "All I want for Christmas is you. Please call me. I love you. S.S."

Suzanne stared at the note and the gift in dismay. "I don't want them. I don't want him."

The doorbell rang again. Suzanne glanced to the door in dread. "What now?"

She opened the door with caution. A leafy poinsettia in Ben Gardner's hands hid his face. "A tree for thee from me," he quipped and shifted the plant to one side.

"Whoa..." Bennett exhaled the word with the exuberance of a deflating balloon. He set the plant aside, glanced at the box in Suzanne's hand and at the signature on the note.

No funny one-liners, no comical quips rushed to his rescue. Bennett stood silent with the lost look of an abandoned child.

"Ben... Ben, I'm so sorry."

God, no! Please no! I don't want an apology. I want a wife!

Bennett fought back tears and bit his lip. He stared into Suzanne's eyes and prayed that he did not look as pathetic as he felt.

"I, I didn't know. I never expected," she said and reached a hand to Bennett's face. "Ben. Don't look so forlorn...."

She buried her face in his shoulder and wrapped her arms around his neck. "I don't want his gifts. I don't want him! I want you, only you. I love you Bennett Gardner!"

A sob escaped from Bennett's throat as he crushed Suzanne in his arms and returned her lingering, passionate kiss. He slowly released her and whistled. "You look like an angel in that white mohair sheath and white leather boots."

"Ben...?"

"Yes, Ms. Claiborne?" He smiled, a genuine, heart-felt, *Merry Christmas, God bless us everyone* smile. She was his.

"I was going to say something...." Suzanne shrugged. "Come on, Handsome. We'd better get going."

"How much of this booty do I need to load?" He yelled after her as she headed down the hallway.

She returned in a moment with a mink stole over her arm. "We need to load all of it," she said with a laugh. I'll help."

With the last of the packages loaded, Ben bowed and offered his arm to Suzanne. She turned to lock the door when the phone rang.

Ben's anxious look confirmed that he and Suzanne shared the same thought, *Stalworth!*

"Nah," Suzanne said, as though to the ringing phone. She laughed, took Bennett's hand and raced with him through the snow to his car.

Stephen slammed down the phone. Disappointment and frustration gnawed at him.

Adrian entered the library carrying a snack tray. "Stephen would you like egg rolls, or something a bit spicier?"

"Neither!" Stephen shouted. "I would like a scotch on therocks. Make that a triple!"

"You can't mix your pain medication with alcohol, Darling," Adrian said.

Stephen glared at Adrian. Feeling certain that her patronizing smile would nauseate him he cried, "Don't tell me what I can or can't mix! I'm a doctor damn it and I want that scotch NOW!"

"Stephen!" Victoria ran into the room with a dishtowel in her hands. "You don't have to be rude to Adrian just because you aren't feeling well."

"I'm feeling fine. I'm feeling perfect!" Stephen's face twisted in anger.

"I don't mind being restricted to this sofa or being confined with a bunch of women clucking around me like barnyard hens. I don't mind playing brain numbing board games or stuffing my face out of sheer boredom. But I do mind her going out with him!" He screamed.

Stunned, Adrian spun to face him. She held a green bottle of J&B in one hand and a crystal glass in the other.

Reeling from the shock of his heartless betrayal, she dropped the bottle of scotch and the glass from her hands. "Her? *Her!* You can't mean...!" Adrian screamed over the sounds of shattering glass.

"Stephen!" Victoria screamed. "You're out of control! Tell Adrian you didn't mean it. You're not yourself!"

Ignoring Victoria, Stephen curled his lip. He raised chilling eyes to Adrian. "No. Not *her*, you're right Adrian, *Dear*. I don't mean *her*, I mean Suzanne, Suzanne Claiborne!"

Victoria wadded the dishtowel and fired it at Stephen. She kicked at the sofa, aiming for his injured leg. "You are despicable! And you call that poor wretch from the hollow ill-bred!"

With tears in her eyes, Victoria encircled Adrian with her arm. "I'm sorry Adrian, I don't know what's come over him, but we don't have to stand for this. Come on, let's get out of here!"

"Maggie!" Stephen screamed.

Breathless, the maid raced into the room.

"Get me a scotch, find those damn crutches, and tell Dwayne to bring the car to the door!"

Dwayne *swish, swished,* into the library, the starched fabric of his uniform rubbing at the legs as he moved in measured, dignified steps. "Sir?"

"Get me some scotch, ice, and a couple of glasses. Help me to the car!"

Dismayed, Maggie fought her tears and watched. She pitied Dwayne who wrestled Stephen, his crutches, a bottle of scotch and a bucket of ice out the door.

Her frayed nerves snapped. With a shudder she burst into tears as the door to the Stalworth mansion slammed for the third time this evening.

Twenty-One

"If all this comes with having a family, I'm getting me one," Bennett cried. He took in the grandeur of the Richardson estate with a long, low whistle.

The home, a sprawling three story English stack stone, sparkled with multi-colored lights on the roof, in the trees, and across the fence line.

Bennett pushed a teetering package back in the stack in his arms. "Where's that sleigh when you need one?" He joked as Suzanne pressed the doorbell.

"Suz! Welcome, Darling, and Merry Christmas!" The pretty brunette who answered the door gushed. "And this must be Bennett," she said, hugging them both.

"No, we left him in the car," Bennett said, straight-faced.

"Ignore him, Claire." Suzanne poked a finger in Bennett's ribs. "He takes some getting used to."

"That's why we left him in the car," Bennett said, poker-faced.

"Well, I'm Claire and I'm pleased to meet you anyway!" Claire's pretty face crinkled with smiles. She shook Bennett's hand, winked at Suzanne, and said, "I think I like this stranger, whoever he is, a lot."

Suzanne and Bennett followed Claire to a cavernous room filled with noisy guests. "Ross is in there somewhere," Claire said.

She nodded to the packages in the new arrivals' arms. "You can stash those under the tree, anywhere you can find room."

Before Suzanne could voice her protest, Bennett squatted before a mound of packages that spilled in every direction. Like a card dealer dealing cards, he fired her carefully wrapped packages onto the mound.

Suzanne told herself that she would save the second armload from Bennett's enthusiastic disposal when she heard someone call her name.

"Suzanne!" Pick squealed. She ran all smiles and open arms to Suzanne.

"I been waitin and waitin fer you. I reckoned maybe work was keepin you late and you changed yer mind. Look what Miss Claire done." Pick pulled her hair that was neatly braided in a single braid, over her shoulder. She rubbed the green velvet bow that fastened her braid and continued like an excited child.

"She fixed my hair and bought me these fancy clothes. I'm takin folks' wraps fer 'em." The bright sparkle vanished from Pick's eyes. She leaned close to Suzanne, whispering, "Wraps is coats, ain't they?"

Suzanne hugged Pick and whispered back. "Yes, wraps *are* coats." She held Pick at arm's length. "Pick, you look stunning!"

And Pick did look stunning in a turtleneck of green mohair with a pleated skirt and jacket of cream wool crepe, and black patent flats.

With her copper hair braided, Pick looked elegant and sophisticated. Dark lashes that Claire had tinted with mascara framed Pick's green eyes and made them sparkle like emeralds in her flawless face.

Pick pulled Suzanne close. "Miss Claire bought fine things for Olivia, Buddy, Willie, and Jimmy Joe, too. I told her flat out I ain't got money to pay fer such and she said it's done paid fer."

Confusion troubled Pick's eyes. "What is she sayin?"

Suzanne took Pick's hand. "Pick, we pay for gifts in many ways. Making someone happy can be a sort of payment."

"You made Claire happy by allowing her to buy these things for you and your family. You owe her nothing. My sister believes that the happiest people on Earth *give without remembering and receive without forgetting.*

182

Suzanne met Pick's eyes with a smile. "Claire lives by these words."

"Miss Claire's fancy folk, but she's God-fearin and good, ain't she?"

"That she is," Suzanne agreed with a nod and started for the great room with Pick.

Pick hesitated. "I'm takin folks' wraps so I better stay put."

Suzanne's reply was lost in shouts of "Aunt Suzie! Aunt Suzie!"

Anthony, age six, and Yvette, age four, tackled Suzanne as other guests waved and shouted greetings from across the room.

Clinging to Suzanne, the Richardson children chattered nonstop as she made her way through the crowd, introducing Bennett to friends and family members.

"Claire, you've outdone yourself this year!" Suzanne exclaimed. She craned her neck to see to the top of a soaring blue spruce.

The tree sparkled with hundreds of lights and shimmering icicles that illuminated the beautiful, rare ornaments that Claire had collected through the years.

"This is the adult's tree," Claire said, nodding at the spruce. She pointed through an arched doorway. "The children's tree is in the dining room."

"You're kidding. Two trees?"

"We needed more room for gifts. Gifts belong under the tree, so...." Claire led the way to the dining room and to the fragrant Scotch pine that towered before a bay window.

Unable to resist, Suzanne touched the delightful items that dressed the splendid tree. Miniature Raggedy Ann and Andy dolls, striped candy canes, and clusters of red, gold, and green glass balls hung from every branch. Red velvet bows graced the tips of the branches.

Multicolored lights twinkled off and on all over the tree that stood like a cheerful sentinel, guarding the mound of colorful packages beneath it.

"Claire! This place looks like the North Pole. The only thing missing is Santa himself!" Suzanne exclaimed.

"He's on the guest list," Claire said. She took Suzanne's arm and said, "Let's join the others for a drink before dinner, shall we?"

Whispering, giggling children of all ages made dinner a lively event as the joyful spirit of Christmas filled the house.

After dinner, the children remained in the dining room, circling the Raggedy Ann and Andy tree. They pointed to package after package with excited squeals. "That one's mine, and that one!"

With the children happily occupied, the adults made their way to the great room where they sipped eggnog and caught up on the past year's events.

Overwhelmed by the sheer size of the Richardson family, Bennett squeezed Suzanne's hand. "What was his name?"

Anthony had blurted earlier, "That's Uncle Joey, Uncle Ben."

"Did you hear that? He called me Uncle Ben. I've never been called Uncle. Family gatherings have never been a part of my life, but I think I could get used to them,"

Bennett said as he brushed a strand of dark hair from Suzanne's face.

"Think you could, huh?"

Bennett nodded then answered with a kiss.

Having finished his eggnog, Bennett took Suzanne's empty mug. "Want another?"

"Please, *Uncle* Ben," Suzanne teased.

Bennett put the mugs on a table and wrapped Suzanne in his arms. "I like the sound of that. I could get used to being Uncle Ben, or Daddy, or Father, or Papa."

"What are you saying, Uncle Ben?" Suzanne asked, glowing.

"I...." Bennett stuck out his lip in a pout as Ross Richardson yelled.

"Your attention! Your attention, please!" Ross tapped a spoon against a clay mug.

"We have children here who insist that it's time to open gifts. Being a democratic family, I think we should take a vote. Those who think our rug runners have behaved themselves with sufficient decorum to justify the opening of presents, so say!"

Bennett crossed his eyes. He muttered to Suzanne. "I thought you said he's a doctor. You sure he's not a politician?"

"Boo! No!" Suzanne and Bennett giggled. They yelled and wagged their heads with the other adults.

The children shouted their disappointment.

"Shall we give them another chance?" Ross asked as he retreated from the children who threatened to tackle him.

As they moved to the crowded dining room with the other guests, Suzanne warned Bennett. "Get comfortable. This may take a while."

Chapter Twenty

"Whoa. I think I'm rusted," Bennett groaned. He twisted his head side to side and rolled his shoulders. He scooped a handful of pistachios from a sterling dish.

"I see what you mean about it taking a while," he said as Suzanne pulled him to his feet.

"You're worse than the children," she said, then cringed as Bennett cracked a pistachio with his teeth.

Bennett rubbed his backside. "That was an ordeal. I'm all in favor of exchanging gifts at Christmas, but when kids get so much stuff they refuse to open it, you'd think Mommy and Daddy would get the message."

Suzanne agreed. "The extravagance is …."

"Obscene?" Bennett blurted.

"Ow, Ben, I think my foot's asleep." Suzanne clutched his shoulder. "I agree with you, there should be…." She glanced into the foyer. "Is someone crying?"

"What?" Bennett turned to look.

"Oh, Ben! Pick's crying."

"Oh, Suz," he said with a face as miserable as Suzanne's.

"How could I have been so stupid?" Suzanne groaned.

"Pick's family barely survives with the basics and I bring her here to see these kids get everything the North Pole can crank out. What do I do?"

"Whoa! Hold on there, sport." Bennett cradled Suzanne in his arms. He lifted her face to his. "The sleigh's still hitched to the North *Post*. We can shop in the morning. I've got a few pennies in the bank," he said, bouncing his brows and grinning.

"Oh, Ben!" Suzanne cried. "We'll give them the best Christmas they've ever had! You stay put, I'll tell her."

Frowning, Bennett marched backward like a nutcracker soldier. He paused beside the pistachio dish, dropped his hand, and mechanically grabbed a handful of pistachios.

Suzanne rolled her eyes and darted off. Sometimes she found Bennett's boyish behavior frustrating.

Pick sat at the top of the stairs, looking out the circle head window at the falling snow.

"Hey, Suzanne." Pick wiped her eyes with the heels of her hands and scooted over to make room for Suzanne on the step. "It ain't fair," she said, wagging her head at the small children who played in the foyer below.

"That's what I want to talk to you about," Suzanne said softly.

"They're just little uns. It ain't fair," Pick repeated.

Suzanne smiled into Pick's eyes. "Pick, will you let me and Ben make it up to you?"

"Make up what?" Pick blinked. "What are you talkin about?"

Suzanne hugged her knees and cast a sideways glance at Pick. "For tonight, for being so thoughtless. I'm sorry you had to see these children receive so much more than they could ever need. Such excess! I'm so sorry, Pick, I just wasn't thinking."

Pick scrunched her eyes and searched Suzanne's face. "Suzanne, I ain't got no notion what yer sayin."

Suzanne placed a hand on Pick's knee. "I saw you crying, Pick, and I feel so bad. I didn't realize how it would hurt you to see these children get so much when you and your sister and brothers have so little. But Ben and I...."

Pick pulled away with a look of surprise. "But I ain't sorry fer us! Me and mine, we got plenty. We got each other, our friends, and the Good Book."

She squeezed Suzanne's arm, smiling. "And you to teach us to read it. We got plenty and it ain't no burden."

"But them little uns.... " Pick nodded to the toddlers who shrieked and raced after one another.

"They got too much and they ain't got no notion what to do with it. Their folks want em to be happy right enough, but they was burdened, like the rich young man in the Good Book. He couldn't follow Jesus cause he had too much and he was sad with it. Fancy things ain't what makes kids happy, Suzanne. Look at 'em now."

Pick pointed to the laughing youngsters who had abandoned their new toys to chase one another through a large cardboard box.

"Why do rich folks think fancy things make younguns happy?"

Suzanne shrugged. "I don't think any of us know the answer to that, Pick."

"Everything all right?" Bennett called from the bottom stair.

"Better than all right," Suzanne said. "Pick's giving me lessons on human nature."

"That'd be the finest thing ever," Pick said. "Giving lessons."

Suzanne yanked Pick's braid playfully and followed her down the stairs. "You can be anything you want to be, young lady." She looped her arm through Bennett's and added with a smile, "Ben and I will be your cheerleaders."

"Want me to do a cartwheel?" Bennett raised his arms above his head and pointed a toe to the floor.

"Don't you dare!" Suzanne cried, laughing.

"Suz, are you coming? We're waiting for you," Claire called from around the corner. "Bring Pick."

Pick waved Suzanne and Bennett on, but Claire yelled for the three of them again.

Pick poked a finger in her chest. "Me?"

Suzanne nodded and took Pick's hand.

"Geez, look at this crowd," Bennett said. He noted that every chair, sofa, and cushion in the room was taken. "Quick, grab it!" He dived for a piano bench, pulled Suzanne onto his lap, and Pick onto the bench beside them.

"Whew!" Bennett leaned his head on Suzanne's shoulder. "If this is gonna be another gift grab marathon, I want my blankie and pidow," he said and stuck his thumb in his mouth.

"Behave!" Suzanne hissed through her sealed lips.

Ross and Claire knelt beneath the adults' tree, sorting packages, reading names aloud, and passing gifts to children who carried them to the intended receiver.

"Miss Pick McKinley," Claire called out.

"What do I do Suzanne?" Pick cried.

"Accept the gift," Suzanne said with a nod to the child who stood before Pick, holding a wrapped package.

"Oh, thank you," Pick said to the little girl.

At Pick's uncertain glance, Suzanne tapped the package. "Open it."

Pick tore through the red foil paper, opened the box, withdrew the contents, and looked to Suzanne in horror.

"It's all right. Give them to me," Suzanne said. With a wink, she took the stack of elegantly inscribed cards from Pick and read:

"This card entitles Early Mae Johnson to one free eye exam and one free pair of prescription glasses when presented to Dr. Lewis Cooper."

Pick's eyes and smile grew wider as Suzanne continued reading the cards that represented free medical services and visits for Pick's family and neighbors.

Suzanne, Bennett, and Olga had solicited the services of physicians, surgeons, and dentists, including a heart specialist for Mama John and an orthopedic specialist for young Eli O'Connor.

Each professional had volunteered his time. There would be no charge for anything.

Tears filled Pick's eyes as the faces of those whom she loved flashed in her mind. She could see and hear Olivia and Buddy coughing, and young Eli limping on his twisted leg, and Mama John with her spells, blind as a bat, and laboring to breathe.

"Thank you, thank you so much," Pick gushed, hugging Suzanne and Bennett in one squeeze.

"Every doctor I approached cheerfully volunteered then asked if they could spread the word. It was amazing. My phone never stopped ringing," Bennett said.

Suzanne snuggled in his arms. "It's wonderful, isn't it? This is what Christmas is all about, joyful, selfless giving."

When the family members and guests had opened the last package, Ross pulled Claire to her feet. "That's it, folks," Claire announced. "Please help yourself to desserts or freshen your drinks."

Bennett stood, stretched, laced his fingers, and cracked his knuckles. He limped his wrists, shook them, and said with a lopsided grin, "It's been a while."

"You play the piano?" Suzanne shook her head in amazement as Bennett lifted the keyboard cover from the gleaming Steinway baby grand and began softly playing *White Christmas*.

"Save our places. Pick and I are going to help Claire clean up," Suzanne said.

"That man's a wonder," she confided to Pick. They gathered crumpled paper, bows, and discarded boxes and stuffed them into bags for disposal.

Together, they cleared empty glasses, wiped spills, and in no time, they had finished. Sounds of carols and laughter drifted from the great room. The two women returned to find Bennett entertaining the crowd.

Guests with drinks in hand called out requests. Bennett played carol after carol and sang along.

Pick exchanged glances with Suzanne. "He sings, too," Pick said with a giggle.

Seeing Suzanne, Bennett patted the bench. "I kept it warm just for you."

"What are we playing next?" Suzanne asked.

"You play?" Bennett's smile stretched across his face. "Just follow me."

Playing the piano together, Suzanne and Bennett delighted the crowd through a prolonged round of children's' favorites. As the children wandered off, Claire requested *Oh, Holy Night*.

"*Oh, Holy night, the stars are brightly shining...,*" a chorus of voices sang. One by one, the voices fell silent. A single voice continued, singing with notes so sweet and powerful, it stirred the souls of the captivated guests.

Pick blushed when she realized that she had finished the song alone. She looked to Suzanne with fearful eyes as the guests swarmed her, applauding with enthusiasm.

Suzanne wrapped her arm about Pick's shoulder. "Please, sing another."

With a shy smile, Pick spoke in hushed tones to Bennett.

"Perfect," he said, and then added, "Sure can."

Pick fixed her eyes on Suzanne's eyes. She said shyly, "This ain't a Christmas song exactly, but it was my Mama and Papa's favorite."

When Pick finished singing *How Great thou Art*, the room erupted in enthusiastic applause.

"Her voice is heavenly."

`"She sings like an angel"

"Suzanne, that girl needs a manager. With a voice like that, she can pack a stadium anytime. Why, she's good enough to entertain the president or the Windsors."

Suzanne's cheerful smile at the crowd's genuine appreciation of Pick's singing vanished quickly.

A matronly woman pointed to Pick's departing figure and said in loud tones to her companion, "Isn't that the red-headed heathen from that horrid Widows Hollow? The same one who made a spectacle of herself dancing with Jan Vandeventer after she wreaked havoc at Vivian's ball?"

The woman shook her head. "She's not fooling anyone dressed in that finery! She probably stole it!"

Suzanne's eyes blazed with anger.

"Uh, oh!" Bennett cried. He grabbed Suzanne and pulled her back from what was certain to be an unpleasant encounter.

"Let me go!" Suzanne seethed. "Pick is no thief and she's not a heathen, either! Pick may not be able to read but I bet she knows *Judge not lest ye be judged* better than that old hag!"

Suzanne's words came out so loud and strong, Bennett clapped a hand over her mouth.

Claire approached. She questioned Bennett's behavior with a wordless stare.

Bennett glanced from Claire's scowl to Suzanne's face. "There, Sweetie, I got it," he said and tapped his mouth. "Got any chocolate on mine?"

Still fuming, Suzanne replied "No, but I can fix that if you like!"

Bennett grabbed a dish of chocolate covered cherries from the piano and thrust them at Suzanne. "Fire away!" He said.

Suzanne looked at the chocolates, glanced from Bennett to Claire, and burst into laughter.

"Thanks," she said to Bennett through her laughter. "That could have been really bad!"

"No kidding!" Bennett said and shook his head.

"Did I miss something here?" Claire asked, confused.

She bid the other guests goodnight, then saw Suzanne and Bennett to the door where they exchanged hugs and wishes for a "Merry Christmas."

Suzanne and Bennett walked Pick to her truck where Bennett stowed packages and containers of leftovers.

They waited hand-in-hand while Pick tried repeatedly to start the old Chevy. She pumped the accelerator and pounded the wheel. "Dang truck, don't do this again!"

Bennett closed the hood and wiped his hands. "Probably needs a battery," he said. He had scraped corrosion from the battery cables, but the truck was not going to start.

"Sorry Pick, you'll have to come with us. We're stopping by Olga's. I'll fetch your rusted bucket of bolts tomorrow if that's fine by you."

"I thank you, Mr. Gardner, and I'm sorry to be such a bother," Pick said. She climbed in next to Suzanne on the front seat of Bennett's cherry red 1950 Ford Convertible.

"Did you hear that? She called me *Mister* Gardner. It's good to know somebody respects me." Bennett quipped and slid behind the wheel.

Chapter Twenty-One

"Welcome! Excuse the mess. I'm Joy Bardo, in charge of new recruits." The friendly stranger who answered Olga's door shot out a hand in greeting to Bennett, Suzanne, and Pick.

The pretty, petite blonde spied brown smudges on her red-tinted hand. She snatched her hand back and licked the chocolate from her fingers. Her friendly smile made it plain that she felt no need to apologize for any perceived breach of etiquette.

"Cherry juice and chocolate frosting," Joy said with an impish grin. "We have plenty more where this came from and plenty of cookies to frost and decorate, so consider your selves recruited."

Suzanne introduced herself, Bennett and Pick.

The three followed Joy to a kitchen filled with fresh-baked aromas and busy, laughing women.

Olga stood at the stove stirring a bubbling, heavenly-smelling concoction.

"Suzanne! Welcome. Who is dis handsome man and dis beautiful young lady?" Olga asked, playfully hugging Pick and offering a cheek to Bennett who gave her a loud smooch.

"Miss Olga," Pick said with a shy smile. She could not take her eyes off the photo gallery that was displayed on the common wall between the study and the kitchen.

Jan at various ages accepted ribbons and trophies beside his horse, in front of his horse, and sometimes, leaning from his saddle.

Pick looked at the photos with varying degrees of pleasure. She stared at a colorful, double matted eleven by fourteen that hung front and center of the collection. Her smile fled.

There was Jan, sparkling in a sequined western outfit, sitting tall and upright in his saddle, leading the grand entry into a rodeo arena with the stars and stripes flying from the pole he carried. Beside him, dressed in a matching outfit, tall and erect in her saddle, and carrying the flag of the Commonwealth of Kentucky, sat Margaret.

Pick felt an unfamiliar kick in her stomach and frowned. *What do I care if Margaret's in a picture with him?*

"The cider's ready, help yourselves," Olga announced to the mothers and daughters of the women's league who frosted cupcakes and decorated cookies at Olga's oversized, antique harvest table.

Olga waved a hand over her counter top. "De cubs are here vis lemon and cinnamon sticks."

"Yea! Reinforcements!" Friendly voices called from the table to Suzanne.

"You want to cut or paint?" Joy invited. She patted the empty chair to her right and tapped an assortment of ceramic bowls. "Chocolate. Vanilla. Strawberry frosting. Glazed fruit. Nuts." She met Suzanne's eyes and said with a chuckle, "Get busy."

Olga slid a sheet of cookies in the oven and set the timer. She pulled the oven mitt from her hand and said to Bennett "Klaus is in ze stables. Our groom, Dana, he get married and move away. We have hired nobody yet. Come dis way." She pulled open a door that led to the stables and pastures beyond the house.

Bennett flashed Olga a grateful grin, dragged his finger through a bowl of chocolate frosting, and popped his finger in his mouth.

Mortified, Suzanne smacked Bennett's hand as he reached again for the frosting.

"Ow! Suz!" He yelped and hurried out the door.

Olga said with a laugh "Bennett reminds me of my Klaus. He is so cude!" She cut her eyes to Suzanne. "Dat man is in love vis you."

Olga wiped her hands on her apron and circled Pick's waist with her arm. "Peek, I did not expect you tonight. You look so pretty."

Pick dropped her defenses in the warmth of Olga's smile. She replied, "Papa's truck wouldn't start, so Suzanne and Mr. Gardner brung me with 'em. This is the best Christmas ever. My younguns is at Mama John's and I'm just bustin to tell 'em Suzanne and Bennett's doctor friends are gonna see to Olivia and all the folks up home, and they ain't askin no wages fer doin it," Pick added, beaming.

"How wonderful for you, Suzanne is great friend, yes?"

"Oh, yes, Maam." Pick nodded with enthusiasm.

With a childlike twinkle in her eyes, Olga took a large, gift-wrapped box from a corner cabinet. "Olga has surprise for you, too," she said and presented the box to Pick who eagerly tore away the wrapping.

"Roses!" Pick cried. She lifted the crystal bowl of roses from the box to smell their fragrance.

"These have no smell, Peek. These are silk roses, but they will do until we get you some real ones in the spring."

Pick hugged Olga. "Oh, Miss Olga, these are the finest roses I ever seen. Just like my Mama wanted. Thank you."

"Wait," Olga said, tapping a finger on the envelope that lay inside the box. "Open."

"Wha...?" Pick cried at the stack of green bills she pulled from the envelope.

"This is for the bread and jerky you and your friend Mule made for ze ball. Our friends, dey buy all of it and dey want more."

Speechless, Pick wanted to hug Olga and shout with joy, but whispers from the table prevented her.

Beautiful young women dressed in clothes Pick could not imagine owning stared at her with the same look that Pick gave stray cats that deposited stiff, squashed toads, or half-eaten mice at her door.

Pick felt confused. She was not dressed in her tattered rags, nor in a maid's uniform, so why were the unsmiling women with their icy stares whispering about her?

She tore her eyes from the gawking women as the back door burst open.

"Where's the potty?" Bennett mouthed the words to Suzanne who blinked from Bennett to the sea of manicured hands that pointed the way to Olga's guest bath.

"Think about my offer, Klaus. I want that yearling," Claude Olliphant said and clapped a hand on Klauses' shoulder.

"Isn't she cude in dat apron?" Klaus smiled an adoring smile at Olga. He kissed her on the cheek and snatched a warm gingerbread cookie from a baking sheet. He bit into the cookie and said to Olliphant, "I'll discuss it vis Mama and ve vill let you know."

"That yearling's as good as Papa's," Margaret, who followed her father into the kitchen, announced. Flanked by Jan and Jacques, she said with an air of confidence, "Papa always gets what he wants."

She lifted her chin to sniff the spicy aroma that filled Olga's kitchen. "Mmm, Jan, that's your mother's heavenly cider." She squeezed Jan's arm and locked her eyes on his. "Can I get you a cup?"

Jan did not answer. He riveted his attention on the tall figure that hurriedly disappeared around the corner into the study. Jan's pulse quickened. *She's here, I can't believe she's here, dressed like that… She's gorgeous!*

Margaret glimpsed the object of Jan's sudden interest. In a temper, she speared Jacques with her elbow. "Isn't that the clumsy domestic that spoiled Vi's ball?"

"Please tell me that Jan didn't hear you say that!" Jacques hissed. He rolled his eyes and braced himself for Jan's tirade.

But Jacques needn't have worried. Jan was oblivious to everyone and everything—but *her*.

Starting after Pick, Jan hesitated. He turned to Margaret. "Weren't you getting cider?"

Margaret dazzled a smile for the uncharacteristically quiet women at the table. She broke from Jacques' side like a Derby contender at the starting gate and poured two cups of cider.

In a loud voice she confided to her friends who could not take their eyes off Jan. "He's so helpless…."

She stirred the cider with cinnamon sticks and returned to Jan. "Just like you like it, Jan."

"Thank you Margaret." Jan took both cups. He nodded to Jacques, cocked a smile, and said to Margaret, "Now why don't you get some for yourself and Jacques?"

Pick appeared to be absorbed in viewing the photo gallery when Jan raised a cup of cider to her with a nod.

"No thank you, I don't want none," she said, careful to keep her eyes on the photo wall.

Jan pressed a cup of cider in her hand. With his fingers, he turned her face to his.

"I didn't ask if you wanted any. Try it, you'll like it," he said. His dimples sank deep in his cheeks while his mind registered her expression—she had been crying.

Pick sipped the cider and forced a tiny smile.

Jan glanced at the photos and grimaced. "If I marry and have kids some day, I'll make them a promise. No cameras. I used to cry because someone flashed a camera in my face every time I turned around. I think Mama's filled a couple of warehouses with albums." He was trying to calm her. Was it working?

Pick's eyes fell on a photo.

"I was barrel racing in that one. I'm not very good at it, but I like to rodeo. All that English and dressage stuff is not for me."

Jan pointed to a photo of Klaus, dressed in a helmet, jacket, breeches and knee boots, mid-air above a fence on a gleaming, muscular horse.

"Papa and Mama love it. This farm has produced a few of the Grand National champions."

Pick's eyes fell on the photo of Jan and Margaret leading the grand entry. She tried to look away before Jan noticed.

Jan noticed. *You didn't want me to see that. You're jealous...*

Jan's cheeks dimpled. He smiled at Pick and tapped the photo. "And this one is me and Margaret. We're leading the grand entry at Will Rogers in Ft. Worth, Texas."

Pick lifted her chin and stiffened her back but kept her face expressionless. She met Jan's eyes for one brief moment before turning again to the photos. "Oh!" She squealed, reaching eagerly to frame a photo with her hands.

Startled by her sudden enthusiasm and equally curious to know what excited her so, Jan stepped behind Pick, consciously moving as close to her as he dared.

Jan groaned. *Oh, no, another of Mama's Kodak moments I wish she had skipped.*

There he was, a small boy in overalls, waving from his little red wagon in the middle of rows and rows of bright colored flowers, roses, gardenias, and lilies, amidst blooms and flowering shrubs of an infinite variety.

"It looks like heaven," Pick breathed and turned so quickly that she collided with Jan. Cider from her cup splashed all over him.

Horrified, Pick clapped her hands over her mouth. ""I'm, I'm so ...."

"Hey!" Jan yelled, wanting only to stop Pick from feeling guilty.

"Jan!"

"Zhan!"

"Pick!"

Margaret flew to the study.

Pick stood with one hand covering her mouth and the other holding her empty cup.

Jan stood with the far-flung arms and shocked expression of one who has been suddenly doused in hot cider.

Jan waved a hand at his breathless mother who had apparently raced Margaret to his rescue. "I'm all right, just clumsy."

Suzanne and Bennett stepped lively to clear a path for Margaret who dashed to the kitchen and returned in an instant with a damp towel.

Flashing Pick a look of contempt, Margaret brushed past her to wipe cider from Jan's sweater.

"She obviously hasn't spent a lot of time mingling with the upper class," Margaret said in a loud voice.

Suzanne dropped her jaw and started for Pick.

Bennett shot an arm around Suzanne's waist and took Pick by the hand. "Pick, Sweetie, you've had a long day. If you're ready, we'll take you home now."

"Good!" Margaret muttered.

"Stop!" Jan commanded, reaching for Pick's hand. He yanked the towel from Margaret, took his and Pick's cups, and gave them to Olga.

"Mama, would you please get me a fresh shirt?"

Feeling Pick squirm her hand in his, Jan tightened his grip and widened his smile. "Bennett, if you and Suzanne don't mind, I promised to show Pick Mama's greenhouse. We won't be long, if you can wait."

Bennett and Suzanne exchanged glances. Bennett shrugged. "Sure, if it's all right with Pick."

"What?" Margaret demanded.

"You've seen the greenhouse." Jan's voice was dismissive.

With a smile playing around her lips, Olga tossed Jan a clean shirt.

Jan pulled his sweater over his head, tossed it to Olga, and pulled on the clean shirt.

His mother's smile stretched wider as Jan, with Pick in tow, darted past her to snatch cookies from a plate.

"Great gingerbread, Mama. We'll be in the greenhouse."

Chapter Twenty-Two

Jan led the way through the greenhouse. If Pick liked it, she was doing a great job of hiding it.

After a silence that stretched too long to suit him, Jan asked, "Don't you like it?"

Standing with her back to Jan, Pick answered in a hollow voice. "I like it fine."

Jan reached a hand to stroke her copper braid when Pick turned on him.

Bristling like a treed coon, she cried, "What did you bring me here fer? Ain't nobody here to laugh at me now. I know I ain't much use to nobody outside the holler, less yer wanting yer winders cleaned or yer supper served. I may not read or write *now*, but I kin figure folks party good."

Her eyes glittered with anger. "I ain't figured you out yet, but I'm studying on it. If you think you'll be having yer way with me cause uppity folks call me white trash and hillbilly, you'd best forget it right now cause them that's tried picked their selves up dustin off their britches and rubbing their jaws!"

Pick slammed her arms across her chest, glaring at Jan with eyes that dared him to move one inch.

But inside—she groaned. *Lord, fergive me fer them words. I don't know how to talk to 'im. He ain't got no reason fer bringin me here but the devil's own and I got a family to mind. It don't matter if I like 'im. Jimmy Joe, Willie, Buddy, and Sissy's what matters. Please help me....*

"Hahahaha," Jan laughed. He could not stop laughing. Helpless, he watched Pick's scowl grow black as a storm cloud.

She darted for the door. He reached for her shoulder to stop her but missed and accidentally pulled her hair.

"You keep your hands to yerself!" Pick cried, whirling to snatch her braid from his hand.

With tears filling her eyes, she started again for the door, feeling miserable, lost and confused.

"Pick! WAIT A MINUTE!"

Pick stopped.

"You are not getting away this time until I say what I have to say! You don't know anything about me, and what you think you know is wrong. And I didn't mean to pull your hair. I just wanted… I just wanted to touch you."

Pick stood inches from Jan, mesmerized by the vanishing storm in his blue eyes. His jaw relaxed. His face softened to that of a small, guilt-ridden boy, caught in his misdeeds, anxious to repent.

Jan towered over her by a foot. He was dressed in a blue polo shirt, creased Wranglers, cowboy boots, and a soft leather jacket.

Pick would have thought him handsome in burlap. Everything about him was beautiful: his thick blonde hair, rugged face, and sky blue eyes. His powerful, broad shoulders, muscled thighs, and narrow waist would set any woman's heart pounding. Pick had never met a man as handsome as Jan.

"Let go my hand," she said softly, and to herself; *This ain't no time fer tears, but I can't stop 'em.*

She sniffled and raised her eyes to Jan's. "I know that yer rich and that you and your friend go to the university to be lawyers.

I know that everbody knows yer name like you and yer folks is famous. I reckon you even got horses what's famous. And you got one women in yer Mama's kitchen doin yer fetchin while another pack of 'em sittin at 'er table is waitin like buzzards on a fence post to…"

"Please, let me talk," Jan interrupted. "We can sit if you'll follow me." Jan's boots echoed across the cobblestone floor of Olga's greenhouse.

The musty smell of weathered wood, plant decay, and soil reminded Pick of the woods at home. She followed Jan past plants, shrubs, and trees, to a gazebo lined inside with wooden benches.

Rusted garden tools leaned against a wall beside a three-wheeled wooden cart. A stone wishing well rose from the center of the gazebo. Pick wanted to peer into the well but Jan motioned her to the wooden bench. "Sit. Please."

Beckoning her closer, Jan rubbed his damp palms on his jeans. "I won't bite," he said, looking into her eyes.

Women had never stirred emotions in Jan. Now, sitting here beside Pick, he did not know whether to laugh or to cry, to touch her like he wanted to, or to fold his hands in his lap.

"Want I should read yer mind?" Pick asked after an awkward silence. She pulled her braid across her shoulder and rubbed the soft velvet bow. When she raised her eyes to Jan's, a tiny smile played about her mouth.

"Pick, I never laughed at you. You thought I laughed at you at Stalworth's shindig."

"I heered ya! And I know you just done it agin!"

"But Pick, I wasn't laughing *at you*. You catch me off guard. You're so different, I never know what to expect. I don't know anyone who speaks the truth as plainly as you."

"Ain't nothin wrong with speakin the truth."

"You're right, Pick, and believe me, I wouldn't laugh at you for any reason. And as for the woman in the kitchen," he said, adding with a laugh, "And the buzzards on the fence post..."

Pick smiled to his surprise.

"They don't know me. They know my family name and that we've had some success raising and racing horses. Most of these women would act the same with any rich man's son. I think that if they really got to know me, they'd be very disappointed. I don't fit their preconceived notion of a *Genteel Southen' Gentleman*."

Pick made a face. "Why're ya talkin funny? I don't know them words yer usin."

208

A smile lit Jan's face as he looked into her eyes. *She is beautiful. And innocent. And so* naïve. Really naïve. *There is not a phony bone in her body.*

"Ya gonna answer me, or ain't cha?" Pick elbowed Jan to his surprise.

"You're just so real! You don't put on airs or pretend to be something you're not. And you don't make excuses for who you are or where you come from. And you don't whine because life's been difficult for you. You accept circumstances as they are and work to make them better. You're remarkable. Turn around."

"What?"

"Turn around. I want to unbraid your hair. Do you mind?"

"I ain't sure. Ain't no boy ever messed with my hair." She eyed Jan, hesitating. "I guess it's O.K." She turned from him, feeling that kick in her stomach again.

Jan talked as he removed the bow and unbraided her silky hair. "I'll never know what you did with those twins, but whatever it was, you saved the life of that dying baby. People call you a miracle worker."

"I ain't!" Pick turned to see Jan's eyes. "Can't nobody work no miracle but the Good Lord. I asked Him what to do about Mose and Amy Beth's youngun and He told me. I ain't no miracle worker."

"I ain't nothin but the oldest child of James Joseph and Isabel Mckinley, borned and raised in Widows Holler. I ain't ever had no schoolin and I got four younguns to raise what ain't had no schoolin neither. I know where I belong, but ain't no work fer wages up home so I come here lookin fer work like my Mama done. That's all my story and I still ain't heered your's. And you never said why you talked funny and you never told me what them big words was you was usin."

"I think yer about the handsomest boy I ever knowed and I think ya got a fine Mama and Papa. Fairy tales is somethin that happens in picture books and in stories like my Mama made up fer us, but fairy tales is just made up, they ain't real. And I could like ya, but I won't, and even if you took a shine to me and come to the holler tippin yer hat, I'd tell you to git on yonder cause the Good Book says so."

"Yer city and I'm country, yer rich and I'm poor, and yer university educated and I can't read a lick, but Suzanne's gonna start teachin me this week. That's three yokes that ain't even. And the Good Lord says it ain't to be when the yokes ain't even. So if you'll excuse my callin ya handsome, I didn't mean nothin by it. It's gettin late and I gotta git back to Suzanne and Mr. Gardner."

"Bravo, Peck! The girl knows her place, after all!"

Crimson-faced, Pick scrambled to her feet with Jan at her side.

"I have to agree with you, Peck, he is handsome," Margaret said, looping a possessive arm through Jan's.

Jacques, Suzanne and Bennett hung behind.

Catching the last of the conversation, Suzanne and Bennett knew only that Margaret had hurled more insults at Pick. They hurried to Pick as Jan extricated his elbow from Margaret.

Jan turned to Margaret and said in anger, "Her name isn't Peck, Margaret. It's Pick, Pick McKinley. She is a guest in my home. I expect you to remember that and to treat her as such."

Jan chucked his chin to Jacques. "Jacques! Take Margaret back in the house. I'll be in after I see my guests to their car."

Jan pulled Pick's arm through his, continuing their conversation as if they had not been interrupted.

"The funny talk is called an exaggerated Southern drawl. And preconceived notion is when somebody expects you to behave in a certain way. But honest, Miss McKinley, is when you say and do what you really feel in your heart. And honest is the way I'm behaving. Right now."

Jan took Pick's hands in his, pulled her to him, and gently kissed her forehead.

"Thanks for bringing her, Suzanne, Bennett," he said as the three piled into Bennett's car.

"Oh, and Pick-- the grand entry? That picture was a gift from Margaret's mother. She and Margaret helped Mama decorate that wall."

Pick stared at Jan's face, feeling hollow and empty, certain that she would never see him again. She flashed him a fleeting smile and climbed into the front seat after Suzanne, grateful for the darkness that hid her tears.

"Jan wants to come with us tomorrow night, doesn't he?" Suzanne braced her feet on the floorboard as the car belly-flopped and roller coastered over the rough roads out of Widows Hollow.

"Not exactly," Bennett huffed, tiring of the endless bouncing. "He wants to go with me to get her truck in the morning."

"I'm afraid for her, Ben. Jan and Pick have nothing in common. I don't think I could stand to see Pick hurt. Being a Good Samaritan and being in love are two different things. Jan may be confusing the two. Perhaps we should discourage him."

Bennett squeezed Suzanne's hand. "We can try."

"Ben!" Suzanne shrieked, spotting Stalworth's limo in her drive.

"We're in your ballpark, darling. You say. I'll do," Bennett said.

"Come with me, Ben."

As they walked in silence to the limo, the driver's door opened. Dwayne stepped out and said over a yawn, "I'm sorry, Sir, Madam, but Master Stalworth insisted that I *stay put* until you arrived. I cannot be certain, but I believe he is, uh, passed out."

Bennett pulled open the back door. "Phew!" He fanned the stale air and picked up the empty J&B bottle. "Did he drink all of this?" He asked with a nod to Dwayne.

"I'm afraid so, Sir!"

"And he's on pain medication!" Bennett cried, grabbing Stalworth's limp wrist. He spewed a lungful of air. "Looks like your Master's pulse is as strong as his stomach."

"He insisted on speaking with Ms. Claiborne before we depart, Sir."

"I'm pretty sure your Master won't be speaking with anyone this evening. You look like you could use some rest yourself. Let's take him home and put him to bed, what do you say?"

The weary chauffeur agreed with a nod.

"Suz, do you mind?"

"Of course not, I'll be right behind you."

Bennett kept silent on the drive back to Suzanne's. His merry mood had changed, fear gnawed at him once again. Stalworth was not going to go away.

Bennett had enjoyed every minute of this evening, feeling that, at last, he had found someone who could fill the gaping hole in his life. He had fantasized all night.

The Richardson Estate had become the Gardner Estate, himself and Suzanne, the happy host and hostess. And the lively Anthony and Yvette--cousins to the children he and Suzanne would parent, love and spoil with adoration.

Even when he was in Suzanne's house, Bennett could not let go of her hand. He hoped the dim light of her Christmas tree would hide his fears.

Shivering, Suzanne pulled her hand from his. "It's freezing in here, would you mind building a fire?"

Bennett's wilting heart rallied. *Anything to stick around a little longer.*

Chapter Twenty-Three

"Advertising, are we?" Jacques asked, amused. "You hate driving the ranch van."

"My Jeep's too small," Jan replied.

"I refuse to ask the obvious," Jacques said, squatting close to the ground. "It's Christmas vacation, and I plan to enjoy it." He scooped a handful of snow, packed it tight, and fired it at Jan.

Jan snatched the black Stetson from his head and, positioning it like a catcher's mitt, caught the snowball.

"You better get your law degree, Jacques. I don't see any major leagues in your future," Jan teased, swatting the Stetson against his leg to spill the snow.

"Too small for what?" Jacques asked in an afterthought as they sped down the tree-lined lane from Jan's home. "No horse is gonna fit in here. I'm worried about you, Buddy. You've been acting weird lately."

"Don't be so nosy."

"Please tell me we're not gonna waste the whole day messing around with that truck," Jacques said with a glance. He tuned the radio to the McGuire Sisters singing

Sugartime and croaked a couple of bars. He looked at Jan and snapped his fingers.

"That reminds me, Daylon Coopersmith's entertaining the sorority babes tonight at her place. She wants us to stop by, or we can corral some cowgirls at Mavericks." Jacques drummed on the dash, waiting for Jan's reply.

In his mind's eye, Jan could see Pick dressed in a white Stetson, white jeans, shirt and boots. Fringed sleeves adorned her leather jacket. Her copper hair cascaded down her back like fine silk.

When the waiter asks if she is ready to place her order, she will say, "I reckon I ain't. I can't read this menu." And they will laugh. Damn them, they will laugh!

"It doesn't matter to me. We'll go wherever you like. I just don't want to be stuck in that hollow—the place gives me the creeps!" Jacques said. He stopped drumming to glance at Jan. "Well?"

Jan tapped a tin of Copenhagen on the steering wheel, pinched off a chew, and stuck it in his mouth. With his jaw bulging, he said, "Jacques, you don't have to go. I'll drop you off at home so you can spend time with your brainless beauties."

Jacques hated this conversation. He and Jan agreed on everything but women. "You have a bad attitude toward women, Jan. They're not going away. Sooner or later you'll have to face it."

"Jacques-- tell me why I should waste my time playing the dating game when there's no future in it? I know what I want, so I'll know when I find it."

"I want a real woman, a partner who'll share my life, someone who can pitch hay or saddle her own horse and rodeo with me. I'm not looking for genius or beauty-- I just want a woman who's real."

"Margaret's real. And the crush she has on you is real!" Jacques goaded.

"You want to walk?" Jan snapped.

"I take it back," Jacques said, laughing. "She's just so, so...."

"Pathetic!" Jan barked. "Margaret has sequined outfits in fifty colors. Seen one, seen 'em all. They're boring. All she talks about is shopping, what she bought, what she's going to buy."

"I don't care who broke up with whom or who's vacationing in the Hamptons. What does any of it have to do with my future? Why should I drink beer that I don't want, dance when I'd rather clean stalls, or listen to gossip when I can witness miracles with a real person?"

Jan grimaced. He had said more than he had intended.

"Jan! You're not falling for that hillbilly, are you?"

Jan hit the brakes so hard he laid rubber for a hundred feet and slammed Jacques into the dash.

In a fury, Jacques demanded, "What was that all ab…!"

Jan leaned toward Jacques with his pointer finger straight up, close enough to Jacques' nose to touch it.

Jacques had seen Jan angry before, but the look on Jan's face painted a brand new picture of Jan Vandeventer—a picture Jacques did not like.

"If you want to end our friendship here and now—you call her a hillbilly one more time! I'm sick of it! You and

216

any one of the rest of our so-called peers pick a label, any label, and it's official! Margaret and Victoria call Pick a hillbilly, so she's a hillbilly, right?"

Jacques shrugged—which only fanned the flame.

"What gives any of you the right to call her names, to insult her, when you don't know a thing about her?" Jan demanded.

"And let me tell you something else, her beauty has nothing to do with price tags and makeup. Read the papers lately? Anything about a miracle worker--Guess who?"

"People say that she's done it before but Pick denies it! Imagine Margaret, Victoria or Daylon miraculously saving a dying infant then refusing to take credit for it."

Jan cranked down his window and spit a stream of tobacco juice on the asphalt. He felt calmer now that he had vented his anger.

He put the van in gear, glanced at Jacques, and said with a burst of laughter, "Cheer up, Jacques, you look like somebody kicked your puppy."

"Anybody seen Jan Vandeventer?" Jacques mumbled.

"What's that supposed to mean? I'm right here."

"Not the Jan I know. The Jan I know would never have threatened our friendship over a woman. And... Let's see." Jacques counted on his fingers. "You are city, she is country. You are rich, she's a pauper. You are educated, well-bred and sole heir to a family empire with a lot at stake where your mating is concerned. She can't put together a decent sentence."

"For God's sake, Jan, she can't even read a sentence. Couple that with her barnyard whistle and the girl might destroy the house the Vandeventers built. Wake up, Jan! It's not like you can't have anyone you want. Your name alone..."

"She doesn't care about my name!" Jan snapped.

"Oh, that's it! Take me with you, buddy, take me with you. Jan Vandeventer has fallen for a woman from the wrong side of the tracks. I wouldn't miss this for the world!" Jacques cried glumly as he crossed his arms and slumped in his seat.

Chapter Twenty-Four

"Ah! Santa's helpers have arrived." Bennett greeted the boys with a handshake at the restaurant where they had agreed to meet. The three of them ordered breakfast, wolfed it down, and left together in Jan's van.

"I think her old rust bucket needs a new battery. Jan, pull in here at Ashford Auto. I'll get one," Bennett said.

Jan parked in front of the auto parts store. He drummed his fingers on the steering wheel while Bennett went inside.

"You've never been there, have you Jan?"

"Widows Hollow? No." Startled by the look on Jacques' face, he said, "You look scarier than Bela Lugosi in a morgue. It can't be that bad, Jacques."

"Widows Hollow is *that* bad, Jan," Jacques said, looking morose. "Don't say I didn't warn you."

Pick's truck started easily after Bennett installed the new battery. He closed the hood and wiped his hands on a towel.

"This old jalopy's about worn out. She won't see many more miles," he muttered.

"What will they do then?" Jan asked, ducking a flying snowball.

"I don't know, Jan. I'm sure they can't run to the bank and finance another one."

Jan and Jacques helped Bennett gather his tools, then they packed snowballs and pounded each other.

Soon Bennett joined in as well. "Missed me!" He yelled. Snowballs exploded against the open door as he dived into Pick's truck. Waving and laughing, he took off for Widows Hollow with Jan and Jacques following.

Traveling off the smooth blacktop into the wilderness of briars and brambles, Jacques shuddered. "This place spooked me when I was a kid, and it spooks me now."

Jan's heart sank. Dilapidated shacks and shanties lurched into view. Whatever paint these humble dwellings had once boasted was gone, blistered by the sun, peeled by the wind, or erased by the finger of time.

Shingles had fared no better. The few that remained sagged or buckled in a mismatch of hues pasted together with thin dribbles of tar. Some of the shanties hid behind a patchwork of tarpaper, cracked clapboard, and quarter inch sheets of plywood.

The evidence of long sustained poverty took Jan by surprise.

"I didn't expect it to be this bad." Jan's teeth chattered with the van's rough bouncing through one deep pothole after another. He locked his jaw and said with a scowl, "How can anybody put up with this? Is this the only road they have?" He swore with some frequency as they bounced and sank past barren trees and gutted pits that had long ago regurgitated the last of their coal.

Grateful for signs of life, Jan looked from the stark landscape to kids who hollered and screamed.

"Papa's truck!" Willie yelled, running to keep up the truck.

Bennett cranked down the window. "Hey there, I'm Ben Gardner, looking for Pick McKinley."

Willie darted a wary glance at the strangers in the van behind Bennett. "Them yer friends?"

Bennett answered with a nod.

"Follow me," Willie shouted, sprinting off with a pack of noisy children.

Bennett and Jacques stood in the doorway for a brief moment, looking across Pick's tiny shack. A fire flickered in the fireplace. Ragged quilts covered bunk beds in one room, and a larger bed in another.

The stark cabin offered no hint that people the world over celebrated this day as Christmas Eve. No holiday aromas or festive bustle marked this most blessed day of the year. Modest furnishings huddled in every corner that holiday symbols might have claimed.

The dull thud of Jan's boots echoed on the wood floor. He traced the carved letters in the back of the rocker with his finger when a charcoal drawing on the mantel caught his eye. Something in the drawing of a beautiful woman smiling from the clouds at people gathered about a barren tree stirred Jan.

With the drawing in hand, he walked to the door. That's the tree in the picture. The people must be neighbors. There's no mistaking the woman—but why would someone draw Pick as an angel?

Carrying the picture with him, Jan walked about the cabin that was smaller than his bedroom. He could not imagine the life Pick must live. She drew water with a rusted pump and cooked on a wood burning stove.

He rubbed the uneven fabric of the patchwork quilt that hung like a curtain across one corner of the cabin. He pulled it aside and stared at the hand-stitched quilt on the neatly covered bed. *This is her bed, I can feel her presence.* He inhaled deeply of Pick's lingering scent when he heard Bennett's voice.

"What's your name?" Bennett asked their young guide.

"I'm Willie and I'm eight," the boy answered, smiling a shy smile. Emboldened by the friendly stranger, Willie pointed to the mountain.

"Jimmy Joe's up Old Gum Tree, Sissy and Buddy's with Mama John and Pick's with Papa and Mama."

"Your sister's where?" Jan took long strides to the door where he squatted eye to eye with Willie.

"She's with Mama and Papa," Willie repeated.

"Can you show me?"

Willie answered with a trusting nod and placed his hand in Jan's hand.

Jan responded with a genuine smile and a deep, satisfying sense of pleasure.

"Bennett, Jacques, I'll be right back." He replaced the drawing on the mantel and hurried out with Willie.

Willie ran sure-footed as a mountain goat up the steep slope that led to the church and the overgrown graveyard.

"Ssshhh!" Jan whispered. He pulled Willie beside him into the tall weeds that hid them from Pick's view. "Thank you, Willie," Jan whispered. "If you don't mind, I'll wait for her here."

Willie grinned, enjoying the secret, but was glad to return to the friendly strangers back at the house.

Jan stretched out on his belly in the weeds. Pick's face was shining. Her copper hair swung to her waist as she moved about the cemetery.

"…and Sissy's cough's better. Suzanne and Mr. Gardner give us cards that's the same as medicine and doctors fer the folks in the holler. Miss Olga seen I got lots of work and Mr. Gardner's seein to Papa's truck this very morning."

"We ain't gonna be heathens, Mama and Papa; Suzanne's gonna teach us to read. Jimmy Joe's refusin so you might speak to the Good Lord about it seein how Jimmy Joe kin be so stubborn. The younguns is behavin and Mule and Mama John keep a close eye on us. Jimbo's needin work, he's wantin sorely to help his folks."

"Remember the promise I made you Mama, on the day of yer buryin? These here are silk roses that Miss Olga give us. They's beautiful red roses in a fine glass bowl that sparkles like diamonds. Mama, they's our Christmas gift to you and Papa."

"Come spring, me and the boys will be cleanin up yer buryin place. We'll plant real roses, roses that smell good and bring the birds with 'em, just like you wanted, Mama-- like in Rosemillion's garden. I love you Mama and Papa and the youngun I never knowed. Merry Christmas from me and Jimmy Joe and Willie and Buddy and Sissy."

Tears sparkled on Pick's cheeks. She placed the bowl of roses on the small mound beneath the marker that said

Isabel McKinley and brushed black soot from the marker. Straightening one marker and then another, Pick sang.

Jan remained silent, hidden in the weeds, listening.

"Sing, Rosamond, sing. Send your magical notes echoing... We await the glad tidings they bring, songs of love from our Father, the King."

"Sing, Rosamond, sing, songs that chase darkness away, songs that bring sunshine to stay, and robins and sparrows to play. Sing, Rosamond, sing, sing soft as a butterflies wing, sing sweet as rose petals op'ning, sing, Rosamond, sing! Sing, Rosamond, sing! Hearts are filled with the gladness you bring, sweet spirits reach down, scattering...love and joy, Rosamond, when you sing!"

"Oh, Mama!" Pick fell to her knees on the mound of frozen dirt that covered her mother's coffin. "Mama, I remember 'em! The words you sung to us, the words to Rosamond's song! Oh, Mama! You give it to me fer Christmas, didn't you? Thank you Mama! We love you and we'll be there quick as the Good Lord calls!"

Pick turned from the graves and started down the hill singing in a loud voice.

"Aaaah!" She screamed, startled by Jan's presence.

She looked so beautiful. Jan wanted to touch her, feel her soft skin, run his fingers through her hair-- and *explain what I'm doing here, hiding in the weeds, but I can't find my tongue.*

"I..., I didn't mean to scare you!" He managed at last. His hair was in his eyes, his typically neat appearance abandoned. Leaves and twigs clung to his wrinkled shirt and grass stained his jeans.

"I came to tell you your truck's running and that, uh, we brought it home." He added with a sheepish grin, "I'm really sorry if I scared you."

Pick stared at him. Her face was blank, her eyes so bright and clear, Jan could see his reflection in them.

She was unreadable. Jan did not know if she might scream any minute or perhaps slap his face for intruding on her private moments.

His heart rate shot up like mercury in a thermometer on July asphalt. His mouth felt like cotton.

"You think I'm ignernt, don't ya?" Pick said, folding her arms and lifting her chin.

"What? No. I'm the one who feels like a fool."

"Don't you reckon I'd a knowed Papa's truck was back when I got home and seen it? That ain't why you come here, is it?"

She had a stubborn streak, big as Texas, but somehow, it did not bother Jan. It emboldened him.

"Are you a witch or an angel?" *Good grief where did that come from?* Jan wanted to stare into her green eyes but the goose bumps marching along his arm distracted him.

"Neither."

Jan paled. *Can I be having a panic attack?*

"You didn't answer my question. If you say you don't think I'm ignernt, then yer a liar. Yer jumpy as frog legs in a fryin pan so just tell me why you come here, you'll feel better." She was grinning at him.

Jan pushed his hat off his forehead. He wiped sweat from his brow, caught Pick's eyes and held them. "Do you know that I never had a problem talking to anyone until I met you?"

"I reckon ya didn't."

"I'm not a liar. I don't think you're ignorant. I came here because I wanted to see you, talk to you." *There. Is that honest enough?*

"Why?"

"Why...? *Why?*" Jan blinked. He felt like little boy lost again.

"Is that a hard question?" Pick's eyes bore into him.

Jan stared mute and helpless.

Pick looked past him. "I got to git back," she said in a rush and started down the slope. When Jan did not follow, she turned, reached her hand to him, and said with an impish grin, "You comin or not?"

Her hand... Her hand! Jan shot out his hand.

Pick's hand felt weightless, soft. His pulse slowed. His head cleared. He inhaled her scent of wood smoke and mountain musk.

A sudden gust blew strands of her hair in his face. He brushed them away and turned to her.

She stared into his eyes—and captured his heart.

"You asked why I came here. I came because I wanted to be where you are. You're beautiful. You're raw and rugged. You have a primitive way about you that's fragile and good. You make me feel peaceful, like there's no chaos in the world, like there's nothing but the river and the mountains and the forest. You make me feel like I could stay right here and never want for another thing as long as I live."

Pick laughed. "That's the way I been all my life. It's the only way I know."

Jan could not respond. The beauty of her copper hair mesmerized him. Like an invisible breath blew it about, her hair rose and fell softly on her shoulders.

They walked on, hand in hand, like old friends, comfortable together, talking easily, laughing often.

Pick pointed out the homes of neighbors and friends, introducing Jan as if he was no different than the gaunt figures that opened their doors wearing patched shirts, worn overalls, and hardship carved in their faces.

Neighbors waved from their porches. "Merry Christmas, Pick, we'll see you this evenin."

After a number of "See you this evenins," Jan asked, "What are they talking about?"

Pick turned and looked back up the hill to the little cemetery. With her eyes fixed on the markers on her parents' graves, she lifted her chin a little higher. "Suzanne's startin the readin lessons tonight. Tonight, the change this holler's been waitin fer is comin right through the McKinley front door. I don't care if the town folks call us white trash and hillbillies, but they ain't gonna call us no heathens. I reckon I know a fair mite about the Good Book, my mama and papa seen to it."

She spoke now with a fire that drew a smile across Jan's face. "And I'm gonna see to it my own and others know about it, too. I'm gonna read it to 'em and teach 'em to read fer theirselves. Younguns in this holler's gonna git schoolin one way or another! Everbody's comin tonight. We celebrate special times together and tonight's the most

227

special of all. Mama John's younguns, and Eli, and me and mine, we's all gonna learn to read together."

Jan usually spent Christmas Eve at home with family and friends. Klaus and Olga would not mind if he spent his Christmas Eve here, with Pick. But, he realized with disappointment, *I haven't been invited.*

"You come, too," Pick invited, spinning to face Jan. She grabbed his wrists and skipped backward like a child, bouncing her hair on her back.

Jan laughed aloud, whether because she made him feel so carefree or because his mind teased him with images of Margaret and Victoria behaving with such childlike innocence, he did not know.

He searched Pick's face for a hint, for some indication—and found nothing but her laughing eyes and simple eagerness, the same countenance that Pick shared with her neighbors.

Jan felt a pang with the question that formed in his mind; *what do you want from her? More than this,* he thought, staring into her bright eyes. *As far as she's concerned, I might as well be Jimbo or Mama John.*

Pick released his hands. Her smile vanished.

Jan blinked, bewildered. *Why are you looking at me like that? Did you read my mind?*

Pick shuttered her eyes. Her tone was apologetic. "But you kin read already. And yer frends'll be wantin you to spend this evenin with them."

"No, no, I'll come!" Dimples burrowed deep in Jan's cheeks. His mouth formed a lop-sided grin. He did not care if he looked like an idiot or if he sounded *ignerant*. He wanted to be near her.

Pick scrunched her brows and narrowed one eye to a squint. "I know you got better things to do."

"No, nothing, I'll be here!" Jan exclaimed. He could not wipe the grin off his face. He would be spending this Christmas Eve in Widow's Hollow *with her*.

Back near Pick's cabin, Mule, Mama John and their brood swarmed Bennett and Jacques.

Mule hung his head and addressed Pick with a sheepish face. "Pick, I'm needin the use of your Papa's truck to do some shoppin uptown."

Mama John added with a wave of her hands, "And Honey, don't you worry none about the gas bein returned, I'll see to it myself!"

Pick gave Mule a squeeze. "Mule, yer welcome to Papa's truck. I ain't worried a mite about no gas. I'm fine ain't I? You best let go them notions you done me wrong with this old truck, you hear me?"

"You sweet Chile!" Mama John gushed. "He's been worryin hisself sick fer causin you hurt."

Pick nodded to Jan. "Mama John, Mule, this here's Jan. I can't say his last name, it'd gag a gator. Ain't he handsome?"

"Vandeventer," Jan said. He shook his head, laughing. He could not get used to Pick's unbridled honesty.

"Mule, Mama John, pleased to meet you," Jan said, and shook hands with the friendly couple. He frowned at Jacques who fluttered his eyelashes and mouthed the word *handsome*.

229

"Kin we go with Mule?" Buddy, Sissy and Willie pleaded.

"Well, seein it's Christmas Eve and all…"

Her siblings did not wait for Pick's answer.

"C'mon, Petey," Willie and Buddy cried and sprinted for the back of the pickup.

Lucy took Olivia's hand. "You kin sit with me and Lottie."

"It's gonna be cold back there. Get yer coats on and get some quilts, yer gonna need 'em!" Pick cried, then cut her eyes to Mama John who wrestled Jasmine on her hip.

"Come here, Jaz, we'll stay in by the fire while yer Mama and Daddy wrastle that wild bunch."

Bennett stroked Jasmine's chubby cheek. "You're pretty busy these days, Pick, you sure you've got time for reading lessons?"

"Yes, sir, I truly do."

"And you'll be ready for us tonight?" He tickled Jasmine.

"Yes, sir!"

"I'm in trouble!" Bennett glanced at his watch. "I'm late picking up Suzanne."

Jan raised his chin to see beyond his hat brim. "So I guess I'll see you tonight, Pick," he said, his grin going crooked. "Can I bring anything?"

Pick made fish lips at Jasmine who chuckled aloud. "I can't think of nothin," she said, glancing at Jan. "Tell Ms. Olga Merry Christmas and may the Good Lord bless her and yer Papa real good."

After dropping Bennett off at his car, Jan headed home with Jacques.

"I can't believe you're spending Christmas Eve in that place," Jacques moaned. "Not me. I'll be spending this evening with some lovely and *literate* ladies. You sure you won't change your mind and come with us?"

"Nope." Jan shook his head. "But if you change *your* mind Jacques, you know where to find me."

Chapter Twenty-Five

Jan found his mother in the kitchen basting a turkey. He inhaled the spicy odors of sage, sausage, and onion, then helped himself to a handful of cookies.

"Vell?" Olga's face crinkled with smiles.

"I promised her I'd be there tonight. Do you mind?"

Olga's smile widened. "Dat vill be very different for you, Son."

"Mama, it's unbelievable. They don't have electricity, they pump water from a well, and she cooks on a wood burning stove."

Olga brushed melted butter mixed with poultry seasoning and sage on the turkey. "I told you dat."

"She acts like her brothers and sister are her own children."

"Remember Zhan, she doesn't have to…"

"They act like they don't know it's Christmas. They have no trees. Nothing is decorated; nobody's baking cookies or anything. Mama, they know it's Christmas, don't they?"

"Of course dey know, Zhan. Dey do things differently than ve do. You'll be surprised tonight. Nobody forgets Christmas."

"I want to take them something. What can I take them?"

Olga cut her eyes to a large box on the harvest table. Wrapped packages filled the box. "Suzanne tell me about Peek's family. Those packages are for dem. Peek loves roses; she wants to make garden for her mother."

Jan glanced at a shelf of cookbooks. "I know, I'll get her a book on roses, a book with all the varieties and how to plant and care for them. She can't read now, but she'll be able to soon. Until then, I'll read to her if I have to."

Olga's face grew solemn. "It is good that Peek ees your friend, Son, but be careful. Peek lives in vun vurld, ve live in another."

Jan cut his eyes to his mother as he reached into the skillet of simmering sausage, sage and onion. He picked sausage from the skillet and dropped it in his mouth. "Ouch! That's hot!"

Olga laughed. "Vot did you expect?"

"I'm off to shop. Can I pick up anything for you?"

"Box, maybe."

"Box? Box for what?"

"For dis dinner I'm cooking for dem."

Jan squeezed his giggling mother. "I should have known. Mama, have I told you you're one in a million?"

Olga tugged on Jan's shoulder, kissed his cheek, and said, "Few times."

The sounds of happy voices drifted up to meet the first stars in the night sky over Widows Hollow. Doors slammed, neighbors tromped back and forth between houses, helping one another prepare for the holiest night of the year.

Candles flickered in the windows. Lamps burned bright inside the cabins. The air was heavenly, smelling of fresh cut pines and holiday spices.

Pick inspected her fresh scrubbed and dressed family. "You younguns look like yer dressed fer Sunday meetin."

"Kin I have another cookie?" Buddy asked, tugging at the neck of his new sweater.

"One more," Pick replied, adding, "I ain't gonna be up all night if you make yerself sick with sweets."

Jimmy Joe, Willie, and Sissy were dressed in the new outfits that Claire had bought for them, too.

Jimmy Joe draped the last of the evergreens on the mantel. He carefully arranged shiny red apples at intervals.

The porch creaked with heavy footsteps. "Make way, Make way!" Kenneth O'Connor yelled. He and his brother Levi thumped and banged into the cabin, carrying sawhorses. They placed the sawhorses along one wall and covered them with a sheet of plywood. Willie and Olivia covered the plywood with an embroidered linen tablecloth.

Neighbors carried in steaming pots, dishes of fruits and vegetables, and trays of candies, cookies, and mouth-watering pies.

Mule returned from Old Gum Tree in Pick's pickup with Stump who hauled fifty–pound burlap bags of potatoes and onions to the back porch. He carried bushel baskets of apples, oranges, grapefruits and gaily decorated tins of hard candy into the kitchen. He and Mule placed rough wooden benches end to end about the cabin.

Brother Lester, his wife Lydia, and her mother arrived. Heavily laden as the others, they called out greetings to the gathering neighbors.

Exclamations of "Look how they've growed!" and "Ain't they the purtiest sight you ever did see?" announced Mose and Amy Beth with their twins.

Bennett and Suzanne arrived just ahead of Jan, who gave Bennett a hand unloading Bennett's car. "I didn't expect to see this many people," Jan said. He added, "It smells like they've all been cooking all day."

"Good thing," Bennett said. "I'm hungry."

Bennett, Suzanne, and Jan entered the cabin together. "Wow!" Jan exclaimed, fixing his eyes on the beautiful tree that glowed from a corner of the cabin. Light spilled from candles affixed to the tin star that adorned the loftiest tip of the stately cedar. Angels with embroidered faces and hand crocheted dresses and wings smiled from the branches.

Handcrafted ornaments hung from the tree amidst colorful tiers of popcorn and dried cranberry garlands.

Jan whistled, walking closer to inspect the unique ornaments. There were cornhusk dolls and cornhusk dogwood flowers, delicate crocheted snowflakes, and tiny, hand carved wooden animals. Miniature charcoal likenesses of close neighbors hung inside pine frames, among paper chains of children, angels, and St. Nicks.

"Mister?" Young Eli O'Conner leaned on his crutches with a parchment rolled in his hands. "This is fer you," the boy said.

"Thank you," Jan said of the unexpected gift. "What is your...?" Jan blinked. The boy was gone.

Jan unrolled the parchment and stared at a perfectly rendered likeness of himself: His piercing eyes, his Stetson, perfectly angled on his brow, his rugged features in exact detail, looking into the eyes of the woman in the charcoal portrait he had carried from Pick's mantel this morning.

"Hey Jan my man, you feel all right? You look pale," Bennett said, and cracked an almond with his teeth.

"Look at this. A young boy on crutches gave it to me. He can't be the artist."

"Wow!" Bennett exclaimed. "He is good." Bennett picked the almond from the shell and popped it in his mouth.

"The artist is Eli O'Connor. He's twelve now. A tree fell on his leg when he was young, busted it up pretty bad. His folks had no idea he had so many multiple fractures when they tried to set it. A buddy of mine, Dr. David Haymes, from Medical City, Dallas, is visiting next month. He's close friends with the best ortho surgeon in Big D. David put in a few good words and his buddy is gonna fix young Eli right up."

From the second chapter of Luke, Brother Lester read the story of Mankind's Greatest Gift. He asked everyone to bow their heads and join hands for the blessing of the meal.

At the prayer's end, Jan felt a thump in his hand.

"Somebody's got to keep an eye on you," Jacques said, grinning.

After a wonderful dinner and quick clean up, Bennett lit the coal oil lamps.

Neighbors called out names and presented children with dried apple dolls, carved wooden toys, crocheted slippers, deerskin moccasins, pens, pencils, crayons and coloring books.

Suzanne, Bennett, Jan and Jacques blushed at their unexpected gifts.

Mrs. Lydia Lester beamed as Jimbo carried in a large package for Pick.

Pick removed the wrapping from a heavy quilt. The beautiful quilt, hand stitched with red roses centered in white squares, had an embroidered border of green leaf and vines. Overcome by the extravagance of the beautiful quilt, Pick pulled it to her face and cried.

"We all done it," Lydia said, nodding to her neighbors. "Mule made us the frame. Kenny, Luke, and Jimbo hung it. Mama John and her girls, Mrs. Brewster, Amy Beth and my own Mama helped stitch it. We figured the hardest part was keeping it a secret and not one youngun snitched."

She smiled her approval at Pick's youngest, and at Mama John's brood.

Bennett made his way to the front of the room. "If anyone's still hungry, we'll wait while you eat."

Moans and laughter filled the air.

"That pretty lady there is handing out tablets and pencils. Raise your hand if you want one and don't mind a couple of greenhorns teaching you to read."

Suzanne passed out tablets, pencils, and a card printed with each student's name. Bennett drew and recited the letters of the alphabet on the board.

"Pick McKinley!" Pick exclaimed. "My own name, I'm readin' my own name!"

Jimmy Joe turned his card face down, refusing to look at it.

The students recited letters from flash cards Bennett turned one by one. He and Suzanne helped each eager student print their first letters. When Bennett finished the lesson, he assigned homework for practice until the next lesson. He added that school would continue into the evening, as there would be no shortage of coal oil for the students.

Erasing the chalked letters from the board, Bennett caught a glimpse of Suzanne in Isabel's rocker. Suzanne rocked one of the tiny Tate twins.

Bennett could not count the Christmases he had spent alone, insulating himself from the loneliness, working double shifts and volunteering wherever he could. With his quick wit and lively humor, invites had never been the problem.

But he was always the third wheel, the three that crowded two's company. He had no heart for shopping for champagne and specialty bakery items for those Samaritans that took him in on days that were clearly stamped *family* in his mind.

The few holidays he had spent with female companions gave him hope. Maybe a spark would burst into a flame that would light the way to the ceremonial forever after. It had not happened.

Lots of Mommy's little girls were too well tutored on how to marry a doctor. Others armed with their own medical credentials had shot him down with modern woman mindsets—You doctor. Me doctor. Period.

But Suzanne.... Bennett turned to the chalkboard and scrawled a new message.

Jan elbowed Jacques. "Look!"

"Hey, hey!" Jacques cried. They passed the word until the excited whispers drew Suzanne's attention.

She glanced at the chalkboard. Overcome with emotion, Suzanne covered her face with her free hand. She nodded an affirmative nod and finally managed a faint, "Yes," followed by "YES!"

She stumbled from the rocker holding Edward Moses and fell into Bennett's arms.

"In case you're wondering, this fella Bennett ain't askin for more apple pie with them words," Brother Lester explained.

He read aloud; "Suzanne Claiborne, I love you! Will you be my wife?"

Bennett withdrew a tiny box from his pocket. "I hope this isn't inappropriate, but I can't wait!"

Suzanne opened the box and gasped. "Oh, Ben, it's beautiful!"

Bennett slipped the ring on Suzanne's finger and kissed his wife-to-be.

Cheers and whistles erupted from the crowd as the old, the young, the crippled and the whole of Widows Hollow rose with Jan and Jacques, to congratulate the newly engaged couple.

Stump said with a grin, "I reckon I ain't never knowed a finer Christmas, nor finer pie." He offered his congratulations and headed to the table for another piece of Mama John's apple pie.

As the friends mingled, laughing, and talking, helping themselves to second servings of the tempting desserts, Pick addressed them.

"I talked to Mama and Papa today. They's so proud of the folks here in this holler that Mama give us a present. It's her words I thought was lost. I'd like to sing 'em fer you and fer Mama and Papa."

"Sing, Rosamond, sing…."

With the song ended, Mama John beamed. "Baby, you sing like an angel. And if I didn't see it was you singin, I'd allow it was my own Isabel."

Her voice softened, sweet smiles creased her face. "Baby, I hear yer Mama sing that song since the day you was born. I hear her singin it after the sickness done settled in her bones. You rememberin that singin, Honey. But 'Ol Mama John don't forget nothin bout my Isabel. You mostly got her words, Pick, Honey, you shore do."

Mama John squeezed Pick and stared into her eyes. "But it ain't Rosamond she was singin, Chile. Yer mama was singin *Rosemillion*.

"Rosemillion? The same's in our story about the roses?"

"Oh, yes, Chile. Ain't no other. Yer mama loved her story 'bout the roses, she loved it so powerful, she made the song, too."

Pick kissed Mama John's cheek. She turned to young Aaron Moses who fretted in Amy Beth's arms. Pick cradled the baby against her chest, smiled into his tiny face, and sang *Rosemillion's Song*.

The crowd in the cabin fell silent except for the sound of Pick's voice. Flames in the coal oil lamps leaped as the door suddenly flew open.

Jacques nudged Jan and whispered. "There's no wind."

Though she had not heard Jacques' remark, Pick sought him with her eyes. "Don't be afeared," she said, "It's just angels comin' in."

Brother Lester stood. "What a night this has been," he said. "God is smiling on our community so let's remember to thank Him for what He has done and continues to do. Good night folks, may God bless you all."

As some of the neighbors made their way home, others lingered to help clean up.

Jan and Jimbo lifted opposite ends of the heavy plywood and carried it out to the porch.

"Mr. Jan, you got fine horses, don't cha?"

Jan looked to Jimbo in surprise. "Yes, we have a few."

"It shore must be somethin, raisin fine horses," Jimbo said.

Jan knew next to nothing about Jimbo, only that no one had to ask for his help. Jimbo hurried to help despite his limp. He was patient and gentle with the younger kids and young Eli clung to him like a shadow.

"Jimbo... It is Jimbo, isn't it?" Jan asked, meeting the young man's eyes.

"Yes, sir, Jimbo Johnson. I'm my Ma and Pa's oldest at eighteen, and I kin out wrastle any man in this holler. Just axt 'em!" Jimbo said with a proud grin.

"Can you out wrastle a horse?"

Jimbo hesitated. "Ain't no call to wrastle no horse."

"You're right, Jimbo. But they do have to be fed, bathed, brushed and exercised. We're short-handed at our stables. How would you feel about coming to work for Vandeventer Farms?"

Jimbo stood shock still. He did not know if this city stranger was dangling carrots that he would quickly reel in with a vicious laugh-- or if the offer was genuine.

Feeling uncertain and defensive, yet not wanting to pass up an opportunity to help himself and his family, Jimbo raised tormented eyes to Jan.

Jan watched the look on Jimbo's face change from eagerness to suspicion to defeat. He recognized the faces. He had seen them on Pick.

Jan stuck out his hand. "You can trust me, Jimbo. The offer is real. We need a ranch hand. You can accept or not, that's up to you."

"Ain't nothin I'd like better!" Jimbo shook Jan's hand with enthusiasm, short- lived enthusiasm.

Jimbo dropped his head. "But I 'spect I can't do it nohow, unless, that is, if it ain't too fer to walk. I ain't never minded walkin," he said hopefully.

"Can you drive?"

"Yes, sir! I kin drive, and me and Pa kin fix anything that kin be drove!"

Jan pumped Jimbo's hand. "You're hired! You start tonight. You can drive me home and keep the van to get to work. Bring your Pa along. We can always use a good mechanic, too."

Jan returned inside and heard from the porch, "Thank you, Lord, from me and my family. You know Ol' Jimbo's gonna do right by 'em." And though he could not be certain, Jan thought he heard— dancing.

Jacques loaded Pick's truck with the bounty Stump would be taking home.

Stump hugged his friends and neighbors, smacked his battered hat on his head, and departed with a shout. "Merry Christmas, the Good Lord and Stump loves ye all."

Making her hugging rounds, Mama John near hugged the life out of Jan. Holding him in the crook of her arm, she said, "God bless you boy, I know my Jimbo will make you proud."

She surprised Jacques, giving him a hug and saying, "Yer gonna be a right fine lawyer, son, the Lord's strong arm fer them what's weak."

Jacques exchanged quizzical glances with Jan. They had told no one of Jacques' plans to become a lawyer.

When the neighbors had departed, Jan added logs to the fire.

Pick retrieved the charcoal picture from the mantel. Staring into the picture, she felt transported there, among the roses with her Mama and Papa. She walked to the tree and touched the faces that Eli had drawn.

As if she were alone in the room, Pick sang softly, "*Oh, Holy Night*."

Jacques fixed his eyes on Jan, who never took his eyes off Pick. There was a longing in Jan's eyes Jacques had never seen before. He and Jan had shared many holiday evenings, whispering together during solos, duets, even orchestrated chorales. Jan was not whispering with Jacques now.

Pick finished the song. "Sometimes, yer heart's so happy, you just gotta sing!"

"Pick, I thought you might like this," Jan said and offered Pick his gift.

Pick tore through the wrapping. With a gasp, she ran her fingers over the book's glossy cover, and then quickly thumbed through the full color pages. "Thank you, Jan. I love it, truly!" She glanced at Suzanne and Bennett. "And 'fore long, 'cause of them, I'll read the words in it, too."

Jan waited with sweaty palms. He felt certain that Pick would thank him with at least a hug.

Pick smiled at him with the sweetest smile—then hugged the   book.

Chapter Twenty-Six

"Master Stalworth, it's your uncle." Gloom weighted her voice as Maggie fumbled the phone to Stephen.

Wild-eyed, Stephen demanded, "Claude, Claude! Have they found it?"

Claude's voice broke. "Stephen."

No! No! Don't do this to me! Stephen held his breath. Clutching Maggie's hand, he squeezed it colorless.

"About an hour ago, in the mountains near Santa Fe."

Stephen's heaving chest confirmed to Maggie the news that Claude Vinsant confirmed in hoarse whispers. "None of them...made it...Stephen..."

"No! No! God help me, no!" Stephen screamed. "Claude, it's a mistake! It's not theirs. For God's sake, Claude, tell me there's been a mistake!"

"Son, I wish I could! Holy Jesus, I wish I could! But the logo...the logo on the tail section confirmed-- it's their plane. There's no mistake." Claude rasped. "Three bodies...recovered... your parents...and Max."

"Not my parents, please, not my parents!" Stephen bellowed.

"Son, it was fast. Low clouds, no visibility, storm came up unexpected. They did not suffer. Plane...too low," Claude mumbled in broken sentences.

"We're on our way. Asad's here. Be coming with me... bringing bodies..." Claude broke down, heaving hoarse, intermittent sobs. "Bringing bodies back with us... Oh, God! Vi...! Clay...! Stephen, Tory, I'm so sorry!"

Claude sniffled. After a moment, "Stephen, where's Tory?"

"I, I don't know. She and Adrian have been gone...gone for days."

"Stephen, find Tory! They're notifying Max's family now. Find her. Do not let Tory hear this on breaking news!"

Claude waited for Stephen to gather himself. "Son, we need to make arrangements...Call Reid Garrison, tell him to get over there. Asad and I will be arriving at the airport *with them* in a few hours....Santa Fe says the weather is clearing. Asad's pilot will be flying us in his Lear. Let Reid handle things until we get there. You just find Victoria!"

Stephen dropped the phone. Maggie hastened to hang it up and reached a comforting hand to her devastated young master.

He recoiled. "Mommy! Daddy! You can't be gone! You can't leave us like this!"

The brave face Maggie wore for Stephen shattered. With a howl, she pulled her apron to her face and wept.

Logs splitting in the fireplace drew Stephen's attention to the fire. Hatred blazed through his tears. That fire had no right to go on burning, no right to make a mockery of warmth and comfort. There was no warmth. There was no comfort.

With lips that quivered in a snarl, Stalworth slit his eyes to colorless gashes. He snaked his hand around a crystal vase, then hurled it into the fire. The vase splintered into shards, spewing water on the glowing logs with a *hiss*.

Drained, Stephen panted. He sucked in vapors of a venomous cold that slithered through his body and iced his bones to their very marrow.

He tuned hollow eyes to the portrait. Henry Claymore Stalworth and Vivian Vinsant Stalworth were not smiling. They stared at him with empty, desolate eyes, eyes of strangers—strangers who had deserted him.

Everyone that Stephen had cared about and loved in his life had deserted him. Suzanne. His parents. Victoria. He was alone. In his most desperate, desolate hour--Stephen Stalworth was alone.

Fear crept into his soul. They laughed. Those strangers above the mantel with the cold, barren eyes, they laughed at him.

The citizens of Ashford laughed at him, mocked him. There he lay, humiliated and exposed on the front page of his family's own newspaper, his undignified kodochrome likeness captured forever in file cabinets and newspaper morgues.

He had no one to turn to...that image...beckoning... A jester. Bells rattling. Taunting. "Hide and seek! Come find me!" He had to get out of here. He had to have help. He had to find someone. Someone who would hold him in her arms, tell him everything would be all right.

"Maggie! Dwayne! Maggie! Dwayne!" Stalworth screamed.

Folding himself at the waist, he hobbled to the bar. Like a blind man in unfamiliar surroundings, he groped for support on sofa backs, chairs, and credenzas. He snatched a bottle of whiskey, yanked out the cork, raised the fiery liquid to his lips, and chug-a-lugged in loud gulps.

Maggie, wet-eyed and sniffling, huddled beside Dwayne in the doorway—silent witnesses to their distraught master's manic behavior.

"Maggie, call Reid and tell him to get over here! Tell him to wait here for me!"

Dwayne squeezed Maggie's shoulders in a comforting gesture.

"Damn it, Dwayne, help me! Get on the phone and find my sister!"

Dwayne retrieved the family address book. He began dialing numbers when his hysterical employer interrupted. "Give me the damn phone, you get the car!" Stalworth jerked the phone from Dwayne's hand. He dialed a number. Waiting impatiently for an answer, he gulped more scotch.

"Where are you, damn it?" He slammed the phone back into its cradle.

"Maggie, bring some ice and another bottle of scotch to the car!"

He pushed himself from the sofa, limped to the foyer, and glared at his reflection. Unwashed, disheveled, wearing shoes and no socks--the reflection staring back at him looked like a skid row bum. The eyes appeared bloodshot, the face, stubbled and choleric, the hair, greasy and uncombed.

With a snarl, the newly orphaned Stalworth hurled the scotch at the disgusting visage, shattering both bottle and mirror.

Cringing, he ducked the rain of glass and liquor. He grabbed at the brass umbrella stand. The stand toppled, sending him sprawling.

He tried to push himself from the floor. His hand slipped, driving splintered glass into his soft flesh.

"Dwayne! Maggie! Quit standing there like imbeciles, damn it! Get me out of this!"

Crunching through broken glass, Maggie and Dwayne struggled together to lift Stalworth. Circles of wet stains splotched his pants and shirt. Bits of glass and mirror clung to his clothes.

"Sir, perhaps you should wait here for Mr. Garrison, you're in no condition..."

"Shut up! Don't tell me what I should or shouldn't!" Stalworth's rage stopped any further attempt by Maggie or Dwayne to prevent his leaving the house. They had no choice but to help him to the limo.

Stephen jerked the bottle of scotch from Maggie. He tried to pour another drink. Scotch spilled in his lap and on the limo floor.

Dwayne crawled behind the wheel and fixed his eyes on the rearview mirror.

Stalworth jerked the car phone from its cradle. He dialed a number. "Damn it! Where the hell are you?" He dialed a second number. It too, went unanswered.

Maggie watched from the front steps, twisting her apron in knots.

Dwayne gawked from the rearview mirror.

"Oh, to hell with both of you. I'll drive myself!"

Stalworth staggered from the back seat, shoved Dwayne out of his way, and fell into the driver's seat.

Chapter Twenty-Seven

Pick hummed as she worked, pausing to recite the words that Suzanne had printed on index cards and attached to objects throughout her home.

Pick coupled her reading chores with her house cleaning chores. She had changed the linens on the b-e-d. Now she was ready to hang garments in Suzanne's c-l-o-s-e-t.

Pick had no shortage of work now. Olga saw to it and kept Pick busy cleaning houses and helping caterers with banquets and special events.

Suzanne found that she liked coming home to polished furniture and fresh linens, too, and had engaged Pick's services.

Pick had showered and washed her hair earlier. She enjoyed these privileges when she cleaned Suzanne's house.

Pick hung a blouse in the closet then scraped hangers along the rod, admiring Suzanne's elegant wardrobe. Pick had never seen such beautiful clothes. She had never touched such fine fabrics.

She turned from the closet to the gleaming bathroom. Pretty, scented bottles sparkled from the dressing table. Pick picked up a bottle, pushed the spray top, and inhaled the sweet scent that fell on her shoulders.

She thought how wonderful it would be to smell like this anytime she liked. She returned to the closet and wrapped herself in the garments, rubbing the soft sleeves of a cashmere sweater against her skin, then the black mink, leathers, and silks.

I ain't always gonna dress in rags, Pick promised herself. *Someday, I'll be a fine lady like Suzanne. I may never have no schoolin, but I'll know how to read and I'll teach myself with books. I'll teach others, too so they kin git work what ain't cleanin or mendin.*

She caught a glimpse of herself in the mirror. "Who am I foolin? I ain't never gonna know nothin but hard times."

"My chance fer getting out of Widows Hollow is gone. I'll be dressin in second hand rags fer the rest of my days. The only fine homes I'll see is the ones I'm cleanin fer the rich folk, and the only younguns I'll ever have is the four I got now. Ain't nobody gonna want me with four younguns, not even that honery Luke O'Connor who thinks he fancies me."

Pick stared at her reflection, absently playing with the buttons on her faded flannel shirt when a sudden impulse took her.

She unbuttoned the shirt and tossed it on the bed. Overalls, shoes and socks followed. Pick stepped into the closet and reached for the white mohair sheath. She slipped into the elegant dress and returned to the bath.

She rummaged through compacts, bottles, and tubes, selecting and applying make-up and glossy lipstick. When she finished, Pick stared into the mirror, open mouthed—stunned by her own reflection.

The image staring back at her was not that of a ragged orphan. It was a beautiful young woman with skin that glowed, eyes that sparkled, and copper hair that shimmered.

Pick padded barefoot across the bedroom to Suzanne's dresser. Framed photos displayed on a mirrored tray sat on top of the dresser beside a doll that Pick supposed was a keepsake from Suzanne's childhood.

Pick took the doll, cradled it in her arms, and returned to the mirror. She admired the image of herself with the doll in her arms. *This is what I should look like,* she thought. *My hair's shiny as new pennies, my skin's fine and smooth, and ain't nobody kin see my big, ugly, hipbones in this dress. It's soft as lamb's wool and it makes me look like them fancy ladies in the Sears catalogs Papa used to bring home....*

Pick lost herself completely in her fantasy. With her eyes closed, Pick hugged the doll close and danced in slow, dreamy circles. She envisioned herself in that grand ballroom, but unlike before, she was no domestic this time.

She was one of them, one of the fancy folk. Jan was her husband. And this was their child cradled in her arms.

Pick smiled, imagining herself with Jan's arms about her, her head on his shoulder, their child between them. So real was her fantasy, she sang, filling Suzanne's house with the sweet melody of *Brahm's Lullaby.*

Hugging the doll, Pick waltzed in slow circles, singing, *"Lullabye and good-night, with pink roses bedight…."*

Lost as she was in her fantasy and singing so loudly, Pick did not hear Suzanne's front door open. She did not hear the besotted, staggering drunk that lurched down the hall following the sounds of her singing.

Reeking of scotch, his mind muddled, Stalworth stumbled toward the sweet sounds. The lullaby cradled his soul. It comforted him, soothed him, made him feel small and safe.

Suzanne…dressed in white, with that baby cradled to your chest you look like an angel… Stalworth reached for her and kissed her tenderly.

"Aaaahhhhhh!" Blood curdling screams seared through his being. They stupefied his senses in their ear-splitting terror.

He cowered, covering his ears. *I can't think! Mommy! Mommy!*

Bleary-eyed, he searched through the fog. *Suzanne! You're not gone, you can't be! But…* "SUZANNE!"

"Lemme go! Git yer hands off me!" Pick screamed. Repulsed by his vile breath, she shoved him away with all her strength.

"No! No!" Stalworth lunged. Heaving like an angry bull, he tore the doll from her arms, lashing out at Pick in his rage.

"I'm warnin you, git outta here!" Pick cried and shoved him backward.

Stalworth lunged again. He grabbed for her and tore the white sheath.

Realizing that Stalworth was not going to go away, Pick threw up a hand to stop him. With her free hand, she grabbed a lamp, aimed for his forehead, and swung. *Crack!*

Pick jumped back from the spewing blood and the flying glass. She never took her eyes off Stalworth.

He stared at her with a brief, disbelieving glance—then dropped to the floor like a corpse.

Chapter Twenty-Eight

"She's going to be fine, Mom. These will take care of her congestion and her cough," Suzanne said. She scribbled prescriptions for the wailing three year old. Suzanne lifted the toddler from the examination table and into her mother's arms.

"Thank you, Dr. Claiborne," the mother said and left the room.

Suzanne had seen patient after patient today, dispensing prescriptions, and dispelling fears with the cheerful optimism that made her a favorite at the county hospital. She jotted quick notes for the file when the sudden, strong smell of liquor drew her into the hallway.

"Stephen!" She cried.

Wild-eyed, he gaped at her. Unwashed, unshaven, with his clothing wrinkled and stained, his torn shirt half-tucked, Stalworth tried to focus on her face. Blood seeped from a gash in his forehead. Ugly slashes crisscrossed his puffy face.

"What are you doing here, looking like this?" Suzanne's mind spun in turmoil. Had he suffered a breakdown of some sort? She glanced up and down the hallway, telling herself *I can't let anybody see him like this,* as he tottered, then collapsed in her arms.

Groaning, Suzanne dragged him out of the hallway and into her private office. She propped his limp body against the stainless examination table.

"Sending Dwayne to my home with gifts is one thing, but coming here to my office in this shape, it's, it's inexcusable!"

"I, I needed someone to talk to. They were all gone. But I knew you'd listen, Suzanne." Stalworth spoke with his head bent, his eyes averted, playing with his fingers like a distracted child.

"I won't be listening long. I have work to do. Do you want me to call you a cab?"

Suzanne's anger showed in the hard lines of her mouth and in the harsh tone of her voice.

"Suzanne.... Mommy and Daddy...." Stalworth stared at her, mumbling something about his parents.

Suzanne bit her lip. "How am I going to get you out of here before someone notifies administration? I could call security, but that would end your career for sure."

"They're dead, Suzanne! Mommy and Daddy are dead!"

"Both your parents-- dead?" Suzanne gasped, reeling from the shock.

"Is everything all right, Dr. Claiborne?" A young nurse asked.

"No. No, I don't think so," Suzanne said, shaking her head. *Henry and Vivian dead! That explains a... But...*

257

Bewildered, Suzanne grabbed her files and clipboard. She thrust them in the nurse's hands. "Cancel my schedule. I'll be out the rest of the day." Careful to keep herself between Stalworth and the nurse, Suzanne added in haste, "If anyone asks, tell them I had a family emergency."

"Come on, Stephen, we've got to get you out of here," Suzanne cried, feeling increasingly dismayed.

"Tory doesn't know," Stalworth whimpered. "I, I can't find her."

"What? How long have you known?" Suzanne cried.

Stalworth stared at his hands. "Since this morning. Mommy and Daddy's plane was missing. Searchers found them. Uncle Claude and Asad are flying them back today. It might all be on the news before we find her."

"What?" Suzanne shook him by the shoulder. "Do you have any idea where we can find Victoria? We've got to find her before this story breaks!"

"No. She's with Adrian somewhere," Stalworth said, playing with his fingers.

"Have you called Adrian's house?"

"Yes."

"They're not there?"

"No."

"When did you last see your sister or Adrian?"

Stalworth hesitated. "Before Christmas."

"You haven't seen them since before Christmas?" Suzanne's head throbbed. *This isn't making sense. Nothing is making any sense.*

"No. I called you, Suzanne, but you wouldn't answer. I needed you, I needed you so bad!"

Suzanne tried to think. She needed help. Stephen was drunk. He was behaving irrationally, and most likely, he suffered from shock. She had to get him home.

Suzanne had no choice but to call a security guard. He helped her get Stalworth to his limousine. She dialed the Stalworth home while Stephen spilt himself another drink.

"Reid, this is Suzanne Claiborne. Stephen's fine, he's with me, we're on our way there. Have you seen Victoria?"

"No," Garrison replied, agitated. "But I just saw the news…"

"Oh, God!" Suzanne cried. She disconnected and dialed another number. No one answered at Adrian's home.

Garrison was very fond of Maggie. It distressed him to see her so overwrought. He hugged the little woman. "It's going to be all right, Maggie. We're here for them. We'll help them get through this."

The phone's constant ringing since the news broke wore on Maggie's nerves. She allowed Garrison to lead her to a plush wing chair and fix her a drink. "Here, this will help."

Garrison's gesture came none too soon. Victoria called, sobbing and screaming in hysterics.

"Suzanne? They heard it on the news at LaGuardia. They'll be landing at Ashford Regional in about an hour. Can you meet them and bring them here?" Garrison asked in a curt, business-like manner, correctly assuming his young employer was in no shape to handle anything.

Suzanne glanced at the man. Slumped in the seat with a precarious grip on his scotch, Stalworth looked so pathetic and vulnerable. She could not help but feel sorry for him.

In his day-to-day business dealings, Dr. Stephen Stalworth appeared formidable, demanding, unapproachable, a Goliath in a world of Davids.

Nothing could be further from the truth, Suzanne surmised. Behind his intimidating facade, Stalworth was, in reality, an insecure little boy who was lost without his mother.

At the airport, Suzanne had her hands full keeping Stalworth upright. He burst into tears at the sight of Victoria, sending her into renewed howls of remorse.

Garrison dispatched police security to escort his clients home from the airport and past the media that mobbed the front lawn.

Smelling faintly of scotch, he ushered Stephen, Victoria, Adrian, and Suzanne into the Stalworth home.

Victoria collapsed in Maggie's arms, allowing Maggie to lead her to the great room where the Stalworth family doctor waited with a sedative for Victoria.

Adrian headed for the bar.

And, having sufficiently tranquilized himself with scotch, Stephen passed out.

Friends and neighbors arrived in a steady stream. The phone and doorbell rang incessantly. Floral arrangements and containers of living plants quickly filled the great room and spilled down the hallway.

In ever-growing numbers, film crews and insensitive reporters assembled on the lawn. Clamoring loudly, they waited to snap photos of the bereaved family members or to record any statement they might use as a lead on the evening news.

Traffic threatened to become a problem, as did the growing crowds at the Stalworth estate.

Among the first to arrive, Olga took charge. She instructed Maggie to retire for a nap. Olga would answer calls, receive guests and serve drinks. She greeted and was happy to welcome Mayor Beau Brittany and his wife. Klaus, Jan, and Jacques arrived soon after.

The mayor huddled with Garrison in close conversation. They agreed to post security at the door and to draw up a list restricting those who could enter.

While Stephen and Victoria slept, Garrison made phone calls. He instructed the airport to call when Asad's plane landed. He advised Ashford's most prestigious funeral home to stand by at the airport with black hearses.

Mayor Brittany ordered the city police to "Guard that plane and keep the media at a distance. Escort Vinsant, Asad, and the family members here to the estate."

Ladies of the Ashford Women's League arrived with covered dishes, bouquets, and delicate hankies.

Clay's business associates phoned, anxious to know who would fill the vacancy created by the death of their CEO. Stalworth Enterprises throughout the city and nation closed early with no explanation other than the black wreaths that appeared on their doors.

Stump Simpson waited with Mose Tate outside the wreath-draped door of the Ashford Citizens' Bank.

Others approached the door, noted the closed sign, and turned away. Stump stood unmoved, facing the door with his hat in his hand.

"These doors wouldn't be a closin early fer nobody but Clay," Stump said, as if he talked to himself. "I'm gonna have to get a move on. Storm blacker'n these flowers'll be follerin Clay's passin."

Mose touched Stump's arm, suggesting that it was time to go. Stump remained. After a few minutes, a bank officer glanced at the two men in passing. Recognizing Stump, he hurried to unlock the door.

Mose followed Stump inside. "Zat feller know you?"

Stump snorted. "Ain't none of em knows nobody ner nothin but money."

Mose waited alone in the lobby for what seemed like hours.

"I'll be needin to make one more stop if you ain't mindin," Stump said upon his return.

"What? She left this morning? Did she say where she was going?" Having just returned from a medical conference in Dallas, and being unable to find Suzanne, Bennett interrogated the floor nurse at the County Hospital. He found her answers unsettling.

He hurried to a phone in his office and dialed Suzanne's number. When she did not answer, he thumped his watch. He had the correct time. Suzanne should be at work. Something was wrong. Suzanne would not simply vanish without telling him.

With an uneasy feeling, Bennett hurried to the office of an associate. "Take over for me, something's wrong. I can't find Suzanne."

Bennett raced to his car. He drove with uncharacteristic speed to Suzanne's. When he did not find Suzanne's car in the drive, Bennett let himself in her house with his key.

Inside, everything appeared to be normal. He found no note penned in Suzanne's hand on the counter. Maybe she left work early for reasons she would explain later. It was not like her, though. She knew he would be calling.

Feeling foolish for rushing to conclusions, then finding no cause for alarm, Bennett started from the house. But something insisted that he return.

I'll check her room to see if she came in earlier and changed. Playing toss and catch with his keys, Bennett hurried down the hallway and pushed open the door to Suzanne's bedroom.

He recoiled in an instant from the rank odor of scotch. He fanned the fowl air with his hand, feeling someone had kicked him in the gut and simultaneously zapped him with an electrical current. Somebody had ransacked Suzanne's bedroom.

The bedspread lay crumpled on the floor beneath a smashed lamp, pillows, and bed linens encrusted in glass shards. Horrible and headless, Suzanne's doll lay tossed against the wall, its vacant eyes staring from its severed head. Next to the doll, discarded in a disheveled heap, lay the white sheath Suzanne had worn to Claire's dinner.

Suffocating with fear, Bennett reached unsteadily to pick up the dress. There was no mistaking the red stain on the dress—it was blood.

"No! Suzanne!" Bennett screamed, forced to let go the breath he was holding. He ran from the house like a sightless man, bumping walls and furniture, berserk with fear.

Stalworth mumbled in his sleep. He worked his jaw in agitation and yelled out, waking himself. Slowly, he recollected the foggy events of his most recent hours. "Reid! Reid, where's Victoria?"

"She's asleep, sedated, right there." Garrison pointed to Victoria's sleeping form across the room.

"Has Claude arrived with...?" Stalworth pushed himself to his elbows, his bare chest exposed, his hair, wild.

"Not yet. Any time now." Garrison threw a handful of peanuts in his mouth and met Stalworth's eyes.

Hung-over, disoriented, and appalled at the number of people milling through his home, Stalworth felt in no mood to deal with the hordes. *Spectators. Vultures.*

He forced himself upright. "Suzanne! Suzanne, where are you?"

Suzanne ran from the kitchen. "Stephen, what is it?"

"Get me out of here!" He growled.

"Stephen!" Garrison barked. "Your Uncle and Asad will arrive at the airport in an hour with your parents. You need to clean yourself up and meet them!"

Stalworth looked stung. "Suzanne, will you help me?"

With a nod, Garrison prompted Suzanne to agree. He turned to a commotion at the front door. Men wanted to enter whose names did not appear on the list. Quickly identifying Stump and Mose, Garrison nodded his O.K. to the guard as Bennett shoved to the front of the crowd.

The guard dropped his arm like a turnstile before Bennett.

"He's with us," Stump insisted and slapped at the guard's arm.

Holding the door, Garrison welcomed the three men.

"I come to pay my respects," Stump said and whipped his hat from his head.

Respects... Bennett's heart leapt to his throat. Like a mad man, he searched the room for Suzanne or Stalworth. *The crowds, the flowers, the security...*Bennett's lip quivered. He could not find Suzanne.

"I'm sorry about Clay and the Missus."

Stump's words to Garrison wormed their way into Bennett's consciousness. The traffic jam. The news vans and media. *Stalworth's parents are dead?*

Bennett drew breaths in erratic gulps. *Suzanne. Suzanne!* He searched the faces of the quiet company. He walked through the kitchen, unaware of the curious glances that followed him.

Trying to slow his pace to one of dignity, Bennett hurried down the hallway.

"You just sit there. I'll do this!"

Suzanne's voice! Bennett's pulse quickened as he raced to the sound and shoved open the bathroom door.

"Hello, Gardner." Stalworth, his face slathered in shaving cream, grinned from the chair.

Suzanne stood at his side, holding a razor.

Not trusting his legs to support him, Bennett slumped against the door. He fixed his eyes on Suzanne and said, "Hello, Stalworth. I'm sorry to hear about your parents."

Melting in the warmth of Suzanne's smile, Bennett let his words out in a rush. "Hello Darling. I was so worried when…"

"Darling?" Stalworth glared at Bennett in the mirror. "Who are you calling Darling?"

"Suzanne. We're engaged," Bennett answered innocently.

"Engaged?" Stalworth spun to Suzanne. In a fury, he slapped the razor from her hand. "How dare you pretend to care about me, about my parents—when it's a lie!" He slammed his fist so forcefully on the marble counter that his weight shifted in the chair. The chair pitched forward, dumping him to the floor in a sprawl.

Suzanne raised helpless eyes to Bennett.

He sidestepped Stalworth's prone body, tucked Suzanne's hand in his, and led her from the room.

"He's all right, Reid, a little emotional," Bennett said to Garrison who came running at the sound of loud voices.

Suzanne and Bennett said their good-byes with hugs for Klaus, Olga, and Jan. They waved from the door to Stump and Jacques, who sat huddled together in deep conversation.

Chapter Twenty-Nine

"BEENEEETTT!"

"Oh my God!" Bennett dropped the fireplace poker with a loud clatter. In his haste to get to Suzanne, he fell over a footstool.

"Wha...?" Suzanne's face froze in horror. She stood in the midst of the shambles that was her bedroom with the bloodstained sheath in her hands.

"You haven't seen this room? You weren't here when...?" Bennett cried, confounded.

"No!"

"Suzanne, I...I...thought..."

"Bennett!" She grabbed his shirt in both fists. "Bennett, I forgot her!

Bennett went limp. Dishrag limp. Too many assaults to assimilate. Too frequent. This input would not digest...

Suzanne shook him like a rag doll. "I forgot Pick! Oh my God, how could I? Bennett, look at this room! Look at this dress! Where is she? Where is she?"

"I picked her up to clean the house. Was supposed to take her home. Then Stephen, then Stephen.... That *was* blood in his hair! This room smells like... He couldn't! It's freezing and she... Oh Bennett, we've got to find Pick!"

Suzanne shifted her eyes from Bennett to her closet. Grabbing Bennett by the wrist, she pulled him close. With her free hand, she shuffled clothing. With her foot, she lifted pillows and blankets from the closet floor. Suddenly, she let go of Bennett. Punching garments with her fists, she cried, "Nooo! Not Pick! Not Pick!"

They searched the house, the grounds. No Pick.

"Damn weather!" Bennett swore. Holding Suzanne close, he steered her across the icy walk to his car and into the seat. Suzanne slumped against the car door in mute silence. After a moment, she touched his elbow. "Ben?"

"Suzanne, Suzanne..." Bennett's words stuck in his throat. He was just getting past the idea that the shambles in her room had anything to do with Suzanne. And now Pick?

Suzanne patted Bennett's shoulder. She jumped when he blurted "Rape!" "That is what we're thinking, isn't it? That word branded itself in my brain when I saw your room, smelled the liquor, and couldn't find you. I didn't race to Stalworth's to pay my respects. I raced there to kill him! Then, when I saw you, some mystical, magic eraser simply blanked the whole thing from my mind."

"But maybe we're wrong. Maybe Pick just stumbled and ransacked your room in the fall, broke a fingernail and bled on your dress..."

The commiserating continued, Suzanne and Bennett each equally certain that his/her lone and independent actions or omissions had set the stage for the diverse disasters, both real and imagined, that had brought them to this moment.

Seized with sudden shivers, Suzanne edged closer to Bennett, remarking in her mind how the giant shadowy trees loomed like black robed judges in powdery wigs of cirrus snow.

"Bennett, are you sure this is the way?" Suzanne's voice was taut with apprehension. In the best of conditions, the way to Widows Hollow was forbidding, but on a moonlit night in a blinding snowfall, it could be fatal.

"I'm sure." Flickering lights far below in the distance confirmed Bennett's words.

"Bennett, what are we going to do if she's...? I mean if she was..."

"Raped?" Bennett shoved the brake pedal with rigid muscles, slowing the car's careening, downhill fall. "Whew!" Bennett spewed a breath. He steered the car to a sideways stop in a snow bank on a steep ridge above the hollow.

"I can't answer that, I don't have a plan. But we know something happened in your bedroom today. We know Pick was alone in your house. We know Stalworth called, looking for you and that he was drunk and disoriented, very possibly in shock because of his parents' sudden death."

"Your room reeks of liquor, it looks like a struggle took place, there's definitely blood on your dress. We both assume that Stalworth raped Pick or at the very least, that he frightened her to the point that she had to defend herself. Whatever happened, the answer is right down there. And we're going to have to walk the rest of the way if we want to get out of here tonight. Think you're up to it, or you want to wait here for me?"

The sound of Suzanne's door scraping open answered Bennett's question.

"Ben, I don't know what to say to her, how to begin."

"It'll come to us, I'm sure. That is, if she's even here. But no matter what, we'll handle it together. Agreed?"

Suzanne nodded and took Bennett's arm for the slippery walk downhill.

Willie opened the door, looking a little bit miffed. "We been waitin and waitin!" he said, backing against the door to allow Suzanne and Bennett entrance.

"I reckon they didn't fergit," Pick cried. She stood beside a chalkboard before neighbors that sat crowded together on benches with tablets and pencils in hand.

"We didn't know if you forgot about the lesson tonight or if you was off the road in a ditch somewheres," Pick said with a teasing smile.

Suzanne and Bennett exchanged guilty glances; they had forgotten about tonight's lesson.

Pick took their coats as the two greeted the quiet people who looked upon them with a fondness that gentle folks usually reserve for heroes.

Bennett quickly printed two and three-syllable words on the board. Suzanne took a seat beside Amy Beth who printed letters on her tablet with Edward Joseph fast asleep on her shoulder.

Suzanne took the baby, lifted him to her shoulder, and looked to Pick with searching eyes. She saw no hint that anything was amiss. Pick behaved in her usual what-you-see is what-you-get way.

She raised her hand gladly when Bennett asked if anyone wanted to read aloud from the board or from one of the many easy readers he and Suzanne had left on earlier visits.

Pick read from Dr.Suess's *The Cat in the Hat*. Her reading drew loud applause from the crowd as she read each page with confidence and without error.

"It looks like somebody's been doing their homework," Bennett said, applauding Pick's progress with enthusiasm.

"Would anyone else like to read?"

Jim Johnson waved his hand. When he finished reading the first page of Anna Sewell's *Black Beauty*, the listeners kept their silence.

"Would you read us some more?" Mose asked. He stood with his hat in his hand and directed his request to Jimbo. "Them's 'bout the most beautiful words I ever heered! I'd shore like to hear more 'bout that horse."

Jimbo smiled. "Ain't nothin I'd like better Mose, than to read some more to you, but Lottie's 'bout bustin her buttons to give it a try. He nodded to his younger sister, "Go on, Lottie, you read now."

As Lottie stood to read, Suzanne and Bennett exchanged glances. These young people were reading well ahead of the instructions they had received from the pair.

Lottie finished reading the second page of *Black Beauty*. She never faltered nor stumbled on a single word.

"What, are all of you getting together and reading every day?" Bennett knit his brows. "You're making progress that we can't explain."

Jimbo said shyly, "When we rest a few minutes from seein to the Vandeventer's horses, or when we eat dinner,

Mr. Tanner teaches me some. He give me this book." Jimbo held up *Black Beauty*. "When I git home of an evenin, I share what I learn from Mr. Tanner."

Bennett smiled. "Looks like we have some competition, Suzanne. We'd better be on our toes!"

"You ain't a mindin, Mr. Bennett?" Jim gave Bennett an anxious look.

"No, *Mister* Jim, we don't mind a bit. In fact, we are very pleased to hear that others are pitching in to help you and the rest of our friends here to learn to read. If others want to volunteer, we welcome them, too"

Bennett looked across the crowd. The neighbors exchanged pleasantries and chatted amiably among themselves.

They were all dressed in worn clothing. Many coughed and wheezed. Their speech was simple, unhampered by correct grammar, and equally often, unhampered by correct pronunciation of even the simplest words.

For some of the older folks, none of this would matter. They would continue on, unchanged, and would live out their lives in Widows Hollow, safe among others who spoke their language and lived similar, destitute lives of uncomplaining, quiet acceptance.

But the younger ones.... Bennett glanced at Eli, Lucy, Lottie, Willie, Buddy, Jimbo, Jimmy Joe, Peach, Petey, and others. It would matter to them. Education was their ticket out of Widows Hollow, their path to a better life. Bennett cleared his throat.

"No, Jimbo, we don't mind if others help you learn to read. I say this to you and to all who are gathered here, if you don't have a teacher, find one. It's all right to ask. I've found that most people are willing to share a little of their time to help others."

"Once you learn to read, you can teach yourself just about anything you want to know. All it takes to be a success in life is a good education and a willingness to work hard to achieve your goals."

Bennett glanced at Suzanne. "Pardon me if I get out of line here, but I want to share my personal philosophy with all of you. I believe there are three great powers on planet earth. The first and greatest is God. I don't think anyone here questions that. The second is education. The third is money. Have you ever heard, "A fool and his money are soon parted?" It's very easy for an educated man to take a rich man's money."

"So, if you follow the directions of Power number one, and work hard to get power number two, power number three will come fairly easy. I can't tell you how proud Suzanne and I are to be a part of all of this. We have no doubt changes will be coming soon to Widows Hollow, good changes."

Bennett glanced at his watch. "If anyone has questions, I'll try to answer them. If not, Suzanne and I had better get out of here. Getting up a slippery hill is a lot harder than getting down it."

"Mr. Bennett…"

"Yes *Mister* Jim?" Bennett smiled.

"What about these words we kin say but ain't got no notion what they mean?"

"I'll answer that for you in just a minute, Jim. It's great that you're learning to read, but nobody will know it if you keep saying things like "but ain't got no notion what they mean.""

Try asking your question like this: "What about the words we can pronounce but have no idea what they mean?""

"Hit sounds right uppity to me," Mose said.

Amy Beth raised her soft brown eyes to Mose. "Then our younguns is gonna talk uppity. I'm aimin fer 'em to read and to talk proper, too. 'Less you want to sleep in the barn, Mr. Mose, you'll help me see to it our boys kin read and talk proper."

Mose gaped at Amy Beth. "I ain't sleepin in no barn!" Amy Beth smiled a smile that melted Mose. He dropped his head, mumbling, "Hit wasn't all *that* uppity…"

Suzanne caught Bennett's eye. She raised her hands beside her face, silently applauding Amy Beth's fire. Bennett shook his head.

"Now, you want to repeat your question, Jim?"

"What about the words we kin pronounce but have no idea what they mean?" Jim smiled, please with himself.

Bennett wrote the sentence on the chalkboard. He crossed out kin and wrote can above it.

"We'll start here," Bennett said. He pointed to the word he had crossed out. "Kin is a word, but it is not the word you want to use here. The word you want is c-a-n, can. Instead of saying I kin run, say I can run, I can read, I can write."

"And for those words that you don't know or cannot define—we'll save that for the next lesson. We didn't expect you to be so far ahead of us. We'll be ready for you next week, with a dictionary. A dictionary will tell you all about the words you don't know."

Tiny Joseph Aaron began to squall. "I guess he thinks it's time to go," Bennett said. "It sounds like his lungs are pretty well developed now."

Bennett erased the chalkboard and carried it to Pick's back porch. He and Suzanne lingered until all the other guests had departed.

Suzanne glanced at Pick at every opportunity. The oversized flannel shirt Pick wore with her overalls left nothing to see but her face. A thin layer of makeup could hide bruises and whelps or black grease paint for that matter in the dim light of the coal oil lamp.

"Pick, are you sure you are all right?"

"Sure I am. Why wouldn't I be?"

Olivia wrinkled her face, making it plain that she had something to say.

Pick's hand on Olivia's silenced the little girl.

"Willie, you and Buddy tend the fire," Pick said, heading for the kitchen with empty coffee cups.

Suzanne followed. "Pick, let me help with the dishes."

"No!" Pick snapped. She dropped the cups in a basin filled with soapy water. Her heavy hair hid her face—but not before Suzanne glimpsed the sparkle of a tear.

"Pick! Please tell us what's wrong! We came to help you. Are you... Did somebody hurt you...at my house? I'm so sorry, I forgot you! Stephen Stalworth's parents died. There was an emergency at the hospital and I just forgot everything. I'm so sorry. Are you all right?"

Olivia clung to Buddy on the hearth. She watched Pick and Suzanne in silence.

Pick lifted her chin and threw her hair off her shoulder. The smile she smiled could not have been brighter.

"I done told you Suzanne, I'm fine. Just wore out, I guess. There ain't much to do when the snow comes 'cept sit inside and wait fer it to go away. A body gets to thinkin on things it wouldn't be thinkin on if the sun was shinin."

"Time was, on nights like this, our Mama and Papa would sing to us and tell us stories. We didn't pay no mind to the cold. But the Good Lord seen fit to take 'em and I'm just missin 'em, that's all. Their restin place is a shame and I can't fix it up like I want to. Soon's spring comes, me and these younguns'll fix it up proper, with roses, like our Mama wanted."

Pick washed out the cups. She placed them on a dishtowel to dry. "At least I kin read to the younguns." She glanced at Olivia and Buddy. "They're waitin fer me to read to em now."

"Did you get the idea that she dismissed us?" Suzanne asked as she and Bennett slipped repeatedly in the snow, trying to get back to Bennett's car.

"Yeah, I got that idea. Pick was working hard to convince us that everything is all right, but I'm more convinced than ever that something is wrong. Very wrong."

That night, Pick did not join Olivia, Buddy, and Willie in their Mama's bed. Their request to Pick to tell them about the roses fell on deaf ears.

Jimmy Joe lay on a blanket with his chin on his hands, staring into the fire.

Olivia, Buddy, and Willie huddled together as close as they could. No sound disturbed the stifling silence in the little cabin, no sound but the crackling fire, the pounding of young hearts, and Pick's wrenching sobs.

Two days later, the Stalworth funeral procession wound through the city. With funeral flags waving from their antennas, limo after black stretch limo followed the Ashford Police motorcycle escort.

The Stalworth family led the procession behind the twin flower-draped hearses.

City, county, and state officials attended the memorial service with Stalworth Enterprise executives, employees and friends, and with others whose names appeared with some frequency in the allotted column inches of Ashford's society pages.

A lone black limo with tinted windows waited beside the tent that sheltered the two new gravesites. The vehicle's occupant did not join the mourners who gathered under the tent.

He watched the bereaved wipe their tears and comfort one another as the minister spoke the final words over the deceased.

The mourners filed quietly past the coffins, offered their condolences, and departed the cemetery. Reid Garrison with Prince Asad waited patiently before urging Victoria, Stephen, and Claude from the site. Victoria and Claude acquiesced.

No one heard the silent mechanism that lowered the dark window in the limo. No one glimpsed the back seat occupant who inclined an ear toward the tent.

"Stephen, son...it's time to go," Garrison said with a hand on Stalworth's shoulder.

"Noooo!" Stalworth screamed. "Mommy, Daddy! You can't be gone! You can't leave us like this!" He hugged the flower-draped coffins, shoving roses, orchids, and camellias into the gaping pits.

Screaming and sobbing, Stalworth finally allowed Garrison to lead him away. Suddenly, Stalworth wrenched free. He spun to face the coffins.

"Mommy, Daddy, as God is my witness, they will pay! Those despicable heathens drove you from your home. They exiled you from your beloved Ashford. I promise, I swear on the Stalworth name, I will avenge your deaths. I will exterminate the vermin in Widows Hollow, every one of them, down to the last cockroach. As I live and breathe, I swear it!"

Garrison tightened his grip on Stephen's shoulder, dismissing his threats as empty words, hysteria brought on by grief and despair.

The occupant who engaged the silent mechanism that raised the limo's tinted window would not make that mistake.

Chapter Thirty

"I'm quitting medicine."

Stalworth delivered the message dressed in a navy suit, blue dress shirt and blue silk tie. His Italian leather shoes gleamed with a high shine, every hair in his salt and pepper mass lay neatly smoothed in place.

"What?" Across the desk, Reid Garrison sat in a plush leather chair with his legs stretched before him. "You can't mean that. Jacoby just finished your office."

"Jacoby can sell the office. You can sell it. I don't care who sells it. Just see that it's done. The estates are not for sale, the staffs remain. Find another pilot; put him on payroll. As soon as he's hired he can help you find another airplane."

"You want the final decision?"

"I do not. You make it. I'll sign the check."

"Your father left a lot of CEO vacancies," Garrison said, reading from a yellow legal pad.

"I want quarterly statements. I'll sign whatever you draw up. You sit in my father's place on the boards."

"That's not possible in every case. There are board members, stock holders to consider."

"Again, don't bother me with details. If Victoria wants to involve herself with running companies, that's up to her. If you're not up to the job, maybe I need to find an attorney who is," Stalworth said, leveling his gaze at Garrison.

"Is that a threat?" Garrison stretched his lanky frame from his chair. He stood, lacing his fingers, directing his steel blue gaze at his arrogant young employer.

Stalworth understood he could not afford to lose Garrison. The attorney knew the Stalworth business better than anyone else did, including the new owners.

"No threat, Reid, just handle it," Stalworth said, favoring Garrison with a smile. "Now, let's get down to some important business. "I'll need more cash. Liquidate anything you can and draw up a complete list of the horses at both estates. Blood lines, val..."

"You don't have horses at both estates." Garrison met Stalworth's eyes with a cool stare.

"What? What do you mean we don't have horses at both estates? I've seen them, damn it!"

"The horses at the country estate do not belong to you with a few exceptions."

"Then what's that double "S" brand on their flanks?"

"Their owner's brand."

"If we don't own those horses, why are they in our pastures and our stables? Get them off my property. Tell their owner I want them removed immediately."

Looking to pacify Stalworth for the moment, Garrison muttered, "Will do."

The truth was that he had already spoken to the owner. The owner had arranged to move them, not as fast as Stalworth wanted, but Stalworth could do nothing about it. Garrison chose to keep that information to himself.

"I want advance notice of any meetings scheduled by local, county, or state groups that involve Ashford or Titus County." Stalworth's briefcase lay open on the desk. He read from notes of his own.

"I also want a list of those who are politically active with any degree of prominence here locally. If they can pull strings, I want their names, interests, financial status, hobbies, whatever I might find useful."

"Include those officials who have anything to do with roads, utility construction, tax assessing, zoning, city planning, alcohol licensing, and anyone else who might prove helpful." Stalworth bent his head to make additional notes.

"Helpful for what?" Garrison dropped into his chair, leaned back, and tapped his pen on the desk corner.

"You, my friend, already know that. And if you ever divulge another secret when I've told you to keep your mouth shut, you may consider yourself unemployed." Stalworth leered at Garrison. "I think we can both agree that, no longer the tail, I am now definitely the dog."

Garrison rolled his eyes. He muttered under his breath. "Definitely. The dog."

Stalworth leaned back in the plush leather armchair, formerly occupied by none other than Henry Claymore Stalworth.

Unlike his father, Stephen found this office and others like it depressing. Plaques, honorariums, and citations for civic services decorated the wall. Henry Stalworth smiled from behind non-glare glass at ground breaking ceremonies, winner's circle photos, and eighteenth hole celebrations.

A set of Clay's golf clubs leaned in a corner beside a coat rack. Stephen looked across the room and picked up a family portrait from the desk. He found himself suddenly steeped in loneliness.

He turned to the familiar odor of his father's ever-present cigar—but there was no cigar. There was nothing but the memory. He could see his mother's smiling face, feel her embrace, and hear her words. "It's no bother, Stephen dear, we'll take care of it."

She had spoken her final words to him through her tears. Her meticulous orchestration of Ashford's elites into one final gift-bearing gala for the children had ended in a catastrophe. Havoc in headlines. HELL. Hell recklessly heaped upon her by one of the lowbred heathens from Widows Hollow.

Stalworth's jaw muscles tensed. They would pay for desecrating the Stalworth name.

He would rid that hollow of every one of them and raise up a monument to his parents, a monument that would enshrine the Stalworth name atop the highest rise in the county.

Stalworth Sterlings. Nothing could stop his dream from becoming a reality now.

Or so he believed. Sometimes, the simplest things in life make all the difference. Stalworth would have found the idea amusing, however.

It would not be power, prestige, or money that would stop him. It would be one of the simple things, a fairy tale—Isabel McKinley's fairy tale—that would stop his dream from becoming a reality.

He replaced the picture. "I'll need a secretary."

Garrison doodled on his legal pad. It had become a habit over the years. When clients tended to be long-winded, Garrison amused himself drawing caricatures. He had been drawing one now while Stalworth took his mental excursion.

"Am I interrupting you, Reid?" Stalworth jabbed a finger at Garrison's pad.

Garrison scratched a couple more lines on his drawing. Not about to dance on Stalworth's strings, he took his time flipping the page.

Stalworth leaned forward in his chair and absently drummed his fingers on the desk.

Annoyed at the sound, Garrison raised his eyes to Stalworth.

"By the way, did you happen to begin the title search I requested?" Stalworth aimed a smug grin at Garrison.

"No!" Garrison's reply was sharp.

"Would it be too much if I asked you to accomplish that task now?" Stalworth was enjoying his new powers.

Garrison wagged his head, studying Stalworth. He pitied the man. "Every acre, tree, and mineral right belongs to one person," Garrrison said.

"Have I heard this before?" Stalworth's grin was Cheshire-like.

"Probably."

"Every man has his price," Stalworth said, drawing dollar signs on his pad. "So that makes your job fairly simple."

"How so?" Garrison's face was rigid.

"Simply find out the man's price! Do some market comparisons. Bring me the fair market value of that land. Do some research on those bodies, too."

"Bodies?" Garrison's eyebrows lifted with his voice.

"Bodies! Graves! Call them whatever you like! We'll need permission to exhume. Get it."

"Permission to exhume who?" Garrison held his tongue and his temper. The effort was valiant. He felt like a pressure cooker with gauges swinging wildly in the red zone.

"You don't think golfers will be comfortable teeing off of headstones, do you? That ratty little graveyard has to go. Those ignorant hillbillies will jump at any offer! We'll move the graves, plow the whole place under and Widows Hollow will be history."

Stalworth cart wheeled a pen in his fingers. He thumped the pen and sent it flying across the room. He leaned forward and said with a grin, "Just like that!"

Chapter Thirty-One

"Hey Jacques, it's not noon yet, what brings you out so early? "

Jacques swatted at Jan's black Stetson. "I'm checking up on you, my friend. I haven't seen much of you lately." Jacques opened the metal barn door for Jan who led a handsome thoroughbred through the barn to the practice track.

"What are you doing now?" Jacques asked, patting the horse on the rump.

"I'm waiting for Jim to put this one through his paces. This boy is a wedding gift to a very special lady. Papa wants to do a dog and pony show for the new owners when they arrive. Jim's getting his papers."

"Whoa, boy!" Jan commanded. He led the spirited animal to a fence and tied the reins to a post. He took a currycomb from a bucket that was nailed to the fence and stroked the animal's sleek neck.

"Hey, Jim!" Jacques shouted, chucking his head at Jim Johnson who emerged unsteadily from the house carrying papers.

Jacques elbowed Jan. "Hey, what's wrong with Jim?"

Jan pulled the currycomb through the horse's silky coat and glanced at Jim. He looked winded. His shirt was soaked with perspiration despite the early hour. He did not move with his usual slight limp, but seemed to be dragging one leg.

As Jim drew nearer, the boys saw sweat beads on his face. His eyes looked faded and glazed. He stopped beside the horse and gave him a pat on his rump.

He looked up with Jan and Jacques as a stretch limo followed by a shiny new truck and matching horse van pulled up near the track.

The driver exited the limo and opened the back door. A beautiful, elegant, black woman stepped out, followed by an entourage of richly dressed men.

"Wooee, that's one good-lookin mama!" Jim exclaimed.

"That good lookin mama is Mrs. Claudette Robinson, Smokey Robinson's new wife. He's the gentleman holding her hand. They, along with their friends there, are *Smokey Robinson and the Miracles*, a new and popular singing group that's topping the charts. This fella is Smokey's gift to Mrs. Robinson."

"And I can't sing a lick!" Jim moaned. "That must be some fine feelin, buyin a horse like this for yer lady!"

Jan looked at Jim with concern. "You don't have to be a famous Motown Artist to buy a horse like this, Jim. You can raise them and buy them if you want."

"All it takes is the desire, a little planning, and lots of hard work. Are you sure you feel up to delivering this guy to his new owner? You look like you aren't feeling well."

Jim bent closer to the fence rail. "Oh, yes sir, Jan, I feel fine. These horses done gave me a workout this morning, that's all." Jim kept a firm grip on the horse's bridle and stretched himself upright.

Jan was not convinced. Jim's breathing was erratic. Jan suspected that Jim's grip on the thoroughbred's bridle was not so much to secure the horse as to secure Jim's upright stance.

Jan stepped forward to feel Jim's forehead when Klaus shouted from across the track. "Jim, could you bring the gray, please?"

Jim led the gray off the fence, between himself and Jan, forcing Jan to step backward. Jan crossed his arms and watched as Jim released the horse to Klaus. "Oh well, Jim's a grown man. I'm sure he'd tell us if he wasn't feeling well."

Heading back to the stables with Jacques, Jan said, "You never said what got you up before noon."

Jacques pulled the hay straw he chewed from his mouth. "I have to run an errand, thought I'd see if you want to come along. I thought we'd take the Jeep but we haven't been out on horses in a while."

Jan removed his hat and wiped his brow. "Where you going?"

"Old Gum Tree."

Jan shot Jacques a look of surprise. "Stump's place?"

"Yep."

Jan wiped his sweaty palms on his jeans and cast Jacques a sideways glance. "I can't think of a single reason you would be visiting Stump Simpson. We've heard the rumors since we were kids. Stump Simpson is the craftiest, most elusive and most famous moonshiner in all of Kentucky. I can't confirm the rumors myself, how about you? You're not into…."

"No, I'm not!" Jacques said. He swatted Jan with his hat for implying that Jacques might be visiting Stump for some of Stump's famous moonshine.

Trading playful jabs, they ignored the approaching pickup and horse trailer.

"So?" Jan waited for an answer.

"Somebody told Stump that I'm a law student. Can't imagine who that might have been," Jacques said, narrowing his eyes at Jan.

"Anyway, he wants me to check into a couple of things for him." Jacques made a face.

"Stump's got more brains under his hat than all of our professors combined. You wouldn't believe the things that old man knows, or who he knows…" Jacques ducked and threw up an arm to catch the bridle Jan tossed at him.

"I'll take Sage. You take Tinker," Jan said. He opened a stall door beneath a plaque inscribed Dark Sage. The beautiful horse was the smoky charcoal color of the spice that inspired his name.

"Tinker gets antsy on asphalt, we'll have to stay off the road as much as possible," Jan said as he tightened the cinch on Sage's saddle.

Jacques walked the chestnut roan called Tinker to the insulated metal barn doors. Jan followed on Sage.

"Hello boys!" Claude Olliphant called in greeting. He jumped out of the way of the barn doors that Jacques swung open. Margaret followed her father and Klaus into the barn.

"Why, hello Jacques, Jan," Margaret said to the boys. She cast her father a pleading glance that was anything but inconspicuous.

Jan and Jacques exchanged looks of dread.

"Margaret, why don't you join the boys for a ride? Klaus and I have some business to attend and I'm sure the boys would love your company."

"Of course, we'd like nothing better," Jan lied. He scowled at Jacques who did a poor job of hiding his mirth."

"You can take Dolly," Jan said, dismounting.

Margaret caught her father's eye like a practiced spider.

"Ah, Jan, Margaret took a fall a while back and her wrist isn't quite what it should be. I'd feel better if she could ride with you this once, until her wrist gets stronger."

Seething, Jan hid his anger. He swung into the saddle and extended a sweaty palm to Margaret. Without waiting for Jacques, Jan toed Sage in the belly and left the barn at a full gallop.

Despite the laughter that shook him, Jacques mounted Tinker and raced after Jan.

The riders took the main road to a busy intersection. They waited at a light to cross the four-lane to the grassy shoulder beyond.

Cars whizzed by. Men honked and women squealed at the sight of Jan, Margaret, and Jacques on horseback.

One such car idled in the stopped traffic. As the driver geared into motion, she sounded a long, loud horn blast, startling Sage who reared in fright.

Margaret screamed and clung to Jan.

"Shut up, Margaret!" Jan snapped.

The offending driver and her female companions panted at the sight of Jan Vandeventer rodeo-ing right before their eyes.

Jan jerked his head upright and braced himself, rippling the muscles in his powerful arms and legs.

"Whoa, Sage!" Jan commanded, snapping the reins downward. The frantic horse reared again and sidestepped. Anticipating the horse's movements, Jan leaned with him, going easily with the motion.

"Whoa, Sage!" Jan repeated. Sage tossed his head and stilled to an abrupt halt with four feet on the ground. Never looking to identify the offenders, Jan's face remained unchanged.

Within a short time, they reached the Hollow.

"Mama would faint dead away if she knew I was in this shanty town," Margaret complained.

Jan leaned forward in his saddle, sweeping the landscape with his eyes. He smiled and waved at Lucy, Lottie, and Olivia, who waved from Pick's yard.

"Jan, Chile! Come on down off them horses, Honey. Lemme git you a nice glass a tea," Mama John invited before disappearing inside with a bang of her screen door.

Jan dismounted and reached a hand to Margaret.

"You know these people?" She asked with a look of horror.

"We do," Jan said, nodding with Jacques.

"Surely you're not going to accept tea from that woman, are you Jan?"

"I surely am," Jan said. He held the door for Mama John who returned with a tray of glasses filled with tea.

"How are you boys?" She asked, smiling and passing them each a glass. She placed the tray on the porch, reached into her cleavage, and withdrew her kerchief. She wiped her brow and raised curious eyes to Margaret.

"Mama John, this is Margaret. Margaret, this is our friend, Mama John," Jan said. He pushed his hat off his forehead and took a long gulp of the tea.

Mama John's face creased with smiles for Margaret, but smiling for Jan was a different matter. Mama John watched with anxious eyes, knowing that Jan was looking for Pick.

"She ain't home, Jan, Honey," Mama John said with a glance at Pick's house.

"Pick ain't home much lately. Lord fergive this meddlin ol woman." Mama John rested a hand on Jan's shoulder. "But I spect somethins wrong with my Pick. She's risin early, goin up to the cemetery and the woods beyond and she's stayin 'til it's past time fer speakin to."

Mama John glanced to Old Gum Tree. "Pick's got herself a heavy burden that she ain't sharin, not even with my Jimbo. He and that baby, they been close all they lives," she said, meeting Jan's glance with troubled eyes.

Uncomfortable in her tight jeans in the heat, Margaret spewed an impatient breath.

"We're heading up to Stump's place. Maybe we'll see Pick there," Jan said. He returned his empty tea glass to Mama John.

"God bless you boy. Now you go on up there if you've a mind to."

Jan hugged the dear old woman despite feeling distracted. *What's going on? Why is Pick hiding on the mountain, avoiding everybody?"*

He put his foot in the stirrup, swung in the saddle, and reached a hand to Margaret.

Mama John patted Jan's knee. "Are my boy and my ol' Mule doin right by yer sweet folks?"

Jan's smile was quick and genuine. "Couldn't be doing better, Mama. I don't know how we managed without them."

The riders waved good-bye and spurred their horses up the steep climb to Old Gum Tree. Jan did not like it.

Something worried Mama John, something about Pick who had turned her back on everyone and everything she loved. Why? What could have happened?

The riders dismounted as they approached the top of the rise near the cemetery.

Jan and Jacques walked side by side, leading the horses.

Margaret spewed curses. She slapped Sage on the rump to shove past the horses and walk beside Jan.

Jan scowled. Pick did not need to see Margaret here with him. He stopped suddenly and reached behind his back to place a hand on Sage's muzzle.

"What are...?" Margaret huffed.

Jan dropped to one knee in the grass. A soft breeze blew off the rise, carrying with it the sound of Pick's voice.

"Verily, verily, I say unto you, He that heareth my word and be..., believe..., believeth on him that sent me hath everlasting life and shall not come into con-dem-na-tion; but is passed from death unto life. ...the hour is coming and now is, when the dead shall hear the voice of the Son of God: and they that hear shall live."

Jan strained to hear, but could not make out the sounds that followed.

Margaret fumed. "Will somebody tell me...?"

Jan's heart raced. He hoped to see Pick if only for a moment so he scrambled to the top of the rise.

"Hello!" Willie shouted with a wave and a smile.

"Hello!" Buddy echoed.

"Hello there Buddy and Willie," Jan said. He did not want to appear unfriendly to the little boys, but more than that, he wanted to find Pick. He traded playful jabs with the boys and then asked, "Where's Pick?"

"She's not here," Willie said.

"Pick's not here," Buddy echoed.

"Was she here just a minute ago?"

"No," Willie said.

"No," Buddy echoed.

Jan knew better. He had heard her reading from the Bible. "We're on our way to Stump's place. Will you tell your sister we said hello?"

"O.K." The little boys exchanged mysterious smiles. They seemed to breathe sighs of relief before they raced off down the hill.

"That was weird," Jacques said.

"She was here, I heard her. I don't know what's going on, but I intend to find out." Jan strained to see the grounds of Old Gum Tree but trees obscured his view. He gathered Sage's reins, put a foot in his stirrup, and pointed to

Margaret. "She can ride with you, Jacques. I'll meet you at Stump's."

"Why, I never!" Margaret cried. Stomping her foot, she stared after Jan who clicked his tongue, flicked the reins, and tore off for Old Gum Tree at a gallop.

"You'd 'a liked my boy," Stump said to Jan as Jacques and Margaret joined them.

He sat on a rough-hewn hickory bench whittling what looked to be a large cross from a chunk of oak. He pointed his knife at the cabin. "Pull yerselfs up a chair, young fella."

Jacques walked to the back of the cabin where two twig chairs leaned against a wall. He dragged the chairs close to Jan and seated himself and Margaret.

Listening to Stump's tales, Jacques took in the surroundings with the eerie feeling that he had stepped backward in time a hundred years.

Stump's house was made of split logs chinked with mud. The house had small windows, a small door, a huge stone chimney, and a roof made of split wood shingles.

A smokehouse stood nearby with a springhouse and barn far below. The view was breathtaking. The primitive structures of Widows Hollow stretched along each side of the rut to the wild tangle of overgrowth that kept the valley like a secret.

Behind Stump's cabin, the Cumberland Mountains soared to the clouds in heavily forested peaks. Looking deceptively close, they lay far away, beyond miles and miles of dense forest.

Stump pointed to a thicket of trees. "Them yeller ribbons is markers, me and Buster tied ever one of 'em. The marked trees is goin to the mill. Them saplins need light and sunshine so's they kin take their grandpap's place...someday."

"My Lizzy loved this spot. This was 'er flower garden. When the Good Lord called 'er, my Will wouldn't have it no other way, said he wanted to plant his Mama amongst the flowers she loved, high up on this ridge so's she could keep an eye on us."

"When them in the uniforms come a callin, midway of the war, I planted Will alongside his Mama. I reckon I've tarried too long. These ol' eyes has done seen all they's wantin to see."

Margaret fidgeted.

Jan and Jacques listened with rapt attention as Stump continued.

"Folks ain't changed much near as I kin tell. Used to be, this land belonged to them what found it and cleared it fer their corn crop and fer homes fer their families."

"The first settlers in these mountains was run-aways, all of 'em. The king sent em on ships from England agin their will; black folks and white, and orphans what the king didn't see no use in feedin. They was all put to work on the rich man's plantations."

"Them what could, run away-- high up in these mountains where them that'd chain 'em couldn't get to 'em. They come with nothin but growlin bellies and hatred fer them with the chains. They worked the land and the forests to eat, got what little they knowed from the Indians."

"The Indians weren't no farmers. Corn'd grow til the patch was used up and they'd move on. Moved on 'til all the patches was used up, wore out. Hunger come and war—the Civil War--agin them with the chains."

"The mountain men took off, choosin sides 'til their dyin and when the war was over, didn't nobody fergit their choosin."

"Them from the north and them from the south kept it sourin in their memories 'long with their hatred. They begin feudin, killin one another, brother agin brother, family agin family…carried on like that fer generations."

Jan interrupted. "I can't imagine generations of families being torn apart because of their ancestors' loyalty to either the Union or the Confederate Armies."

"Ain't no *imagine* to it, son. These mountains is full'a folks what would shoot a Yankee or a Rebel on sight yet today." Stump gazed into the distance as if lost in his thoughts, and then he continued.

"When folks thought times couldn't get no harder, coal come. The coal companies bought up the land fer near nothin.

Throwed up houses and commissaries and them what worked fer 'em spent their pay fore they got it, ever cent back to the company store."

"Come a callin on my kin, they did, offerin cash fer mineral rights. My kin done seen what sellin mineral rights done fer others. They didn't have nothin left, the land was useless and bare, ruint!"

"Next, them fast talking city slickers come fer the trees, takin all of 'em in a lot, leavin behind nothin to put back what they took."

"The history of Appalachia's southern highlands is pretty bleak," Jan said.

"Bleak?" Stump grunted. "Them coal mines worked the men folk to their dyin, leavin widers with no notion of how to earn a livin, tendin younguns. Couldn't live off the land, teachers couldn't be got, no money fer gettin 'em. What come belonged to the company store like everthin else, and wadn't fit fer teachin."

"My kin wouldn't be bought. What little corn could be growed after the rains washed the land into the river, they growed. Them what owned the company stores had a powerful thirst fer that which could be made from the corn and with the Good Lord's help, we kept it hid all these years in His own trees. Right up yonder..." Stump pointed through the dense treetops overhead.

Jacques whistled. "How many jugs do you have hidden up there, Stump?"

Stump said with a grin, "Never you mind, boy."

"Oh, my Lord!" Margaret cried. "I'm sitting here with a moonshiner!"

"Little lady, yer a site better off here with a moonshiner what will tell it like it is to yer face as well as behind yer back."

"Them high minded city slickers can't give ye a howdy do what you kin trust in and won't give ye the time of day less ye pay fer it, neither!" Stump cried, his eyes blazing.

Falling silent for a moment, Stump glanced down the hill. He peeled off more shavings from his carving and continued. "Flood come and took 'em all. Washed them, their company store and the likes a what they called houses, right down the river. Didn't leave nothin behind but Stump and Old Gum Tree."

"But these mines have been active recently, haven't they?" Jacques asked.

"You don't miss nothin, do ya young fella?" Stump asked, smiling at Jacques.

"Yer right. Young Colter showed up and opened the mines agin, him and others, bringin their coal and their burnin slate dumps, cloudin the sky and everthin in it with their sufferin blackness. Them what passes calls this Big Black Mountain cause of the coal turnin livin things to dead..."

"Look around ye. See them trees? They's poplars, white-oaks, black oaks, red oaks, chestnuts, hickories, beeches, maples, basswoods, ash, black-gum, sycamores, birches, willows, cedars, pines and hemlocks. Good Lord planted and tended ever one of 'em and left 'em to my seein to. I kept 'em fer 'Im. Ain't no harm come to 'em in my time..." Stump got a faraway look in his eyes and fell silent.

After a moment, he said to Jacques, "I believe we got business to tend to." Leaving his carving behind, Stump headed for the cabin with Jacques.

Jan picked up the carving. He ran his fingers over the smooth wood, gazing in silence to the hollow below.

Margaret shook her head. "It must be true, what they say."

Jan turned to Margaret. He lifted his brows to appear interested. He was neither interested nor was he listening. A single thought occupied his mind. *Where is Pick?"*

"He must really be demented," Margaret said. "No one in their right mind would bury their wife and son in the front yard. He acts like he's talking to them, it's morbid! These mountains and the people who live here are spooky. Who cares if a flood washes Stump and his Old Gum Tree away tomorrow? We have better things to do than name all the trees in Kentucky!"

"Ain't many folks no more what kin name the trees, like this hackberry here."

Jan spun to the sound of Pick's voice."I beg your pardon?" Margaret said. She glared at Pick.

"Was these trees what built Stump's house. It's them what keeps him warm in winter and cool in summer. Yer sittin on a bench and chairs what the trees give ya. In their roots is medicine and in their leaves, too. Squirrels and birds live up top of 'em, rabbits down under 'em and deer in the thickest of 'em. It's them what fed Stump and the other folks in Widows Hollow all our lives."

"It's the trees what keep the mountain tops on the mountains. If they wasn't here, the mountains would wash into the river and the river would turn to mud."

Jan felt oddly aware of the blood that pumped through his veins. When he heard Pick's voice, he was certain it pumped faster. He kept still, listening, fearful that if he moved, Pick might run away like a frightened deer.

Pick continued, playing with a twig in her hand. "The dirt's special, too. Time was, Stump had a old hound dog, called him Cooney. He weren't no proper coon dog, but he could tree a coon good as any hound in the county."

"Old Cooney come limpin up one day, swelled bigger'n a bull frog, his eyes shut, and his breathin thin and scarey-like. Bout broke Stump's heart, seein his old dog painin so. Stump knowed Cooney'd been snake bit. Weren't nothin Stump could do. Cooney took his leave and went off into the woods by his self. Stump figured on runnin across his carcass sooner or later. Pined for 'im sore."

"We was here, puttin up the summer harvest fer Stump, when we heerd him a hollerin like he done saw the Good Lord sittin on his roof. Weren't the Good Lord, it was Cooney, thinner'n a spider's web, 'ceptin fer the mud he was a wearin. Looked like he'd done burrowed his self inside a hornet's nest and was carryin it on his back. Cooney knowed the dirt was special. Pulled the poison clean out of 'im."

"Ain't no school house teached Cooney bout the dirt. Don't reckon they'll be teachin the younguns bout the trees neither. There's lessons can't be found in books. Lessons what's learned in the hearts of them what love the trees, the river, and the dirt." Margaret crossed her arms. With a tilt of her chin, she assumed an air of superiority. "Perhaps they'll learn in the schools that we have doctors for the humans and veterinarians for the animals."

Margaret crossed her arms. "If we all go around naming trees and nursing dirt and we just let nature grow wild around us, there won't be any room for progress, for advancing civilization, for, for promoting gentility!"

Stump, who had returned with Jacques, stopped where he stood. He looked at Margaret with eyes that blazed.

"Then I reckon you wouldn't be a mindin if they come with their noisy machines, a' mowin down the trees so's they kin plant their little green carpet and scatter them little white balls so's they kin chase 'em and put up one of them fancy eatin houses so's a man can trade a weeks' wages fer the privilege of guessin what's on his fancy eatin plate or what's in his sparkly glass or which of them fancy little thread spitters sewed the outfits the rest of 'em are a paradin!"

With a gasp, Margaret reached for Jan's hand.

"Ain't nothin civilized about no man what's got to pay another'n fer carryin his toothbrush cause he's soused and got his pockets loosed and offers up his hard come by wages to be a sleepin in a bed harder'n a oak stump and wakes himself to find there's another'n in the same bed he ain't even a knowin the name of!"

Jacques and Jan exchanged worried looks. Stump look winded, his face red, but he continued.

"Gentility? I'll tell you 'bout gentility! Gentility's a good woman in a sunbonnet teaching her daughters how to bring the vegetables from the garden to the cellar to the table."

"It's a good husband, walkin tall and proud alongside his son, teachin 'im to build a cabin, chop the wood and keep the fire goin when the cold wind's howlin! It's a family takin supper together, carin fer one another, and knowin there's a time to work, a time to play and a time to pray!"

"City folks ain't got time fer such! They're bored in their leisure and busy destroyin what is ...a lookin fer what ain't!

301

And now they got their eye on Old Gum Tree! They're a wantin to pull it down, plow it under, and waste it along with their days!"

"This land was country when I was a comin and it'll be country when I'm a goin! And I'll be planted in my own front yard right next to my kin so's I kin keep an eye on it and on them THAT AIN'T GONNA GIT IT!"

Stump fired off his angry words like a volcano belching lava, frightening Margaret. He looked to her like the devil with a pitchfork. With his teeth clenched, his eyes fiery, and his face glowing like hot coals, he held a guitar over his head, thundering it back and forth, emphasizing his words.

He waved it now as he approached her, crying, "And let me tell you somethin else, young lady, most times, the dead hear a site better'n the livin!"

Stump patted his chest. His rage left him short of breath, coughing a violent cough that wracked his body.

As the old man bent his gray head and lifted a forearm to hide his tears, Pick and Jan ran to support him.

With a loud *"Eee Awww"*, Buster nuzzled between Jan and Stump. Stump wrapped his arms around his beloved, gray-bearded mule. "Don't you be a frettin, Buster, Ol' Stump ain't gonna be a fergettin his friend, no sir!"

Stump wiped his eyes with the back of his hand and said to Pick, "I promised Buster you'd see to 'im…if need be. I know I kin count on you to make good my promise."

Stump thrust the Gibson J-45 acoustic flat top guitar at Jan. "You take this, young fella. It was my Will's. You'll be takin you a Missus what gits her singin from the angels and if yer wantin to 'company 'er, you'd best be learnin to play it since you can't strike nary a note."

Thinking of Pick's extraordinary voice, Jan took the guitar then stared at Stump in mute silence.

At the same time, Margaret quickly forgave Stump's outburst. "Why, how could that old man know that I've been taking voice lessons since I was six?"

"Ain't nothin civilized about no man what's got to pay another'n fer carryin his toothbrush cause he's soused and got his pockets loosed and offers up his hard come by wages to be a sleepin in a bed harder'n a oak stump and wakes himself

Chapter Thirty-Two

"Tanner, where is dat Jeem?" Klaus asked his ranch foreman.

"I'll get him, Klaus." Tanner tipped his hat to Klaus and hurried to the stables to find Jim Johnson.

"Jim. Jim!" Tanner called. Hearing no response, he quickened his pace to the tack room, inclining his ear to one of the stalls as he passed. "Jim?"

Again, there was no response, but Tanner Pruitt left nothing to chance. He was responsible for every heavily insured animal on this world famous ranch and for every ranch hand as well. He retraced his steps and shoved open a stall door.

"Jim!" Tanner threw off his hat and fell to his knees beside Jimbo Johnson. The boy lay curled in the hay, sobbing, his body drenched with sweat, his breathing labored, and his face the color of ash.

"I'm sorry, Tanner, I can't get up-- I can't walk."

"You don't owe anybody an apology Son!"

Jim was in bad shape. Tanner did not want to let on to Jim just how bad. He placed a hand on Jim's leg. Jim screamed, writhing in pain. Tanner pulled a knife from his pocket, ripped through Jim's pant leg, and carefully removed the boot from Jim's foot.

"Oh my God, boy! Oh, my God! Why didn't you say something? Why didn't you say something?" Tanner bellowed, staring at the grotesque infection that swelled Jim's foot and leg beyond any recognizable form or shape.

Tanner gently touched Jim's leg, and screamed. The hot, rancid, rotting, purple-black flesh fell away at his touch, unleashing a current of sickening, oozing pus.

"Maggie! Maggie!" Stephen Stalworth pounded his fist on the morning's Ashford Sentinel.

Maggie's nerves felt raw as an open wound. Her cheerful demeanor had become as brittle as old bones. Stephen's mood swings were taking a toll on her.

His self-absorbtion was so complete; he took no notice of Maggie's metamorphosis. Impatient and petulant, she appeared in the doorway of the breakfast room. "Yes, sir?"

"Call Garrison. Tell him to get over here now! I pay the thief a king's ransom to keep me informed and then I read in a twenty five cent newspaper what I pay him to tell me!"

Victoria burst into the breakfast room, her eyes swollen, and her feet bare. Her paisley silk pajamas were rumpled, her long blonde hair wild with snarls. She looked like she hadn't slept in days.

Slumping into the seat across from Stephen, she cradled her head in her laced fingers. "Stephen, what's wrong now?"

With her face propped in one hand, she poured herself a cup of coffee. She raised the cup to her lips and spilled it with a start at Stephen's exclamation, "I'm firing Reid!"

"WHAT?" Victoria pulled her coffee-soaked pajama top away from her body. "Firing Reid? You're not firing anybody! I forbid it!"

"Tory, look! Look at this!"

"County to have new school," she read aloud. "Unnamed benefactor donates land and windfall grant to Titus County for the construction of new school...."

"Stephen, I have enough to think about! I don't care if the county gets a new school!"

Victoria felt overwhelmed running the companies, the estates, and the various staffs. She needed all the help she could get, and now Stephen was threatening to fire Reid Garrison?

"You will not fire Reid, do you hear me, Stephen? You will not fire anybody! You will not threaten anybody! You keep this up, and the next one leaving will be me! Look at you! You haven't shaved in days. You haven't dressed in days!"

"Look at *me*? I can't remember the last time I had a decent night's sleep or the time to properly dress. Whatever happened to dressing for breakfast? Or good manners? Or keeping a civil tongue, for that matter?"

Victoria missed sleeping late, waking to Maggie's cheerful smile. She missed her father and his boisterous, good-natured laugh. She missed the smell of his cigars. She missed the freedom and security. Now, they were gone, leaving her with—chaos.

Maggie placed a steaming basket of muffins on the table. She poured Victoria a cup of coffee. "Miss Tory, you're soaked!" She cried, noting the wet coffee stains on Victoria's shirt.

Maggie left the coffee carafe on the table. She fetched a wet cloth, wiped the stains from Victoria's shirt and folded a soft towel between the wet fabric and Victoria's bare skin. Maggie smiled at her young Mistress and refilled Stephen's cup.

"Thank you Maggie," Victoria said, patting her hand.

Maggie smiled, giving Victoria's shoulder a gentle patbefore she departed.

"And you might try a "Thank you, Maggie" once in a while yourself!" Victoria snapped at Stephen.

Stephen mumbled a belated "Thank you, Maggie."

"You are so consumed with this memorial fantasy that you're letting everything our parents loved fall to ruin. Our parents' *lives* were a memorial! They were industrious, hard working, and responsible. They were generous, community-spirited, and kind-hearted. They, they..." Victoria burst into tears.

Stephen wasted no time. Catching Victoria in a weak moment these days was a chore.

"You're right, Tory, I am sorry. I will do better, I promise. You're right about Mommy and Daddy, too. They dedicated themselves to seeing Ashford and its citizens flourish. They lead the way in living an exemplary, community-spirited lifestyle that made this country great. Look at this community. Look at our neighbors."

"It's simply more than I can bear, Tory. Watching all that our parents worked so hard to establish and protect being threatened."

"We must preserve this community for our parents, for ourselves, and for our children. Think of it, Tory. When we have children, Ashford will be their home."

Encouraged by her vague look of interest, he continued.

"If we allow that white trash to invade Ashford, God only knows what may happen. Who can predict the horrors of their incestuous inbreeding?"

"Help me, Tory, please help me." Stephen patted her hand and smiled.

"For our parent's sake, you must promise to help me protect Ashford from the likes of that, that, Pick person and that poxed population that she incites. I'll do anything you ask if you'll just help me!"

Chapter Thirty-Three

Sitting in the dingy waiting room of the county hospital, Tanner chain-smoked. Sitting was not something Tanner did well, especially in a cooped-up space. He felt like he had been here for hours, but the clock he stared at told him different.

The boy's eyes haunted him. And his words—"I ain't afraid, Tanner-- I know you won't let nothin happen to me." They hung over him like a gathering storm.

Klaus and Olga huddled nearby over lukewarm cups of machine-dispensed coffee. Klaus paced, watching the door open and close to the hallway where strangers in white gowns and plastic booties had disappeared with Jim.

Mule Johnson had gone with one of the hands on a road trip to bring back a new truck. "Damn rotten timing," Tanner muttered. "If these guys in the gowns and booties come back with bad news..."

The hallway doors swung open. A young stethoscope-draped doctor with a brisk walk and a clipboard in his hand called out "Johnson family?"

Klaus, Olga, and Tanner hurried forward.

Staring at the three white faces, the doctor glanced at his notes and repeated, "Jim Johnson family?"

"This is Klaus and Olga Vandeventer, Jim's employers. I'm their foreman, Tanner Pruitt, Jim's bos..., Jim's friend."

The doctor took in the elegant couple, Klaus in his angora sweater, ostrich quill boots, and a sterling belt buckle—Olga in diamonds that could fund a medical complex. Money.

"Vandeventers, from ...?" The doctor's smile was dazzling.

"Vandeventer Farms. What's the verdict?" Tanner asked, hoping to skip the question, "*The* Vandeventer Farms?" and wanting only to get out of this place.

Though his face said he did not appreciate Tanner's blunt manner, the doctor knew better than to risk offending *The* Vandeventers.

He drew a resigned breath. "Mr. Johnson's family needs to be notified immediately. The infection in his foot and leg is in the advanced stages of gangrene. If we don't amputate that leg within twenty four hours, he could die."

A cry escaped Olga's lips.

Klaus squeezed Olga's hand tighter. "Thank you, doctor, ve get his family now."

Tanner glanced to the ceiling. He shook his head to stall his tears and clamped a hand on the doctor's shoulder. "Did you tell him?"

"No, not yet."

"Don't!" Tanner said in a voice that commanded respect. He glanced at his employers. "And don't spare any expense; I'll be responsible for his bills."

"No, Tanner," Klaus placed a hand on the man's shoulder. "Let me and Mama do this for Jeem."

The doctor shifted his eyes between Klaus and Tanner.

Wanting to be alone with those closest to him, Klaus said to the doctor, "Dese people know vere to send de bill, dey can call if dey like."

Staring at the floor, Tanner drug a fist across his cheek. "What do you want me to do, Klaus?"

"Please go get Zhan and Jim's modder. Mama and I vill stay vis Jim."

Olga sniffled. Wiping at her tears, she clutched Tanner's arm. "And Peek. You must bring Peek."

Leaving a wailing Mama John to change while he picked up the others, Tanner drove on to Stump's, heading the Jeep up the hill in a cloud of dust.

"I ain't afraid, Tanner. I know you won't let nothin happen to me." Tanner could not get the words out of his mind. Tanner did not have a family. He had never wanted one, had never needed the tangle of those ties that bind. Now-- this damn boy was breaking his heart.

If that boy's leg is amputated, his ranching life is over, he thought. Wrangling's tough enough on two legs. One leg— no way.

Tanner choked. "God, I'm not sure if You're up there, and I'm not sure You care to hear from me anyway, but it ain't for me I'm asking. It's for Jim. If You could just see fit to help him out here, God. I'd be obliged. Most obliged. I don't reckon we've been introduced, God...Sir. My name's Tanner. Tanner Pruitt." Tanner knotted a fist beneath his eyes and wiped his face on his sleeve. He had one more stop to make.

Stump and his visitors watched the Jeep stop at Mama John's and the sudden commotion that followed.

Jan yanked open Tanner's door. "Tanner, what's wrong?"

"It's Jim, Son. I've come to get his mother and you and Pick."

With Jacques and Margaret following, Jan hurried with Tanner across the yard to Stump.

Tanner nodded to the horses. "Leave them, I'll send a hand to pick them up."

Stump slowly raised his eyes to Tanner's.

"Mr. Simpson, Jim Johnson's at the county hospital. His leg's infected and the infection has spread. It's gangrene. The doctor says Jim could die if they don't amputate his leg by morning."

Stump dropped his head in his hands. After a moment, he stood to walk Tanner and Jan to the Jeep. "You folks get a move on, I'll see to yer horses. Tell Early Mae and the boy, Stump's prayin fer 'em."

Tanner slid behind the wheel.

Margaret, Jacques, and Jan piled into the Jeep as Stump moved to close the door.

"Wait! Where's Pick?" Jan cried. He glanced across Stump's property. She was gone from the bench, gone from the yard, and gone from the trees where she had been earlier. Jan grabbed the door handle and hit the door with his shoulder.

Pressing against the door with his stubby arms, Stump raised solemn eyes to Jan. "Go on, boy. Pick ain't comin."

"But she… Jim needs her!" Jan darted his eyes from Stump to the grounds Pick had deserted. A second glance at Stump confirmed his words. Pick was not coming.

Suzanne and Bennett met Olga in the waiting room. They tearfully convinced her that a second opinion would change nothing. The raging infection would kill Jim Johnson unless doctors amputated his leg.

Time was running out. The doctors waited for Jim's family to arrive. Jim had to be told.

Suzanne, Bennett, Olga and Klaus shared their concerns, each preparing the other for the trying moments ahead. A commotion at the door signaled the arrival of one of those moments.

Mama John shuffled into the waiting room on the arms of Tanner and Jan.

Bennett hurried to assist. Suzanne left to advise the doctors that Jim's mother had arrived.

Bennett led Mama John to a chair, trying his best to calm her as the surgeon approached. Hearing the news from Tanner was one thing, but hearing it from the doctors was another. This was final. Early Mae and Mullen Caine Johnson's beautiful, strong son would be a one-legged man by morning.

Mama John shook her head violently. "Naw! Naw! It can't be, Sweet Jesus, Lord! It can't be! Not my b..." Staggering to her feet, Mama John lifted her face to Heaven. Jumping up and down she flailed the air with her kerchief.

"She's going down!" Bennett cried. "It's her blood pressure! Get a gurney in here!" Bennett issued orders, straining beneath Mama John's weight until attendants rushed in with a gurney. Bennett followed the gurney and Mama John down the hallway with Suzanne and Olga right behind.

"Somebody's got to tell him. Asking his mother is no longer an option and we cannot amputate his leg without permission." The doctor stared back at the solemn faced men he addressed.

"I vill tell him," Klaus said.

"No, Papa, you stay with Mama, I'll tell him," Jan said, exchanging grim glances with his father.

"No!" Tanner said, shaking his head. He edged between Klaus and Jan and wrapped them fiercely in his arms. "Let me do it. I'll tell the boy."

Klaus gave Tanner a grateful nod. Jan protested but Tanner waved him to silence. Tanner headed down the hallway that led to Jim's room, scowled at the rumbling he felt in his gut, and pushed through the door.

"Tanner!" Jim's smile was weak. When the taut muscles in Tanner's face did not relax, panic replaced Jim's smile. Tanner looked like a condemned man.

"Tanner..." Jim's voice broke.

Tension charged the waiting room. Jim's friends and family paced with dry throats, taut lips, and eyes that darted from face to face, hopeless eyes that mirrored despair.

There was no hope to cling to, no fifty-fifty chance, and no critical time period to survive.

The three Vandeventers, Jacques, and Margaret paced. Mama John slept in a room down the hall with the aid of an injected tranquilizer.

"Naw! Naw! They can't take my leg, Tanner! They ain't goin take my leg! Naw! I ain't givin nobody p'mission to take my leg! I'd ruther be dead! They ain't goin take my leg I tell ya! Where's my Mama? Get my Mama!"

Suzanne fed silver coins into a vending machine, trying desperately to block out Jim's screams. She lifted the plastic cover and removed a Styrofoam cup filled with coffee. Suzanne carried the coffee to Olga who thanked Suzanne, lifted the cup to her lips, and dropped it to the floor with a *splash!*

Tears streamed from their eyes as the two women embraced one another.

Rapid, uneven steps thudded up the hallway. The double swinging doors slammed against opposite walls as Tanner bulldozed through them, stormed through the waiting room and out of the hospital.

Jan started after Tanner.

Klaus raised a hand. "Leaf him alone, Zhan."

Jan swept his eyes over the tearful faces. He crossed his arms against the vending machine, dropped his head on his arms, and cried.

Jim's condition grew worse with each hour that ticked by. Following a conference with Jim's surgeon, Bennett agreed to ask Mama John to give her permission for the surgery.

Mama John granted her permission, sobbing. "I rather have my boy hate me…than leave me." She became inconsolable, refusing to rest, insisting on remaining by her son's side. "He ain't never gonna forgive me. I'm goin lose my boy sure's he's goin lose his leg!" She cried.

"It will be all right, Mama," Suzanne said in a whisper. "Jim will realize you did what you had to do to save his life."

Jan returned to the hospital after driving Jacques and Margaret home. He found his mother with Suzanne and Mama John in Jim's room.

"Mama..."

Mama John pushed herself from her chair and stepped to Jim's bedside.

"Mama... Where's Pick?"

Certain the heavily sedated boy mumbled in his sleep, Suzanne patted Jim's arm.

He opened his eyes and fixed them on his mother. "Where's Pick? Mama, where's Pick?" A single tear splashed from his eyes before he closed them again.

Mama John squeezed Suzanne's hand and looked to Jan.

Jan tried without success to avoid Mama John's eyes.

"What is it, Jan, Honey?" Mama John squeezed and released her knotted handkerchief. "Why you tryin to hide yer eyes from me?"

"She ain't comin!" Mama John cried. "My Pick ain't comin. That's why yer hidin yer eyes from this ol' woman, Jan?"

Startled, Suzanne and Olga glanced at Jan.

"Go on boy, Pick ain't comin!" Stump's words had left no room for argument.

"I, I'll..." Jan floundered. He glanced helplessly at Jim's ashen face and at the weeping women.

Olga turned away and dabbed at her eyes with her handkerchief.

"Quit crying!" Jan barked. He shifted his eyes from his mother to Mama John and to Suzanne. He slapped his Stetson on his head, brushed a kiss on Olga's cheek, and turned to his sleeping friend. "You're going to be all right, Jim. You just sleep peaceful until I get back. With Pick!"

"They're needin ye, Pick." Stump filled the pail at his feet with grain and carried it to the stall where he settled Sage for the night.

"Ain't like you Pick McKinley, turnin yer back on them what needs ye. What's come over ye, causin you to shut out everbody? I've knowed you since you was no bigger 'n a cricket and I ain't never knowed you to sull up fer such a spell. Ain't no point yer tryin to hide in that corner. I knowed you was there all along. You gonna keep me talkin to myself or you gonna come out and tell me what's takin ye?"

"Gangrene's a serious matter. I reckon you know that's well as me. You got neighbors and family a countin on ye. The Good Lord seen fit to give ye somethin special they ain't got and they's needin it sore right now. You gonna git yerself up there or you gonna stay put in that corner lickin yer wounds and buryin yer mite like a dog with a bone?"

Pick stepped from the dark corner into the lantern light. Her face was swollen from crying, she clutched Isabel's Bible in her hands.

"It is buried! It's buried fer good 'n keeps just like them bones in the cemetery box! And I couldn't dig it up if I wanted. The Good Lord done took it back and ain't likely to answer if I was a callin and I ain't gonna be a callin!"

Stump continued feeding the horses with his back to her. "Jimbo could die, ye know. Ye wantin to be left with that?"

"I can't help 'im! I can't help nobody! I ain't fit and I ain't never gonna be agin!"

Stump had had his suspicions concerning Pick's leaving off her friends, and now, she confirmed by her actions that his suspicions had been right. Tears of guilt swelled into the old man's eyes with the sorrow that shrouded his soul.

"Two wrongs ain't no fix, Pick McKinley! One of em's mine and the Lord'll be a callin me to answer fer it soon enough. The other'n's yer's to be a rightin whenever ye choose!"

"I can't be a rightin it! The Good Book says so. I'm blacker'n a swallowed up coal mine and buried as deep. And I didn't ask fer it, I never! I didn't choose it, but I can't let it go!" Pick screamed.

"I hate him! I hate him and I can't fergive him! And the Lord ain't gonna fergive me because of it!" Pick threw the Bible to the ground and dropped to her knees, shaking with sobs.

Stump picked up the Bible and clutched it to his chest. He closed his eyes, muttered words over the Book, and kneeled beside Pick.

Stump circled Pick's shoulders with his arm. "Pick, you got to hate me if you're gonna hate him. I'm equal to fault, God fergive me, I'm equal to fault!"

Pick wiped at her nose and raised startled eyes to Stump. "I ain't got no hate fer you Stump."

Stump lifted Pick's chin with his trembling hand. "The Good Lord'll reveal my wrongin of ye in His own good time, but I'll go to my rest burdened forever 'lest ye tell me I'm fergiven, Pick. Me and the other'n as well!"

"Stump, I, I can't make sense of yer words."

The sorrow in Stump's eyes moved her. She knew as well that his pleas for her forgiveness were genuine—and conditional. To forgive Stump, she had also to forgive Stalworth. Stump had done nothing that could make Pick withhold forgiveness from the kindly old man.

But Stalworth—that was another matter. Pick felt sure she wore her hatred for Stalworth like sackcloth. She did not speak of it. Had never. But that hatred--like a black cloud—cast a shadow over everything in her life. How could she love her family and neighbors when hatred filled her soul? Hatred and love cannot exist together in a single soul.

"Love thy neighbor as thyself."

Tears spilled from Stump's eyes, breaking Pick's hardened heart. She felt nothing but love for Stump Simpson--nothing but love for everybody she knew or had ever known.

"For if ye forgive men their trespasses, your heavenly Father will also forgive you; But if ye forgive not men their trespasses, neither will your Father forgive your trespasses."

Pick knew the verses from memory. Her hatred for Stalworth had robbed her. She had not been able to eat, to sleep, to laugh, or to face those she loved. Now, Jimbo needed her, needed for her to be right with God.

Pick lay on her face in the hay and prayed. "Jimbo's needin us Lord-- and Stump, I ain't got no notion what he's sayin but it's him what's askin my fergiveness—fer himself and the other'n. So I'm askin now. Fergive me fer hatin Stalworth and fergive me fer not fergivin. I forgive 'em now, and ask you to forgive me. Help me keep to it Lord, cause I can't never without you. And please show me about Jimbo, Lord. I'm askin in the name of Him who brung pardon to us all. Amen."

Pick pushed herself from the floor, scraping hay stubble from her face. Feeling like a heavy weight had been lifted from her shoulders, she smiled into Stump's watery eyes and said with a hug, "Stump, yer forgiven forever!"

Stump hugged the girl to his grateful heart. He pressed his wet cheek to hers and said, "God bless ye, child, God bless ye."

Pick wiped her eyes and helped Stump finish his chores. He gathered the lantern, and together, they walked to the barn door. "You look a mess, Pick McKinley," he said with a laugh. Plucking hay straws from Pick' hair, Stump raised the lantern.

Jan stood in the doorway.

"Reckon she'll be a comin with ye now," Stump said. He gave Pick a nudge and walked with them, lighting their way in the darkness.

Wordless, Pick followed Jan to his Jeep. She did not know what he had heard or if he had heard anything. But she could not think on that now, she had to think on Jimbo.

"Jim's asking for you, Pick. They're going to amputate his leg in the morning. There's no other way to save his life." Jan glanced at Pick, hoping for a reply.

Pick sat staring out the passenger window as if she were far, far away.

Jan drove in silence, wrangling with his thoughts. *What was it about Pick?*

She turned to him, staring, plowing him like a cornfield with her green eyes. Every vain thought and shallow pretension Jan possessed fell before her gaze like corn stalks before a Harvester. She could ask him anything and he would tell her.

But she's not asking, he realized with a start—she doesn't need to ask.

Jan pulled into the hospital parking lot, fearing his legs would fail him. His throat felt parched, his nerve endings fired off like fireworks. He felt he had survived the inquisition, and Pick had never spoken a word.

"Turn around!"

Jan jumped like he had been poked with a cattle prod.

"Turn... Do... What?" He muttered, confused.

"Turn around," Pick repeated.

Jan gripped the steering wheel and turned his body in the seat to face Pick. Her green eyes searched his like lasers. Her mouth stretched in a wide grin. "What are you so afeared of? I ain't gonna bite ye."

"I wasn't, I'm not...." Jan pulled straw from her hair. "You haven't said one word to me since we left Stump's place. So…"

"Turn yer car around. We got to git back to the holler."

"Back to the hollow?" Jan blinked, more confused than ever.

"We don't have time. It's almost sunrise. They'll take Jim's leg soon. He and Mama John are waiting for you. I can't let them down, they're desperate to see you, Pick. You have to come inside with me, now. Please."

"They ain't gonna take Jim's leg--if we git back to the holler. Now." She spoke the words so quietly, with such certainty. Had anyone else suggested such madness, Jan would have jumped from the Jeep calling for help. But this was Pick...

Jan shifted into reverse. "Pick, how do you know? How do you know you're doing the right thing? How can you be so sure Jim won't lose his leg if we do this?"

"He told me."

"Who? Jim?"

"No," Pick said with a laugh. "The Good Lord."

Jan watched the road in his rearview mirror. This was no time to chance being pulled over for speeding.

"Don't be afeard fer yer speed," Pick said, like she had read his mind.

Jan shoved the accelerator to the floor. He was a simple chauffeur here. He stopped at Pick's house as she instructed.

Pick disappeared inside, ran back out the front, and disappeared behind the house. She returned moments later carrying something wrapped in burlap.

Jan put the Jeep in reverse again and headed back to the hospital. He told himself he would not, but, nodding to the burlap bag, he asked. "What is that?"

"Better you don't know," Pick said, avoiding his eyes.

"Pick! Pick chile, yer too late. They done taked my Jim and him a callin yer name!" Mama John cried. She looked haggard and spent, her wet eyes-- defeated.

"I ain't too late," Pick said, giving Mama John a peck on the cheek. "You be still and peaceful now."

Pick looked over the crowded waiting room. Spotting Bennett, she crooked her finger and said, "Come with me."

"But Pick, they've taken Jim to surgery. I'm not a surgeon, I can't interfere."

"You comin or not?" Pick said, meeting Bennett's eyes with an even stare.

Suzanne pushed Bennett. "Go!"

"Take me to Jimbo," Pick instructed.

Bennett had reservations, but something told him to do as Pick asked.

Pick, Bennett, and Jan ran to the elevators. Exiting on the fifth floor, they ran down a hallway to metal double doors with small glass windows.

"This is as far as we go," Bennett said. "That's the operating room. We can't go in there."

Pick peered through the window. Nurses and doctors arranged silver instruments on a tray and checked monitoring equipment. A nurse thumped a plastic line that ran from a bag filled with liquid into a needle in Jim's hand. Another pulled back sterile sheets to expose Jim's leg and thigh.

Doctors and nurses moved aside for the surgeon. He approached Jim with what looked to be a power saw in his hand. Noise like a buzz saw rattled the air.

Pick yanked on Bennett's shoulder. Whispering and gesturing frantically, she shoved the burlap-covered object in his hand.

"I can't do that, Pick! I'll lose my medical license!" Bennett cried.

Staring into Bennett's eyes, Pick realized he had made up his mind; he would not do as she asked. She delivered her words like a thunderbolt. "He's gonna die if they take his leg. You be deciding!"

Bennett fired a desperate glance from Pick to the surgeon that bent over Jim with the droning saw. Bennett threw a hand in the air. "Stop." The word squeaked out.

"STOP!" he repeated with a roar, tearing through the doors like a man possessed, past stunned nurses and doctors. He grabbed the surgeon's wrist as the saw blade rotated inches from Jim's leg.

With frantic gestures, Bennett repeated Pick's instructions to the surgeon.

The surgeon stared at Bennett. He stripped the mask from his face and shoved Bennett backward.

Bennett shoved back, shouting, "Do you want to be responsible? My responsibility ends here and now!"

"Gardner, you're out of line! My God, man, infection is eating the boy inch by inch, and you want to, you want to...!"

"Save his life. I just want to save his life!"

"And if this insanity doesn't work?"

"I'll take my chances!" Bennett cried, his chest heaving.

The surgeon peeled the sanitized gloves from his hands. "Call the chief. I'll have no part in this and I want witnesses."

Nurses summoned the hospital's Chief of Staff. An angry and animated confrontation followed. The chief read Jim's chart and agreed with the surgeon. "Bennett Gardner has lost his mind."

Shoving angrily through the doors, Hollingsworth collided with Pick. "Pardon me!" He snapped.

"Jimbo will be dead by mornin if you don't," Pick said quietly to the man.

Images of a dying infant coming back alive flashed through Hollingsworth's mind, images of a tiny blue body turning pink. All thought processes deserted Dr. Dan Hollingsworth-- all thought processes save one. *Do what she asks.*

Blinking like one waking from a deep sleep, Hollingsworth turned on his heel and pushed through the doors, re-entering the surgical ward. He spoke in a mechanical voice to Bennett who quickly leaned over Jim Johnson's body with the object Pick brought from Widows Hollow in his hand.

Moments later, nurses and doctors stampeded from the ward. Wild-eyed, they ran with hands covering their mouths and hands clutching their stomachs as if they had witnessed some obscene, grotesque horror.

Chapter Thirty-Four

Stalworth tossed and turned in his sleep. Stomach acid spewed its searing ruminations like a geyser into his throat, triggering his gag reflex.

The numbness held him, forcing his tortured eyes to search like beacons through the fog that enveloped him night after night. He strained. Veins pulsed in his neck. His heart hammered, louder, louder.

The fog thinned. Faint, faceless shadows, the figures danced, faster, faster, whirling recklessly, feverishly—too fast. Stop. Stop!

His impotent mouth gaped in silence. He wanted to scream to make them stop, but could not.

"No!" Stalworth screamed, clutching his stomach with clammy hands as he heaved, stoop-backed and stumbling like a bent old man, to the bathroom.

He fumbled the toilet lid open and vomited. Groaning, he reached for a cloth to wipe the bile from his mouth. Haunted, bloodshot eyes stared back at him from the mirror. He backed away, turned, and ran.

Cursing in frustration, glancing repeatedly in the rearview mirror, Stalworth drove like a maniac to Reid Garrison's office.

"May I help you, sir?"

Ignoring her question, Stalworth raced past the startled receptionist and burst through Garrison's office door.

Garrison was on the phone. Disgruntled, the attorney pulled the phone to his chest. "I'm sure you have a reason for barging into my office," he snapped.

"Hang up the phone!"

"What?"

"Hang up the phone damn it, this is an emergency!"

Garrison hesitated. *Stevie's in big trouble.* "Let me get back to you, something's come up...." He dropped the phone in its cradle.

"Get rid of her!" Stalworth growled, glancing at the receptionist who stood at the door with her hand on the polished brass handle.

"Gail, please go file those answers and pick up some ink cartridges for the printer. Put the phones on the machine."

Garrison closed the file on his desk and swept it into a drawer. "Stephen, what's going on?"

Stalworth poured himself a drink from the mini bar behind Garrison's desk. He lifted the bottle with a nod to Garrison.

"No. It's too early for me," Garrison said, watching in scorn as Stalworth gulped down the first and poured himself a second drink.

Stalworth paced, rolling the glass in his hands. "Reid, I think I'm in trouble."

"You think?" Garrison laced his fingers on the desktop.

"I'm not sure, damn it! Maybe. I can't remember! I've been having these dreams that keep me awake. Last night I realized I wasn't dreaming. It happened."

Stalworth lurched unsteadily, searching the paneled walls of Garrison's office as though he expected something to jump out and grab him.

Garrison rose from his chair. He crossed the plush carpet of his office to Stalworth, took the man by the shoulder, and steered him to the black leather chair before Garrison's desk.

"Now. Calm down and tell me about it."

"Ho-ly Je-sus!" Garrison let go the rubber band he had stretched over the tip of his pointer finger and thumb with a *snap!*

Stalworth finished the story he had related in a drunken narrative.

Garrison chewed his lip. He spun his chair to the window and the welcome distractions beyond. But, needing to think, he spun to face Stalworth and found an empty chair. Garrison turned to the sounds of clinking glass, Stalworth had returned to the liquor cabinet. *And with good reason,* Garrison told himself.

"And you haven't heard anything...from anyone?" Garrison posed the question over the rattle of ice and the slosh of liquor.

"No one."

"She must have told somebody. I think we would be foolish to underestimate her at this point. She has made some fairly influential friends around here. I'm sure they'll be advising her.

"Oh God!" Garrison dropped his head in his hands with a groan.

"What?" Stalworth shouted.

"Stephen, we could get around an assault, attempted rape, whatever it is you think you might have done in your drunken stupor but can't remember... We could make her an offer, shut her up, but..."

"But?" Stalworth demanded.

"But things could get complicated, damned complicated, if..." Garrison's voice trailed off.

Stalworth slammed a fist on the desk, sloshing scotch onto the polished cherry wood. "If what?" He spluttered his face choleric.

Garrison reached into a drawer and pulled one, two, three Kleenex from a box. He mopped up the spill, fired the wad of Kleenex into a wastebasket, and raised steely eyes to Stalworth.

"If, Mister Stalworth, as a result of your mindless, drunken act of indiscretion, that is, if as a result of your possibly *raping* her, Miss Pick McKinley is carrying your child!"

Stalworth charged the unsuspecting attorney like a raging bull determined to skewer a matador. He came close to knocking Garrison senseless, smashing his skull with a head butt while choking the man with both hands crushing his windpipe.

Roaring in fury, Garrison sprang to his feet. He peeled Stalworth's fingers from his neck, grabbed two hands full of Stalworth's shirt, lifted him into the air like a rag doll and threw him across the room.

"You little bastard! You try that again and I'll hang you myself!"

Stalworth slumped against the wall, unconscious.

The commotion in Garrison's office prevented anyone from noticing the old man who waited outside the door. No one heard his whimpers. No one saw him raise speckled hands to his chest, hands that trembled to the tips of their faded, yellowing fingernails.

Chapter Thirty-Five

"Ees everybody here?" Olga swept through the crowd of young people dressed in a filmy blue pants suit with a blue satin shell and silver beaded sandals.

Helping themselves to crisp finger foods and icy drinks from a poolside buffet, the young people answered in chorus. "Yes."

Olga caught Jim Johnson by the elbow as he trotted past on his way to the stables.

"What about ze cars?" She asked, shading her eyes with her hand.

"All hidden behind the stables, Miss Olga," Jim said, flashing a wide smile.

Despite the skeptic physicians, Jim's recovery had been swift and complete. He ran with no pain and no limp. When persuaded to tell the story, he cautioned his listeners they would need strong stomachs to hear the miraculous tale.

Brother Lester had similarly cautioned his congregation the previous week before delivering the sermon, "God's ways are not our ways."

"When man is defeated, when the educated members of the medical community with its advanced technology are defeated, The Lord delivers the victory using what He will."

"Psalms 42; 5: Why art thou cast down, O my soul: and why are thou disquieted in me? hope thou in God; for I shall yet praise Him for the help of His countenance"

"Had we lost hope? Did we agree with the doctors who said there was no hope? How many of us turned to the countenance of God, to God's face?"

"And what was God's reply to our hopelessness? Did He turn to the surgeon with the buzzing saw? Did He turn to the druggist for a magic elixir? Or did God in His infinite wisdom turn to the humblest of His creatures?"

"What is impossible with man is possible with God who proved it once again using only the larva of his humblest creatures."

When his congregation did not respond with gasps of comprehension, Brother Lester added "Almighty God turned His countenance toward us. He heard our pitiful cries, and Our Lord God Almighty, whose ways are not our ways, fed Jim Johnson's gangrene, along with our doubt and disbelief—to the maggots!"

Olga smiled. Jim looked especially handsome today. He looked forward to showing his mother and siblings around the beautiful ranch. He and his father had taken the family shopping last night. Jim laughed at the memory.

Mule sat at the supper table with his hands laced over his stomach, smiling a mischievous smile at his wife. "What is you up to, old man? You a grinnin like a possum in a hen house."

Mule shook his snowy crop of wiry curls. "You doan reckon we should refuse to attend Mister Jan's birfday party?"

With Jasmine tucked in the crook of her arm, Mama John slapped a hand on her hip. She narrowed her eyes at Mule. "I does not!"

"Don't suppose you'd want to be embarrassin them good folks, taking these raggity rascals we done got ourselves in they wore out play clothes with they ugly toes sticking clean out of they shoes?" Mule's grin had been maddening.

Mama John squeezed one eye closed. She arched a brow. "Old man, don't you be a sittin there, a grinnin in yo' leisure, wastin my too little time talkin me in circles like I ain't got no babies to be bathin or dishes to be washin!"

"You got somethin on yer mind you better spit it out flat. This baby don't weigh nothin and I kin still take a broom to yo skinny backside!" The ire in her face and Mama John's waggling finger set Mule to laughing.

"I done noticed some of them uptown women lookin right sharp in they pressed britches and shirts. Ain't nothin like them old wore out house dresses you always puttin on."

Mama John scraped her chair from the table and shoved Jasmine in Jim's arms. "This ol' man done gone crazy!" She yelled. "A tellin me 'bout them uppity town women and they right sharp dressin. I'll show this crazy sinner what right sharp dressin be all about! I'll be dressin him like a

Thanksgiving bird and stuffin him with his own uppity feathers!"

Mule howled with laughter. He said to Jim, "Yo Mama ain't lost none of her fire with all them pounds she done got rid of!"

"The only pounds I'm gonna be gettin rid of is them what's stuffin yo shirt, *Jack-Ass* Johnson!"

Jim jumped to his feet. "Mama! Mama, Daddy's playin with you cause he's bustin to tell you that with the money Daddy got fer his jerky and with our wages workin fer the Vandeventers, we's goin shoppin tonight and buyin new outfits fer the whole family."

Chuckling at the memory, Jim smiled at his mother. She had shadowed Olga all morning, prissy as a schoolgirl in her new outfit and shoes. With eyes that sparkled with pride, Jim spied Mule across the lawn.

"Mama, I've got to help Tanner with the horses, you stay close to Miss Olga. She ain't slowed down all day."

After a few moments Olga announced, "I guess ve are ready, Jeem. I'll call Zhacques." She winked at Mama John. "Zhacques keep Zhan busy for us dis morning."

"Now Miss Olga, Honey, you tell me what you need fer me to do," Mama John said, following Olga into the house. Balloons, streamers and a banner that said, "Happy Birthday Jan," hung from the exposed beam ceiling. Poster sized enlargements of Jan's smiling face at various ages decorated the walls.

"Zhan was cute baby, wasn't he?" Olga giggled, passing a poster of baby Jan sitting in a washtub with a washcloth on his head.

334

"He's still a cute baby and there's more'n us what thinks so. I ain't never seen such preenin and powderin in all my born days. Them young ladies out there reminds me of a pack a hounds just waitin to be set off after a fox".

"Not all of dem," Olga replied. She glanced out the window to the magnolia-shaded lawn where Pick played on a quilt with Jasmine, Buddy, and Olivia.

"Does Peek speak of my Zhan?" Olga asked, straightening rows of sterling forks and spoons on the indoor buffet.

"Oh, yes 'um. Pick speaks of Mr. Jan. She says Mr. Jan is one fine young man. She goes on and on bout his hirin my Jim and my Mule. Yes Mam, Pick thinks the world of that boy."

With a look on her face that surprised Mama John, Olga asked, "Is that all she says about Zhan?"

Olga's pleading eyes wanted more than Mama John offered. Mama John had lived too long to miss that look. She knew what Olga was asking. The notion sent shock waves through the old woman.

"Miss Olga, pardon dis ol' black woman's askin, but why is you concernin yo'self with Pick's thinking on Mr. Jan?"

"You do not know?" Olga asked with innocent eyes.

"I reckon I don't." Mama John's eyes looked troubled.

"My Zhan is in love vis your Peek."

Mama John knit her brows. Swinging her head side to side, she blinked, widening her eyes above the soft flesh of her plump cheeks. She would do anything for Olga who ranked right up there with the saints in Mama John's eyes. But Olga's words had come as a staggering blow.

335

"Cain't be, Miss Olga! It cain't be! My Pick don't know nothin 'bout easy livin 'mong fancy folk. She's only just learnin to read and she gots a fambly."

"Mr. Jan, he's getting hisself a college education, he knows easy livin and he belongs 'mongst the rich folks. He ain't ready to be no daddy and Pick cain't be no other than mother to them younguns."

Sorrow welled in her eyes with Mama John's cries. "No, Miss Olga! Jan cain't be lovin my Pick. Her home is Widows Hollow. Mr. Jan don't want no holler fer his home. He cain't be lovin my Pick--and hurtin her. Naaaaw, Naaaaw!"

Thunder-struck by Mama John's reaction, Olga turned to reassure the old woman. But Mama John was gone.

"I'm sorry Olga, we're a little late," Bennett said. He glanced from Olga to Suzanne who ran after Mama John.

"Oh, Bennett, Olga make big mistake. I ruin my Zhan's party."

"It can't be all that bad," Bennett said.

Tearfully, Olga told Bennett how Mama John had reacted to the news that Jan was in love with Pick.

Bennett sucked air between his teeth. "Whoa, that is some news!" He added, "I think I need a drink."

Olga shot him a look of dismay.

Bennett added quickly, "Not alcohol-- liquid, cold, wet, liquid."

Olga filled a cup with punch from a bowl on the buffet. After emptying the cup in a gulp, Bennett met Olga's troubled eyes.

"How do you feel about it, Olga? Does Pick fit in the plans that you and Klaus envisioned for Jan?"

"No, nod really," Olga said quietly. "Ve tink Zhan vill marry somebody like Margaret, or Victoria, someone who lives like Zhan, someone who likes horses, and has university education, maybe."

"Does Jan know how you feel?"

"Ve tell him but he does nod listen."

"Jan doesn't strike me as being impulsive or foolish," Bennett said, refilling his cup. "What does he say? Why has he chosen Pick?"

Olga gave Bennett a sheepish grin. "Zhan says that if Peek had money and university education, she vould be just like…me."

Bennett said with a grin "Can't argue with that."

"Zhan says Peek vill make good life partner, she is nod selfish, she is nod afraid to verk. He says he knows no other voman like her."

"So your boy is determined?"

Olga nodded.

"And if Pick were suddenly wealthy, had a horse ranch of her own, hired a tutor, went to college, dressed in those pricey duds you women wear?"

"Dat vuld be very different. Dey vuld have a lot in common."

"And Pick's brothers and sister? They're gonna be around for a long time. Money and education won't change that."

Olga smiled. "Ve have big house. Ve love children."

337

Bennett gave Olga a hug. "So how can we help? You want us to discourage your boy?"

Olga took Bennett's cup. She said with a sigh "You can try."

Overcome with a sudden urge to protect her from the world, Mama John ran to Pick. Pick was safe in Widows Hollow. She could live a contented life in Widows Hollow, but not here, not in Jan's world. Pick did not belong here.

Mama John and her family did not belong here. They were visitors, guests for the day. Mule and Jimbo were employees. The relationship ended there. Why couldn't Jan fall in love with one of those eyelash flutterers, one of his own kind?

Pick saw Mama John running toward her, breathless, with her kerchief flying. Pick scrambled to her feet. "Mama, what's wrong? Why are you crying?"

Mama John smoothed Pick's hair. "Nothin's wrong, child. Just this foolish old woman gettin the sentiments, seein all these young folks what's come to celebrate Mr. Jan's birthday."

Pick hurried after Jasmine who toddled off the quilt.

"She's getting faster," Suzanne said with a laugh.

"Hey Suzanne, where's Bennett?" Pick asked. She bent to capture Jazmine. She grabbed the baby and hauled her back to the quilt.

Suzanne dropped to the ground beside Pick. "He's probably raiding the refrigerator," she replied, laughing at Pick who whirled in circles, holding Jasmine like an airplane while the baby squealed with delight.

Mama John stared with sad eyes at the young people who milled about the pool.

"What's wrong, Mama John?" Suzanne followed Mama John's eyes to the fashionably dressed young people. Most were college students whose designer fashions were purchased with funds from bank accounts that ensured a life of luxury.

Mama John shook her head in misery. "Mr. Jan could have any one of 'em. He could walk right up and choose his self one of them pretty ladies what's got his same learnin and his same money."

She glanced at Pick. "But naaaw, it ain't one of them he's a wantin. He's wantin my baby, my Pick. Miss Olga herself done told me Mr. Jan's in love with Pick."

Suzanne darted her eyes to Pick who burst into laughter. "Mama..." Pick laughed so hard she was breathless.

"Mama...," she said, laughing louder, "I heered you tell Suzanne Jan's in love...with me." Pick rolled backward on the quilt, laughing so hard Jasmine toddled over to investigate.

"And so I did!" Mama John huffed.

"That's the funniest thing I ever heered." Tears streamed from Pick's eyes.

"Ain't no funny to it!" Mama John exclaimed with a scowl. "Miss Olga done tole me herself."

"She was just funnin ya, Mama. I ain't nothin but a old hound with a litter 'a pups and them up yonder's what folks call pedigreed."

"Jan's my friend, true enough, but he's got eyes fer Margaret. When he brung 'er up Stump's place, Stump said

Jan would be takin 'er fer his wife. Look at 'er. She's fancy dressed and's got university schoolin just like Jan."

"*That* Margaret, up there?" Mama John narrowed her eyes. "The one what ain't shut her mirror all mornin? Her eyes ought to be 'bout wore out, the way she's a flutterin 'em."

"And what about Pick?" Suzanne asked.

"My Pick's got herself some gumption. She ain't asked nobody to be doin fer her and them younguns. She ain't a worryin herself with fancy dressin and she's first a showin up when anothern's needin a hand. She ain't never fergittin the Good Lord nor her neighbors and truth's the only speakin she ever done."

A smile curled Suzanne's lips. "And Pick would be the same, whether she lived in a fancy house or in the hollow, wouldn't she?"

"Pick ain't never goin change," Mama John said, reaching to squeeze Pick's hand.

"But we are!" Willie said, red-faced and panting from playing chase. "Me 'n Buddy 'n Sissy and Jimmy Joe, we're gonna change and go to school and be all growed up some day."

"So are we," Lucy and Lottie said, swinging their arms, hand in hand.

"You younguns stay put and wipe yer faces. Miss Olga said Jacques and Jan are on their way and we need to come inside," Jimmy Joe announced, panting hard after herding the children to the quilt.

Suzanne smiled at the children. "You will be going to school and growing up some day." She shifted her eyes to Mama John.

"Ain't no matter," Mama John said. "Pick ain't in love with Mr. Jan nohow. Is you Honey?"

Pick plucked a blade of grass and stuck it in her mouth. She tried to ignore the taunts in her mind. *You'll never be Jan Vandeventer's wife; you'll never be anybody's wife.*

They refused to leave him alone. "Come on, Jan, we can't let these women beat us in water volleyball!"

Jan might as well have remained in the barn with Pick. His mind was there. He saw nothing but the tangle of her hair beneath Jim's massive hand.

The hours blurred as afternoon wore into evening. Water volleyball turned into waltzes, swimsuits into sundresses, music and voices growing louder.

Margaret smiled like the consummate winner in a game of musical chairs. When the music stopped, she was at his side.

Jan had surrendered in silence. Caught like a coon in a trap, he would have gladly chewed off his leg if doing so would guarantee his escape.

He smiled at Olga when she asked if he was having a good time. He smiled at hearing repetitions of the latest campus gossip. He smiled at the amateurs who predicted the season's Triple Crown contenders. He smiled at Margaret.

They had him at last—or so they believed.

But the reality was that Jan had escaped. He had pushed his auto pilot buttons and now performed simple robotics.

His head turned from side to side, his face smiled, his arms and legs moved forward, one in front of the other, nicely.

His friends' faces had long since lost all distinguishing traits. They had become clattering clones, each a remarkable likeness of the wind-up toys that Olga collected.

A lone gladiator, Jan had no shield and no weapons to aid him in his solitary battle. His heart screamed *Yes!* His family, his peers, *society*, screamed No!

Stalworth had had his hands on Pick, his mouth on hers, and Jan did not give a tinker's damn. She remained undiminished in his eyes.

And Stalworth. Jan wanted to scream aloud, "The son of a bitch assaulted Pick!" Somebody had to defend her. Jan felt it was his duty. But he could not. He was damned if he did and damned if he didn't.

Twain understood. He painted the dilemma in *Huckleberry Finn* where Huck wrestled with his conscience.

To confess Huck's sins, committed in order that he might aid his black friend, Jim, in unlawful escape, and in so confessing, endanger Jim, or live with the guilt of his deeds and with the assurance of Divine retribution for the non-confession, thereby assuring his friend's safety.

Huck chose his friend. And hell.

"Vengeance is mine!" *Thank God,* Jan breathed the words, *Thank God.*

But Pick *would* be his.

A cloud, floating past the moon, cast the stables in a silvery light. Jan watched with leaden eyes as the doors swung open. He saw Pick and his heart leaped.

Jim emerged leading an albino named Casper. Pick followed with a buckskin named Sandman. They tied the reins to the fence rail and returned for more horses.

With his eyes fixed on the stables, Jan's pulse pounded in synch with his racing heart.

"Jan. Jan, did you hear me?" Margaret insisted.

"Yes, yes I heard you," Jan replied, watching the stable.

"Well?"

"Well, what?" Jan huffed, irritated at the intrusion.

"They're bringing the horses out. It's time to go riding," she said, resting a possessive hand on his shoulder.

Jan rose gladly from the chair. Soon, he could be near Pick, if only for a moment.

Young people scurried to change into riding attire. Jan excused himself to hurry upstairs with Jacques following on his heels.

"I cannot wait for this nightmare to end. Mama means well, but I hope I never have another birthday party as long as I live," Jan vowed, heaving his tee shirt across the room in anger.

Looking through Jan's closet for a shirt, Jacques cut his eyes to Jan. "This may be none of my business, but I'm dying to know. Why has Pick camped out in the barn all day?"

Jan slapped Jacques on the back of his head as he reached past him for a shirt.

"She thinks she's out of place here. She's not ready for a coming out party."

Jacques buttoned the snaps on the shirt he borrowed. "Well buck up, Buddy. Maggie suffers from no such delusions. The girl has wedding bells in her ears, Daddy's money in her pocket, and nobody other than yourself hamstrung dead center of her cross-hairs."

"There are a few things in this world that Claude Olliphant's money can't buy," Jan said with a grunt as he pulled on his boots. "And I am one of them!"

Abandoning this conversation before their moods soured, Jan turned to Jacques. "So, which lucky lady has her noose around your neck tonight?" He asked as they took the stairs by twos.

"Jan, my man, this neck has no noose, these reins are loose," Jacques said with a laugh. "Besides, I think it'll be fun to tag along with you and Maggie."

Jan threw a playful jab at Jacques. "You have a very warped sense of fun."

"Margaret, he's so handsome in his riding clothes!" Loretta Vandergriff squeezed Margaret's wrist and gushed over Jan.

"I'd give my right arm to be on a horse with him," Melody Maschotte sighed.

Margaret favored Melody with a brief smile and a tilt of her chin that suggested that the very idea of Jan being with anyone other than herself was *impertinent.*

"Please let me ride with Jacques, please," Janie Bunker clasped her hands and looked at the sky as if in supplication.

The women giggled, anxious for the moonlight trail ride to begin.

Montana Yates rounded the corner from the back pasture with a group of friends. "I think I'm going to be sick!" She cried.

Her friends clutched their throats, mimicking Montana's repulsed expression.

"It was ghastly!" Montana's eyes watered--her shoulders lurched forward, her stomach heaved. She groped for the nearest shoulder. "That poor animal! I am going to be...sick!"

Young people scattered. They grabbed their stomachs and their mouths as Montana heaved.

Jan and Jacques laughed at their citified friends who assumed the two would ride horses dressed in shorts.

Arriving at the stables, Jan said to Tanner, "I'll take Rogue, give Jacques Starbuck." He looked inside the barn. There was no sign of Jim or Pick.

Jan boosted Margaret onto Rogue's back when the thought occurred to Jan thatTanner Pruitt had better things to do than saddle horses for kids.

Jan grabbed Tanner by the elbow. "Tanner, where's Jim?"

"Jim and Miss McKinley left, Sir, on J.J., your father insisted."

Jan frowned. "Left? Jim left my party?"

"Yes, Sir, they all did--all the people from the hollow," Tanner said, answering Jan's next question before Jan asked.

"Tanner, what's going on?" Jan pulled the man close to speak in confidence. He waved a dismissive hand at Margaret who called his name.

"What's wrong, Jan?" Jacques leaned from Starbuck's saddle to hear.

"They left with that pathetic creature!" Montana cried.

"What's she talking about?" Jan demanded.

"The mule," Tanner said, his face clouding. "The old mule showed up here, soaked in blood. Looked like something attacked him, chewed his legs up bad.

"I don't know how he got here in the shape he was in. We tried to load him in a van. No way. That mule was going home the same way he came. Miss McKinley and Jim were pretty torn up when they saw him, said he belongs to Mr. Simpson."

"That mule wouldn't let anybody near him but Miss McKinley. She got a lead on him and they're taking him home."

Jan clapped a hand on Tanner's back and met his eyes. "River?"

Tanner replied with a nod. "Jan, can I help?"

Jan shook his head. ""Put her on Dolly," he said and pointed to Margaret.

Tanner pulled Margaret, spluttering, from Rogue's back.

Jan grabbed Rogue's reins and swung into the saddle. He chucked his head at Jacques. "You coming?"

Jan yelled to Tanner, saying with a wave of his hand, "Make our apologies, tell everyone an emergency came up, and not to wait for us."

Jan glanced at Jacques, jerked the reins, and pivoted Rogue into a muscled pirouette of panting, pawing horseflesh.

Rogue's hooves struck the ground and bounced like sparks from a blacksmith's anvil as horse and rider disappeared into the night.

Leaning low on Starbuck's neck, Jacques flicked the reins and whistled as he pounded across the lawn after Jan.

Jan's heart thundered as he gave the stallion full rein. He drove the animal at frenzied speed out of the city and to the river that wound into the dark wilderness of Titus County.

Wild animal. It had to be a wild animal of some sort. Jan talked to himself, thinking that a wild animal had attacked Buster.

The woods were full of marauding wildlife. This explained Buster's injuries, but it did not explain why the mule showed up at the Vandeventer's alone.

Where was Stump?

"Stop, Jimbo, stop!" Pick cried, feeling resistance to the rope tied around her wrist. She shoved against Jimbo's back to push herself off the horse.

"Jimbo, he can't go on. He can't git up!" Pick cried.

"Buster. Buster…. It's all right, boy." Pick knelt beside the mule, stroking him, speaking softly. "You rest, Buster. We'll get you some help. You shouldn't 'a tried it, boy. We'll get ya home, Buster, don't you worry, we'll get ya home."

Tears splashed her cheeks. "He ain't gonna make it, Jimbo. We shudda got him in that truck."

"But, Pick, we tried," Jimbo said, close to tears himself.

Buster flailed. He struggled, pushing against the ground with legs that looked like patches of bloody flesh dangling from raw bone. He tried to stand, wobbled weakly, and fell to the ground where he lay panting, his sides heaving, wild-eyed with pain.

Helpless, Pick and Jimbo watched, certain there were tears in the old mule's eyes, but he refused to give up.

"Jimbo, we've got to..." Pick turned to the sound of pounding hooves, and Jan and Jacques racing to them, closing the distance at a full gallop.

Jan saw Pick and Jim kneeling beside the mule in the moonlight, and saw Buster struggle to stand.

Jan reined Rogue to a stop, dropped the reins, and jumped to the ground.

Jan knelt beside Pick, shouldering himself between her and the suffering animal. Buster panted in short, shallow breaths.

"Jacques, bring Rogue up here!" Jan shouted. "Unsaddle him, get him on his knees."

Jim and Jacques unsaddled the big stallion and coaxed him to his knees. "Now, help me lift Buster across his back."

Together, the three men pulled Buster's front legs and chest up and over the kneeling horse. Jan coaxed Rogue to his feet and carefully tied the mule across the horse. "We'll have to take it slow. Buster's in bad shape," he said, patting Buster as he spoke.

Jim swung into J.J.'s saddle and reached a hand to Pick.

Jacques centered his foot in Starbuck's stirrup when he felt a light pressure on his shoulder. Turning, he met Jan's eyes. "You ride with Jim. Pick's riding with me."

Jan climbed in Starbuck's saddle, braced his legs in the stirrups, and reached a hand to Pick. With one powerful jerk, Jan pulled Pick resolutely into his arms.

Comforted at last by the feel of her body against his and the beat of her heart against his, Jan vowed in silence, *Nobody, nothing, will ever again keep her from my side!* This endless day had been unbearable because a wall had separated her from him. Never again. As soon as they returned Buster safely home, Jan would tell her.

He locked his muscled arms around Pick's waist. He did not feel tongue-tied now and would never again. Life with Pick was going to be interesting. There would be obstacles, many obstacles--but they would manage, he was certain.

Jan clucked to the horse, urging Starbuck slowly forward.

Buster tolerated most of the ride with little protest. As the riders neared the highest rise in Titus County, the mule struggled against his bonds. Buster thrashed and jerked violently against the rope that secured him. He brayed pitifully as the horses drew near to Old Gum Tree.

"Now Lucy and Lottie, Me and yer Pa got to git ourselves on up to Stump's place and see what that mule of his has done got into. Stump's gonna have enough on his mind a'ready.

He ain't gonna need no rowdy children pesterin 'im. You keep a close eye on my babies, you hear?"

"Miss Suzanne and Mr. Ben goin with us to see can they help that poor ol' mule. We'll be down directly." Mama John said.

Mule took Mama John's hand in the crook of his arm and headed for Stump's place.

Suzanne smiled at the pair. She and Bennett were very fond of them.

"Dat ol' mule gonna make it, ya reckon?" Mule asked of Bennett.

Bennett shook his head. "I'm not sure, Mule. It looked like something powerful got a hold of him. I don't see how he walked at all, much less all the way to Jan's."

"Buster's always been just as stubborn as Stump," Mule said, grinning.

"And that's sayin some for stubborn." Mama John added with a laugh.

With Stump's cabin in sight, Pick feared Buster would further injure himself-- he struggled with such violence to be free.

Dismounting close to the cabin, Jim and Jacques coaxed Rogue to his knees. Jan quickly untied the mule. Buster wobbled for a moment and fell to the ground. Struggling to stand, he brayed pitifully, his cries desperate and urgent.

Mama John heard the mule and let out a shriek. Suzanne and Bennett exchanged solemn glances. They picked up their pace to keep up with Mama John and Mule.

Feeling uneasy, Pick looked across the moonlit grounds. Something unfamiliar and unwelcome lay heavy in the trees, darkening the shadows, silencing the night music of the mountains.

Pick patted Buster as panic overwhelmed her. She broke into a terrified sprint, charging the cabin door, crashing into it with her shoulder, shoving it open.

Chaos met Pick's fears. In the moonlight, she could see that someone had invaded the cabin. Stump's table and chairs were overturned. His supper dishes lay scattered over the floor. His lamp lay crumpled in pieces of glass in a puddle of coal oil and scattered papers.

Pick reached with trembling hands to retrieve and upright the lamp. Her body quaked as she fumbled along the window ledge for matches. She lit the lamp and lifted it above her head as Jan and Jacques entered the cabin. The flickering light swelled and grew brighter—then crashed from Pick's hand.

Jacques stumbled and grabbed for the lamp, sending Jan sprawling into Pick who screamed an anguished, mournful scream that tore through the heart of Widows Hollow.

It echoed across Old Gum Tree and into the darkening shadows of the trembling trees that moaned like grieving humans at the base of the Big Black Mountain.

"Oh! Sweet Jesus!" Mama John cried as Mule pulled her along.

Racing through the door, Suzanne and Bennett found Pick on the cluttered cabin floor. With her head bent, wailing pitifully, Pick rocked the lifeless form of her beloved friend, Stump, in her arms.

Jan was at her side, absently stroking her hair.

Mama John fell to her knees and buried her face against the still, cold chest of her dear friend and neighbor.

Silent tears splashed off Mule's quivering lips. He sobbed in stutters and circled his wife's grieving form with his arms.

Bennett righted the table and chairs and searched the cabin for clues to the identity of the intruders. He stacked oil soaked papers on the table, replaced pens and pencils in the empty Mason jar.

Bennett's subconscious mind joined in the search, busying itself cataloguing and analyzing while it waited for Bennett's conscious mind to catch up.

His impatient brain forced Bennett's hand to drop a pen. Bennett bent to pick up the pen. He dropped his jaw and stared. With caution, he approached a huge hole in the cabin wall. The jagged hole tore through logs that caved inward.

Bennett lit a lamp on Stump's bedside table. He ran his hand over the broken logs, gathering hair and splintered pieces of what appeared to be rock. Staring at the evidence in his hand, Bennett walked to the cabin door and looked outside. "Nooo! Nooo! It can't be!" Bennett leaned his head against the doorframe and cried.

"What's wrong? What is it, Ben?" Suzanne cried.

Bennett slowly opened his hand.

"What does that mean? I don't understand."

Bennett's voice broke with his sobs. "His mule, it was his mule...trying- to- get- to- him."

"Bennett, No! No!" Suzanne cried and clapped a hand over her mouth. She exchanged mute stares with Bennett as they wept together for the brave little mule that sacrificed himself trying to reach his dying master.

Bennett wiped his eyes. "Hurry, maybe we can save him."

Without lifting her head, Pick said in a whisper as they passed, "Will you cover 'im fer me, please?"

Suzanne pulled a quilt from a wardrobe. Bennett stooped with it to cover Stump's body.

Pick shook her head. She raised her eyes to Bennett's and whispered through her tears. "Not Stump. Buster."

Chapter Thirty-Six

"Lord, grant us your wisdom in this dark hour. Strengthen us and go with us as we do battle with the foe that Satan has unloosed in our midst. In Jesus' name, we ask it. Amen."

Brother Lester closed the Sunday morning meeting with his prayer. The church glistened in the sunshine in its coat of new white paint. The cemetery outside boasted fresh cut green grass and roses.

The church bell sounded this morning as it had in recent weeks, to a full house. Though fervent and fiery, Brother Lester's sermons did not ignite the common flame that burned in the souls of the anxious congregation.

It was not a sermon at all that had gathered the wanderers back into the fold. It was a stranger, one of the outsiders who came uninvited to Widows Hollow. One whose presence was preceded with pinpricks of apprehension and mute mountain Morse tapped in heartbeats, house to house, wary eye to wary eye, long before his person arrived.

Brother Lester welcomed the stranger and thanked him for the envelope he delivered. He waved to him from his porch with a smile and Christian good will as the stranger pulled away in his sleek black Mercedes.

Brother Lester had opened the envelope and had read the letter with enthusiasm. Concerned, he continued reading with knit brows and narrowed eyes.

He read it again, replacing concern with disbelief. He read it a third time, wildly waved the letter in the air and called his wife and mother-in -law to witness that which a lone soul could not bear.

The church bell ringing in the middle of the week had alarmed them. Neighbors in the hollow and scattered folks who lived a ways off had responded.

They had come running with buckets and shovels, prepared to battle flames that threatened homes and hearths. Fighting fire would have been easier.

Brother Lester had read the document aloud, word for word, in all its cumbersome judicial jargon. His congregation's blank faces suggested they needed a summary so he had summarized:

"Friends, this here paper says that if ye have kin buried in yon cemetery, ye got to git down to the court house, claim 'em as yer own, and find another restin place fer 'em. The ground they's restin in now is bein' purchased fer other uses."

"And that ain't the worst of it. We all got ninety days from this very day to find ourselves other places to be livin 'cause this land we live on is also bein purchased fer other uses."

"We kin keep the church house if we've a mind, but we got to find another place to keep it 'cause this ground we're meetin on today has also been purchased fer other uses."

"These houses what we're livin in is gonna be shoved over. This paper come from the law at the courthouse and we're obliged to be a' doin what it says."

The Titus County Eviction Notice continued to be the reason Brother Lester spoke to a capacity crowd each Sunday. His *Amen* today had barely passed his lips before the roar of excited voices once again filled the little church.

"Ain't there no way to stop this Stalworth fella from shovin over our homes and turnin Widows Hollow into a playground fer rich folks?" Mose Tate asked, looking to Bennett with hopeful eyes.

"Where are we supposed to go? This is the only home we know!" Levi Thompson shouted in anger.

Bennett stood. "Folks, Suzanne and I are doing all we can. We have attorneys looking into this so-called purchase, to see if we can find a way to stop it. The Vandeventers tried to counter the purchase offer. The buyers refused. They said the agreement was non-negotiable."

Jan listened as Mama John addressed a haggard knot of neighbors. "I knowed when all them fancy cars paraded through this holler up to Stump's place fer his buryin that the devil was done up to mischief. What business the mayor and the governor hisself got with Stump?"

Jacques gave Mama John his full attention.

He's doing that a lot lately. Jan noticed.

What was going on?

Chapter Thirty-Seven

Three Weeks Earlier

Stephen Stalworth's morning had not gotten off to a good start.

Maggie had become impossible. Her tantrums were getting on his frayed nerves. He smacked the rolled up Ashford Sentinel against his palm, resolving to fire her—as soon as he had his coffee.

"Maggie! Is it too much to ask to have a cup of coffee THIS morning?"

Maggie gritted her teeth. She had taken all she could take. The quiet lunches she prepared for Victoria and Stephen became business luncheons for company executives with little or no notice. And Stephen did not know the words "Thank You."

The only tone Stephen used was that of a terrorist addressing his subordinates. She had had enough. *I will take him this last cup of coffee and exit this place—forever.*

Maggie jutted her chin, placed his coffee on the table beside the newspaper Stephen read, and straightened her shoulders to deliver some news of her own.

"Mr. Stal..."

Stephen sprang from his chair, grabbed her, and swung her in the air. "Maggie, my mean little mistress of the manor, you need a day off. Take two. I insist. I've treated you abominably lately. Let me make it up to you. You deserve a raise, consider it done."

"Just do me this one little favor." Stephen pulled a rose from an arrangement on the table.

"Take this to my sister and ask her to come down. Do that for me, Darling, then be off to do anything you like." Stephen's smile was broad, his eyes bright.

Maggie was speechless. *Two days off and a raise?* Maybe she could stay a few more days...

Victoria flew down the stairs.

"Today is the first day of the best of our lives," Stephen said with a grin. "It is ours Victoria, it is ours!"

"Stephen, whatever are you...?" Victoria halted, mid-sentence. Stephen waved the newspaper before her.

"There was never any question that it would be ours— but now; it will be ours for a song." Stephen ran imaginary scales with his fingers then bowed as though answering a curtain call.

Victoria scanned the paper. She saw nothing to prompt her brother to this kind of childishness. Her questioning eyes brought Stephen to her side. He made circles in the air with his pointer finger before nose-diving it midway of the obituaries.

Victoria read the paragraph aloud, exclaiming, "Why, why that's the old hermit who owns all that glorious land!"

"Precisely my dear sister, precisely."

"Oh Stephen, it is ours! Our dream is coming true!"

Stephen gloated. "Indeed! Get Reid on the phone, shall we? Gentlemen, start your bull dozers!"

Reid Garrison had dreaded this day. He knew he would get the call as soon as Stalworth learned of Samuel Simpson's fatal heart attack.

The strings that ran from Stalworth's bloated bank account to key political puppets and civic chameleons stretched like a detonator wire across city, county, and state lines.

One forgotten favor, one rogue resister could ignite headlines powerful enough to blow the elected pillars of the community to pea gravel.

"Stephen, there are laws and ordinances involved here. For starters, there is the fifty-ninth minute of the eleventh hour to consider. Anyone who has or might have claim to that property can wait right up to the last second to claim it."

"All that you can legally do to secure title to that land is to wait for the past due tax notice to be posted and then pay the delinquent taxes. You will then own no more than the tax lien itself."

"There's also the little matter of the auction on the court house steps. You will have the opportunity to bid against others who share your interest in this property. Samuel Simpson's intestate real estate will be disposed of properly, according to the dictates of the Commonwealth of Kentucky; there's nothing you or anybody else can do about it."

Garrison waited, bracing himself for another Stalworth tantrum. Stalworth did not take the word *no* very well. Ever.

Stalworth laced his fingers beneath his chin. "Reid, why don't you run by Jacoby's and see if he's made any progress on those plans?"

That was it? Reid, run by and check on plans? Garrison was not buying it. This was too simple and too unlike Stephen Stalworth. Reid was getting off light. Too light. And it bothered him all the way out the door.

"Maggie!" Stephen screamed before he remembered that he had given her two days off.

"Damn!" He swore and pushed himself from the sofa to get the address book. He flipped a couple of pages, pulled the phone closer, and dialed a number.

"Give me Clark McDonald. Clark? Stephen Stalworth. I need a favor, friend."

Jan could not concentrate. He had heard nothing prior to Professor Ison's, "We will continue our discussion tomorrow, ladies and gentlemen."

Thank God. Jan raced to his car. Jacques had not been in class today. He had missed two days last week, too, so Jan decided to pay him a visit.

Jacques' mother showed him in.

Jan hurried up the stairs to Jacques' bedroom, knocked, and pushed open the door. Stacks of newspapers cluttered the room. Jacques had one spread open before him.

"You have a paper route? That's why you're missing class?" Jan shook his head.

"Ah, English assignment," Jacques said as he folded the paper that he had been reading.

"English? We're in the same class. We don't have any assignment that requires newspapers from all over Kentucky," Jan said, noting papers from distant counties. "You've missed a lot of school lately and you seem to know everything that's going on in Widows Hollow before the people who live there. It's making me nuts! What's going on Jacques?"

Jacques shoved a stack of papers aside. "Come on, let's get a burger. I need a change of scenery."

Jacques led the way down the stairs, saying with a laugh, "I'll drive, you relax."

As they approached his gleaming black Corvette, Jacques crouched to peer in the side mirror. "Look out ladies, here we come," he said with a grin.

"You are so vain!" Jan said with a laugh. He pulled open the door and pounded his fist on the roof. Glaring at Jacques, he scooped an armful of newspapers from the seat.

"You're up to something, friend. You cancelled a date last Friday and Daylon saw you at the mayor's office. You showed up an hour late for the game Saturday. Why all the mystery? What's going on?"

Jacques took the papers from Jan and tossed them in the trunk.

Jan climbed in the two seater, crossed his arms, and demanded, "Well?"

Jacques turned the key, pushed the accelerator, and shot Jan a look that Jan did not recognize. "I'd tell you Jan, if I could, but trust me—I can't."

"You're not getting married, are you?" Jan asked, slumping in the seat.

"Not without telling you, Buddy," Jacques replied with a grin.

Jan was not impressed. Jacques' answer did nothing to quell Jan's suspicions.

"Dwayne! Dwayne!" Stalworth yelled. "Bring the car around we're going for a little ride."

As the limousine crept through Widows Hollow, Victoria whispered. "Stephen, it's ghastly."

"Yes, it is, isn't it?" He said, patting her hand. "Soon, this nightmare will be nothing more than a bad memory.

"Look at them, peeping out their windows like cockroaches. I would love to have seen their faces when their little bumpkin of a preacher read them their eviction notices." He waved his hand behind the tinted window. "Bye bye, blight."

"I can still see that demented derelict threatening me. The gall of that old miser was monumental."

"Sir, I believe we will have to walk from here," Dwayne said and turned to face the Stalworths.

"Our pleasure," Stephen replied.

Victoria pressed close to her brother who picked his way carefully up the steep rise. "Feast your eyes, Tory. You are walking on the future site of Stalworth Sterlings."

A sudden gust of wind scattered dried leaves in their path. Victoria batted at the leaves. "Stephen, this place gives me the creeps."

Stephen laughed a brief laugh. A bent figure inside the cemetery fence rose. Pick turned and stared at the Stalworths from the gravesite.

Dwayne whipped his hat from his head and stuffed it under his arm.

Stephen glared his disapproval at Dwayne's show of respect.

"Miss McKinley, I believe?"

Stalworth's sneer did not come off with quite the edge he had intended. His heart thumped his rib cage. Why didn't she scream and shout accusations at him? Why didn't she run? Why hadn't she served him papers, called him to court to answer for his sins against her? What was she waiting for, public showdown?

Stephen glanced at Victoria. Her smile indicated that she did not detect anything amiss. It also bolstered his arrogance.

"How crude of us, we are interrupting your prayers."

Pick remained silent for a moment. Then, she walked boldly toward him as if an invisible hand pushed her forward.

Stephen had not anticipated this. What was she doing? Had the girl gone mad?

Pick kept coming, closer, and closer. She could not have stopped if she wanted to. After a moment she blurted, "God don't mind."

"Wh... What?" Stalworth's tongue felt thick in his mouth.

Close enough to touch him Pick stared at Stalworth. "God don't mind if you interrupt my prayers. Some of 'em are for you."

Stalworth stumbled backward, tongue-tied. He felt sick to his stomach, feared that he might heave any minute. In a panic, he clutched for Victoria. His arms would not move. Immobilized, he cried, "Stop her, she's a witch!"

No sound escaped his throat. He panicked. Pick exercised some kind of power over him that he could not defend against.

"Stephen?" Victoria called his name. "Stephen..."

"What? What!" He growled.

Victoria did not respond.

"Well?" Stephen demanded in anger.

"Well what?" Victoria spluttered.

"Why do you keep calling my name?" Stephen screamed.

"I never called your name!" Victoria exclaimed. Her eyes grew wide and fearful.

Stephen spun to face Pick and very nearly collided with her. Frightened and disoriented, he tripped over his own feet and fell.

Pick stood staring above his prostrate body. Her copper hair lifted and fell in the breeze.

Her face shimmered like a mirror in the bright rays that made her hair appear to flame.

Dwayne rushed to assist Stalworth. A glance from Pick stopped him in his tracks.

Reaching her hand to Stalworth, Pick's whole body seemed to flame.

The nightmare! The flaming fingers! It was her!

Stalworth cringed. "I'm sorry! Forgive me! I didn't mean it, I'm sorry!" He rolled to his knees with his face in the dirt and sobbed.

"He's having a breakdown!" Victoria cried. She scrambled to take Dwayne's outstretched hand

Stalworth wiped tears and dirt from his face. He felt embarrassed and tongue-tied. Stalling, he brushed dirt from his pants. He felt that he had to say something. At last, he lifted his eyes to her-- but Pick was gone.

Another sudden gust whipped up so violently that it rattled the heavy bell in the steeple. The bell responded with a loud, vibrating, *boooong!*

Dwayne shepherded Victoria and Stephen before him up the rise to Old Gum Tree.

When they reached the pinnacle, Stephen let go Victoria's hand. Thunderstruck, he stood and stared in disbelief.

Heavy equipment and trucks lined the far slope beyond and below Stump's cabin. Less than a thousand yards from the primitive place, a roaring bulldozer pushed mounds of dirt. The dozer appeared to be cutting a road from the back of the old cabin into the tangle of forest that stretched for miles before it disappeared into the lap of the Big Black Mountain.

Flatbeds stacked high with spiked wrought iron fence sections stood parked side by side. The sounds of machinery and power saws filled the air.

Stalworth doubled his fists. He ran to the bulldozer, planted himself in its path, and waved his hands. "Stop!"

The operator chugged the dozer to a halt.

"Who are you? What do you think you're doing? You're trespassing on private property! I order you to cease and leave this property! Immediately!" Stalworth blustered.

The big stubble faced operator climbed from the seat. He had a sunburned nose, a parched throat, and prickly heat that itched the back of his neck. He tugged off his hard hat, wiped his forehead on his grimy sleeve and glared at Stalworth.

"And just who might you be?"

"I'm Stephen Stalworth, owner of this property," Stalworth shouted.

"Well, Stephen," the big man spoke as though he addressed a child. "You're a liar! You're the one who's trespassing on private property. I suggest you take your delusions and your little wind up toy," he nodded at Dwayne in his starched uniform, "and get out of my way unless you're entertaining the notion of becoming road kill!"

"Who is your employer? I demand to know, who is your employer?" Stephen blustered, red-faced.

The burly man put his hands on his hips and grinned. He enjoyed toying with this puny little peacock. The man reached to the back of his neck, scratched at the itching heat, and waved to the graphics on the side of the bulldozer. Stalworth Enterprises.

"It's one of ours!" Stephen choked. "Who could...? Who?"

"What does this mean, Stephen?" Victoria asked, her voice incredulous.

The dozer operator laughed.

"We'll be back, with a court order!" Stalworth vowed.

The operator grinned. He shot his eyebrows higher. "Well, I'll be right here, too, with your bulldozer, Stephen!"

Suzanne, Bennett, Jan, and Jacques gathered in Mama John's yard with neighbors to celebrate Pick's seventeenth birthday. They bowed as Brother Lester asked the blessing on the meal that the people of Widows Hollow felt certain would be their last supper together.

Pick opened her gifts and thanked her friends. She tried hard to smile and to appear light-hearted. She smiled in gratitude when Suzanne addressed the crowd.

"As you know, like many of you, Pick is learning to read. She has practiced very hard and has advanced very quickly. In less than six months, she has completed a number of primary and intermediate workbooks on many subjects."

"If she continues at this pace, she'll be studying at middle school level in no time. Once she masters the high school subjects, the sky will be the limit for Pick, and Widows Hollow may have its first college student."

The crowd applauded with enthusiasm. Suzanne presented Pick with a Certificate of Outstanding Achievement from the Board of Education, Commonwealth of Kentucky, along with a stack of books.

Jan whistled and applauded loudly. "I knew she could do it!" He cried, grinning at Jacques.

"Hey, who's he?" Jacques speared Jan with his elbow and nodded in Pick's direction.

A tall, slender cowboy shoved a bouquet of flowers in Pick's hand and planted a kiss squarely on her lips.

Jan started for the stranger.

"Whoa there, boy! This is Pick's party," Jacques cried as he clamped a hand on Jan's arm. "Maybe your girl forgot to mention that she has a boyfriend."

"Levi Thompson! You ain't never gonna learn!" Pick yelled. She wiped her mouth and spit, shifted the flowers to her left hand, doubled her fist and landed a punch squarely on Levi's jaw.

"Whoa! Did you see that? Your girl served him a knuckle sandwich that about took his head off!" Obviously impressed with Pick, Jacques turned to Jan for Jan's reaction.

"Jan?"

Jan made his way through the milling guests to Pick. He took his new UK class ring from his finger and a gold chain from his neck. He threaded the chain through the ring, and locked the clasp as he approached Pick.

Before she could protest, Jan took Pick's hand, turned it palm up, and dropped his necklace in her palm.

Jan locked his eyes on Pick's eyes and spoke quickly. "I have to say this fast before I lose my nerve. I love you. I know you don't know me very well and I'm willing to wait until you do. I don't want to rush you into anything, but I'm asking for your promise."

"Promise me that you will let me be part of your life, no matter what happens here. I have another year of school, and then I plan to marry you and raise horses and kids."

I know you think that a relationship between us is impossible. Give me a chance to prove you're wrong.

That's all I ask. And...," he smiled a smile that sank his dimples deep, "I hope you don't slug me!"

Pick glanced from Jan to the crowd that watched in silence, and then fell into his arms as Jan pulled her close and kissed her squarely on the lips. At the same time, someone shoved Jan. Hard.

Jan staggered, stunned.

"Get on back to the city where you belong! Pick's my girl and she won't be needin this!" Levi Thompson snarled. He snatched Jan's necklace from Pick's hand.

Jacques plowed through the crowd with his fists doubled. "Hey! You don't shove my friend!"

"Come on, city boy, let me teach you a country lesson you ain't gonna fergit!" Levi threatened. He taunted Jacques with raised fists.

"Stop it!" Pick threw the flowers to the ground. "I ain't nobody's girl!" She shifted her eyes from Jan, who looked contrite, to Levi, who looked like he was ready to take Jacques' head off.

Overcome with her conflicting emotions, Pick covered her face and fled across the rut to her home.

She bumped the little table before she fell to her knees by her mother's bed. With covers knotted in both hands, Pick buried her face in the quilt and cried.

"Lord, I'm happy and sad and more skeered than I ever been. This holler's been my home all my life. They're wantin to take it from us, and we can't do nothin to stop 'em. Settle us with it, Lord. Let us know yer thinkin on it so's we kin do what we're needin to do."

"And Lord, you know that I love Jan with all my heart. I ain't fit to be his wife and even if I was, the yoke you speak of in the Good Book ain't right between us."

"He ain't needin fer nothin and I ain't got nothin 'cept a family to see to. He's got college schoolin and I'm learnin to read. I ain't wantin to hurt him, but the yoke ain't right and I don't see no way to make it right. Please show me what to do with it, Lord. I ain't got words to tell 'im. In Jesus' name. Amen."

An ominous, eerie sound split through the cabin walls before Pick got to her feet. She cried out in fright and covered her ears with her hands. The sound was like nothing she had ever heard. A sickening light filled the cabin. Pick was terrified. Something horrible was in the hollow and she was alone with it.

"Come with me, Lord!" She cried.

Pick raced from the cabin, looking for the light. It seemed to be coming from Old Gum Tree. With her heart pounding, Pick ran toward the light and the noise.

She raced ahead of the footsteps and voices that followed as she stumbled up the hill.

"No!" She screamed. "No! No! Noooo!" She screamed again—then collapsed.

Anxious, frightened neighbors clambered up the hill. They raised their voices in despair. Their beautiful little church with its proud coat of new paint and newly restored bell no longer stood where it had been since time forgotten.

Its empty windows stared, silent, and forlorn from the elevated platform of a flatbed truck.

The red lights mounted on top of the cab spun in sporadic revolutions, cloaking the hollow in its hells-afire neon. The eerie, high-pitched wail screeched from the truck itself.

Pick remembered hearing nothing but Mama John's cry. "Oh, Jesus

Lord, they're takin our church house!"

Chapter Thirty-Eight

"Excuse me, Professor. There's an emergency. I need Jan Vandeventer."

Professor Ison peered over the rims of his glasses at the panting figure that interrupted his lecture.

"Jacques, what's going on?" Jan did not welcome the curious stares that Jacques' announcement invited.

"Come on, Jan, we have to go!"

"Go where?" Jan made no move to close his book or to gather his notebooks.

"I'll explain later, we have to go now!" Jacques cried as he leaned on Jan's desk to catch his breath.

"Jacques, I'm not going anywhere until you tell me what's going on!"

Jan had become withdrawn and moody since Pick's declaration, "I ain't nobody's girl!" He seemed to have lost interest in everything. He raised empty eyes to Jacques and said nothing.

Annoyed, Jacques filled his lungs and repeated. "Are you coming?"

Jan hesitated.

Jacques leaned across the desk, his face determined. "Do you love Pick McKinley or not?"

"What's she got to do with this?"

"Everything!" Jacques shoved a book across the desk at Jan.

Jan wasted no time. He gathered his books and raced from the lecture hall with Jacques. "Where are we going?"

Jacques ran so fast, he did not hear Jan's question. Jacques sprinted across the campus to the parking lot, abruptly reversed himself, and darted to a pay phone.

"Hello?" Jacques gulped air. "Could I speak with Dr. Gardner?" After a short silence, he insisted, "This is an emergency. Tell him I'm Jacques Champeaux."

"Hello, Dr. Gardner, please, I have no time to explain. Bring Suzanne and meet me on the Titus County Courthouse steps at eleven o'clock."

"Jacques, I have patients."

"Please, Dr. Gardner, I need both of you there at eleven."

"I'll try, Jacques."

Jacques slammed the receiver in its cradle and sprinted off again with Jan on his heels.

"What are you driving?" Jacques yelled, approaching the parking lot.

"My Jeep, why?"

"We have to pick up Mama John and Pick. You're driving."

Asking no further questions, Jan drove like a madman, weaving in and out of the early morning traffic.

Startled and somewhat frightened by Jacques' urgent request, Pick and Mama John left the children with neighbors and piled in the Jeep.

The courthouse clock said ten minutes to eleven. The parking lot was full, the closest available space blocks away.

"Park in the "No Parking" zone, I'll pay the ticket," Jacques insisted.

Jan nosed into a space as Jacques threw open the door. "Run!"

At the top of the courthouse steps, Stephen Stalworth flashed dazzling smiles at every acquaintance that passed by. Stephen looked resplendent in his Armani suit of navy blue pin stripes, with a powder blue shirt and matching silk tie.

At his side, Victoria waved to those same acquantainces. Her golden tresses fell across the shoulders of her powder blue silk Chanel suit.

Stephen Stalworth spotted Pick, Jan and Jacques and his smile stretched wider.

A court clerk approached the microphone. He raised his hand for silence, read from a document, and asked if there were any questions.

Jacques searched faces in the crowd as though he sought someone that he could not find. He shaded his eyes, looked down the street, and broke into a grin when he spotted a long, black limo that rounded the corner.

The limo, with its flags of state flying, rolled silently to the courthouse. As the car pulled alongside the curb, a roar went up from the excited citizens.

Jacques cut his eyes to the top of the steps where both Stalworths and the court clerk seemed to pale.

The crowd parted in noisy anticipation, making way for the Governor of the Commonwealth of Kentucky and for the Mayor of the City of Ashford.

The officials made their way quickly to the top of the steps where they conferred with the court clerk. Peering into the crowd, the governor crooked a finger at Jacques. Jacques hurried up the steps and presented an envelope to the governor.

The governor opened the envelope and read in silence before he turned to address the crowd.

"I'm sorry, folks, if any of you have been inconvenienced today by the legal notice of a land auction that was to be conducted here this morning."

"The county has cancelled the auction due to a recent discovery concerning the land in question. Mr. Samuel Simpson did not die intestate, as we believed. He did, in fact, leave a will."

"That's impossible! That old hermit had no heirs!" Stalworth exclaimed.

As the governor unfolded a lengthy legal document and read page after page into the microphone, Jan and Jacques exchanged startled glances. Stump Simpson's wealth had been far greater than either of them had imagined.

The governor continued to the last page. "And in summation, the estate of Samuel Llewellyn Simpson is hereby granted and bequeathed in its entirety as herein specified in the foregoing, to Ross Mueller McKinley."

The governor smiled. The mayor smiled. Jacques Champeaux did not smile. He looked stricken. He darted his eyes from the governor, to the mayor, to Pick.

With a glance at Jacques, who looked as though he had been struck by lightning or some similar catastrophe, the governor's smile vanished.

He beckoned Jacques closer. After a short conference, the governor's face fell, his eyes pinched like one who had forgotten his reading glasses, yet attempted to read from a tele-prompter.

"I don't know, Sir. I followed Mr. Simpson's instructions to the letter."

"I watched the papers, kept an eye on events in the hollow and brought the people here today that he instructed me to bring. But something is wrong, something is terribly wrong!" Jacques exclaimed.

Having watched and listened to the proceedings with interest, Mama John noted Jacques', the governor's and the mayor's looks of confusion.

All of a sudden, she bounced her bulk in the air with a shout. "Halleleujah! Halleleujah Jesus!" Her voice boomed. "That ain't no Ross Mueller Stump be talking 'bout! No sir! Rosemillion! That's who Stump be talkin 'bout!"

Pick's face turned crimson. Perhaps the excitement of being so close to the mayor and the governor was too much for Mama John. She had taken leave of her senses.

Pick reached for the dear old woman and hugged her tight. She glanced about, frightened for Mama John.

"Mama, there ain't no Rosemillion for real. Our Mama made her up. Rosemillion's our fairy tale what made Mama happy."

"Oh, Chile..." Pricked to her heart, the old woman's eyes filled with pity. Pick did not know. This blessed child of Isabel and Joseph McKinley truly did not know that she was the child whose loving smile and angelic singing had turned darkness into light, bleakness into rainbows and dried, dead stubble into roses.

She had no idea that sunshine, happiness, and music had come to Widows Hollow--with her birth.

Mama John stared into Pick's green eyes. She said tearfully, "The first time I put you in yo sweet Mama's arms, she hugged you tight, kissin yo face and carryin on."

"I won't never fergit my sweet Isabel's words. "This youngun right here's better'n a million roses," then she breathed yo name, "Rosemillion.""

"That baby looked at me and said, "If I could have my ruthers of all the roses in all the world, this 'un right here would be my Pick," and we been callin you that ever since."

After hearing Mama John's words to Pick, Jan raced up the steps to Jacques.

Stalworth growled to Victoria. "You wait here. I'll call Garrison. If this so called "Ross Mueller" can't be found, that will is void!"

Jacques repeated Mama John's story to the governor. The governor conferred with the court clerk. The clerk disappeared into the courthouse and returned shortly with a hand scribbled note. The governor, the mayor, the court clerk, and Jacques nodded and pointed at the words on the note.

The governor asked Jacques a question.

Jacques looked perplexed. Confused, he turned to Jan, who, in turn, turned to Mama John.

Jacques crooked a finger, beckoning Mama John to join them.

"I ain't goin up there with the mayor and the gub'ner," Mama John cried, balking at the idea.

"You can do it, Mama John," Bennett urged.

"They're people just like us, go on up there," Suzanne encouraged.

"You kin do it fer Stump," Pick said.

Mama John hesitated. She smoothed her hair and nervously mounted the steps.

"Miss Mama John, do you know of any official record of the birth of this "Rosemillion" who is also known to you as "Pick?""

Mama John trembled. She was talking to the Governor. Her heart pounded like a hammer on a railroad spike as she tried to recall the details of Pick's birth.

She had delivered Pick while Joseph, Stump, and Brother Lester waited on the porch. Brother Lester had fallen a week earlier and had broken his arm while helping to repair the O'Connor's leaking roof.

Mama John appeared lost deep in thought when she abruptly shouted, "I does!" "I surely does!"

Jacques gently rubbed her shoulders. "Where, Mama, where is it?"

"It's in the ol' Bible in the church house." Her voice rose to hysterics. "Our church house what's done gone...."

Jacques grinned from ear to ear. Hugging Mama John, he exclaimed happily, "Somebody would have called me if that flatbed with the church on board had moved one inch. It's not gone, Mama!"

Following another brief conference, the governor lifted his head to address the milling crowd. "This meeting will reconvene in one hour at the place known to many of you as "Old Gum Tree."

Racing with Jacques, Pick, and company, Jan prayed that they would beat the tow truck back to the Jeep. He had parked in a No Parking Zone as it had been the only available space. Agitated and impatient, Victoria paced, waiting for Stephen to return.

An hour later, the governor's limousine wound through the ruts and ditches of Widows Hollow. Curious neighbors ran from their homes, following the car to the highest rise in Titus County.

Leaving the cars parked below, the occupants scrambled up the steep hill to Stump's place with the court clerk and the mayor assisting the governor.

"It's just beyond the cabin," Jacques said. He pointed to the little church that sat on the flatbed.

The Stalworths, Dwayne, and Reid Garrison topped the hill, red-faced and panting.

The bulldozer belched black smoke as it smoothed a wide stretch of red clay soil. Construction workers guided a crane as it placed wrought iron fence sections on the distant perimeter. The stubble faced dozer operator spotted Jacques and switched off his noisy machine. He jumped from the seat, whisked his hard hat from his head, and said with a nod to Jacques, "Mr. Champeaux."

"Please ask your crew to take a break, we won't be long," Jacques instructed the man.

The operator placed two fingers in his mouth, whistled an ear-splitting whistle, and waved the other workers to a shady area.

Stalworth plucked burrs from his pants leg. "Somebody better tell me what's going on here, and they better tell me quick!"

The governor led the way to the flatbed. He stopped a few feet from it and lifted his bushy brows to Mama John.

"It be right there on that shelf 'neath the pulpit, yer Gub'nership, Sir." Mama John smiled and dipped in a half curtsy.

The governor watched the court clerk with interest as the clerk scrambled onto the flatbed and disappeared inside the church. He broke into a wide smile when the clerk returned, waving a thick, well-worn Bible.

The governor took the Bible and thumbed through its yellowing pages to a page marked "Births." He scanned page after page of names, all neatly penned in Brother Lester's handwriting.

The governor turned a final page, read the names, marked a line with his pointer finger, and beckoned to the clerk.

The clerk stepped closer and read the line. He nodded in agreement with the governor who raised his hand to quiet the waiting crowd.

"The court wishes, at this time, to enter a correction for the record, to the instrument known as the Last Will and Testament of Samuel Llewellyn Simpson. The name as before read and understood, Ross Mueller McKinley, shall be struck from the document and replaced with the correct name, Rosemillion McKinley."

"Objection!" Reid Garrison barked. "Sir, how do we know that the name penned by Mr. Simpson in his will is one and the same as that of this so-called, "Rosemillion" as reflected in this church birth record?

The governor, the mayor, and the court clerk exchanged glances. They huddled together, pointing and nodding once again.

"Mr. Ah...," The governor addressed the Stalworth's attorney.

"Garrison, Sir, Reid Garrison."

"Mr. Garrison, it is the opinion of the Clerk of the Court and the Mayor of Ashford and myself, representing the State of Kentucky, that the two names as recorded in two separate documents are indeed one and the same."

"Those who question this decision please come forward and examine the documents."

Clutching Victoria's arm, Stalworth approached the clerk who placed Stump's handwritten will beside the birth record in the Bible. He pointed to the words "Born July 24, 1943 in Widows Hollow, Titus County, Kentucky to James Joseph and Isabel McKinley, daughter, Rosemillion McKinley."

Stalworth's mood blackened as he read the name on both documents. The two names were identical. No two individuals had recorded the name, "Rosemillion."

A single hand had penned the name in both documents, the hand of Samuel Llewellyn, "Stump" Simpson.

"Your attention! Your attention please! I will not detain you further with repeating the reading of Mr. Simpson's will. Let me sum it up briefly."

The estate of Samuel Llewellyn Simpson as specified in the foregoing is hereby indisputably granted and bequeathed in its entirety to Rosemillion McKinley," the governor said. He added, "Known to most of you from birth, I believe, as Pick."

The neighbors from Widows Hollow exchanged uncertain glances.

Mama John threw her hands in the air with shouts of "Hallelujah, Thank You, Jesus!" Bennett and Suzanne shared enthusiastic hugs and congratulated Pick and her neighbors.

Jacques elbowed Jan. "So you thought I was up to no good, missing classes, canceling dates, and showing up late for ball games. I think you owe me an apology."

"I might let you worm your way back into my good graces by buying our dinner and helping me burn all those newspapers!"

"Jacques, you knew all along that Pick would inherit all of this?"

"All of this?" Jacques laughed. "Plus a couple of six figure bank accounts, stocks in a few companies, and at least one quarter of what Stalworth believes is his finest breeding stock, which is why Stump ordered the crew down there to clear land for Pick's new home, stables, pasture, and of course, her garden."

"But, how did he know?"

"There's not much Stump *didn't* know. Your father told him I was going to law school. He suggested that Stump ask me to help him get his legal affairs in order. Stump knew that he was dying and made me swear not to tell anyone. He sat up here one night and predicted what Stalworth would do and how he would go about it. He told me to watch the papers for notice of the auction. He knew that Stalworth would have his buddies post the notice in papers in far away counties so interested parties could not make the courthouse deadline."

"Stump had some pretty powerful connections, too. Two of his childhood friends grew up to become the mayor and the governor. And if Stump was right," Jacques said, scanning the crowd for Stalworth, "Stalworth isn't finished yet…"

Chapter Thirty-Nine

The governor made his way to Pick. "Congratulations young lady, this is a big day for you," he said, taking her hand.

Pick pumped his hand. "Thank you Sir, I ain't ever talked to a governor."

The governor smiled. "I think you may have some nervous friends and family here. Is there anything you would like to say to them, Rosemillion?"

Pick wiped her tears. "I reckon the first thing I got to do is learn my name."

The crowd laughed.

"I asked the good Lord last night to help us. I didn't have no notion what was gonna happen to the folks of Widows Holler or how we'd be lost one from another."

She sniffled and swiped at her tears with a knotted fist. "I know now," she said and turned to her anxious neighbors. "You kin go home and unpack them boxes and suitcases, ain't none of us goin nowhere. We're stayin right here in our home!"

Pick smiled a broad smile. She yelled to Jacques over the jubilant crowd. "Kin we pay fer 'lectricity?"

Jacques said with a laugh, "All the 'lectricity you want!"

Pick's eyes lit up. "We're gonna get 'lectricity and our younguns are gonna get real schoolin."

Tears sparkled from weathered cheeks. They leaked from eyes gone dim with age.

Fathers and husbands with quivering lips gathered wives and children in their arms. Their cautious smiles broke into sobs of relief with the realization *We're safe. We're home to stay.*

Children whooped and hollered. Their best friends would not be leaving after all.

Wives and mothers hugged babies to their breasts and whispered through wet eyes, "Thank you, Pick. God bless you, Pick."

"Now, Chile." Mama John opened her hand to Pick.

Jan's class ring sparkled from the golden chain. "I had a talk with Mr. Levi Thompson," Mama John said with a mischievous glint in her eyes.

Pick searched for Jan over the sea of jubilant faces. She wanted to accept his ring. She would make him that promise now, but...

"Miss McKinley!" Reid Garrison shouted. "My clients, Stephen and Victoria Stalworth intend to contest the court's decision on the grounds that Mr. Samuel Simpson was not of sound mind when he executed this will."

The crowd fell silent. Jan clenched his fists. "Unbelievable! I've wanted to punch that arrogant snob for a while!" He said and started for Stalworth.

Jacques stepped in Jan's path. "Let me!" He insisted.

"I don't think you want to do that, Mr. Stalworth," Jacques said. He pulled an envelope from his pocket and waved it at Stalworth.

"I don't care what you think!"

Jacques shrugged and made his way to Garrison. He spoke in quiet tones to the attorney and then turned again to Stalworth. "Are you sure you want to do this?"

"I am!" Stalworth repeated.

Garrison motioned the Stalworths closer with his hand. "Stephen, Victoria, we need to accompany Mr. Champeaux. It seems he has some privileged information to share with us."

"What now?" Stalworth demanded. He trudged up the hill with Victoria to a shady spot beneath a sprawling gum tree. Stump's cabin was clearly visible below.

Jacques opened the envelope, removed papers from it and read:

The young woman, Isabel Carter, was a orphan. The black lung had kilt her father and the pneumonia took her mother. The old man found her shiverin and hungry in his barn. He and his wife took 'er in and raised 'er.

Isabel brought sunshine and music to Old Gum Tree. One day, her singin was stopped. A stranger, lickered up and half crazy, took 'er and had his way with 'er.

Summer, 1934. Rains battered the cabin. Trees were scattered like twigs across Old Gum Tree. The holler was knee-deep in floodwaters. The old man was wore out, pullin calves, horses and mules to higher ground.

With the storm howlin outside, Isabel lays inside, taken with the fever, 'bout to birth a youngun. Elizabeth Simpson's taken with the fever beside 'er.

James Joseph McKinley is seein to the two of 'em when the storm grows worse and James Joseph drops with the fever.

By his self, the old man returns.

Isabel hollers and screams with 'er breathin gettin thinner and thinner. The boy is born. Weeks pass 'fore James Joseph takes his new wife, Isabel, up the hill to the buryin place at Old Gum Tree and her a 'cryin 'afore the marker what says to this day "Baby McKinley."

"God fergive me, there ain't no baby McKinley 'neath that marker! Never was! I never counted on Isabel's livin past the boy's birth."

"Thought it'd be her marker I was carvin. I took that boy and delivered him in a basket to his true Pap with papers what his Pap needed fer savin his own life—tied up in a ribbon."

"And the boy's pap took his own and Isabel Carter's son with the rising of the noon sun on the boy's birthplace, Widows Holler, in Titus County, Kentucky, May 8th, 1934. The boy was called Stephen Claymore Stalworth after his own father, Henry Claymore Stalworth."

"It's a lie! It's a lieeeee!" Stalworth screamed, jabbing a finger at Jacques.

Jacques leveled his gaze at Stalworth and then continued:

"And the writing of this confession was the last willful act of Samuel Llewellyn Simpson before his death from a fatal heart attack, right over there in that cabin, where you were born, twenty-seven years ago."

"It's a lie!" Tears streamed from Stalworth's eyes.

"No, Son, it's not a lie," Garrison said quietly.

"You knew? You knew and you didn't tell me?" Stephen raged.

"I did as Henry instructed."

"You're lying! You're both lying!" Stalworth sobbed.

"Every word of the story you just heard is documented and signed by your father. There are copies in the floor safe in your library. I have copies in my office."

"Stump Simpson carried the burden of this secret from the minute Isabel Carter recovered from the fever that he had felt certain would kill her."

"He had already given you to your father when she recovered against all odds. He carved and placed the marker in the cemetery and never told another living soul. It was years before he told your father that your real mother, Isabel Carter McKinley, was alive in Widows Hollow."

"That's why your father took such pains to keep you away from here. It was to protect Vivian, Isabel, and you. Vivian never knew the true identity of your father, she never knew about Henry's, ah, indiscretion."

"Because of you, Stephen, Stump felt responsible for all of the people in this hollow. He learned of your recent, ah, unfortunate encounter…with Pick. It made his secret burden all the greater to bear and caused him to move swiftly to secure their home and their way of life from what he felt certain would be your treachery."

"Today, his final offer is on the table before you. All that you have heard here is unknown to anybody other than myself, Jacques, and now, you and Victoria."

"She doesn't know?" Stalworth nodded to Pick.

"She does not."

"Jacques and I are legally bound not to divulge any of this to anyone. Jacques is the executor of Stump's will. Stump also hired him as a legal assistant. That leaves you and Victoria, unless...."

"Unless?"

"Unless you choose as you have indicated, to contest Stump's will. If you contest his will for any reason following this meeting, all that you heard here today will be headline news tomorrow."

Victoria gasped. She darted her eyes from her brother to Pick.

"Oh my God! She's your sister! Stephen, you're one of them!" Reeling from the shock and overcome with emotion, Victoria sobbed on Garrison's shoulder.

Stephen patted her back. He looked down the hill at the people who milled anxiously about. He searched for Pick. At the same moment his eyes fell on her, Pick glanced up the hill at him.

"She's my sister... I'm one of them!" Stalworth looked stricken.

Garrison watched him closely. Did he see a hint of softening in his young employer's eyes? That notion was short lived.

"No, no, it's not possible!" Stalworth screamed. He turned to Garrison with a snarl. "If you want to see another paycheck with my signature on it, you better find a way out of this nightmare! As of this minute, the documents my father supposedly signed no longer exist! I will burn those in my possession as soon as Tory and I get home and I demand that you do the same with the copies that you have!"

"Stephen, you don't know what you're asking!" Garrison retorted in fury.

Stalworth leveled his gaze to meet Garrison's. "I know exactly what I'm asking. My father is Henry Claymore Stalworth and my mother is Vivian Vinsant Stalworth, not some low class, heathen, white trash!"

Stalworth thrust a finger in Garrison's face. He spewed his threat between clenched teeth. "And if one word of this vile, fraudulent conspiracy shows up on any page of any newspaper, I will bury the perpetrator with lawsuits and legal fees!"

"As long as I live and breathe, no one, and particularly no heathen white trash from Widers Holler will impugn the Stalworth name! Do I make myself clear, counselor?"

Victoria sniffled. She released Garrison, and took Stephen's hand. She glanced down the hill, lifted her chin and announced "My brother has my full support, Reid. As Stephen has indicated, we will contest Simpson's will!"

Garrison shook his head. "I should have resigned the minute I learned of Henry's death! I knew this little monster was capable of wreaking havoc but I never realized he was capable of pure, unadulterated, evil!"

Garrison berated himself in silence. He raised defeated eyes to Jacques who approached with long, determined strides.

"Jacques, I can't tell you how miserable I feel. I know that Ms. McKinley and her neighbors desperately needed for you to win. Believe me, if I had known that Stalworth would go this far, I would have bailed out a long time ago."

"Those people down there can't afford to fight him and he has tied my hands. I have no choice but to follow his instructions." Garrison shook his head. "I really am sorry, Jacques."

"Mr. Garrison, I have all the respect in the world for you, Sir, but if you will allow me to clear up one little misconception here."

"You told Stalworth earlier that you and I were both bound not to divulge any of the privileged information that was revealed here today. As Henry Stalworth's attorney, you are bound to keep Henry's confidence. As Samuel Simpson's attorney, I am bound to keep *or, according to his wishes,* divulge *his.*"

It was difficult at this point to tell who had the bigger grin, Garrison or Jacques.

Garrison clapped Jacques on the back. "I am so going to enjoy this, Mr. Champeaux!" Garrison half bowed. "Please, be my guest!"

Jacques looked at the attorney long enough to contain himself, to replace his grin with a solemn, dignified air. "Mr. Stalworth…"

"Yes, what is it?" Stalworth snapped.

"The documents that you instructed Mr. Garrison to destroy and those in your possession are copies. I have the originals, along with a very detailed story regarding your birth and your legal identity. They are kept in a sealed envelope in a safety deposit box."

"Since neither you nor your father ever signed one of my paychecks, I am in no way bound to keep your confidences. I am, however, legally obligated to execute the orders given me by Mr. Samuel Simpson who made his wishes perfectly clear. "Protect the people and property of Widows Hollow.""

Jacques glanced at his watch. "You might want to note the time, Mr. Stalworth. I will give you exactly forty eight hours from this minute to deliver a court-approved document declaring your agreement to cease and desist and to void forever any claim you have made or intended to make, to any property formerly or currently owned by Mr. Samuel Simpson."

"Further, you or your assigned agent will bear full responsibility for the health and welfare of every thoroughbred branded with a double "S" that is now stabled or pastured on any Stalworth property, until such time as they are transferred to their new home," Jacques nodded down the hill, then added, "which is currently under construction."

If Reid Garrison's ever-widening smile served as proof, he was impressed with Jacques' performance.

Victoria's sniffles had become noticeably louder.

Stalworth's fury teetered on volcanic. He glowered at Jacques in rage and stared with contempt at the impoverished people below.

"Are you finished?" He sneered at Jacques, and barked to Victoria, "Come on, I've had enough of this!"

Stalworth started down the hill, dragging Victoria behind him, when he hesitated. He turned to Garrison.

"Oh, by the way Reid, you're fired!"

"That's a surprise," Garrison muttered under his breath.

"Not to Stump," Jacques said.

"Here." He pulled a folded document from his jacket pocket and gave it to Garrison.

Garrison scanned the papers to discover an employment agreement. Upon his release from Stalworth and all the various Stalworth entities, Reid Garrison was to become the attorney for the people of Widows Hollow.

He would be compensated through a trust funded by Samuel Simpson. Garrison's duties were to include discovering and exposing every bribe made by Stephen Stalworth to city, county, and state officials who had impeded or tried to halt the construction of the new school in Widows Hollow.

Garrison sought Stump's grave with his eyes. He turned to face the grave and said quietly, "You can count on it, friend."

Pick turned to an approaching automobile that bore the Vandeventer Farms logo on both sides.

Klaus, Olga, Tanner, Mule, and Jim Johnson exited the van. Together, they made their way up the hill.

Mule and Jim looked for Mama John.

Tanner, Klaus and Olga sought out Jan.

Suzanne and Bennett joined Pick in anticipation of another confrontation with Stalworth.

The typically humble and complacent people of Widows Hollow, with their raised voices and angry glares, looked to be taking on the characteristics of a lynch mob.

The mob fell suddenly silent.

Stephen Stalworth, with Victoria in tow, stormed down the hill, careful not to make eye contact with anyone. The Stalworths headed straight for their limo where Dwayne waited in military posture.

Dwayne ushered his charges into the limo, dived behind the wheel, and sped away.

Voices roared again as the people of Widows Hollow expressed their concerns.

Garrison and Jacques made their way down the hill. "Don't bother trying to look dignified, Jacques. It's rough going down this thing. Just be grateful that you don't fall on your face before we reach the bottom."

He grinned at Jacques. "You want to tell them?"

Jacques shook his head. "You're their attorney, you tell them."

"Ah, folks…. Ladies and gentlemen…. If I could have your attention please, just for a moment."

Garrison tried to spot Pick in the crowd. "Pick, ah, Rosemillion McKinley, will you come up here, please?"

Pick wiped her hands on her overalls and smiled at the neighbors she passed on her way to Garrison.

"Are you nervous?" Garrison asked.

"Nervouser than a treed coon!" Pick replied.

Garrison laughed. "Well, maybe we have some news that can calm a lot of nerves.

He addressed the noisy crowd. "You folks can stop worrying. Start unpacking. Widows Hollow is your home for as long as you want it to be." Garrison raised his voice to be heard over the shouts and cheers.

"Your church will be returned to its original location. And Stump Simpson's property, which includes your community of Widows Hollow, will be deeded to Rosemillion McKinley, just as he wished."

Cheers and joyful shouts echoed off the Big Black Mountain.

Jacques turned curious eyes to Jan. "What do you think she'll do now, Jan? Pick's got money and she will be getting an education."

With his eyes fixed on Pick's face, Jan shook his head. "Look at her. Even in that flannel shirt and overalls, she's beautiful. I've never met anyone like her. Everybody knows that I hate to dance, but I could dance all night with her."

"She makes me laugh, the kind of laugh that makes you glad to be alive. And she already has an education, one that shames the rest of us. She knows the important things, the things that really matter." A lump swelled in Jan's throat. "But she rejected me. After today, I'll probably never see her again."

Jacques had never seen Jan get emotional. For the first time in their lives, Jacques did not know what to say.

"What am I going to do?" Jan sniffled. A single tear leaked from his eye. "I love her."

"Papa, vot ees wrong with Zhan? Look at him!" Olga cried. Hand in hand with Klaus, she hurried to her son.

"Come on, Jacques, I've got to get out of here!" Jan cried. He gave Jacques a shove and started for his Jeep.

"Where ya going?" Pick yelled.

"She's talking to you," Jacques said and stopped so fast that Jan plowed into him.

"What?" Jan swung his head to Pick.

She walked to him in long, rapid strides, swinging her arms like a carefree child.

Olga ached for her son. He was so obviously, truly in love with Pick. She took Jan's hand as Pick spoke.

"Miss Olga, Mister Klaus, I got money, now. I've only just started, but I'm learning to read. I got four younguns and that ain't never gonna change, but I am. I'm gonna change, go to college, and become a teacher, or maybe a doctor like Suzanne."

She glanced at the neighbors who had quieted. All eyes were on Pick.

"There's folks what'll always call me white trash and probably hillbilly, too. But the folks what matters won't call me names."

Pick swung her eyes from Jan to Olga. "I'm askin you yer thoughts. If you want Margaret fer yer kin, I'm done, and I'll be on my way."

Olga would do anything to see that the desolation and despair that she had seen on Jan's face a moment ago never returned.

She reached for Pick and hugged her tight. "Peek, I vant only what makes my Zhan happy."

"Mister Klaus?"

Klaus squeezed Olga's hand, and then kissed it. "If my Mama and my Zhan are happy, I am happy."

"Jan?" Pick met his eyes with a mischievous twinkle in her own.

"What?" He tried not to smile.

"You gonna help me make my Mama's garden?"

"Yes."

"You gonna teach me and Jimbo and Mama John's and my younguns how to care fer fine horses what we'll be raisin here?"

"Yes."

"You gonna behave yerself 'til I get my schoolin done and learn to talk proper and dress proper?"

"Yes."

"You gonna buy me a kitten?"

"What?" Startled by her unexpected request, Jan smiled into Pick's eyes.

"Yes!" He cried. "Anything you want!"

Pick reached a pointer finger beneath her collar and speared Jan's class ring. She swung the ring back and forth on the gold chain and met Jan's eyes with a smile. "Promise?"

"She's wearing my ring!" Jan cried and back handed Jacques in the chest.

"I can see that!" Jacques cried, grinning.

Jan shook his head. He laughed and hugged his parents.

"Vis our blessings," they said.

Jan let out a *whoop!* That echoed off the Big Black Mountain. He threw his Stetson in the air, grabbed Pick McKinley in his arms, and kissed her

33733613R10226

Made in the USA
Middletown, DE
25 July 2016